HOUSE OF DARKEN

SECRET KEEPERS SERIES #1

JAYMIN EVE

Jaymin Eve

House of Darken: Secret Keepers Series

ISBN-10: 1719114307

ISBN-13: 978-1719114301

STAY IN TOUCH

Stay in touch with Jaymin:
www.facebook.com/JayminEve.Author
www.jaymineve.com

For Regina, my great-nan.
She read every single one of my books. Right up to the age of 95.
I wish I told her more often how much her support meant to me.

It was everything.

I miss and love you, Great-nan.

NOTE FROM AUTHOR

I had to change some locations, schools, and landmarks of the town used in this book. To fit with my world building. I did thoroughly enjoy my research of Oregon, though, and hope to visit one day. :)

1

—————

"*A*re you okay, Emma?" Turning from the window, I was more than happy to get out of my own head. The endless forests of the Pacific Northwest were keeping me somewhat entertained, but I couldn't wait to finally arrive at our new home and escape this car. Let's just say it had been a long trip from Roswell, New Mexico.

"Yeah, I'm good," I said, my lips curving up. "Just over-thinking. You know me." My smile was still a little shocking – to me and Sara both judging by her widened eyes. Until recently I rarely smiled.

As she reached back to give my hand a squeeze, I took a closer look at her and felt concern tinge my emotions. She was pale, eyes puffy, and her normally rich brown skin was washed out. Her dark corkscrew curls were a mess.

"Are *you* okay?" I asked, leaning forward in my seat as she let go of my hand.

She nodded, and I was relieved as her weary features relaxed. "Just ready to get out of this car. We're close now. Only another twenty or so minutes."

Leaning back, I wrapped my hands around my necklace, the

only thing I still possessed from before the fire. It was an opal ... maybe. No one actually knew what the oddly shaped and textured stone was, but it had faint opal coloring, so that was what I went with.

It had been my mom's. She gave it to me on my seventeenth birthday; I still couldn't believe that had almost been a year ago. I remembered the day so clearly, each moment as it flashed across my mind was sharp and biting. We'd gone to the beach and gotten ice cream. I'd picked out my first car later that afternoon.

A perfect day.

Next month I would turn eighteen. The first birthday without my parents. I was dreading it with every fiber of my being. Flames tore apart my world last New Year's Eve – a time for new beginnings, but for me it was the end.

Eight months since the fire and I was still haunted ... tormented. Summer was almost over and I was moving to a new town. Again. Sara and Michael, my guardians, were the only two of my parents' friends who gave a damn about anything to do with me after the fire, and since I had no other family to speak of, I was grateful to them. They took in a grieving, broken mess of human and somehow provided me with what I needed to claw my way from the darkness.

Space, then support. Warmth and love followed.

I'm not sure I would have survived without them, which, frankly, scared the hell out of me. I didn't want to rely on anybody anymore. Knowing they could be gone in an instant was terrifying, and there were plenty of days I was tempted to run from them, to escape their cheerful faces and happy world. But as those moments of panic passed, I remembered how lucky I was. I was not in the system. I was not alone.

Michael shifted forward, squinting through the front window, focused upwards for a minute. He was very Irish in coloring: pale skin, hazel eyes, and carrot orange hair. He only had to walk across the yard and he burned, unlike his wife who could sunbake for hours. I loved the diversity between him and Sara. Not to mention how epic their love was.

In a world of broken people and marriages, those two gave me hope.

"Hopefully we'll beat this storm," Michael finally said as he straightened. "I don't like the thought of moving in during a downpour." Dark, angry clouds were awash in the sky, which had been blue not ten minutes earlier. The turbulent masses swirled and dotted about, trying to eclipse the last light of the afternoon.

Storms never bothered me. I quite enjoyed the heavy crash of thunder, the spark of lightning, the soothing pitter-patter of rain as it washed across the land. It felt like the earth was cleansing, a new start.

Michael turned a worried look toward his wife. "Think we'll make it in time?"

Sara began reassuring her storm-hating husband that we'd have plenty of time, and I had to hide my smile. We had a box and a suitcase each. Even if a hurricane sprang up it really wasn't going to be a huge problem to move in. Except, of course, there was no chance any rental we could afford would be able to withstand a swift wind, let alone a serious storm.

I had already moved twice in the eight months I'd lived with the Finnegans, and both times our furnished rentals were one step up from slums. But hey, it was a roof over our heads. Growing up I'd lived solidly middle class, always thinking my parents had plenty of money. After they died, I learned there was only enough left to cover their bills. After losing your only family, though, being poor was sort of insignificant. When I was hungry, I put things into perspective and dealt with it like an adult.

"What's in Astoria, Oregon, anyway?" I asked, dropping my necklace back beneath my tank and pushing my wavy hair behind my ears. Already the humidity from the storm had my hair going haywire. It was long, a mixture of curls and waves, in a rich auburn color. The red explained my temper; the curls were from parts unknown. My parents were both straight-haired brunettes.

Michael's freckled face lit up, hazel eyes shining with excitement as he shifted to see me better. "Astoria is it ... the one! I think we really have something this time, Em. There have been multiple eyewitness accounts. Multiple. And they're from legitimate sources."

My guardians were two of the nicest people I'd ever met, but they were crazy. Complete batshit crazy. They believed there was something other than humans out in the world. They referred to themselves as supernatural chasers. I had no real idea what exactly they were searching for, but they spent their lives scouring the internet, hunting down leads, and moving all around the country. Which was why we had no money for a new car. Michael was very good with computers, and had an online tech-support business that made just enough to sustain their lifestyle – but their focus was definitely not on making money or settling down in one place.

I had been born and raised in California. At the time of the fire, Sara and Michael were living in Vegas, so my first move was to their small place there. Then we moved to New Mexico for five months. And now to Astoria. I hadn't been back to school since the fire, having taken some time off to grieve before eventually homeschooling to finish my junior year. Astoria would be my first new school ever. Senior year. To say I was nervous was an understatement, but I was a tiny bit excited about it too.

I returned Michael's grin, trying to adopt some of his enthusiasm even though I didn't believe a word of his insane theories. "I still don't know how you guys have moved so often. Was there ever a time you just stayed in one place?"

I leaned forward, elbows resting on my knees. Sara's smile was gentle as she exchanged a lingering look with her husband. "When we first got married, we lived in California for five years. That's how we met your parents."

My heart tightened. Sometimes the pain just hit me like a bullet. Grief was a strange thing, ebbing and waning without any reliable pattern. Some days I was okay. I could talk about them, think about them. Other days I was a mess.

Today was somewhere in the middle, so I was brave enough to push for more information. "I know Mom and Dad missed you both when you started moving around. Your visits were always a highlight in our house."

Sara's light brown eyes got shiny then; her throat worked as she swallowed hard. "It was a highlight for us too, honey," she finally said, her voice barely above a whisper. "We miss Chelsea and Chris so much." She cleared her throat and spoke again, louder this time: "And this time we will be staying in Astoria for your entire senior year. We promise. It might be nice for us to have some stability for a while too."

That was a relief. I didn't want to have to navigate two schools during my senior year. Still, Astoria seemed like an odd choice.

"It's a fairly small town, right? Are you sure there could really be much supernatural activity?" It was hard to phrase these questions without letting my skepticism show. Even the word "supernatural." What did that refer to? Was it ghosts? Vampires? Werewolves? What exactly did they think was out there? Any time I asked they just said, "Other than human..."

So basically it could be anything.

Michael lifted one hand off the steering wheel, waving it animatedly. "I can't wait to find out, but so far all the signs look really positive. Unusual activity is picking up in the area. Reports of energy spikes. Missing people. Strange occurrences with natural landscape formations. This is definitely the one!"

I smiled, but internally I was shaking my head. It was hard to actually believe that my accountant father and science teacher mother had put aside their level-headedness to become best friends with the Finnegans. That in itself was bordering on the crazy, but I wasn't going to complain. This kooky pair had saved my life and I would owe them forever.

Turning back to the window, I let the scenery capture me again. I expected the natural landscape to really thin out before we hit Astoria, alert me to civilization approaching, but one minute it was trees and the next ... we were in the town. I sat up in my chair, moving closer to the window. The back seats were old and threadbare, springs digging into my spine if I shifted too far out of the center, but it was worth it to catch a glimpse of this picturesque little place. Despite the grumbling skies and rolling clouds, there was something truly beautiful here. Something which almost felt familiar ... homey.

"What do you think, Emma?" Sara twisted again, her teeth bright against the dark of her skin. She looked happy and more energized already.

I didn't reply straight away, choosing to focus on the world flashing by the window. Tiny fishing shacks gave way to large mansions scattered along the water. A huge bridge could be seen far off in the distance, looking like it disappeared out over the water. Fishing boats shared the water with huge barges. And so much greenery. Everywhere I looked it was lush and natural, pockets of forest scattered among the city. Eventually I had to say, "It's perfect. Just perfect."

From the corner of my eye I could see the Finnegans exchange beaming smiles, but I was too enthralled to care. I never believed I'd ever feel at home anywhere again after losing my parents. They had been my home. But Astoria was definitely special; maybe this was the place to heal a little of the heavy ache in my heart and soul. It would be nice not to hurt so much all the time.

When we were passing through what looked like the main town of Astoria, Sara started trying to direct her husband toward our new house. She was terrible with maps, which was comical considering how much they traveled. I'd asked them if they'd ever like a navigation system in their car. I had gotten a solid no from both of them. Apparently they trusted their paper maps more, saying electronics could be manipulated.

After about thirty seconds of her rotating the map, I leaned over her shoulder. "Do you want some help?" I asked.

Without hesitation, she thrust the paper toward me. "Yes, please, this damn thing makes no sense. It's upside down or something."

Michael chuckled, very used to his wife's lack of map-reading skills. "We're on Marine Drive," he told me, before pulling out a piece of paper from his pocket. "And our house is on ... Daelight Crescent." He squinted in the dim light, repeating it: "Fourteen Daelight Crescent."

I scanned across the map, searching for both streets. I found the one we were on easily enough, but the other was not jumping out at all. After a few minutes I was about to tell them they had the wrong address when I finally noticed it. The name was tiny, almost unreadable.

It was across the other side of town, near the water. I figured out the quickest route from where we were and directed Michael. The storm was hanging lower now, which gave me almost no visibility in the back seat, and since there were no interior lights I had to hold the map very close to my face while lifting it up near the window to capture the final rays of the dying light. I memorized the route as best I could.

After driving for about fifteen minutes I leaned forward. "Should be around here somewhere." I had abandoned the map. It was way too dark to see.

"There!" Sara gave a shout.

She must have picked up the flash of a sign in the lightning sprinkling the sky, because there were very few streetlights out this far. Michael and I had missed it completely; he had to swing the car around and go back again. This time he approached slowly, indicating to turn before we realized that Daelight Crescent was actually barred by a huge, imposing wood and iron gate. The design was intricate and expensive: shiny wood, polished metal accents. It towered into the sky, making me feel small and insignificant.

We all stared in silence. Michael and Sara exchanged a look.

"This can't be right," Michael murmured, turning from his wife and leaning forward to see better through the front windscreen. "This was the cheapest rental we could find here. It's only seven hundred a month. They didn't mention security gates. There's no way we can afford this street."

Michael wasn't kidding. Our place in New Mexico barely had a front door, let alone something that resembled the sort of gated community movie stars hid away in. A tap at the window then made us all jump. The man standing outside of Michael's window had taken us by surprise.

He was a large, imposing guy, holding what looked like a heavy-duty LED camping lantern. Michael slowly rolled down the clunker's old sticky window. It stopped about halfway, unable to go any lower.

The man inclined his head toward Michael and I caught a glimpse of dark skin and eyes, and very white teeth flashing as he spoke. "Can I help you, sir?"

His accent was mild, hard to place, and his tone very polite. I studied his dark uniform, trying to make out details in the light from the high-tech-looking lantern he held. The word "security" was finely stitched in white across the pocket, and it all clicked into place.

Apparently this *was* a compound for movie stars, and somehow we had scored a place in there for seven hundred dollars a month. No catch either, no doubt. I slumped back in my seat as I waited for the guard to tell us we were in the wrong place.

Sara spoke up, answering his question from before – which she often did when her husband got flustered. "We arranged to rent a house, 14 Daelight Crescent. We might have the wrong street, though. We only have an old map to navigate from."

"Who did you rent this property through?" the guard asked.

Hmmm ... curious. I expected him to immediately usher our old clunker away, lest it taint the rich folk.

Michael, who no longer looked flustered, leaned over the back seat and yanked up a folder from the floor. Riffling through it, he pulled out a few pieces of paper and handed them over to the security guard. "This was the site," Michael said. "We've already paid first and last months' rent."

The man took a step away and I saw a flash of light as he lifted the lantern closer, reading over the documents. He stepped back to the car window a few minutes later, just as the first drops of rain started to hit. The storm was about to rage at us.

"Well, everything seems to be in order here. You're one of the lucky few allowed to live on Astoria's most exclusive street. There will be security cards in your house, one for each of you. Please keep them on you at all times. And make sure you stick to your side of the street." He cleared his throat. "That's an official rule – don't cross to their side of the street and you won't have any trouble."

With that weird and kind of insulting advice, he turned and marched off. Within seconds, the double gates were silently swinging open.

Our side of the street. *Their* side of the street. What crap was this? Did they segregate people here? Because I was not cool with any sort of segregation.

Except for assholes – they could walk straight off a cliff.

My parents had always drilled the importance of equality into me, that I should treat people as I would want to be treated, no matter their personal circumstances. Despite the fact that sometimes people hit my bitch switch – my redhead temper could get the better of me – for the most part I tried to be a decent human being. I actually tried even harder now my parents were gone. I had to make them proud.

Michael eased the car back into drive, and with a few shuddering lurches we were moving again.

"Where exactly did you find this rental?" Sara asked him as she leaned forward in her seat, a dubious look on her face.

Michael didn't answer at first – he was too busy staring at the street before us – but he did thrust the same papers at her that he had given to the guard. As she silently read through them, I turned my full attention to this street. Despite the darkness, I could tell how stunning it was. The most picture-perfect street I had ever seen in my life, beyond movies and any fairytale world. The road was wide, long, and straight. There were lanterns dotted in even intervals along each side, casting everything in soft light. Hedges and perfectly-shaped rose bushes filled the spaces between the lanterns.

To our right, which I knew from the map was the side on the water, the houses were ... well, not houses. At minimum they were mansions. Some in the distance looked a lot like castles. Huge and imposing, they were the height of beauty and architectural design. No two were the same layout or color, and each seemed to be set on an enormous block of land with solid gates barring them from the street.

"Michael!" Sara's voice was high and stressed now. "This is a mistake, right? We can't live in one of those houses. They're multi-million dollar properties."

It was then I noticed the other side of the street and I started to understand how we'd ended up in here. Not to mention the *our* and *their* side comments from the guard made a lot more sense now.

The left side of the street was the very poor, rundown cousin to the mansions on the right. Each house was small and dark, as if even the streetlamps didn't like them very much and decided not to shine any light over there. The blocks were close together, and many of the buildings looked a little worse for wear. Michael and Sara also noticed "our side" of the street, and relief crossed their faces. This was the world we were familiar with.

"Keep an eye out for fourteen," Michael said as he continued creeping along. The road was deserted. Everyone must have scurried inside to avoid the storm. We were the only crazies driving around. Already a fair bit of water was splattering in through the still-open driver's window. Michael hadn't managed to get it closed yet, although he was still working on it.

"There it is," I said, pointing my arm through the center of the car toward a single level, rickety-looking place with a half-porch.

Outside of the soft lamplight everything looked eerie, shadows awash across that small porch, the wind whipping leaves and debris around the front yard. The clunker eased into the open car space and with one last huff turned off. Michael used both hands then to get his window all the way closed. Well, almost all the way. Then the three of us sat and stared, exhausted from the days of travel, but reluctant to leave the familiarity of the car and step into the dark, creepy house.

Sara pulled herself together first, plastering on her best confident face, turning to Michael and me: "Let's go inside. We can deal with all the problems tomorrow. Fresh sheets on the beds and a warm shower. Everything will seem brighter in the morning."

It was as good a plan as any. I wiggled my legs to get the blood pumping again, before dragging my Converse up off the floor and pulling them on. I was wearing short shorts and a tank. It was summer, and hot when we left this morning. Apparently the Pacific Northwest cared nothing for seasons though; it did what it wanted. Which meant I was going to freeze my butt off trying to get my bag and box from the back.

The three of us dashed to the trunk of the car. Michael yanked it open and started handing things across. Arms full, we all made our way up onto the porch, which provided only the slightest shelter from the rain. It was just shy of a downpour, and we were damp in moments. The front door opened right up and we hurried inside.

Sara found the lights in the front room, flicking them on. As everything came into focus, I sort of wished she would turn them back off again. The house was small and boxy, set out in a square formation. Living room and kitchen in the front half, hallway in middle, and I would guess the two bedrooms and bathroom made up the back half.

We stepped into the living area with its threadbare carpet, two old ragged couches, and a coffee table that looked like it was put together with cardboard. Sara's smile didn't dim; she was used to this life, and had embraced it long ago.

"Great, they actually left some furniture. Even when they say fully furnished, so many times they aren't." Her overly chipper chatter continued as she moved farther into the house, turning on more lights. "Isn't it great that electricity is included in this rental property?"

That was a positive. For once we wouldn't have to worry about that bill getting paid.

"Come on, Em. Let's get settled." Michael briefly dropped his hand on my shoulder. His expression didn't change when I subtly shifted away, breaking contact. I loved my guardians, but ever since the fire I had avoided being touched. Emotions and images would overwhelm me. Like ... I was only able to remain contained if I existed in a world devoid of touch and comfort. If it bothered Sara and Michael, they never showed it; they just minimized the amount of physical affection they forced on me.

They had learned quickly when to push and when to let me be.

We explored the tiny place. Of the two bedrooms, the smaller one with the twin bed was mine. I dumped my box and bag on the floor and took a second to examine my new space. Besides the bed there was a closet, side table, and dresser, more furniture than I was used to having in the last six months. I didn't even care that it had seen better days, the white paint peeling and tattered. It would do the job I needed.

There was no bedding but that was okay. I had my own. Sara said that no matter how many houses you lived in, as long as you had clean, familiar sheets, and a secure roof over your head, you'd be okay. Personally, I wouldn't have minded a sandwich and hot cocoa to go with that, but she was half right at least.

Stepping to the mattress, I wrinkled my nose as a slight smell of stale dampness assaulted me. Glancing up, it didn't seem as if this room leaked, so hopefully it was just from sitting unused. If the increasing heaviness of the rain was any indication, we were in for a bit of a thrashing this night, so I'd find out soon enough on the leaking situation.

"How you getting on in here, Emma?"

Sara popped in, and seeing that I was in the middle of making the bed, strode over to help. It took us a few minutes to get my pale rose sheets on, throw a couple of pillows to the head of the bed, and finish with a simple white knit blanket over the top. Hopefully I'd be warm enough. Something told me we weren't even remotely prepared for the weather here.

A crash of thunder rocked the house at the same time my stomach growled. I thought Sara looked at me closely, probably wondering if she'd heard right. She wasn't used to me wanting food. My curves were long gone, grief and lack of interest whittling my frame down to one that was far too slim. I was just starting to get my appetite back. I really hoped my curvier figure would return with it.

"Are you hungry?" Sara said quietly. "I just realized we haven't really eaten since lunch and those few other snacks. I can duck out and get you something."

I shook my head, forcing a smile across my face. "No, it's okay. I can wait for breakfast."

She nodded a few times, her own smile looking forced too.

"Mike will get up early to grab some essentials. You know him, always up with the birds."

"You talking about me, woman?" Michael's shout came from the living room, where he was no doubt trying to hide from the storm.

With a laugh, Sara turned to leave, a gleam in her eye that told me Michael was in trouble. She paused at my doorway to wink and blow me a kiss, before closing the door to give me privacy, which was my general request.

Sucking in a deep breath, I braced my hands on the dresser. Closing my eyes, it took me many moments to center myself and push off the sadness, the pressing ache in my chest that sometimes literally took my breath away and had me dizzy and shaking. I managed to keep up a happy façade when I was around my guardians; they tried so hard and I knew my pain hurt them. I kept waiting for it to get easier, for the day I would wake up and be able to breathe again. The psychologist had said – during my five forced appointments right after my parents' deaths – that only time could ease my agony. "Give it time," he'd say, over and over.

Clearly, eight months was not enough time because I felt nothing but constant pain.

Miss you guys. Love you both so much.

A part of me hoped they were around, watching over me, that death wasn't the end of it all, that there was something more. Something beyond. I needed to believe I'd see them again one day. We weren't a religious family. Math and science had been our calling, but I was taking a leap of faith for the first time.

There was only one bathroom in this rental, so I gathered my toiletries and pajamas before opening my door and entering the green-tiled room.

Five minutes later I emerged shivering as I dashed to my room. "No hot water," I yelled as I passed the living area.

I heard a few curses; most of them sounded like they were

from Sara, but by this time I had already shut my door and was jumping into bed – which was not much warmer than the outside, but it was cozy at least. Despite the fact I'd only sat on my butt all day, I was exhausted. Tomorrow was a new day. I would hopefully explore the stunning little town that was to be my home for the next twelve months. *Astoria.* For the first time in a long time, I actually fell asleep with a sliver of positivity inside of me.

2
_____

That night I slept solidly. When I woke, I opened my eyes to a dimly lit room, but lingered in bed for a few minutes, enjoying the warmth under the covers. The air was chilly on my nose and cheeks; it was definitely not summer weather here. The worst of the storm had died off during the night, but there was clearly no sun shining on the town of Astoria.

After enjoying the quiet for some time, I eventually stretched out, trying to ease the stiffness from my extremely crappy bed – pretty sure the mattress was filled with sand and rocks – and pulled myself up.

The minutest sounds of conversation drifted through the thin walls. Sara and Michael were awake, which hopefully meant food. As soon as I thought about eating, the hunger gnawing at my belly roared to life. A few gulps of water from the cup on my bedside subsided the cramps for a short time. I was getting pretty good at this minimal food thing. On top of grief killing my appetite, the Finnegans also forgot about food all the time. Neither of them were big eaters, focusing more on their crazy research. Team that with our limited money and there had been more than one night we all went to bed with empty bellies.

God, I missed my mom's cooking, my dad's laughter in the morning when he would read the papers and shout about politics and the world going to shit. I missed my family. I didn't even have a place to visit them. The fire had burned so hot and fast that there was literally nothing left but ash. Some days I imagined they had escaped and were out in the world looking for me, but I knew that was just wishes and dreams. They would never have abandoned me. Which left only one logical conclusion. The fire had ... taken them. The two empty graves back home signified their official deaths.

Swallowing against the painful lump in my throat, I forced the memories down, brushing off a few tears as I hopped out of bed, keeping the blanket wrapped around me to ward off the chill.

Crossing the room, I dropped down beside my box of belongings, ripping off the tape and flipping the top open. I only had a few things I would call personal possessions – including the jewelry box my mom had given Sara as a gift, which she'd passed on to me. I lifted out the heavy box, dark wood with its mother-of-pearl inlay, and placed it on my dresser. Normally I would be worried about leaving it out in the open, especially since I often placed my opal necklace in there for safe keeping, but now we lived on a special magic street with door guards and stuff, which had better mean my belongings were safe.

My clothes took about five minutes to hang and put into drawers, and just like that I was unpacked. The minimalistic life was certainly easy in some ways. Poking my head out around the door, there was no one in the dark hallway. I followed the sounds to find Michael and Sara in the kitchen. A few brown paper bags were scattered across the scarred bench-tops, and I almost shrieked when I saw my favorite cereal sitting there.

I must have made some noise, because two sets of eyes and beaming smiles turned toward me.

"You're awake!" Michael jumped to his feet and hurried around to my side. "How did you sleep?"

I shrugged, but before I could answer Sara interrupted: "There's hot water now. Had to flick the switch on the system. It heated up fast."

I froze, torn about my priorities. What was more important, food, or a long hot shower to work out the kinks? My stomach growled loudly, and then again, angrier this time.

Well, that settles that.

There were three stools at the tiny breakfast bar, I pulled one out and took a seat. Michael dropped down on my right side. "You got Fruit Loops." I could hear the excitement in my voice. "I haven't had that for months."

Sara deposited a bowl, spoon, and small carton of milk before me. "We thought you might like a treat – to make up for the rough trip here."

I beamed at both of them, diving into the box of goodness. "Have I told you guys how awesome you are?" I said between mouthfuls. "This is the best thing I've tasted all year."

I savored each bite slowly. These days I was all about taking pleasure in small things, something I'd never done before the fire. I was different now. Now I appreciated all the gifts.

One bowl filled me, so after rinsing out the dish I excused myself to get ready. Sara was thankfully right about the hot water. Unfortunately the pressure was still crap, but, with a lot of difficulty, I managed to wash my hair. Long, thick waves were a pain, but I'd almost figured out how to control them. Only took me seventeen years.

Rubbing the steam off the old mirror so I could see my reflection, I grabbed my hair cream and quickly ran it through the damp ends. Then the heat protection. Hair dryer was next. It was one of the few high-quality pieces I owned.

Ten minutes later: long, shiny, loose curls. For how long one never knew, but right now "good hair day" was mine. I never wore much makeup; it was expensive and my mom had always encouraged me to avoid it for as long as possible. So I just swiped on some mascara, liking the way it enhanced the cobalt color of my eyes, and pale lip-gloss. My skin was naturally tanned – olive was how my mom described it. My heritage was Caribbean on my father's side, and Australian on my mother's. She had moved to America with her parents at the age of five, and they never left. My father was third generation, born in America. His grandparents emigrated from Dominica.

My mother's parents had died before I was born, and my father's when he was just a child. So I had no grandparents alive, and my parents had been only children. Mom always said small families could be perfect, with more than enough love to make up for lack of numbers.

She was right. It had been perfect.

I shook off the melancholy and forced myself to smile. I had to keep living ... even more so because of the fire – I had to live for all of us. Plus, my parents would not want their deaths to steal anything from me. I knew that logically, but it didn't mean I could just erase my pain.

I was dealing with it. Day by day.

Aware of the weather, I dressed in one of my few pairs of jeans, and a white, long-sleeved, fitted shirt. To finish my outfit, I pulled on a worn-out pair of black Converse that we'd picked up from a thrift shop. They were the most comfortable shoes ever, and until they literally fell off my feet I would not give them up.

Stepping into the living area, I took a second to pay attention to the view outside the double front windows. Someone had opened the old blinds and I could see straight out into the street. Daelight Crescent. Even the name was oddly mystical.

Movement across the other side of the road caught my eye. One of the gates was opening. The house behind it looked straight out of European royalty. A castle, for sure. There was no other explanation for such opulence and beauty. The glimpse I caught was brief: some towering turrets, cream and stone accents, a huge drive, and enough landscaped gardens to keep a team of gardeners busy year-round. A low, sleek car emerged, distracting me. The vehicle was dark, like a rich deep purple or burgundy. It rumbled, intensely powerful, as it slowly glided onto the road. I didn't recognize the make or model, but it was clearly expensive. The engine purring with just enough grunt that I had no doubt it was going to be fast.

I shifted forward, wanting to catch a glimpse of the occupants. But the tint was so dark I saw nothing but a large shadow. Actually two. It was possible someone was in the passenger seat. I realized then that just because I couldn't see them, that didn't mean they couldn't see me. We had no tint on our windows, and if they glanced across to my side of the street they'd have a full view of me gawking like a weirdo. Feeling my cheeks heat up, I sank down into the old couch, hiding myself. After waiting a few moments, I was just poking my head up to check if they were gone when—

"What ya doing?" Michael's voice was close by. He'd crept around the couch and popped up beside me.

I might have let out a bit of a shriek, almost falling face-first off the chair. "Holy heck, don't sneak up on me!"

He let out a loud laugh, shaking his head. He was still laughing as he took off down the hall again, back in the direction of his room. If it was possible, my guardian was acting even odder than usual. I dusted off my jeans and quickly followed Michael. I wanted to tell them both that I was going out to explore.

Even though the door to their bedroom was wide open, I hesitated just outside. We were still getting to know each other, so there was a certain awkwardness in invading each others' privacy. I watched as Sara neatly unpacked their things; Michael was trying to fix the cupboard door that was hanging from one hinge. He wasn't really one for carpentry talent, but he always had a go.

Sara finally noticed me hovering in the doorway. "Hey, Em. Everything okay?" She pushed back her mess of curls. Dust was scraped across her forehead, dark circles under her eyes.

I nodded, forcing that smile again. "Yeah, I'm all unpacked, so I was just thinking about heading out and exploring Astoria. I'd love to see the town."

Sara finished folding the last shirt and closed the drawer. She was a little OCD with clothes, color and style coordinating. Michael was a mess; if clothes were left up to him, everything would be thrown into a pile in the corner.

"That's a great idea," she said. "It looked so beautiful when we drove through last night. I'll have to find some time to explore too." She glanced at her husband. "I'm still trying to get Michael to tell me how we ended up in this town, and especially how we lucked out renting on a gated street. I feel so much better about leaving you alone knowing there's security here, but sometimes when things are too good to be true..." She trailed off, and we all knew what she was thinking.

Michael brushed a hand through his thinning red hair, shooting a smile at Sara. "Like I said, I was chasing up on some reports of weird happenings, energy surges, bright lights, disappearances – the usual things. Astoria has never been on my radar before, and then suddenly I'm inundated with countless news articles from here, some of them dating back at least a hundred years. I have no idea why this area never came up before. I've made that same search numerous times on the dark web, but this time there was all of this new information."

He pushed the cupboard door closed. It was straight for about five seconds before a creak had it lurching back on one hinge. With a curse, he turned his back on the door and faced us. "So I started searching for rentals here, and strangely enough, there was nothing but this one place in our price range. It was a private rental. We got accepted without any fuss, over the phone. Kind of felt a lot like fate."

Fate. That was a funny way to think about it. I mean, the way he explained it did really seem as if someone wanted us to come here ... but that would be stupid. I refused to buy into their theories. No one knew about the Finnegans. They were nomads. Ghosts. They never planted roots, got jobs, or did anything that established them in a town – in and out, leaving very little trail behind.

No one would have lured them here. There was no reason at all for that to happen.

Since Sara and Michael were exchanging their "conspiracy theory" face, I knew they were about to hit their research again, so I bade them one last goodbye before heading to the front door.

"Don't forget to grab your door key and security card, Emma," Michael yelled after me. "They're quite strict in checking you're allowed in here. I passed at least five guards this morning on my way to get food."

Geez, five guards ... overkill much? I grabbed my wallet from my room before making my way to the kitchen to pick up the card and key sitting on the bench. It all went into my pocket.

Cool breezes wrapped around me as I stepped out onto the cement porch and made my way down the couple of stairs. Even though I told myself not to stare, I still had to check out the houses across the street.

The road we had driven in on was at least twice the size of a normal residential street. There was an actual dotted white line right down the center, dividing *our* side of the street from *theirs.*

The guard last night had been pretty blunt in his warning to stay on our side, which only made my urge to run across and touch the forbidden side that much stronger. Of course, I wasn't five, so I managed to restrain myself, all the while feeling a tad annoyed that there was any need for such a divide. Sure, they were rich, probably famous, judging by the ten-foot-high fences, but we were all people. Different but the same. Money shouldn't make anyone think they were better than anyone else.

Of course, I'd love to have more than thirty-five bucks to my name. A few new pairs of shoes. Maybe a car so I didn't have to walk everywhere. But I was aware that the things I valued most in the world could not be bought with money. Which meant, for me, it was not worth chasing.

Shivering in the cool air, I took off at a brisk walk and it still took me ten minutes to reach the front gate. I wasn't stopped by anyone; the street remained empty and quiet. The same guard from last night was waiting in a small booth. In the cloudy light I could see that he was probably only a few years older than me – very handsome, a few inches taller than my five foot eight, and built like a linebacker. Pretty standard for security nowadays. His midnight-dark skin was clear and beautiful, and I had instant envy. My skin was pretty easy to handle for a teen, but was still known to break out on occasion.

"Where are you heading?" he asked, handing my card back after he'd logged me into the system. "A bus rolls by in about fifteen minutes. Pulls up on that corner." He pointed to the right, down a fairly deserted-looking road. "If you use your Daelight Crescent card, you'll get free transport around."

Wow, that was a double bonus. "Awesome." I beamed an actual genuine smile. "Thanks for the info. I'm really just hoping to explore the town. Maybe check out the school. I'll be starting there next week."

Summer break finished up late-August, so early next week I'd be starting my senior year, and I was nervous. Then, once I got through the new school thing, I'd have to deal with my birthday. I was turning eighteen on the fifteenth of September, so I had a lot going on.

"Are you heading to Astoria Highschool? Or Starslight Prep?" he asked, the odd dark gray of his eyes standing out starkly against all of that lovely skin.

"Starslight Prep," I said without hesitation. "It was the only one that offered me a scholarship, and I needed…"

I trailed off not wanting to advise him of our current financial situation. I might not care about money, but most people did. Most people judged. He didn't seem to though; his expression didn't change. I actually couldn't get a read on his thoughts at all, which was somewhat relieving.

Just when the silence got awkward, and I was about to wave and head for the bus stop, he gave me a bright smile. "Starslight is a great school. You don't have to worry. They only offer scholarships to students worthy of attending. It's one of the most exclusive schools in the country, and graduating from there you'll have no trouble getting into college."

Another bonus. They were adding up fast this morning. The only way I was going to college was with multiple scholarships and financial aid, so maybe this new school would have some programs or contacts to help with that. Returning his smile, I nodded and half-turned.

"Well, thanks again…" I paused, waiting for him to fill in the blank of his name.

"Ace," he said with a wink. "You can call me Ace."

"Cool name," I replied, waving and starting across in the direction of the bus stop. I turned back briefly as he called after me: "Take care out there, Emma. Not everything in Astoria is as safe as Daelight Crescent."

I briefly locked eyes with him before marching away. How had he known my name? I definitely hadn't told him it. Must have been attached to the card or something. I pulled it free for a second and had a look, but it just said "Resident of Daelight Crescent," with a barcode to scan. No name.

Maybe it was logged in the computer. I refused to believe there was anything supernatural going on here. Sara and Michael were the only ones living in a fantasy world.

I stood on the corner for a few minutes before a white bus

rolled up. Ace had been right about the card thing; I barely even flashed it before I was waved on. It was empty, so I had my pick of seats. I chose one about halfway, right against the window so I wouldn't miss any of the scenery.

Astoria was just as pretty as it had been last night. Prettier actually, even in the dull, cloudy-day light. Ocean on one side, forests on the other, I felt as if I'd stumbled on fabled faerie lands; surely there was no place on Earth as stunning as this. The houses even seemed storybook-like – cute cottages, sprawling beach abodes. The bus stopped a few times, three people got on, but none sat near me.

Which was fine by me. I was in town-watching mode, not small-talk-with-strangers mode. All too soon the bus entered the "main street." Well, at least according to the driver, who was randomly shouting out information on the town. Seemed we might have been in the historic section, which was why I chose to exit here. As good a place as any to start exploring.

I spent the next few hours strolling around, window shopping, observing the many people who were busy living their lives. They were so happy here, always smiling at me. I didn't trust it; it was bizarre. But at least the scenery was stunning. Early afternoon, I made my way back to the bus pick-up. A different driver this time, a gray-haired woman who looked pretty close to retirement age. Again my card was just glanced at and I was waved on board. There were half a dozen or so passengers seated now, so I plonked down in a free chair near the back, in front of a blond girl who looked my age.

Slumping back into the soft seats – this bus was surprisingly nice – I briefly closed my eyes. I was tired again, despite my decent sleep last night.

"Are you new here?"

I jolted, eyes flying open as I shifted around in my seat to face the blond girl. She had leaned forward and I found myself staring into startling green eyes. If they were real, they were absolutely stunning. From what I could see, she was tall and thin, her features narrow, face angular. Not exactly pretty, but with the interesting look of a model. "I've never seen you on the bus before," she continued on, cheerfully chatting, "and I ride it almost every day."

I pushed back some of my wayward hair, swallowing hard. It was immediately obvious she was ultra-confident, which somehow always made me feel extra-introverted. Finally I found my voice. "Yeah, we just moved here yesterday. I was exploring the town."

She chuckled, revealing slightly-crooked white teeth. "Not much to see. Lived here my entire life, and let me tell you, this is one boring-ass town." She held her hand out to me. "I'm Cara. It's great to meet you."

I shook gently, then pulled my hand back to rest on my lap. "Emma. It's really nice to meet you too."

She seemed genuine and friendly, someone I would have enjoyed hanging out with in my old life. After my parents died I lost contact with most of my friends. They tried to stay in touch, but I was so broken, and after a while they just couldn't deal. I never blamed them. I was depressed being around myself. They at least had the chance to leave.

I knew I needed to put some effort into life again, to make friends. It would be nice to know someone before I started school. Hopefully she was going to the same one as me.

Just as I decided to ask her, she said, "So what school are you going to? I'm at Stars High, senior year."

"I'm going to Starslight too. Senior also." I paused briefly. "I'm extra glad now to meet you. Starting a new school in senior year was not in my ten-year plan."

Cara winked at me. "Don't stress, I'll show you the ropes. I'm not at the popular table or anything – none of us mortals are – but there are some nice people who go there. One or two."

That wasn't exactly promising. Cara pulled out a cell then, the case all shiny and pink; the screen lit up. "What's your number? We should hang out over the next few days, when I'm not working, that is."

Right, cell phone. Something most teenagers had. "I actually don't have a phone. And since we literally just moved here last night, there's no house phone either. If you write your number down, I'll text as soon as I can."

Maybe Sara and Michael had some money in the budget for a cheap cell. Wouldn't hurt to ask. Or it might even be time for me to search out a part-time job. Cara's eyes widened, as if she couldn't even understand what I was saying.

"Girl, how do you possibly survive without a phone? I live on the 'Gram and Snapchat. Every moment is a photo-op, you know?"

I nodded, but I really didn't know. What the heck was a Snapchat? The bus was nearing my stop, so I started to shift forward in my seat, scrambling around to find a piece of paper. "Do you have a pen?" I said, pulling out a receipt from my pocket. My key and card came out too. Just as I was about to shove them back in, Cara reached across and plucked the security card from my hand.

"Where did you get this?" she said, sounding absolutely astonished. "Do you know how much trouble you can get into for stealing one of the elite's cards? A Daelight card?"

I blinked a few times before reaching out and taking my card back and shoving it into my pocket. "It's my card. I didn't steal anything. I live on Daelight Crescent. That's my security pass."

She was staring at me really weirdly now, eyes narrowed, lips pursed. I wasn't sure what she was thinking, if she believed me or not, but there was no time to find out. My stop was next, so I pulled the cord and the bus slowed just before the large security gates.

Cara still seemed to be in shock; definitely no condition to be exchanging numbers, so I just gave her a rueful smile and hopped off. So much for making a friend. Clearly the fact that I lived on Daelight Crescent had freaked the blond girl out. Another odd thing to add to my experience in Astoria.

Stepping up to the gates, I squished down my unease. I'd forgotten how imposing the barriers were until I was standing before them. Like seriously, I was pretty sure Buckingham Palace had smaller fences around it. Ace was no longer manning the security booth. Another hulking man had taken his place, one with a mess of dark curls that hung over his ears, and steely blue eyes. He gave me the creeps as he took an exceptionally long time looking over my card, and then staring at my face.

I already checked, buddy. My face is not on there.

Eventually, after scanning me in through the computer, he let me enter. The entire time he was staring at me, he did not speak one word. For a security guard, he did not make me feel even remotely secure.

My heartbeat remained elevated as I stepped onto the street. I couldn't tell if it was from the security guard, or if there was some other threat nearby. Why did I keep feeling like Daelight Crescent was bad news?

I forced myself not to run, but my steps were rapid as I dashed along the street. Half my concentration was on the world around me, the other half on trying to figure out exactly which house was my new home. A lot of these old cottages looked the same, falling-down porches and all, but I knew mine was across from the European-looking mansion, so as its gates came into view I paid closer attention to the older shoebox homes.

I had just found number fourteen when the deep purr of an engine thundered through the afternoon, and I turned to find the sleek purple vehicle driving toward me. I moved back off the road – even though I was clearly on *my* side. My brain kept telling me to walk, to get into the house and don't draw attention, but my eyes remained locked on the car, which slowed to almost a crawl when it drew even with me. I sensed I was being watched, but again the tint was way too dark to make out anything more than shadows.

The window cracked slightly and I froze, waiting to see what the occupants would do next. The window stopped, leaving only a few inches open at the top. I could still see nothing inside. Finally, when I'd had enough of the weirdness, I turned tail and ran as fast as I could. Screw looking cool and calm, I was terrified and wanted to get my butt out of there.

Something was wrong with Daelight Crescent. I knew it now, and it felt almost like it was too late to truly escape. The Finnegans were lured here, and now we were trapped.

3

$\mathcal{A}$fter my scare, the next few days passed quite peacefully. Sara and Michael disappeared on one of their supernatural hunting trips, leaving me home to read and indulge in my other favorite hobby. Knitting. Yep, I was an eighty-year-old in an almost eighteen-year-old's body. Reading and knitting were my fun times and I would go crazy grandma on anyone's ass who tried to stop me. Thankfully I had found a decent wool site online, getting bulk lots really cheap.

Daelight was still creeping me out, but I couldn't deny how peaceful a street it was. Unlike the usual areas we lived in, I didn't have to deal with domestic violence, gangs, or the randoms who wanted to fight it out in front of my house. The only thing dulling my happiness were the occasional stabs of loneliness, but I was used to the Finnegans disappearing for days on end.

My parents had been a bit on the helicopter parenting side. Michael and Sara were the complete opposite. They believed in freedom, making your own mistakes and learning from them. Plus they seemed to trust me completely. I had no curfew. No rules at all, really. Just make good choices, as they always said to me. When they took off, they had promised to be back in time to

drive me to school on Monday, but since it was Sunday evening
and there was still no sign of them, I wasn't holding out hope. I
would be okay, though. I always was.

Except for the food situation. It was running low, and I wasn't
sure I was up to braving the town on my own again. I had one
bowl of cereal left for dinner or breakfast. I needed to make a
choice now. My stomach rumbled at me – loudly – and no
amount of shooshing or filling it with water was helping. Caving,
I ditched my knitting needles in the basket of wool and got up to
eat my Fruit Loops. Just as I was finishing, lights shone through
the open blinds, and out of habit I pressed myself against the wall
and crept to the window. Peering around the corner, I wasn't
surprised to see a car going back into the royal abode, as I called
it now. I mean, their hedges were pruned into shapes. Who else
but royalty did that?

As weirded out as I had been the other day, I also found
myself strangely obsessed with spying on the rich side of
Daelight Crescent. And since the royal abode was the only one I
could easily see from the front window, it got most of my attention. After some careful and selective stalking, I had learned
some interesting things. First, definitely more than one person
lived there. Multiple cars emerged, often at the same time. So far
there was a white Range Rover, a black Porsche, and the sleek
fancy purple one – which looked a lot like an Aston Martin.
Despite his general academic ways, my father had been a secret
car buff. He'd even had an old Ford Mustang in the garage that he
tinkered with on weekends. So I knew a little about make and
model of cars from him. Enough to know that all of the vehicles
that went in and out were expensive – like feed a small country
for the cost of their tires expensive.

Other cars did drive up and down the street, all of them
expensive and darkly tinted, but they went into the other estates.
I guessed there were about ten mansions on the rich side, and
twenty cottages on our side, all squished together. I almost never

saw any of the people who lived in the cottages, just the occasional old beater in their driveways.

The mystery of this place was slowly driving me crazy. Multiple security people roaming around, mansions, fancy cars. A token side of poor people to even them out. What the heck?

As night fell, the pretty streetlamps lit up along both sides of the road. I wasn't really that tired – what with my big day of knitting and creeping around like a peeping Tom – but I still decided to go to bed early so I'd be well rested for school the next day. Of course, my rock bed, teamed with nerves, had me tossing and turning all night, which meant the next morning I was not only hungry but a tired, red-eyed mess.

It took one hot shower, twenty minutes of grooming, and a failed braid before I threw down my hairbrush and called it a day. This was as good as I was getting today. Time to get dressed and get this first day out of the way. Surely it would be the hardest day, trying to learn all the ins and outs of a new school.

Surprisingly, the sun was shining, so I opted for denim shorts, my Converse, and a black long-sleeved fitted top. No need to wear anything fancy. Starslight Prep had a uniform, which I'd receive when I got there. I grabbed the funky vintage leather schoolbag I'd found while shopping in a second-hand store with Sara. Inside were pens, some notepads, and a few other essentials. I was as ready as I'd ever be.

My scholarship included textbooks, materials for class, and some food. Apparently I would find out all the details when I enrolled properly this morning. At least I had a bit of money to cover me if it didn't, but I would have to be careful what I spent.

The only thing I did already know was my schedule. You could enroll online for that part, and Michael had done it for me before he left. But since there was still plenty I needed to do before class, I threw my wallet, security card, and door key into my bag and hurried out of the house.

It was early, the birds chirping as they flittered about the rose bushes and manicured gardens of our street. Despite the sun, it was still cool out, and I wished I'd grabbed a jacket. I should have known better, having already learned about this state's fickle weather. Sun did not equal warmth here.

I saw no one as I hurried to the security gates. I didn't have to check in and out now; I was allowed to wave my card in front of the magic black box and the barriers would open. Passing the booth, I saw a familiar face.

Ace winked at me. "Well, hello, Miss Emma. Long time no see. Where have you been hiding out?"

I'd finally found the courage to ask him how he knew my name, and he told me it *was* logged in the computer. So at least I didn't have to worry about the guards having a mind reading ability or something, which is what the Finnegans would have guessed.

Smiling at him, even feeling a little confident, I said, "Not hiding, preparing myself for today. School."

Ace shuddered. "I hated school. Almost failed out my senior year. Luckily I knew someone who worked for Daelight and they had this opening. It's been a great job. Pay is fantastic, and as long as I don't ask too many questions, everyone leaves me alone."

Why did they keep referring to the street name like that? Like it was a real person or something. Cara had done it too.

"Well," I said, noticing the bus in the distance. "I better get going. Apparently I have to take two buses to get to this exclusive little school."

Ace winked at me again. He was fond of winking, that was for sure. With one last wave I took off at a run, managing to flag down the bus in time. Breathing heavily, I pulled out a map from my bag and examined the route I needed to get to Starslight. I was pretty sure I knew where to go, but I'd double-check with the driver on my way out.

It was a slower journey than last time. A lot more people were heading toward the main street, and the bus had to make multiple stops. Finally I reached the change-over point, and the driver confirmed that the first of a few school buses would be along shortly.

I need a car. I missed my little yellow VW Bug that had burnt up in our garage. The insurance only covered the house debt. There was nothing left for new cars, so I would have to get used to this crazy trek twice a day. At least it was only for a year, then I was done, off to college hopefully, if I could keep my grades up and snag a scholarship. I was determined to do everything I could to get into a decent school. Even with this fabled Starlight pull, I'd probably still have to join some groups, get involved in extracurricular activities. Apparently, extracurriculars was the one college application area where I was underqualified. Seriously ... how could the fact that I wasn't very social affect me getting a scholarship? Never made sense to me.

But, as always, I didn't make the rules.

A few kids were wandering closer to me now, all of them in uniform. A very fancy, expensive looking uniform, black and white, tailored. The girls wore short, black, pleated skirts and black tights, the boys slacks. I had expected I would be the only one in regular clothes. A seamstress would fit it all properly at the school or something – but still ... it was frustrating to stand out already. Pretty much a beacon advertising I was the new kid. Or that I was poor. I was guessing only scholarship kids had to have their uniforms tailored by the school. Everyone else probably had tailors living in their servant house with the rest of the hired help.

More than one glance was thrown my way; the uniformed kids all looked younger than me. At a school like this, most seniors would have cars. A large white bus roared around the corner then, and unlike the town bus this one was sleek and darkly tinted, the school name and emblem printed on the side. I hadn't seen the symbol before; it had a circle, which almost looked like a shadowy Earth, and another much larger circular world right above it. The second circle had a ring around it, and there was a striking symbol bisecting both.

The driver called out to me and I realized I'd been standing there staring at the side of the bus like a crazy idiot. Everyone else was already on board, waiting for me. Heat blazed in my cheeks as I scurried up the steps, striding past the driver to take a seat about halfway along. Everyone was silent as the bus started up again, and while I didn't want to draw attention to myself, I couldn't stop from glancing around. Most of the kids were on their phones, no one looking at me, which was a huge relief.

With a sigh, I turned back to stare out the window. The bus slowly filled as we got closer to the school. I felt someone drop down in the chair next to mine and turned to find Cara. She was decked out in the uniform, hair up in a high ponytail, makeup subtler than the first time we met, her eyes a chocolate brown now. Again, I had no idea if this was her real color or not.

"Hi, Emma!" she said, all cheerful-like. "I was hoping I'd run into you on here, even though you live on Daelight. I sensed you might be a scholarship kid like me, riding the bus."

She was chatting away normally, like her freaked out reaction over me living on Daelight Crescent had never happened. I decided to go with it.

"Yeah, I'm on scholarship. I have to pick up my uniform this morning."

Cara nodded a few times. She was chewing gum; it flashed as she talked. "I'll go with you. They usually assign someone to the new students, help them get adjusted for the first few days. I'm your girl. I know how to survive in this hellhole when you aren't one of the chosen few."

Okay, that was it. I'd had enough of this town's strangeness, of the millions of questions I had bubbling around my brain, and before I could filter myself I leaned closer, lowered my voice, and said, "I'm going to need you to explain to me exactly what the deal is with this town. With Daelight Crescent and all the weird-ness there. Who are the chosen ones at the school?"

Cara's ran her eyes across me and I thought she seemed surprised. I wondered which part shocked her. Before I could ask, she started talking, her voice barely above a whisper: "I'm aston-ished you haven't run into any of them yet. I don't know a lot, but I will definitely tell you what I do know. Just not right now. We'll talk more later."

Ominous. But at least she said she would tell me later, so I'd have to hold on to that. For the rest of the trip, Cara chatted about everything and nothing. She was one of those people who could talk underwater, requiring very little response from me. Still, I found myself drawn to her, finding true warmth under her flighty personality.

"My boyfriend, Mitch, goes to Astoria High, the other school in this area," Cara was saying. "Do you have a boyfriend? Leave anyone behind? What do your parents do? There aren't many jobs in the area, so they were lucky to find something."

I sucked in a low, deep breath, quiet enough I wasn't sure she noticed the strangeness of my response. Such an innocent ques-tion, and it had literally stolen my breath. After a few more ragged inhales, I managed to reply like a normal person.

"I moved here with my guardians. They have an online busi-ness, so we can live anywhere. My parents ... uh, they died eight months ago. I used to live in California, and no boyfriend. I left no one important."

I skimmed quickly over my parents' death, hoping she would just give me the usual "Sorry to hear that" and then move on. It was when people pushed harder, asked how they died, that I usually lost it.

There were a few moments of silence, enough that it was almost uncomfortable when she said, "I'm really sorry to hear about your parents, girl. I can't even imagine how hard that was to live through. My parents are selfish douches at times, especially Dad, but I would never want to live without them."

Yeah, *dead* did kind of outweigh *douche*, but I appreciated her acknowledgement that she couldn't imagine. Unless you'd lived through something like that, stood beside a pile of black ash knowing your parents had burned to death while you had somehow managed to get out ... well, there was no understanding.

Things might have traveled right into awkwardville then, except Starslight came into view and I leaned forward for my first glimpse of my new school. I knew my eyes were wide, mouth probably hanging open as I stared. Cara laughed at me.

"Honestly, I've been going here for four years now and it still takes me by surprise. My theory is that this is an experiment, like some secret government facility, but instead of guinea pigs they're using teenagers. Socialization experiment on the segregation of teenagers. Rich versus poor."

That's exactly what it looked like. Very government, CIA, NSA, space-center like. Huge, shiny, with lots of gleaming windows. There seemed to be an enormous round building in the center with many connections spanning off that led into smaller buildings. Almost like an octopus, but one that was extremely expensive and luminous, made up from a multitude of different metals.

Cara went straight into tour guide mode. "So, the entire school is indoors. Everything is connected via moving walkway corridors." Her hands were jabbing rapidly as she pointed out things through our bus windows. "The only outdoor parts are the sports fields, and they're way out the back. Even the track field is inside. Olympic size pool is also inside, and state-of-the-art gymnastics arena. Anything you can imagine a school needs, Stars has five of them. It's overkill, but what can you do? This is the home of the elite, and they like to cater to a few of us poorer folk. Gives them good PR."

I wondered if that was the reason for the poor side of Daelight Crescent, to garner some positive public relations. Pressing my face closer to the window, I was hit immediately with the knowledge that I didn't belong here. I was going to stick out like crazy, but Astoria High's scholarship program had not been as extensive. College applications were important too, and according to all of the online forums – and Ace – Starslight was the school you wanted to graduate from.

I repeated this to myself multiple times as I followed the other silent kids from the bus. Cara stayed right at my back as we stepped down to the curb. In front was a huge circular entrance, the American flag high in the center. A second flag on a pole nearby had the same dissected double circle symbol as the bus. It was black and white, the bisecting strike a deep red. Just behind this was an extravagant water fountain. In the center was a hand-carved stone depiction of four huge men standing above a bunch of smaller "student" looking people.

"Those are the four founding fathers of this school," Cara said when I paused before it. "It's been over a hundred years, but we still have to see this ugly-ass fountain every day."

Interesting. More students were pushing past us now. The large clock above the main entrance was telling me it was five after eight, which meant the first bell would be going off in about fifteen minutes. I was running out of time. As Cara linked her arm through mine, starting to lead me toward the entrance, a loud purring roar caught my attention. I spun around to look at the parking lot, situated just behind the bus stop.

"No freaking way," I whispered as the cars came into sight. Well, at least one good thing might come from being at this school. I was finally going to discover who lived across the road from me. There were just two of their cars: the purple Aston and white Range Rover, following each other into the lot, both of them pulling into spaces near the front.

"You know how you were asking me about the chosen ones …

the elite. Well, here's the main group of assholes that run this school," Cara said quickly under her breath, almost like she was worried they could hear us all the way over here. "The Darken boys."

I was about to answer her when the doors to the purple beast opened and two males emerged. A third joined them right after. *What in all holy hell?*

"Are they real?" I finally said, wrenching my eyes from the view and turning to Cara.

She wore a knowing smirk. "I've touched them once or twice, accidentally on purpose. They're definitely real."

I had to turn back. I had to see them one more time just to make sure they hadn't been figments of my imagination. "They're so freakin' tall," I finally stuttered out. They weren't just unnaturally tall, but they also had this intense, dark, dangerous vibe going on. Their hair and aura matched their name.

Cara chuckled, apparently enjoying my astonishment. I just couldn't believe these were the guys I had been spying on for days – I hadn't expected them to be teenagers like me. It made me feel uneasy, and kinda intrigued at the same time.

She leaned in closer. "I don't know much about them. No one does. All I've gotten from the rumor mill is that they're all the same age. They're family but not triplets. Top guess is that they're cousins or adopted. Either way, they all have the Darken name. The one in the middle is Lexen. He doesn't talk much, and..." She shuddered. "He might be sexy, but he is dead-set scary as shit. His reputation..." She swallowed hard. "Just stay out of his way as much as you can. He's their muscle. If anyone causes shit, he steps in and sorts it out. He frankly scares the hell out of everyone here, and I would never want to find myself in a dark alley with him."

I let my eyes linger on him. He was bigger than his brothers both in height and breadth. His muscles were defined under the dress shirt molded deliciously to his body, and I found myself breathing deeper as I ran my eyes across him. His hair was black as night, messily styled on one side, shaved shorter on the other, and it almost looked like there were symbols etched into the shaved side. His eyes appeared to be very dark from here, but I was too far away to really tell. His features were broad and well-honed, with a roman brow, sexy lips, and chiseled jaw. He was distractingly gorgeous, in a rugged way. His brother – cousins – whatever – fell somewhere between rugged and almost pretty for a dude.

"The other two are Marsil and Jero," Cara said. "I can't tell them apart most of the time, even though they aren't twins. All I know about them is that they like the ladies. Jero, at least, has probably gone through half the school. Or so the rumors say. I've never hung with the elite group, so I have no actual empirical evidence of this."

Marsil and his "twin" shifted then; in a single movement the pair turned and looked directly at Cara and me. My new friend let out a low shriek and quickly yanked me into the stream of students entering the building.

"Holy crap, that was close," she huffed. I saw her glance back. "That's not the first time they seemed to hear me from an impossible distance."

I wanted to look back too. One of the "twins" had locked me in his gaze, and I was curious to see if he was still staring at me. We might have been a fair distance apart, but his eyes were such a striking crystalline blue that I had still noticed the color.

"Which one of them has the really blue eyes?" I finally asked Cara.

She grinned, shaking her head, some of her nerves fading and her humor returning as we put more distance between us and them. "Jero. He's the huge flirt. I've seen his charm but never been the recipient, thank God. I would probably pee myself if he talked to me."

I joined her in laughing then, quieting as she continued:

"Marsil has dark brown eyes, which are almost as beautiful. Lexen, though, has the most amazing eyes I've ever seen. They're such a dark brown they almost look black, but I swear I've seen these tiny twinkling little lights that seem to illuminate them."

She shook her head. I was starting to think that for someone who'd expressed such fear and unease she certainly paid a lot of attention to these elites. We made it to the main entrance and cold air engulfed me as we stepped inside. Forcing my mind from the Darkens, I focused on the school. Time to deal with being the new kid.

Inside was as shiny and fancy as the outside, looking a lot like I thought a space station would, lots of steel and metal, high ceilings, large banks of windows and natural light – not to mention it was filled with tons of crazy technology that I had no name for – drones buzzing above our heads; security cameras following students; automated doors that welcomed each person as they entered. As we passed some banks of lockers, I wasn't surprised to see that they used thumbprint recognition for entry. It fit with the rest of the character of the building.

Classrooms spanned off this corridor. Cara led me past all of those, toward the huge center building. "This is the office," she said as automatic double doors swished open and let us in. There was a half-circle desk inside, and behind it were three women, impeccably dressed, typing away.

"Hey, Ms. Sampson, I have a new student here. Emma..." Cara trailed off, flicking her head around to me.

"Walters ... Emma Walters."

Ms. Sampson, who looked to be in her late forties, didn't smile at us. She just glanced down and started typing away rapidly. Her blond hair was pulled back in a tight chignon, her brows dark and severe. Finally, she fixed her watery blue eyes on me.

"Scholarship students use that door there." She pointed

across to the right of the office. "They will enroll you, fix your uniform up, and give you the correct locker and lunch access."

She slid a piece of paper over and Cara gave her a beaming smile as she picked it up. We walked off and I couldn't help but stare back at the office lady. She was still watching me, no smile, eyes narrowed.

"Well, that was a warm welcome," I said, more bite than I expected in my voice. She had kind of got to me, though. Really, nothing had happened, but I felt it – the snobbery and attitude.

Cara glanced back too. "Yeah, those ladies are such bitches. I want to constantly remind them that they are glorified PA's, and that they don't own this school. I swear, Ms. Sampson likes to tell people she's directly descended from the Darkens themselves."

I wanted to ask what the big deal was with the Darkens, besides the fact that they were blessed with money and great genetics, but before I could we were through the door, standing in a less sterile-looking waiting area. They were much friendlier in here. An older man led me to the uniform section and it took no time at all to get me fitted out with two complete sets. No tailoring was even needed, which was great. I changed in the small bathroom, and while the stiff starchiness of my new outfit was uncomfortable, I was glad to finally blend. Stuffing my other clothes into my leather pack, I walked out to find Cara waiting.

"Looking good, girl. You wear the uniform better than most of these rich dipshits." She changed subjects rapidly then, as she often did. "I got your locker number too. It's right near mine, in the scholarship section."

I followed her from the room, the friendly man waving us off. Once we were back in the main part of the school, the bell let out a chiming ring. It echoed around the hall and the masses of people started to clear out, heading toward their classrooms.

Cara must have noticed my slightly panicked look, because she flashed me a huge beaming smile. "Don't worry, I logged our late attendance with the office. They will send it around to all the teachers' palm pads." She noticed my confused look. "It's like their own special version of a tablet device. I've never seen them anywhere but at this school." *Okay, then.* "So we won't get into trouble. And we'll only miss homeroom. After that, your first class is history. I have math, so I'll drop you off and catch you in AP English, which we both have for second."

Schedule, right. I pulled out my copy, which clearly Cara had already checked out. She was right, and thankfully next to each class was a small map that showed me how to navigate the school. She leaned over my shoulder to see it again. "Then we have lunch together, which is great. You don't want to cross that jungle alone."

I nodded, having no doubt now that I'd seen this place that she was probably right.

Pushing our way through some students, we ventured into one of the arms of the building, where I was surprised to see a moving sidewalk in the center, which Cara jumped onto.

"Trust me, you don't want to walk all the way to our section," she called as she started to move away.

Of course not. Wouldn't want to use our legs like suckers.

What the hell was this school? I hurried to jump on after her. The path moved quickly, and when we were about halfway along I started to understand the need for the moving paths. These arterials were huge. After another minute, Cara pointed out our stop and we hopped off at one of the breaks and strode over to a small row of lockers. I counted maybe thirty bunched together here.

"So this is the scholarship section," Cara said, her elegant nose wrinkling. "They stash us down here. It takes us forever to get back to our classes. Thankfully, the teachers rarely care what we do. They don't even notice whether we're there or not."

Lovely. My locker was 1102, and it was already cleared of all previous student information, so all I had to do was touch my thumb to it and then it was mine. Inside, all of my textbooks were neatly stacked. There were even extra notepads and pens. Sara and Michael had assured me that this scholarship included everything, and it looked like they had been right.

Cara crowded close to me and I forced myself not to push her away. She had no concept of personal space at all. I was getting used to it, but this was very close. I didn't want her to know I was a damaged freak yet. I needed at least one friend. So, holding my breath, I waited while she rifled through my things. Finally she grabbed the books for my first few classes, and a small card.

"This card is for your lunch," she said, handing everything to me. "We don't get to eat the same food as the other students, but you won't starve. Keep this on you."

I took it from her, surprised to see my face on the side in a small square. "Yeah, it's also your ID card, and as you can see, ours are red." She whipped out her card too and flashed it at me. "The elite have black, and the rest of the school get purple. The class system here is insane. You need to learn your place fast."

I swallowed hard, tucking my ID into my pocket. An actual class system? What the hell had I gotten myself into?

4

*H*omeroom was just finishing as we made our way back toward the main building. Students streamed out into the hallway again. Cara assured me that they would have already marked me as being present. The school monitored everything through these palm pad devices – they were the size of smartphones, and specifically designed for the Starslight network.

It would be wise for me to remember that every time I opened my locker, or passed one of the many surveillance cameras, I was being watched. It made me feel almost as paranoid as Sara and Michael with all their conspiracy theories.

A lurch of worry rocked my stomach as I thought about my guardians. I'd been trying to ignore it, and a new school was definitely a good distraction, but ever since I'd gotten up this morning to find they were still not home, a decided feeling of dread had settled into my gut.

Something was wrong. I just continued to hope that whatever it was they'd be back by the time I got home this afternoon. Otherwise I'd have to figure out what to do. I had to push that worry down again when we reached the history classroom door.

Cara left me with a wave and I started inside. I always took history; it was my favorite subject, along with archeology and anthropology, which I hoped to study in college. With this school's curriculum, I was a little confused though. It wasn't very clear what sort of history this class was about. There hadn't been an American history course on offer here, or any other kind I recognized. My favorite was ancient history, but I love it all, really. I religiously watched *Indiana Jones* and *Bones* in my spare time. Well, at least I *had*, before the fire destroyed my DVD collection, and my life.

Walking farther into the room, there were about twenty desks spread throughout it. Nice desks, with what looked like real wooden bench-tops. The chairs were padded with a thick dark cushion. Everything looked larger and more comfortable than any other school I'd been in.

As I glanced between the many empty spaces, I wondered if there was assigned seating. I should have asked Cara. Deciding it was better just to sit and move if I was in someone's chair, I chose a spot close to the back, on the left side, furthest from the door. I dropped my backpack on the floor and pulled out the history text, a notepad, and pen. I had a few minutes, so I quickly flipped over the front page of the thick textbook to see if I could figure out what we were studying.

Pausing on the table of contents, the book appeared to be divided into four main sections. Number one was ... "House of Darken." I ran my eyes over the other three sections. "House of Royale." "House of Leight." "House of Imperial." The large bolded title at the top of the four sections read: Starslights' founding families.

Well, shut the history classroom door. Now I understood about the elite and chosen thing. The founding fathers ... those statues out the front ... they were linked to the rich guys from my street.

Still, how could they have an entire class about the founders of this school? How was there enough information here to warrant that?

My interest was rising as I continued to scan the subheadings under each of the sections. One was focused on Astoria, another titled *The Rise of Humankind*. Um ... what? This school was whack. Why did rich people think they could just do whatever they wanted? They had pretty much discounted all history here except that of the four families who'd founded this school. Arrogance, thy name is Starslight Prep.

A few students were trickling into the classroom. I made a concerted effort to keep my gaze on the page, not really wanting to catch anyone's eye yet. Cara's warnings were paramount in the back of my head, and even though it annoyed me that they would even have such a class system, I decided to lay low until I learned the ropes. From beneath my lashes I saw a few glances thrown in my direction, but thankfully most dismissed me without a second look. One or two might have narrowed their eyes at me, but no one sat on my side of the room. In fact it almost looked as if they were all choosing to sit as far from me as possible.

Whatever. I don't care. I stared down at my white knuckles clenched tightly on the desk as I continued to remind myself that I just had to make it through this year. One more year. After the last eight months, I should be able to make it through anything.

My eyes felt hot. I was an emotional crier, especially when I was spitting mad. Somehow my body interpreted fury as a need for a decent cry. Today I wasn't furious, I was nervous. So it was easier to hold back the tears.

From my lowered gaze, a pair of *Testoni* dress shoes came into view. The only reason I knew what that brand was – and the fact these shoes were worth about two thousand dollars – was because of my friend back in Cali whose dad was a lawyer and loved expensive shoes. And so apparently did this person, who wasn't shifting from in front of my desk. With a barely audible exhalation I lifted my gaze to find a pair of piercing blue eyes boring into me. Most of my body froze. Only my mouth worked as I tried to moisten my lips.

Jero Darken stood there, not moving, his head tilted slightly to the side as if he was trying to figure out what sort of creature I was. Up close I noticed all the little details I'd missed outside. His skin was dark, almost copper in tone, and it might have been a trick of the light but it appeared to be softly glowing in the well-lit classroom. His dark hair had streaks of caramel through it and was a little longer than I'd thought, hanging over his ears in styled disarray. His features were masculine but finely honed. Well-defined brows arched over those unbelievable eyes. I wasn't sure I'd ever seen a color like that, blue but light, like the early spring sky. Against his skin they popped out at me, the color mesmerizing, though I did look away from them long enough to notice a small, older and faded scar that ran from his right ear down his jawline, giving him a roughish look. All in all, this was one potent, pretty, glaring, interesting specimen of guy.

Speaking of glaring, his was already starting to annoy me. It's okay to be pretty – you can't help your genetics – but politeness was something everyone was able to offer.

We must have been staring at each other for a while, the moment only broken when a girl walked up and nudged Jero. She didn't move him, but he did swing his head, a lazy grin lifting his lips. "Hey, Aria," he said to her. His voice was deep. "I'm just trying to figure out who this female is and why she thinks she can sit back here in our section." He had a hint of an accent I couldn't place. Of course he would have an accent that sent his words rolling off his tongue with a smooth drawl.

And of course he would be an arrogant ass.

Fighting my anger, I focused on the redhead at his side. She was tall, with legs that went on for a ridiculous amount of time. What the heck did she need legs like that for? She'd better be a pole-vaulter or a hurdler or some crap; put those legs to good use. Of course, as my eyes ran across her golden skin, thin frame, generous breasts, full pouty lips, and huge green eyes, there was a much higher chance she was a model. Figures.

I wanted to hate her on the spot just for being perfection, but that wasn't my style. Jero was still glaring at me, but I was done with his attitude, and I wasn't scared to let him know.

I stood suddenly; the female flinched back, but Jero didn't shift at all. I gathered my books up, flipping my wavy hair back, knowing it was probably a huge mess by now but not caring. "Thanks for letting me know this is *your* section. I definitely don't want to sit here."

My tone made it very clear that I didn't think this section was desirable at all, and he knew it, judging by the darkness that clouded that golden face. Many eyes were on me as I crossed to the other side of the room. So much for thinking they weren't sitting near me. I had apparently sat right in the "elite zone." Thankfully there were still a few seats near the front, which I sank into, keeping my head high as I stared toward the whiteboard. My hands were shaking slightly; I felt riled up in a way that was unusual for me. Especially since he hadn't really said much of anything. It was just the attitude I could feel oozing off him, dripping from each of his words.

I fought the urge to turn and see if he was still glaring at me. What an asshole. Seriously. What world were we living in where crap like this still happened? Where people were segregated in high school because of money? I guess it was reality, happening every day, but that didn't mean I had to like it.

A few more tall and beautiful people arrived then, all of them crossing to sit near Jero and the redhead model. A blond guy in particular caught my eye, mostly because he looked a lot like the Darken brothers, just a lighter version: golden blond hair, golden skin tone, light green eyes, and smooth handsome features. From the corner of my eye I saw him greet Jero like an old friend, taking a seat beside him.

The teacher arriving distracted me from the elite. He was a

portly older man with a receding hairline, two-day growth of beard, and what appeared to be a cluttered, vapid sort of personality. He spilled half the contents of his briefcase across the desk, bumped his head when he went to pick up the pens on the floor, and then tripped over the trashcan. By the time he introduced himself as Mr. Perkins, I was already half in love with him. He was adorable.

"I know most of you have taken some history classes with me before," he said, his voice alight with infectious enthusiasm. "Bear with me while I catch up the newbies to this class."

I had a feeling I was one of the only newbies here. Everyone else seemed to have friends and know each other. I was already wishing that they'd told me before I enrolled that this was a specific class on the history on the school, and that others would have already studied the basics – which I could not have done because, shockingly, this was not a topic in my last school. There we had studied a broader perspective on *actual* history.

Oddly enough, the guidance counselor I'd spoken to on the phone here had been very adamant I take this class. The word mandatory was thrown around, if I remembered correctly.

Mr. Perkins clapped his hands together. "This year will be divided into four sections," he started. "Part one follows the four founders of Starslight School. Part two is the history of Astoria and its development from a two-horse town into the thriving hub we have today."

Thriving hub. That might be a bit of an exaggeration.

"Part three and four will look at some American history in general, and how it pertains to the Pacific Northwest."

Well, at least there was some general history in there also, although still well slanted toward Astoria and this school. Gotta give them points for pride and patriotism. Mr. Perkins spent the rest of the lesson going over the plan for the year. No one around me was paying attention, but I was already enjoying learning about this new world I'd found myself in. The best way to understand this school and its cliquey groups was to learn from the past. Find out how the four founders came to rule this school, and according to Mr. Perkins, Astoria also.

The bell rang and noises echoed as everyone pushed out their chairs and gathered books. I wasted no time, wanting to get out of there before the elite, just in case they decided to retaliate for my little dig before. I expected they had completely forgotten my existence by now, but just in case it didn't hurt to haul ass.

Once I was free of the room I whipped out my timetable, searching for my English class on the little map. A quick glance was all I needed to see that it was on the other side of the main domed section of this building, down another arterial. Picking up the pace, I jumped on a walkway that was moving in the direction I needed to go. These unusual paths seemed to be all over the school. They weren't exactly encouraging exercise here, but I guess in a school this size they had to incorporate some sort of conveniences.

I could see lots of other students zipping past, some ahead of me on my particular path, others jumping on and off via small gaps in the side. I wasn't sure I'd be very good at that part. Most likely I'd fall flat on my face and give everyone here a good laugh. Thankfully, for my first solo ride I only had to step off the end, which was easy. Then I was jogging past the administration office and onto another moving path. I kept an eye out, counting the classroom doors as we passed them, and when mine was next I braced myself for the exit.

There was nothing graceful about my leap and the "ouch" that burst from me as my right knee collided with a poor student who had been just standing there minding his own business. By the time I'd untangled myself and stepped back, Cara was right there at my side.

"Emma! Dude, we need to work on your dismount. You would not even be close to medal contention."

With another groan I rubbed my knee, lifting my head to the

guy I'd smacked. "I am so sorry," I said rapidly. "I hope you're okay!"

The first thing I noticed were his eyes. Seemed everyone in this school was blessed with pretty eyes. His were the lightest of green, sparkling as he grinned down at me. "I have to say, beautiful women throwing themselves at me is not my usual thing, but I'm going take it as a sign that you and I need to become friends."

He stuck his hand out, that smile growing even wider. "Ben Witchard. Senior. Performing arts major. Your new BFF."

Ben was tall and lanky, his stunning eyes surrounded by dark-as-night lashes, skin a pale ivory, and hair a mess of brown corkscrew curls. Everything about him screamed warmth, and I immediately liked him. I placed my hand into his and he shook it with a firm grip.

"I'm Emma Walters. Senior. Bookworm. Poor and on a scholarship."

Might as well give him the dirty truth straight up front. That way he could retract his BFF statement. Instead of backing up as I expected, he wrapped an arm around me. I waited for the urge to wrench myself free, but for some reason it didn't come.

"It's very nice to meet you, Emma Walters. My family has more money than God, so we balance each other out. Although, since I decided to tell them I bat for the team who likes boys, things haven't been so happy in the Witchard house. I'd rather be poor. Can I live with you?"

I snorted, my hand covering my mouth by instinct. "I'm not sure you'd like it all that much. I live on this weird gated street and they have security—" I was cut off as Ben let out a low hoot. "What?" I asked, blinking at him like he'd just lost his mind.

When he didn't answer immediately I couldn't help glance around, worried an elite was about to ambush me, but there didn't seem to be any exceptionally tall and beautiful people in our vicinity.

"You live on Daelight?" His voice was just above a whisper,

each word said slowly, announced with perfect clarity. Like he almost couldn't believe what he was saying.

Throwing both hands in the air, I shrugged out of Ben's hug and faced them both. "What's up with this street? Honestly, the way this town acts, you'd think it was where the Queen of England resided."

That would certainly explain the royal abode.

Cara leaned in closer. "Sooo much better than the Queen of England, girl. It's the kings of Astoria."

Clearly Cara had taken our history class before and was now another person putting Astoria and its history above an entire country. Before I could remark on that though, Ben joined her crazy-party-for-one: "All of the elite live there, those descended from the founding fathers. They make my family look destitute with their money and power. They literally run this school and the town."

"The entire state," Cara added. "I have heard they have an in-line to the president himself, and can get pretty much anything they want or need."

For God's sake, next thing they were going to tell me they peed gold and breathed fire, like magical, mythical creatures. "Look, even though I live on Daelight, I haven't seen any elites. They live on the rich mansion side and we aren't allowed to cross over there."

Cara gave me a look, like the one she had given me on the bus when she mentioned the things she had to tell me later. "Be careful, Emma. They are very serious about their rules in that place. The stories..." She trailed off, shuddering a little.

I expected Ben to laugh also, but instead he also got strangely grave. "My family have these huge parties and sometimes they make an appearance. Don't trust them." He didn't elaborate, but his warning was clear.

I forced out a strangled laugh. "Don't worry, guys, I have no plans to play with the heavy hitters of Astoria. I can barely keep cereal in my house and shoes on my feet. My concerns trump my interest in them."

Their twin looks of worry faded into something which resembled sadness, and since the last thing I wanted was anyone's pity, I opened my mouth to change the subject. Before I could, though, the teacher arrived and ushered us into the classroom. This time I stayed close to my new friends, and was relieved to see that the same back corner was off limits here. That made it much easier for me to know to avoid that area in all classes. As I took a seat next to Ben, I realized that none of the elite were in this class yet, and I wondered if those seats were left empty even if no one came.

Right as the final bell rang, two unnaturally perfect specimens of humans entered the room and headed for the back corner. I recognized one. It was Lexen, the extra huge, extra intriguing part of the Darkens' trio. With him was a petite brunette. She did not have the legs of the redhead, but she was probably even more beautiful, if that was possible. Long, silky hair as dark and glossy as a raven feather cascaded in thick waves to her mid-back. She had ivory skin, and full pink lips, which were pressed together hard as if she was fighting to hold back a scream. Her eyes, shaped to indicate a heritage somewhere in Asia, were almost as dark as the guy's beside her.

Despite all the warnings, and my own internal annoyance at the way they acted in this school and town, I couldn't help but let my gaze linger on Lexen. There was something in the way he held himself. It was fascinating, like a lion waiting patiently in the grass. There was no doubt they had their predator eyes locked on everything. Lexen was like that just sitting behind his desk – making it look ridiculously small I should add. Like the other elites I had seen, he carried no books or a laptop. Did none of them need to take notes? Probably they just paid for perfect grades.

Starlit darkness smashed into me then, our gazes holding for a few beats past comfortable, and I knew exactly how it felt to be prey. Through sheer force of will I managed to tear my gaze away from Lexen's. Everything inside of me was screaming to stay off his – and all the elites' – radars. To avoid drawing even a small amount of their attention. I had to be more careful.

Thankfully the rest of my morning classes passed without incident. By lunchtime I was starting to get a feel for my new school. I had even grown somewhat accustomed to being surrounded by the odd but convenient technology.

Cara was waiting at our lockers. We'd decided earlier we would walk to lunch together. We both dumped everything inside, and with our "poor people" cards clutched in our hands, we took the moving paths toward the cafeteria. The entire school ate lunch at the same time here, which was another first for me. In my last school we'd been split up between different years. Here … well, apparently here they liked to encourage school together-ness. As we stepped into the cafeteria, I understood why it worked so well.

"Holy freaking hell!" My words were a breathless whisper, eyes no doubt as large as saucers while I tried to take in the mammoth structure.

Cara chuckled. "Yeah, they like to impress here at Starslight. Got to make it comfortable for all the future presidential candidates they're teaching."

Comfortable was a slight understatement. This was pure luxury. Everything inside was white and shiny; the building was dome-shaped, the ceiling at least thirty feet above our heads. All of the walls and the entire ceiling were made from thick, octagonal windows that fit into each other, forming the structure. They allowed the room to be filled with light and warmth despite the usual inclement weather of Astoria. There were different levels, and sectioned off areas, and as we moved into the main path Cara steered me toward the center of the room, where there was a huge buffet.

"So ... we're allowed to choose from any food with a red tag. The students who aren't on scholarships can choose from anything in this section, and the elite have their own separate section up there." She pointed to a raised platform above us. It jutted out almost like a viewing stage across the entire domed room.

"Where do the seniors eat?" I looked around, trying to get the lay of the land, figure out the social cliques.

Cara, who was still focused on the upper elite platform, finally pulled her gaze away and returned it to me. "There is no separation by grade here, mostly just elite and the rest of us. Don't sit in the elite section and you'll be fine."

I shrugged. Well, that should be easy enough.

The line wasn't very long. The buffet wound for about twenty feet; students were filling their plates as they walked. When Cara and I reached the start of the shiny silver stand, she showed me where to scan my card, then a red tray drifted along a small conveyer belt to stop in front of me.

"Just in case we forget our place, I'm guessing." My nose wrinkled as some of my awe over this beautiful shiny room wore off. Cara said there was no segregation on this level, but by giving me a red tray they were ensuring everyone here knew we were the scholarship students. Which was confirmed when Cara said hesitantly, "It's more so that the serving staff don't accidentally feed us the wrong stuff."

Right. I was silent as we followed a chatting pair of students. They looked much younger than me but were so filled with confidence, smiles and laughter, talking about parties and shopping for bags, it was like these girls were aliens. I had never felt so out of place in my life. For the past eight months I had lived in a grief bubble, barely even noticing the outside world, basically just forcing myself to breathe, take one step after another, eat my meals, and try not to lose my mind with grief. As the veil of my grief was lifting, I was realizing I wasn't the same person anymore. The death of my parents had changed me. Fundamentally. And now I had to figure out who the new Emma was.

As I followed the path of the buffet, I realized what Cara meant about red food. There were tags above each hot and cold dish stating what it was, and those tags were colored. I tried not to look at the dishes I wasn't allowed. I would focus on the fact that no matter how bad the food situation at home got, I was able to eat something here.

Surprisingly enough, the red section was not bad at all. I tended to prefer fruit, salad, and vegetables, if I had the choice, so I ended up with white-sauced pasta, a bread roll, a cup of very fresh-looking fruit salad, and a small-crumbed piece of chicken for a shot of protein. Orange juice and bottled water finished off my selection. I stepped to the side and waited for Cara. My stomach growled as I stared at my tray, desperate to shovel food in my mouth but determined to not act like a crazy person raised in a jungle.

"God damn, they have ribs in the purple," Cara complained as we walked away. "I made the kitchen staff promise me the ribs would be red one day, but so far it has not happened."

I didn't say anything. This was one of the better meals I'd had in a long time, and since I'd skipped over everything I wasn't allowed, I had no idea what I was missing out on.

Even in here all of the benches were padded and so comfortable. My hands visibly shook as I reached for my cutlery, the hunger pangs almost too bad to handle. Somehow I forced myself to take a long drink of water first, before using my fork and knife to cut off small sections of a surprisingly moist chicken breast, all the while listening to Cara ramble on about everything that came to mind.

I was really starting to like having a bubbly, outgoing friend. She never let awkward silences happen, and expected very little input from me. When I was halfway through the pasta, my stomach started to rebel and I knew I needed to stop. It went against all my instincts to leave food behind now, especially with the Finnegans still missing and my food situation at home standing solidly at zero. But if I ate any more, I would be sick.

Just as I dropped my fork, Ben hopped into the seat on my left. "Hey there," he said, flashing that wide grin of his. "Figured since we're new BFFs, we need to hang out during lunch."

I returned his smile, glancing above his head to find two more girls hovering there, both small and blond. That was where the similarities ended. One had piercing blue eyes that were shrewd and assessing. Ben introduced her as Samantha. The other had thick glasses, deep brown eyes, and a dreamy quality in her gaze. She was Lace, resident hippy apparently.

"Sammy and Lace are old friends of mine. We grew up together in the same asshole neighborhood," he said. He then waved toward a short guy who had just appeared. The new guy had longish brown hair, a serious brow, and glasses almost as thick as Lace's. "This is Derek. He runs the geek squad here, has no problem with me being gay, has never been to a party, and somehow manages to be one of the coolest people in this school."

Derek's surprisingly full lips tipped up as he dropped down on the other side of Lace, both of them across from me and Cara. "It's nice to meet you, Emma," he said. "Ben told us all about you."

"Nice to meet you too," I said as I shook his hand. He then proceeded to pull out a massive textbook, opening it next to his tray.

"Sorry to be rude, but I have a test in a few days and I like to read ahead."

Samantha snorted. "Don't let him fool you. He enjoys reading textbooks, and he's usually a year or two ahead of all class assigned reading." She then picked up her salad bowl. It was the only thing on her tray, which was a dark purple. She could have had her choice from all of that delicious food and had only taken a salad.

I immediately distrusted her.

"Emma, tell us about yourself. Did you just move to Astoria?" Lace leaned across the table toward me as she asked the question. A question which was innocent, but which brought forth so many of the dark memories I was trying to keep contained inside.

Swallowing hard, I attempted to think of something to say that would assuage their curiosity without revealing the last tragic eight months of my life.

"Yes, we just moved here. My guardians travel a lot for their job, but we're here in Astoria for the rest of my senior year. They promised me we wouldn't move again before I went to college."

"Are they in the army?" Cara asked, her tray now pushed to the side as she too was finished.

I let out a bit of a chuckle, giving a noncommittal shrug. "No, they do some consulting, and computer stuff."

I had learned it was better to give answers and be vague than to refuse to answer at all. If you acted like it was a big deal or a secret, it would rouse their interest. With Michael and Sara's crazy theories and lifestyle, it was just easier to pretend they were consultants. No one actually knew what a consultant did. It was one of those jobs that wasn't really a job and explained away lots of business ventures.

Ben changed the subject then; his pale skin lit up as he said, "Are we all going to Trey's on Friday night? The first party back of the school year is always the most epic." He turned toward me, reaching across to grab my hand. "You have to come, Emma. The elite parties are insane. They usually have them at these crazy locations, in the middle of nowhere."

I shifted in my seat, subtly pulling my hand free from his grasp. "I'm not really much of a party person." Something occurred to me then, so I added, "And how do you get invited to the elite parties anyway?"

Samantha answered, a slight softening on her face. It made her look much more approachable. "Our family is the rung below the elite. We're rich – well, compared to Ben's family we are well-off. They are billionaires – so we all get invited to the social gatherings."

"And we can bring you along!" Ben added, still looking far too excited. He was a partier, that was immediately obvious. I'd put my money down on him being the one still dancing at 5 A.M when everyone else was asleep or passed out.

They were all looking at me, Cara included, so I finally said, "I'll think about it. I have to ask my guardians."

I couldn't imagine Sara or Michael ever saying no to something like that, but it was rude to just assume it would be cool. They'd be home this afternoon. They had to be. I couldn't consider any other options.

Cara shrieked as she bounced in her seat. "I'm so excited. They don't allow commoners into Daelight Crescent – outside of the few who score rentals in there – so you'll have to get ready at my place. I might be able to borrow my mom's car to drive us too."

Ben jumped in then. "If you can't get the car, I'll pick you up."

I nodded a few times, keeping my happy face on. That seemed to satisfy everyone. A party didn't sound like the worst thing in the world, and if I still didn't want to go when the day arrived, it was easy enough to make up an excuse.

The rest of lunch passed quickly. The conversation was fun and lively between the other five, and I got to listen and learn all the gossip. I did notice how much time Cara spent looking up at the elite section, sneaking glances whenever she thought no one was watching her. It was definitely time to grill her on the way home. She needed to spill everything she knew about them.

5

My afternoon classes consisted of art, which I was terrible at, and biology, which I loved. Both had elite in them, but none were the Darken brothers. Two blond elites were in my art class, a male and female who could have been twins they looked so similar. I learned their last name was Royale, but other than that they were quiet and kept to themselves.

By the end of the first day I was exhausted. It was like my brain had been on hyper-overdrive as I tried to keep up with this new world, and by the end I was ready to sleep for a week. I could have kissed the moving sidewalk as I jumped on it, zoning out as it zoomed me toward my locker. I stumbled off the end, still not any better at dismounting, and quickly dropped all my books off. No homework had been assigned today, which seemed peculiar, but was probably a first day bonus.

There was a decidedly laid-back approach to learning here. Most of the teachers had asked us to call them by their first name. Textbooks were used, but it was mostly frank discussion that made up the curriculum, and there seemed to be value placed on the opinion and voice of students.

I could get used to that.

"Emma, wait up!" Cara called from the moving path, leaping gracefully from the end and reaching my side in seconds. "We can catch the bus together," she finished breathlessly.

I slung my now very light bag over my shoulder and grinned. "I was planning on waiting for you. You still have to fill me in on the elite."

She quickly glanced left and right, before bringing her gaze back to me. "Yes, we can talk a little about it on the way home."

All day she had been so weird about the elite, seeming to both fear and admire them in equal measure. She'd warned me away from them and then spent half our lunch break watching them. Girl was definitely confused about how she felt. I could relate. There had been a reason I continued to spy on them across the street every day. The fascination was there, no matter how much I wished it away.

There weren't a lot of students on the bus we caught.

"Trials start today for the teams," Cara said as we took our seat in the middle of the bus. "It's really a formality. The same students are always chosen."

That reminded me of something and I let out a low groan. She raised an eyebrow in my direction. "I need a few more extracurriculars for college," I told her, barely holding in another groan. "My last guidance counselor told me how competitive scholarships are, and if I want to be in with a decent chance, I need to pad my application."

Cara dropped her pack between her feet and gave a little nod as she straightened. "I'm the same. Thinking about joining the school paper, and maybe volunteering for one of the committees. Prom or something." She quickly added, "As long as you don't want to be a cheerleader, then we have plenty of time to decide. There's a list near the main office. We can check it out tomorrow."

Relief washed through me; there was still time to decide. When she had said all the tryouts started today, I'd thought I missed my chance. "I definitely don't want to be a cheerleader. I don't have a lot of pep, and my flexibility is about minus fifty." I had never been one of those kids who could put their leg over their head. I was more likely to be found trying to touch my toes and only reaching my knees.

When about half a dozen students were seated across the bus, the driver – a middle-aged man with kind eyes and a cheery smile – shut the door and slowly pulled out of the main parking lot. As we drove by I noticed the Darkens' cars were still in the lot, which probably meant those elite were on the football team. Figures.

As the school disappeared, Cara and I slumped into our seats, and she shifted to face me. The mascara around her eyes was smudged, the fancy up-do in her blond hair falling out, but she still managed to look confident and put together. My last thirty bucks said I didn't look nearly as good.

"What I'm about to tell you is ninety percent rumor and ten percent guesswork from me." Her voice was barely above a whisper.

"So pretty much zero confirmed fact?" I murmured back.

She nodded. "There is something weird about the elite in this town. Weird like ... they're not normal humans."

Obviously they weren't normal humans. They were rich and powerful and connected, like meeting the president, or a movie star.

Cara must have noticed my expression, because she shook her head. "No, it's not just that they are beyond perfect, or that they have enough money to buy most countries, or that there is not a single door in this world which doesn't open for them. It's more ... I don't even know how to explain it. If I had to guess, I would say they were literally not from Earth."

She shot me a look, probably waiting for me to laugh and accuse her of being crazy. I didn't though, because I was very used to this sort of theory now. The Finnegans had me well prepared. "You think they're something supernatural," I whispered, wanting more information. "Like ... vampire or werewolf or something?"

Cara blinked a few times, before she expelled a huge breath of air and sank even lower. "Honestly, I know I sound crazy. I *know* this. And probably the elite are just mafia or something. But if they were vampires it would make so much sense ... explain away their oddness."

I had definitely picked up on that odd vibe. Even the way they garnered so much privilege and respect in Starslight. I mean, football players were treated pretty well in my hometown, but this was an entirely new level.

"Did you know teachers are swapped in and out all the time, sometimes in the middle of the school year," Cara continued. "I don't even remember most of their names."

I wasn't sure what to think or believe, but I was starting to understand what had brought Michael and Sara here. These elites were definitely bringing attention to themselves. Odd that it was happening now, considering Michael always monitored that sort of thing and he had seen nothing until recently.

Could his original theory be right? Were we lured here for some reason? Was that why they were not home yet? My heart rate was starting to pick up, heat rushing my body as panic and adrenalin warred within me. If my guardians were not home when I got there, I would give them until tonight. Then I would have to do something. Talk with the security. Follow their path.

Sucking in deeply, I breathed through my worry, knowing there was nothing I could do until I saw if they were home or not. Cara was looking at me strangely, so I quickly changed the subject.

"So, will they start giving out more homework?"

Tilting her head to the side, she observed me for a beat longer, shaking her head, blond strands swishing across her shoulders. "No, we never get homework. The teachers don't like to mark it."

Third bonus for the week. "You're always staring at the elite? Why is that?" The tactless question exited from my mouth before I could stop it.

I expected a glare, but she just let out a deep sigh. "Last year, at one of the Friday night parties, before Mitch and I started seeing each other, I hooked up with an Imperial. You haven't seen them yet, they never come on the first day – actually, the Imperials only come to school when they feel like it. They fight with the other founding families. Lots of tension."

I flashed back to my history text to those families: Imperial, Royale, Darken, and Leights.

"I don't even know which Imperial it was," she continued, "but before anything could really happen we were separated by Daniel Imperial. He's the leader of his little family group."

She looked wistfully out the bus window. "Ever since then ... I just can't break my obsession with them. With all of the elites. I hate them, Emma, I really do. And yet I crave to be closer to them."

Before we could speak further, the bus came to a halt in the main square of Astoria and I had to change buses. "See you tomorrow," I yelled to Cara as I dashed down the stairs. She was going right to her job at the local diner, so she had no rush to get off. I was running, making the town bus just in time.

I sat right at the front. On the last leg of my journey home I didn't see the stunning scenery of the beautiful town, a town I was already half in love with. I was lost in thought of everything that had happened today. School. Cara's weird vibes about the elite. There was so much mystery surrounding everything here, and I was starting to get a Michael and Sara feeling – Astoria had something extraordinarily strange going on.

I was practically bouncing in my seat as I waited for the bus to reach Daelight Crescent. The Finnegans were at the forefront of my mind. I needed to know they were safe. When the bus finally approached my stop, I yanked on the cord and was already waiting at the front when it pulled up.

"Thank you," I shouted over my shoulder as I hurried down the stairs.

I dashed across the road. By the time I was approaching the gates the sky had darkened and fat drops were landing on my cheek.

"Looks like you'll make it just in time, Miss Emma." Ace's grinning face brought a similar grin to my own. "How was your first day of school?"

I quickly swiped my card, waiting for the gates to open. "It was good. Starslight is amazing and a little intimidating, but I'm enjoying it so far."

Ace's grin turned into a chuckle. "Yeah, they treat you right there. Alright now, hurry inside. It's about to get bad again."

Sure enough, as he spoke, a crack of lightning rocked the sky above us and the rain got heavier.

"See you tomorrow," I yelled as I ran.

"Bye, Emma. Stay on your side of the street, you hear."

The last part he added sounded playful, but it still sent a small flicker of unease through my chest. Reminded me that not all was right in this world. That the elite, who most likely all lived on this street, had far too many secrets for my liking.

My keys were in my hands as I dashed along the rundown side of the street. As my shack came into view I bit back a curse, my heart sinking low. No car in the driveway; the Finnegans weren't back yet. The worry could not be pushed aside any longer; my hands were shaking as I unlocked the front door. Stepping inside, I still checked every room, just in case Michael had dropped Sara off. *Nope.* The house had not been touched since I left this morning.

I'd promised myself that I'd give it until nightfall, so I'd have to wait a few more hours before making a decision about what to do. The Finnegans did not like or trust the police, they made that perfectly clear. But I couldn't think of what else to do. I didn't have money for a private investigator, and I was terrible at computers. No way could I hack in Michael's to try to see if there was any record of their plans here in Astoria.

Please just come home.

I was starting to shiver in my damp clothes, so I hurried to my room and switched out my uniform for the same clothes I'd worn to school this morning. I also unpacked my spare uniform, hanging both in the tiny closet. After this, I dragged the blanket off my bed and snuggled it around me on the couch. Dropping my head back to the barely comfortable cushion, I stared out the front window into the rain-drenched street. The quiet settled around me and I thought briefly of switching the TV on. It was ancient and had five channels, but it would be distracting.

I didn't move. I kept vigilant watch through those windows, hoping the familiar clunker of a car would pull into the driveway. We should have had this discussion as a family, what to do if they didn't show up from one of their trips away. In my old life I would have just gone to the police, filed a missing person's report, and let the professionals do their job. But Michael would never forgive me if I did that. He told me all the time we couldn't trust anyone in council or government, law enforcement as well. They were in the pockets of these supernaturals.

Please just come home.

My eyes got heavy and I decided a little nap might kill some of the afternoon. Stretching out across the couch and wrapping the blanket around me, I drifted off to the pitter-patter of rain. It was one of my favorite sounds, although something told me I could soon become very sick of it living here, and crave the occasional day of sunshine. Quite the opposite from when we lived in Roswell.

A roar of an engine woke me sometime later. I was disoriented for a few moments, finally remembering I was still on the couch waiting for the Finnegans to return. I bolted upright and jumped to my feet, stumbling a few times as the blood rushed around my body. Shaking off the disorientation, I threw a quick glance at the oven to see it was 5:48 P.M. No wonder it was almost dark. The outside was only lit by the pretty streetlights that lined Daelight Crescent.

I scanned our driveway. There was no car, but I was sure an engine had woken me. Grabbing my shoes and coat from the stand near the door, I quickly pulled them all on, lifting my umbrella and opening the front door. Stepping out onto our tiny porch, the icy breezes cut through me. What the hell, Astoria? It felt like it was the middle of winter. I quickly opened the old black umbrella, hoping it would manage to keep me somewhat dry. Then I hurried down the steps and out onto the street. I made sure to stay on the shack side, but it was getting very muddy on the grass, so I walked on the edge of the road.

As I got closer to the front gate, I realized I'd forgotten my ID card, which gave me a moment of worry. What if someone new was on the gate and they kicked me out? I'd be stuck out in the rain. Just when I was trying to decide if I should turn around, Ace's smiling face popped into view. He was on this side of the fence, looking like he was about to clock off work. He had a jacket and umbrella too.

"Ace!" I shouted into the wind, dashing toward him.

He turned, eyebrows raised as though I had startled him. "Hey there. Is everything okay?"

I huffed a few times as I stopped in front of him, my breath wheezing in and out. Ace chuckled this time. "I'm going to guess you're not a runner."

I shook my head, still breathing deeply, managing to huff out, "God no, I prefer leisure activities that include reading, shopping, knitting, lying on the beach, and exploring museums. I'm an indoor activity sort of girl."

"Good to know." His dark eyes glittered in the dying light.

"With that in mind, I'm guessing you have an important reason for running in this storm, then?"

I nodded, my breath finally back. "Yes ... have my guardians come through the gates at all today? They were supposed to be back by now, and ... I'm a little worried."

Understatement of the year. My low-lying panic was starting to really make itself known. I was about an hour off losing my mind completely.

All of the mirth dried up on Ace's face, his blank expression suddenly unreadable. "I haven't seen Michael or Sara for a few days ... did you want me to report this? I mean, there's nowhere in Astoria to really get into trouble. But they did say they were just off exploring the backcountry. Maybe their car broke down and they are trying to get home."

Everything he said was perfectly reasonable, and yet I still felt a shiver of unease trickle down my spine. So many secrets surrounded this street, surrounded the elite. They were up to something here, and I was partly panicking that my guardians had stumbled into a bad situation – sticking their noses into elite business. They were in trouble. I knew it.

I was starting to think that coming to Ace and confessing my worry was a mistake. He could very well be in their pocket. No doubt everyone who worked for them was. What if he was going to "report" it to someone who shouldn't know about us? I could hear Michael's voice in my head cautioning me about sharing any more information.

With that in mind, I pasted on a broad smile and nodded a few times in a careless manner. "I'm sure they're fine. If they aren't back by tomorrow, then I'll go in and check with the police. They have done this before, too. Got caught up in whatever they were doing and forgot to let me know." I winked, which was such a foreign gesture for me that both of my eyes kind of shut at the same time, so it probably appeared I was having a seizure. Still,

Ace seemed to have bought my act. He clasped a hand on my shoulder and with his grin back in place, turned me around.

"Good idea. Okay, then, hurry back to your house now. I think this storm is about to get much worse."

I stumbled away, looking back to find him staring after me. He gave a brief wave, and then the second time I looked back he was gone. There was really no point in running now; I was soaked through, the umbrella zero barrier against rain that seemed to be falling sideways. Talented rain in the PNW, apparently.

Slipping and sliding across the muddy ground, I tried to figure out which house was mine again. I was going to have to tie a big red bow to the front freaking porch soon so I could find it with ease. As I got closer I started to ponder what to do now. There was no other option. I would have to go to the police. I'd just check Michael's computer first, see if I could somehow manage to get information from it...

A roar of an engine close by distracted me, and as my chest clenched I lost my balance and slid into the mud. My umbrella flew off into the wind and I found myself flailing on my belly, trying to gain traction so I could get back to my feet. I managed to lift my head up far enough to see that it was one of the cars from that mansion across the street, slowly making its way along the lane. It pulled up to the front gate and I waited, expecting them to disappear inside, which was their usual thing. But the car's loud engine died off, and the driver and passenger door opened. Two large shadows stepped out, neither of them holding an umbrella. Cara's words came back to me and I wondered if these weird bastards could probably repel the rain with mere thought or something. Those two were joined by another shadow, and then the three of them turned away from their huge front gates and started walking down the sidewalk.

I lost sight of them as I got to my hands and knees, pulling myself up. I had mud in places where mud should never go, coating my face and hair. I could even taste it on my tongue. The rain would have to take care of it, though, because I decided then and there I was not going home. I was following those three. I needed to know what was going on in this street, because whatever the mystery was, my family was caught up in it.

Following them would require me to cross to the other side of the road of course. The forbidden side. But by this point I really didn't give a shit. I was wet. I was coated in mud. I was scared and annoyed and furious at the world for all of its messed up happenings.

So ... I was going over to the elite side.

The sky was lit only by the occasional strike of lightning, yet I felt exposed as I dashed across the main road, streetlight no doubt reflecting off my strained features. The mud running off me in thick dark rivulets was good camouflage, but it would soon be washed completely off, so I stuck to hiding and running between bushes as I followed the three shadows.

They stayed on the path that led right along the front of the elite side of the street, nicely landscaped hedges and small bushy bundles of roses popping up along both sides, which gave me some decent hiding places. Not that I needed them; none of the three ever looked back. I wished it wasn't so dark so I could see who exactly I was following. I had a feeling it was the Darkens, which was almost purely guessed from the size of their hulking shadows, and the car they'd emerged from.

Weirdly enough, the farther we got from the main gate, the fewer street lamps were about, and somehow the harder the storm raged. The wind buffeted me from all sides as I slipped and slid after them, my hands and forearms already covered in grazes from falling into bushes. I didn't care. This was not a chance I was giving up on. I would figure out where my guardians were.

The last elite house was coming up on my left, and as the three shadows passed by it they took a sharp left and then were gone from my sight. Forgetting about stealth, I picked up the pace, hauling butt as fast as I could. Rounding the corner in the same direction they had taken, I found myself in a long laneway. Roses trailed in huge viny masses across the roof of the path; it smelled sweet as I tentatively stepped inside, the damp air ramping up the scent of the flowers.

There was next to no light in here, which had my pulse racing and stomach churning, but I had come this far. I was not turning back now.

Picking up the pace, the grass beneath my feet keeping my footsteps silent, I raced along. After some time, I blinked as a faint glimmer of light appeared in the distance, a pinprick that grew larger as I closed in on it. The roses were thinning above me, the stormy sky visible in small patches as I continued toward the light. It was quite bright, and I kept my eyes locked on, using it as a guide. As the covered path ended, I slowed my steps, afraid I was about to run right into the three elites. If they were standing there at the end of the path, I would just have to play dumb, because there was nowhere to hide.

Hopefully they'd buy my story that I'd somehow gotten lost and stumbled into this secret little area. With my cover story intact, I focused on the light for the first time.

What in the world?

I just stared and stared and stared, trying to figure out what I was looking at.

A swirling portal? A manmade storm?

Whatever it was, it stood at least fifteen feet high, and looked a lot like a tornado of light and energy. It lit up the round, otherwise empty courtyard. The light was swirling and twirling, shooting small rope-like tendrils about. Somehow I made my feet move again, each step slow and deliberate as I walked closer to the swirling mass.

What was it? Some new government technology? Or something ... supernatural?

When I was as close as I felt comfortable getting – there were definite sparks of electricity in the air; I had goosebumps across my arms – I sidled around, trying to see the full scale of this light-tornado.

That's when I saw them. The three shadows.

Only they were no longer shadows. My guess had been right. It was Jero, Marsil, and Lexen.

They stood much closer than me to the swirling mass, not an ounce of unease on their faces as those light tendrils twirled in arcs around their heads. Jero was in the middle, and he had his right arm extended as though he was waiting for someone to take hold of it from the other side.

Which is exactly what happened.

6

My gasp escaped before I could stop it, and even though the noise of the swirling tornado was loud enough to cover a lot, it didn't cover that. Two starlit eyes pierced me, and a plethora of low growls was Lexen's response. Before I could say anything, or run away, which is what my rapid pulse and freaked-out mind was demanding, there was a Darken on either side of me, each capturing an arm and dragging me over to the swirl of light. Marsil and Jero were my captors. Lexen had not moved.

As the pair dragged me right up to the swirling light thing I let out another gasp. I really needed to work on my poker face, but seriously, a person had emerged from within the light.

"You shouldn't have come here," Jero said, his hypnotic blue eyes burning into me. For some stupid reason, I noticed he was wearing a different set of dress shoes, along with a very expensive suit.

Why I should care about something like that, I had no idea, but the suspicious notion of a teenager dressing like a billionaire businessman was not lost on me. I should have guessed from the start that something was really not right with these three. My gut started to churn as light flashed around me. I wondered if any moment now I might actually barf on a Darken. Jero would probably really appreciate vomit on his ten thousand dollar suit and shoes.

"What is this light thing?" I stuttered out.

Jero lifted his gaze to meet Marsil's. No doubt they were having a silent conversation over my head. Here's hoping that conversation didn't involve all the ways they could kill me and make it look like an accident. Realizing I wasn't getting an answer, I turned my attention to Lexen, who was ignoring me as he hugged a willowy girl with long raven curls.

A chick who could apparently travel through light.

As she stepped out of his shadow, she turned to the other two. "Jer, Marsil! I'm so glad to see you! It has been too long!"

Her shrieked greeting grated across my last nerve. That's when I started to struggle. Neither of the Darkens must have expected that, because I managed to wrench myself from their grip, landing hard on the ground. I started to scramble back, but before I got more than a foot away, Lexen took a step forward and snatched me up.

Literally. He jerked me to my feet and up into the air, using just one arm wrapped around my back.

"You're not going anywhere." His words were a low, rumbly growl. His accent was even stronger than Jero's. "Didn't your parents teach you to mind your own business? You've stumbled into something you really should have left alone."

Ignoring that threat, I continued to struggle. "My parents are dead," I spat at him. "And my guardians are missing, so right now I don't give a shit about right and wrong. I want answers."

How dare he give me orders and manhandle me like a child!

"Put me down!" I snarled, feeling hot dampness behind my eyes. I willed my tear ducts to behave themselves for once. Angry crying was not appropriate right now.

To my surprise, he complied, placing my feet back on the

ground. Then he stepped back like he was disgusted just being close to me. "Hold on to her, Marsil," he commanded, before he turned in my direction one last time. "We can't let you go now. You've seen too much. I need to speak with the council. They'll advise what to do about this ... situation."

Great, now I was a *situation*.

Marsil wrapped a big hand around my arm. He was the shortest of the three Darkens, still well over six foot and heavily muscled. I was definitely not going to be able to fight him off.

"Council?" I parroted. "I don't understand ... like Astoria town council?"

Lexen didn't answer; he didn't even look at me again.

"I don't want to hurt you." Marsil's voice was gentle, and I found myself focusing on him fully. Up close I saw why he was referred to as Jero's twin. They looked very similar, but I would say Marsil was not quite as beautiful. Features less refined. More rugged. A little harder around the edges. Which contradicted the softness of his eyes. "Please don't struggle."

I swallowed roughly. "Let's make a deal. You don't rape or kill me and I'll play the good victim for now."

There was a snort of laughter from Jero, but it was Lexen who answered, "You don't need to fear rape from us." Mild distaste was clear in his voice, and I totally hadn't missed the fact he hadn't included death in that statement.

The girl, who was standing close to Jero, watched me silently. I noticed from the corner of my eye, but I was too freaked to really pay attention to her. For some reason, the boys seemed more real to me. Maybe because they hadn't just appeared in a ball of light.

Marsil started to move and I forced my feet to hurry to keep up. He kept his large hand wrapped around my right bicep as we moved along the rose vine path and then back onto the main road. No one spoke as we walked, and when the shacks came back into view I stared longingly at them. Part of me really wished I'd listened to the rules and stayed over there. I understood the world over there. It might have been cold, and lonely, and hungry, but it was mine.

The Finnegans. I reminded myself there had been a reason I'd crossed to the elite side. Hopefully I'd find an opportunity to question these Darkens about where my family was. Maybe their council knew something. If I wasn't killed before getting the chance to ask.

The girl was sandwiched between Jero and Lexen. Marsil and I were just behind. She was a few inches taller than my five foot eight, but somehow still looked small next to the boys. As if she had felt my eyes on her, she met my gaze. Her eyes were a dark blue, and there was a mild curiosity in that look, like she wasn't sure what to make of me. Then she smiled and I almost stumbled over my feet. I hadn't been expecting that.

"*It'll be okay,*" she mouthed to me.

I blinked a few times, but before I could respond she turned back around. Marsil, who no doubt had seen that weird exchange, said nothing. His grip remained firm, but not tight. We stopped when we reached the huge gated estate that the Darkens called home. I looked toward my house. There was no car in the driveway. My breathing got erratic then as I tried to wheeze some air in and out.

"Are you okay?" Marsil asked me, and I found myself staring into his face, focusing on the hard planes in a desperate attempt to calm myself.

He tilted his head, concern emanating from him. I was starting to understand the kind eyes, and his gentle way of maneuvering me. He was a nice guy, that much was clear. And for some inexplicable reason I felt comfortable with him. Wasn't it too early for Stockholm syndrome to be kicking in? Surely I shouldn't trust my kidnappers, even if my instincts were telling me that Marsil at least had a truly kind soul.

"Just wishing I was back in my house," I finally answered him, flicking my head toward the shitty side of the street.

Marsil looked like he was about to say something, but the Darken gates opened then and we were moving. After all of the hours I had spent stalki ... observing their mansion, it was kind of surreal to now be inside the estate. If I wasn't so worried that they were planning on killing me and tossing my body off into the water at the back of their land, it would have been a very cool outing.

I tried the best I could in the dark to see everything, but the rain and wind was making it near impossible.

Wait a minute...

"You're not wet?" I said to Marsil, my brow furrowing as I looked him over. "And the rain is not hitting me..." I was still soaked – at least ninety percent of the mud was gone – but there was definitely no rain hitting me right now. It even felt like the wind was whipping *around* us, not buffeting me like it had done when I was chasing after them.

Marsil ignored me, as I expected he would. No way to explain that sort of weirdness in terms a human would understand. *Freaking supernaturals.* For the first time ever I attempted to wrap my head fully around the concept. I was going to owe the Finnegans a huge apology when I finally figured out their whereabouts.

We continued along the wide, double front drive. Huge trees lined either side, and then off in the dark it looked like flat expanses of landscaped grounds, the sort of place where I would have normally run and frolicked for hours.

If it wasn't the domain of kidnapping assholes, of course.

When we reached a set of huge, ornately detailed wooden front doors, Lexen turned to Jero. "Bring the car in. We don't need any questions from the other houses."

Jero took off then, disappearing into the darkness. I wondered why they hadn't brought the car up when we first passed. Were they worried about separating from me? Because I was such a danger to them? With my ten dollar shoes and threadbare jeans?

I knew the girl had her eyes on me again, but this time I didn't look in her direction. I was not making friends with them, none of them. Lexen moved to the side after he opened the door. Marsil and I stepped into the mansion first, and as the lights flickered on all around me I found myself standing in the most beautiful house I had ever seen. Ever. Including movies and magazines.

Wide, dark oak floorboards spanned out across the open expanse of the entrance, an entrance which continued on into a living and dining room. I even caught glimpses of the large white kitchen bench. The far wall, which was like miles from the door, showcased the dark world beyond with floor-to-ceiling windows. The ocean would be crashing out there, hidden in the night.

Marsil let me go then, the front door closing ominously behind us. I knew there was no way I could escape; I had seen how fast they moved. Even if I did somehow manage to escape, where would I go? My shack was across the street and it had no security. The front gate guards were owned by them. Maybe even the police. Everything Michael had ever told me was hitting with full force now. I might have laughed at the time, but he had been right. I had no power, no ability to fight them. It was the worst kind of feeling, and yet my instincts didn't seem to be picking up on any imminent danger. I decided to see if I could get some answers before panicking too hard.

The three crossed the floor, leaving me near the door. I eyed it for a beat, before Lexen said, "Don't bother. You won't be able to leave until we let you out."

Shocker.

My shoes squelched as I followed their path, water dripping off me. Small shivers brushed across my body as the cold sank in deeper. Their house was styled in a "beach Hamptons, I'm richer than God" look. Expensive, but still seemingly comfortable.

Wide, plump-cushioned, striped couches were scattered around a large ornately-manteled fireplace, facing toward the windowed view. Everything was done in cream and tan colors, and I wanted nothing more than to jump into the soft depths of one of those armchairs and snuggle deep.

Marsil sat, waving at the girl. "Star, sit down, sweetheart."

She practically fell in next to him, the pair slumping together in a familiar way. "I have barely slept for days," she said, her voice low and melodic. "Fighting with Father about me leaving was really frustrating." She shook back her long, thick, shiny hair. "He's still upset, so don't be surprised if he contacts one of you."

Lexen was standing near the window, his back to the view. He swiveled to face her. "We can handle Father," he said. "But I still don't understand why you came at all. We're fulfilling the terms of the treaty."

Star crossed her arms. I was getting a sense of stubbornness from her. "Where my brothers go, I go. Besides, it's no fun on..." She quickly glanced at me. "At home without you."

She was their sister. And they were all brothers. So how the hell were they all in the same year at school? Were they quads? Or ... I had no idea. This family was too weird to try wrapping my brain around. Part of me wanted to remain quiet in the hope I could learn something from their idle chatter, but another part of me needed specific questions answered, and needed them now.

I was about to ask about Michael and Sara when Lexen locked me in his dark gaze. "Why did you follow us? The rules are explained to all who live on this street."

I swallowed hard, his mere presence scary enough to have all saliva disappearing from my mouth. "My..." I had to clear my throat. "My guardians have vanished. They were searching for supernatural activity in this area, and ... something weird is going on in this street!" Somehow I was shouting, so I tried to calm myself. Why was I acting so weird? It was like my emotions had no middle ground. One minute I was calm and collected, the next a raving mess of nerves and anger.

I sensed Star and Marsil staring at me, but I couldn't tear my gaze from Lexen. He was everything I would normally avoid in a man – too tall, too broad, too strong – the shaved side of his hair flashing those symbols at me, and no doubt there were matching tattoos hidden under his sleeves and jeans. He had bad boy written all over him, and unlike a lot of girls I'd known I was not interested in trying to tame myself an attitude problem.

But I couldn't look away.

"There is no such thing as supernaturals," Lexen said, his tone dismissive. "Your guardians are idiots, and are probably lost in the forest somewhere."

He wasn't completely wrong, they definitely could just be lost, but I was almost entirely sure he was lying about the supernaturals part. I was putting all the pieces together now, everything I had ever overheard from Sara and Michael: the strange things in this town; Cara's information; the odd happenings since I was discovered by these Darkens – that ball of light that had spat out a girl. How were they going to explain that away? Even if they could, I had made up my mind. Supernaturals were very much real, and I was in their house. Since it seemed Lexen wanted to pretend this was all a big misunderstanding, I would play along.

"No doubt you're right." I stared at my nails, acting nonchalant. "I've always thought they were a little on the crazy side, but I still love them." Lifting my gaze, I met his unflinchingly. "Do you know for sure they're lost? Do you have any information on them?"

He just shook his head at me, before his attention was captured by something behind me. I turned to find Jero sauntering along, his dark gray suit fitting in perfectly with the beautiful surroundings of their home. "No problems?" Lexen asked.

His brother shook his head. "Nope. It's all quiet out there."

"Sit."

I realized that command from Lexen was aimed at me, but since I wasn't a dog I chose to cross my arms over my chilled body and stare him down.

Screw you, asshole.

His jaw was rigid; I could see a small tic in one corner. "Someone dry her off, and don't let her out of your sight. I will be back once I contact the council."

"And Father," Star piped up.

He nodded at his sister, before turning and striding off.

Jero, who had been heading for the couch with his sister, quickly changed paths. "I volunteer to dry you off," he said, flashing me a wide grin.

I snorted, so elegant as always. "Wipe that smirk off your face, Romeo. This girl is not interested."

It almost looked like he was pouting, even though he flashed a wink at me. "I'm devastated."

Star, who must have moved without me seeing, since she was standing right behind him, let out a little chuckle. "He's never been told no before. You really have devastated him."

She held out a hand to me, not like you would to shake, but sort of like she wanted me to kiss it. I just stared down at it, and she hastily pulled it back. "Oh, sorry," she murmured, sounding a little breathless. "I'm Star. It's really nice to meet you."

I just gave her a nod. "I'm Emma."

Star didn't seem taken aback by my unfriendliness. If anything she got even more animated. "You can borrow some of my clothes. We're almost the same size."

Well, sure, if you discounted me being shorter and fatter than her. Even with my recent weight loss I couldn't compare to her slender figure. I was naturally curvy.

Star turned to Jero and he shook his head. "Lexen won't like it."

She started to plead with him in a low voice. I caught bits and pieces before Jero finally threw his hands up. "Okay, fine. I'm sure

Emma won't try anything." He faced me. "We're very protective of our sister. Keep that in mind."

I wrinkled my nose at him. "I'm not going to attack an innocent girl. You three, on the other hand, I don't care so much for."

One side of his lips quirked up. "I like you," he stated, before turning to Star. "Straight to your room and back, no detours. You better be in this living area before Lexen returns."

She nodded, not commenting on his asshatty way of speaking to her. Maybe I was lucky never having any siblings. I wasn't big on being bossed around. Star linked her arm through mine and began to drag me away, chatting like we were the best of friends.

"This is my first time visiting this house, but it seems to be set out similarly to back home, so I shouldn't have a problem finding my room."

My brain could only handle so many revelations that upset the very fabric of my world, so for now "back home" was a small supernatural community somewhere in the middle of Alaska – still on Earth. It made perfect sense, really. They'd no doubt want to live away from the general population. The Sahara would work too, if they preferred heat.

On Earth. Heat on Earth because they were definitely from Earth. Just like ... evolved humans. God, I hoped they weren't vampires.

Star led me to a staircase off the side of the entrance. It was tucked away, only visible when you got close. I tripped once going up the stairs, my lack of grace and nerves getting to me, but somehow managed to make it to the top unscathed. The first floor had a hallway with a lot of closed doors, so I couldn't see inside, but something told me there were mostly bedrooms on this level.

"This one!" Star declared, halting in front of a white door, identical to a dozen or more white doors we had already passed. I was pretty darn cold, so hopefully she knew what she was talking about. The door swung open without a sound and we were inside in a heartbeat. Thick white carpet squished under my shoes and I ground to a halt.

"Wait, I need to take my shoes off. They're going to make your carpet dirty." I'd never seen carpet so pure, so untouched. It was the sort of flooring that should not be walked on.

Star just waved my concerns off. "Don't stress about it. It's just the floor."

With reluctance I continued into the room, wincing at the trail of black streaks I was leaving behind me. The main part of the bedroom was huge, as big as our entire shack across the street. On top of the pristine carpet was a large bed with a dark purple, velvet and ornate material bedhead. It was huge, rising up and curving inwards at the top. The bed was dressed in whites and lilacs, lace throw pillows giving it a very fairytale finish.

"This is a beautiful room," I said sincerely. It was so light and open, everything feminine but not overly girly.

Star looked around as if only just noticing the room. "Oh, yes, they did a great job making this feel like home. I'm very lucky to have my brothers."

One way to look at it.

"Do they always boss you around like that?"

She smiled at me, seeming unoffended by my question. "The men in my family are very protective. It's part of who they are. I try to only fight the important battles – let them think they win some. I usually get my own way. I just have to be smarter about it."

Dammit. I really didn't want to like Star. She was the sister of my kidnappers. Most probably some sort of non-human being, but ... she was also nice. And smart.

We walked into her closet and I suddenly hated her again. It. Was. Amazing. Like the best thing I had ever seen in my life; I could happily live in this room forever. Some people had all the luck.

"I know it's a little small." Star's brow wrinkled as she looked around. "But we should be able to find something to wear."

A little small? It was official, this chick was insane. The room was the size of a shop, so many clothes I couldn't even take them all in. There was even a white, round, cushioned bench in the center where one could sit and ponder all the delights surrounding them. Above this bench was an intricate crystal chandelier that cast soft light.

She seemed to be waiting for an answer, so I nodded. "Yeah, it'll be difficult, but we'll make do."

Star gave a resolute head bop, like she was preparing herself for battle, then she wandered farther into the room of wonders. I followed, slower, running my hands across everything. It had been a long time since I thought about clothes. I remembered how much I loved putting an outfit together. I might be a book-wormy, indoors, knit-a-scarf sort of girl, but clothes had always been one of my frivolous loves. After the fire I'd told myself I didn't care anymore, that two pairs of jeans and a handful of shirts were all one needed. My butt was covered, and that was the most important thing. But right now my chest was aching in a way I couldn't explain, a similar but far less potent version of the ache I got when I thought about my parents. Like I'd lost something important, a part of myself I was never getting back.

"This is perfect!" Star's exclamation broke me out of my melancholy, and I hurried over to her. She was holding out a dark navy dress. It had long sleeves, a rounded, low-cut neckline, pinched-in waist, and slightly flared skirt. In her other hand was a pair of short black boots. They had a reasonably high heel, which didn't bother me. Don't ever ask me to run, but walking in heels ... I was practically an expert.

I held a hand out, letting it brush against the material. "It's gorgeous. I hope it fits."

She dropped the dress and shoes into my hands, turning and rummaging through some drawers. She was back with a brand new set of black underwear, tags still attached. There was a tag on the dress, too, and I was pretty sure all the blood fled my face when I saw the price.

The dress was worth more than my family's car. "Uh, are you sure it's okay for me to wear this. It's really expensive."

Star laughed, waving her hand at me. "Don't be silly. It's the least I can do after dragging you into this mess." She leaned in closer, whispering conspiratorially, "I really hope the council don't want to meet with you. They're pains ... and you did nothing wrong. You should be free to go back to your life."

Clutching the dress closer, I realized I'd momentarily forgotten my predicament.

I was a prisoner, not just chatting about clothes with a friend. I mean, I was possibly in the house of supernaturals. Something kind of important to remember, because there was a decent chance I might not leave this house alive.

7

I stood in a bathroom fit for royalty wearing five thousand dollars worth of clothes and I couldn't stop staring in the mirror. The dress fit like it had been made for me. The cut of the top gave me more boobs than I knew I had, and the length of the hem made my legs look long and toned. Was this how rich people always looked so awesome?

Don't get used to it, I warned myself, even while I ran my hands across the supple material a few more times. My eyes dropped to the black boots and I had to suppress my little squeal. They were so gorgeous. It turned out that Star and I had the same shoe and bra size, which was a lucky, weird coincidence.

"Are you okay in there?"

I turned at the gentle knock on the closed door. "Yes, all good. Coming out now."

I ran my hands through my hair. There wasn't much I could do about it now. It had dried in long, unruly curls, haphazardly springing everywhere. I had no makeup on, my face plain against the beautiful dress, but I wasn't trying to impress anyone.

My heels clicked as I crossed to the door, and when I opened it I found Star standing on the other side. We were the same height now and I noticed she'd changed her clothes too. Her boots were similar to mine, just with a shorter heel.

"You look amazing!" she exclaimed. "I knew it would be fun to have a girlfriend to share things with."

That gave me a moment's pause. "You've never had a friend?"

She shook her head, long silky cascades of brunette hair tumbling across her shoulders. "No, this is the first time I've left my home. I had to fight for this freedom and I'm going to enjoy every moment of it."

I felt a pang of sympathy for her. "If you can keep your brothers from killing me, then I'd love to be friends," I told her. Despite my previous thoughts about remembering what and who she was, I liked Star. There was an innocence about her that drew me in.

She squealed. "We're going to be best friends, I already know it."

Her gentle nature was very clear, which might have been half the reason I felt a bond to her. Star needed protecting.

"I hope Lexen isn't back yet," she said as we walked into the hall. "He can be ... difficult when his orders are disobeyed. Like Father."

I snorted, which drew her attention. "He's an arrogant asshole who thinks his word is law. But sure, difficult works too."

Star blinked a few times, but before she could say anything, a huge shape appeared in front of us.

"Downstairs, now," Lexen said to his sister, his voice coldly quiet. She jumped, but didn't immediately move.

"Promise me that you're not going to hurt her," she replied, standing her ground. "She's my friend."

His face did not soften; those harsh beautiful lines stayed strong and prominent. "I'm not going to hurt her," he bit out. "I just need to ask her a few questions."

Star threw me a commiserating look. "I'll wait for you downstairs. Maybe we can watch a movie later. I've heard such great things."

They were going to have to work on Star if they wanted to continue pretending they were human. She flounced toward the stairs, giving Lexen a quick hug on her way out.

The moment his sister was out of sight, he turned those dark as sin eyes on me. "Who are you?" he asked, his voice even despite the fire in his eyes. "Why were you really following us tonight? Which of the houses holds dominion over you?"

Okay, then, we were getting right to the point.

"My name is Emma Walters. I followed you because I want answers about what happened to my guardians. And I have no friggin' clue what you're talking about. Houses? Like the history textbook in Mr. Perkins' class? Your family is descended from the House of Darken and the rest..."

I trailed off as he took a step closer. In my heels I was almost up to his shoulders. Which was frustrating. I didn't like him towering over me like that. But I stood my ground, staring up at him without any expression. I would not let him know how spooked I was.

"If you are spying for the Imperials, I will not be happy. They have tried many times over the years to infiltrate our house, but I never thought they'd stoop this low."

He glared. I returned the gesture, following it with my middle finger. "How about screw you? I don't know anything about any Imperials."

Lexen stepped back then, like he couldn't stand to be that close to me for another second. "The council is trying to find out about your family. Apparently the Finnegans have been on their radar for a while, but they don't know what happened to them. They have asked that you stay with us until we can sort out what is happening."

I was already shaking my head. "Hell no. I don't need to stay here. My house across the street is perfectly fine. I'm used to being on my own." The only positive was that someone was now searching for my guardians. I just had to hope those "someones" weren't going to hurt them when they found them. I had to hope I hadn't just made it worse.

Lexen let out a rumble of annoyance. "Trust me, I already argued for you to leave, but the council rules supreme. We're in the midst of a crisis. There is no room to question them. Not with the treaty—" He cut himself off and I found myself stepping closer.

"What are you?" I no longer cared about keeping my knowledge of them a secret. I wanted answers. Of all the Darkens I trusted Lexen the least. His dislike of me, and I would say humans in general, was not disguised, but in some way that was why I directed this question to him. He would give me the entire dirty truth. No sugarcoating it.

His expression went blank. I waited for him to deny it again, but surprisingly enough he didn't. "We're not something you could understand. Your guardians should have left our kind alone. They were warned, and now they will pay the price."

Everything inside of me froze. What price was he talking about? Was the council going to kill them? Or did they already think the Finnegans were dead? Were they searching for their *bodies*?

Before I could let those painful worries spill out, he turned and left. I followed slowly, knowing I had no other choice. As I descended the stairs, I tried not to think about the fact that I might never see Sara and Michael again. I focused on the weirdness of Daelight Crescent. Clearly the domain of these supernaturals.

Why did they allow humans to live in their special gated street? Especially since they seemed to want us to stay away from them. So much of this didn't make sense.

Jero, Marsil, and Star were on the couches, all eyes on me as I crossed behind Lexen toward them.

Jero whistled. "Well, well, you clean up very nicely little hum ... poppet."

I waved a hand in his direction. "You can cut the crap. I know you're not human. Let's not pretend any longer."

Jero's flirtiness disappeared in a heartbeat. He turned narrowed eyes on his brother. "You told her?" His words were clipped with an edge of disbelief.

Lexen returned that stare with one far more potent and displeased. "I didn't tell her anything. She already knew bits from her guardians, and she has clearly surmised the rest from everything she saw tonight. The council is aware of this, which is why they want us to keep an eye on her until they can find her guardians and figure out what to do."

Star jumped to her feet. "She can sleep in my room tonight!" she declared, clapping her hands together. "We should get ready now."

I thought it was a bit ridiculous that she had just dressed me up in these fancy clothes only for us to head to bed. Especially considering it was probably only 8 P.M.

"Absolutely not." Lexen's voice was low and calm; the undercurrent of authority was very clear. "I have a spare room on my level. It's my responsibility to keep an eye on her."

When Star's face fell, his expression softened somewhat, giving a very fallen angel edge to his unnatural good looks. "You can't trust her, S. She's not one of us."

Star swallowed hard, her arms crossing over her chest in a protective mannerism. "Emma is my friend. I refuse to give that up."

I continued standing there, glaring at them all while they talked about me like I wasn't in the room.

Marsil's gentle voice was deep and rich: "How about Lexen watches Emma tonight..." He threw me an apologetic look. Nice of someone to acknowledge my presence. "And then when he sees that Emma is just an innocent victim in all of this, he will be more relaxed with you two breaking some of the rules."

I could already tell the odds of that happening were slim to never. Lexen was not going to bend rules for me, even if they would make his sister happy.

"I have to go out tonight." Lexen's rapid subject change didn't seem to surprise anyone but me. He pointed a finger in my direction. "Which means you're coming with me."

I clicked my heels together and gave him an exaggerated salute. "Yes, sir. Whatever you say, sir."

Clearly I had a death wish. Maybe I'd had one since my parents burned alive, but right in this moment I didn't give a shit that these four could probably disintegrate me with a mere thought. I was done with the elites' superior bullshit.

Lexen blinked a few times at me. I swear there was a flicker of confusion on his face. Then it disappeared and he just looked pissed. "Follow me," he ordered. He strode away and I hurried after him. I felt someone at my back and swiveled my head to find Jero there.

"Are you coming too?" I asked, surprised.

He nodded. "Yes, I watch Lexen's back." He winked at me. "And yours too of course, honey."

"I'm on to you, buddy. You're the suave one. Marsil is the nice one. Lexen is the—"

"Asshole," the man in question interrupted me. I hadn't even realized he had stopped and was waiting for us by the front door. "I'm the asshole."

He held the door open. I watched him with suspicion before I stepped out. We crossed to the front of the house, where his car must have been left by Jero. No doubt there was a garage around somewhere. I knew they had a bunch of cars. Which meant this had been left out deliberately.

"Do you four have parents here? Do you live in this house alone?"

Star had mentioned a father, but it sounded like he was far away. Felt weird thinking of them all alone in this huge house. Even though I was often on my own, I still always knew there were adults around somewhere to do most of the adulting. I might be turning eighteen soon, but I wasn't ready to hand in my irresponsible kid card yet.

"Stop asking questions," was Lexen's hugely helpful reply.

He had definitely been correct before. He was the asshole.

The powerful, low-slung sports car was even more impressive up close. The purple paint shimmered in the dull lights from the house. It had suicide doors, which opened silently.

Lexen stepped aside, gesturing me forward. "Get in the back."

I resisted the urge to salute him again. I tried to crawl my way into the low car without scraping my heels across the leather, or flashing my goods to the world in this short dress.

"You can have the front," Jero finally said, a smirk tilting up his lips. "For all of our sanities."

He reached down and plucked me out of the car – I'd only managed to get half in anyway, my skirt almost over my head. He then sprawled himself out across the narrow backseat, having to angle his long legs to the side. I sort of fell, somewhat gracefully, into the wide wraparound bucket seat in the passenger side. I waited for Lexen to complain, or order me to the back again, but he just slid into the seat beside me and started the car.

The powerful engine thrummed to life. I felt the vibrations go right through my butt and up into my chest. Somehow it was smooth and also rugged at the same time.

"Seatbelt," Lexen said gruffly, and I had only seconds to click it into place before he changed gears and took off down the driveway.

No one stopped us at the front gate. In fact the gate was already open by the time we sped through. "No abuse of power there," I muttered to myself. I could feel dark eyes on me, but I didn't turn to look at him. I would not give that sanctimonious dick the satisfaction of knowing he was getting under my skin.

It was very dark. No doubt another storm was brewing just off the coast to come inland and smash this little town. Still, I couldn't help but strain to see where we were going. The only thing I knew for sure was that we weren't heading into the main town of Astoria. Lexen seemed to take a bunch of back roads, curving and winding into a thick forested area.

Jero, who had been surprisingly quiet in the back, leaned forward between the seats and asked me: "Are you warm enough? You have to remind us of things like that. We forget."

"You don't get cold?" I shot back, somewhat astonished. They still looked and acted like humans, clearly had blood pumping through their veins if the warmth they emitted and healthy flush to their bronzed cheeks meant anything. They also ate, because they had their own food in the cafeteria. I was still rocking the advanced human angle, so maybe one of their advancements was that they completely controlled their body temperatures.

My curiosity about what they were continued to grow. I was almost certain vampires were out, as they didn't fit any of the lore I knew. They could be werewolves, because they were huge and angry a lot. Well, Lexen was huge and angry a lot. Maybe they were something weird and obscure? I hadn't exactly had a chance to research. My theories were so far all formed from movies and television.

Jero chuckled. "We get cold. Just not ... at these temperatures. And you're not wearing a lot of clothes." There was definitely a low rumble in his chest now.

Without thought I slapped his arm. "No! Sit back there and be a good little sleaze."

From my peripherals I caught his wide eyes and slightly open mouth. "Did you just ... hit me?"

He lost it then, laughing hard enough that I swear the car

rocked from side to side. "You have brass ones, girl. I'm kind of glad you decided to friendly-stalk us tonight."

He was just so much like a teenage boy in that moment. Like a human. I turned fully in my seat, watching him, trying to unravel the mystery. I learned nothing from his cocky grin, so I let out a sigh and faced forward again. Staring out as the trees flashed by, Lexen remained silent, which was a blessing. He didn't speak again until the car started to slow. Leaning forward, peering through the front, all I could see were trees, spookily lit up by the play of lights from the car. There was maybe a small clearing up ahead, but it was hard to tell.

"Stay in the car," he said as he opened the door. I didn't know if he was speaking to Jero or me, and it really didn't matter. No way was I getting out in the spooky forest.

A sliver of unease wrapped itself around me and wouldn't let go. For some reason I wanted to reach out and pull Lexen back into the car. I didn't like him going out into the dark either. Which was a really weird thing to feel.

What is wrong with you, Emma?

"You're wasting your worry, sweetheart," Jero said softly. He had moved forward again. "Lex is the predator in this situation."

I let out a low huff, crossing my arms over my chest. "He's holding me hostage. I don't care if he gets eaten by bears."

"And yet you haven't fought that hard to get free. Why is that?"

Jero was starting to annoy me. I let out another huff. "Because I want answers. Because your council seems to know about my guardians. I followed you to figure out what was going on. I still don't know, therefore I will be staying until someone tells me what I need to know."

"Uh huh," he said, sounding not at all convinced. "Don't put your heart in Lexen's hands, honey. Trust me, he's not for you."

I didn't bother to reply again; more protest would only make it worse. I remained silent, my eyes locked on the figure visible in the headlights of the car. Actually, make that figures. Lexen had been joined by three other tall men, all of them pretty much equal to his giant height, all of them broad shouldered and throwing off an aura of menace I could somehow feel from the car.

Jero, losing his relaxed attitude, focused on them as well, his body tense beside me as we stared. Despite the lights from the car, I couldn't really make out the features of the other three. One was very blond; another looked to have a shaved head. The last was hidden in the shadows.

"Who are they?" I asked, not expecting Jero would answer. He just leaned even farther forward, pushing me to the side with his bulk. His scar was shining in the dimly-lit interior, and I looked closer – this was the first time I'd been in close proximity.

"How did you get your scar?" I tried, pausing when I realized how rude it might be to ask that. I was on edge; my brain and mouth were working independently it seemed.

Thankfully Jero just winked at me. "Chicks dig scars, right? Lexen gave it to me when we were younger. He lost control of his ... temper. He says it was an accident, but since I had been annoying him at the time, I wonder if there wasn't a little intention behind it."

Jero didn't seem torn up about it, and he was kind of right. The scar gave a rakish look to his handsome face. It didn't detract at all. "Lexen is a bastard, but ... your scar is pretty cool. I wouldn't go around thanking him for it, though. He could have taken your eye out."

He laughed, tugging annoyingly on a few strands of my long hair. "It takes a lot to scar us. We heal ... fast. Lexen lost control. It happens."

Movement outside the window caught both of our attentions. I forgot what I was about to ask, focusing again on the group of four. My eyes sought out Lexen, feeling some relief that he was okay. *I shouldn't be this tense.* Seriously, it was weird.

Because he was a stranger, a dangerous, scary, supernatural stranger.

I tried to relax. The only thing I should be worried about was this situation getting out of hand and someone attacking me. I did not care about my kidnappers.

Screw you, Stockholm. Screw. You.

Before I could beat myself up any further about my apparently overly huge heart, the little clandestine meeting broke up. The four dispersed off into the shadows. Well, three did, the other bad boy made his way back to our car.

Jero relaxed back, and by the time Lexen opened his door to slide inside, you would never have known that his brother had been worried at all. It was a silent drive back to Daelight Crescent. I bit back multiple questions. I hated mysteries. Even in books it was a genre I avoided, and if I did happen to find one where there was a huge mystery involved, I was sometimes guilty of reading the last page when I was only halfway through.

I made no apologies for that. People should just be straight up.

"How did you end up on Daelight Crescent?" Lexen's question took me completely by surprise. I left an awkwardly long period of time before I answered.

"As you know, Sara and Michael ... my guardians," I added quickly, "search for supernatural happenings around the world. They picked up a lot of signs in Astoria, and packed us up to move here. Apparently a shack in Daelight Crescent was the only rental in Astoria we could afford."

I was really hoping that if I was honest he would be honest, but I wasn't going to hold my breath.

"That's impossible," Jero said. I turned to find him shaking his head.

"Which part?"

"The supernatural signs part. We don't have signs. There are no signs. You won't find a damn sign for a mile..."

"I think she gets the point," Lexen drawled.

I looked between the two of them. "Well, they did tell me that the signs appeared all of a sudden, despite them having run the same checks multiple times in this area over the years."

Lexen's jaw was rigid. "Someone lured your family to Astoria."

That was the theory I was starting to run with. "Why do you have rentals for humans on your street anyway? Especially if you're trying to stay under the radar. And why would anyone lure us here?"

A secret fear I was hiding inside was that we'd been lured here because someone didn't want my guardians poking around in their business any longer, that they brought them here to get rid of them. I was hoping Lexen would have a different theory, one which resulted in them both still being alive.

"We rent to humans because there's a treaty between our kind and yours. It requires a certain level of mingling between us. We chose those who won't cause us much trouble."

In other words, poor people who were just happy to have somewhere to stay.

"And in regards to your guardians," Lexen continued, "they either stuck their noses into the wrong house's business and were lured here to be disposed of ... or there is something more going on, which is what the council is looking into."

Yep, that didn't make me feel better at all.

The car ate up the miles home with ease, and before I knew we were through the huge front gates and pulling into the driveway.

As Lexen opened the door, I reached out and grabbed his arm. I felt a spark under my palm and immediately removed my hand. His eyes met mine, and I realized he was waiting for me to fill him in on why I'd grabbed him. "Oh, I just wanted to say, again, that I can stay at my own house tonight. I won't run or tell anyone. I want answers too. I think sticking with you four is the best way for me to get them."

His gaze felt heavy, his focus completely on me, which was more than a little unnerving. I was barely breathing at this point as I waited for his reply. I wasn't sure if I would be disappointed or not if he agreed to let me leave.

"The council will not be happy if you disappear. It's ... safer for you here."

Then he was gone.

I sucked in a ragged breath, pleased to find my equilibrium returning. His presence was more than a little unnerving.

"Come on, sweets. Time to call it a night. We have school in the morning."

Jero sounded amused, and I was guessing a bedtime because of school was not something he was used to.

I angled my face close to his. "You can't remember my name, right? That's why you call me *honey* and *sweetheart*." I was already getting used to his pet names, but I still had a suspicion about why he used them.

Jero laughed again. "I knew you had a viper tongue after you schooled me in history class, but I didn't expect you to be funny."

I shrugged. "Not my fault you spend no time learning about humans except how to subjugate and exploit us."

His smile didn't fade. If anything it grew wider. We were both out of the car now. He led me through the garage and into a small alcove near the kitchen. Star was sitting at the wide island bench, eating from a small tub of yogurt. Lexen was propped against a wall nearby, keeping an eye on the scene.

"You're back!" Star exclaimed. A genuine smile crossed her face. "I've been waiting up to make sure you were okay." She turned to her brother. "I really think Emma should stay in my room. She would be more comfortable."

Lexen shook his head. "You all need to stop acting like she's part of the family. We don't know a thing about her. We only found her tonight."

I glared. "I'm not a stray friggin' dog. You didn't find me. You kidnapped me and are now holding me against my will."

A ghost of a smile crossed his face. Shock almost knocked me over. He ... he should never ... no smiling. He should never smile because it was way too attractive, and I needed his outside to get less gorgeous. I needed them to match his inner shithead.

Lifting himself off the wall, he closed in on me. For some stupid reason my heart rate picked up as he said, "Weren't you just telling me that you're sticking with us? Doesn't sound like kidnapping to me."

His smile was gone; he gave me a single hand wave, a clear signal to follow him. When he was near the base of their stairs, he even let out a low whistle, no doubt in reference to my stray dog comment.

"Lexen is not going to hurt you," Marsil said. He had just stepped into the kitchen, his phone in his hand like he'd been on it. "He might not like this situation, but he's honorable."

Star nodded her head in rapid bobs. "Yes, the House of Darken is not one you need to fear."

Sounded like some of the other houses weren't so wonderful. Could one of them have taken my guardians?

8
_____

_L_exen was waiting for me at the top of the stairs, arms crossed over his chest, stretching the fitted long-sleeved shirt across his muscles. I wasn't sure I'd ever seen an eighteen year old guy fill out a shirt like that, which only cemented the not-human thing for me. As soon as I was on the first floor, he started to walk along the long hall. We went past his sister's room, and a billion others.

For real? No one needed this many rooms.

I kept waiting for him to stop at one of the doors, but we just continued on. And on. And on.

Like, seriously, this house didn't seem to have an actual ending. Just when I was about to suggest a short rest, because long distance walking was not a favorite pastime of mine, we reached another set of stairs. I traipsed up, exhausted from my long day. School, then stalking, then kidnapping. It had been a lot. And I was hungry. Again.

"Always hungry" should be my new motto.

I'd been so caught up in my thoughts that it took me a few moments to register my new surroundings. The second floor was a single level, not as big as the floor below, but still huge. "This is your bedroom?" I breathed, trying to take it all in.

It was as if Lexen had his own apartment sitting on top of the house. He was watching me, no expression on his face. I moved around him to stare out the windows. Like the living room downstairs, Lexen's windows stared out into the cliffs and crashing ocean beyond. *I don't belong here.* Whatever Lexen was, there was no denying he was way out of my league. Beautiful, rich, and supernatural.

I pulled my gaze from the view to stare at the massive bed that dominated the room. It was piled high with a thick blanket and mounds of pillows. I knew immediately this was Lexen's bed, and it looked so inviting, I almost ran right for it. I didn't, though, because I wanted to stay alive, and I sensed pissing off Lexen too badly was not a way to stay topside.

I followed him as he strode to a door in the back corner of his room. "This is the spare room," he said, opening it up. "You'll stay in here."

Inside there was a king-size bed and a small desk. That was all. It was an odd sort of space, but maybe he had friends or family that crashed in here on occasion. Or maybe he kidnapped people regularly? I was banking on the latter.

"I don't sleep much. There's no point trying to sneak out," he said as he turned to leave, pretty much shutting the door in my face.

"Asshole," I muttered.

Sucking in a deep breath, I tried to calm myself. This was going to be okay. I would stay here tonight, go to school tomorrow, and hopefully after that we would have some answers. How long could it possibly take for their council to follow up the leads? To figure out what was going on with the Finnegans?

It was worrying how casual this council seemed to be in regards to me knowing of their existence. I had expected to be killed on the spot, but with their current attitude I was wondering how big of a secret it could possibly be. I'd certainly never heard anything – except from the Finnegans – about mutants, or supernaturals, or advanced humans. So it definitely wasn't general knowledge.

As I stepped into the small room, I hesitated. I needed to pee quite badly, and I was hungry. The old Emma would have probably sucked it up, dealt with the discomforts, but I was not that person any longer. This new person broke the rules – crossed the street when they shouldn't. I was already deep in it, so what was one more thing.

Walking back to the door on my little room, I reached for the handle, surprised when it opened easily. I stepped out into the main bedroom again. Lexen was nowhere to be seen.

Crossing over toward his bed, I moved cautiously, as if he would leap out of the shadows at any moment. When I was standing beside the decadent bed, I noticed his shirt was draped across it, and in that same moment the faint sounds of running water registered with me.

Great. He was in the shower. Now we were going to have one of those cliché moments. He would be half naked and dripping wet. I would blabber and lose all conscious thought...

Not happening. Spinning as fast as I could, I was hightailing it back to my room when a deep voice cut across the area. "Where do you think you're going?"

Turning back around, I bit back the groan that immediately sprang to my lips. He was wearing shorts. Just a pair of soft black shorts. The rest of his skin was bare, golden, ripped, bare, golden...

My breathing was doing funny things so I forced myself to focus. He was a supernatural. Not a human. We were a different species and I could not lust after him. It was weird, and wrong, and I ... was so going to hell.

"I'm hungry. I have to pee. I need clothes to sleep in." I rattled off my list like they were bullet points, half tempted to close my eyes at the same time. I didn't, because I wasn't keen to advertise his effect on me, but it was definitely tempting.

He crossed the room in a second, bringing with him the heat from his shower. Or at least that was what I was telling myself. "Use my bathroom. You're not permitted to leave this room tonight. I won't have my family put at risk."

I stuck my tongue out at him. I hadn't meant to, but somehow it slipped out.

He growled, getting in close to my face. "Don't. Push. Me."

I pushed him. Literally.

Shit. What was wrong with me?

My shove barely moved him, but since he hadn't been expecting it, it was enough to slide him back a few inches. Absolutely astonishment registered on his face, but only for a heartbeat, before a dark kind of fury descended. I wanted to run, to hide from whatever I had unleashed here, but my feet wouldn't move.

The sprinkles of starlight in his eyes started to brighten, and I would have sworn there was a glow coming from them. As he straightened, he stepped into me and I found my head tilting back so I could take him all in.

"Walk away now, human."

His voice was nothing more than a rumble, and finally I did as I was told. Slipping and sliding across the floor, I sprinted in the direction I thought his bathroom was. I'd already been almost peeing myself. Add in the fear and I really needed the bathroom. Tumbling through the door, I slammed it shut behind me, relieved to find a heavy lock I could slide across.

My chest was heaving as I leaned against the wood door, my body reacting with spurts of adrenalin as it tried to figure out how much of a threat Lexen was. For the first time, I was becoming very aware of what it meant to be sleeping in a house of beings who were not human. It was like I had been in a half-fog since I saw that weird light ball Star had stepped out of, since the Darkens had taken me hostage. I understood what was happening to me, what I was learning, but nothing was really registering. It had been too fast. Too quick. My mind was slowly catching up now.

I was in big trouble.

When my heart finally stopped trying to pound out of my chest, I peeled myself off the door and wandered into the room. It was huge – of course – with tiled floors and walls. Lots of patterns, colors of navy and cream. It was masculine, sophisticated, and boring as hell.

Lexen needed some fun in his life.

The bathtub came into sight and I let out a breathy sigh. "Okay, now that looks like fun."

It was deep, oval shaped, and filled with jets. I wanted to live in there. It had been a long time since I took a bath. Disappointment hit me but I pushed it aside. My jailer was probably standing outside, arms crossed over his chest as he watched the clock. This was no time for a bath.

I quickly used the toilet, and after washing my hands I was about to leave when I caught sight of the shower. There was no time for a bath, but I still really wanted to wash off. And warm up. Parts of me were still chilled from the rain.

I glanced at the door, and straightening my spine I decided that he would just have to deal. Wasting no time, I stripped off Star's borrowed shoes and clothes, leaving them in a pile on the floor. The shower cubicle was one of those glass monstrosities with ten shower heads and gleaming dials everywhere. It was still damp and wet, clearly from Lexen, and I tried very hard not to think about him standing naked here only moments ago.

After multiple attempts I managed to get water to run. As I stepped under, it went scorching hot and I jumped back.

"Shit!" My curse was louder than I intended, but I was pretty sure there were third degree burns on my back now.

There was a loud knock on the door. "Are you okay in there?"

"You have a stupid shower. It's ... stupid!" I shouted back.

The boiling hot water was still cascading down; I had tucked myself right into one corner, which seemed to be the only corner not getting soaked. I heard the door to the bathroom open, and I would have been mortified if all of my attention wasn't currently on staying alive.

The glass was fogged, so I couldn't see anything, but I had to assume it was Lexen. The door swung open and he appeared, his eyes darting over me briefly before he reached in through the water to the control panel. He showed no sign of distress as the boiling water ripped across his skin, and I tried not to gasp too loudly. He hit a few buttons, swiveled a dial, and the water cooled considerably to a medium warm. I relaxed, tension seeping out of me

"Did you get burned?" His eyes were locked on my face. For once he wasn't scowling at me.

I blinked a few times, unused to that look from him. "I don't think so. It hit my back, I ... I'm fine."

"Turn around," he commanded. "Let me see. If you told me you were going to shower I could have changed the temperature. It's programmed to my preferences."

I crossed my arms, trying to hide most of my naked parts. For freak's sake, this was worse than my cliché moment before. Now I was naked in the shower with him. "I'm not turning around. I'm fine. You can leave now."

He seemed to realize then that he had me cornered, naked, and he hated humans. In a flash the glass door closed, and I slumped even further until I was pretty much sitting on the floor, warm water beating down on me. I hadn't for one second felt vulnerable or scared that he might take advantage of me. His eyes had not even drifted below my face. He didn't care. He wasn't attracted to me.

We were not the same species! I was going to keep repeating that mentally until it started to sink in.

Exhaustion pressed in on me and it took everything I had not to curl up under the massaging shower heads and go to sleep. I forced myself to stand, to wash my hair with whatever amazingly expensive shampoo was in here. Then I figured out how to turn the water off, stepping out to find a thick white towel on the sink. Next to it was a shirt.

I blinked a few times, my hand going out to pick up the soft piece of clothing. Had Lexen given me one of his shirts to sleep in? It definitely hadn't been sitting there when I'd got into the shower.

I dried off quickly, gingerly patting the tender parts on my back. It didn't look too bad in the mirror, just bright red, no welts yet. I wished I had some cream to rub on it, but I didn't want to push my luck. Slipping back into the underwear bottoms from Star, since I hadn't worn them for long, I then pulled the huge shirt over my head. It caressed my skin, silky and smooth, falling almost to my knees.

There was a comb on the bench and I used it to tame my mane. The curls would still spring up haphazardly when they dried, but combing it out would help a little. When I had procrastinated as much as I could, I gathered up the rest of the clothing and slowly left the room. I didn't see Lexen anywhere, so I chose to run like a bitch and hide in my cupboard bedroom. When I was safely inside, the door closed firmly behind me, I dropped Star's clothes on a chair in the corner and made my way to the bed. There were a few pendant lights on, as well as a lamp right near the bed. I shut everything off except the lamp.

My stomach gave a rumbling protest. I shushed it. I was not asking Lexen for anything else tonight. Crossing to the bed, I was about to yank the covers down and slip beneath them when I noticed a small white plate resting near the pillow. On top of it was a sandwich.

What in the...? All thought faded as my stomach rumbled again, almost painfully. Uncaring of etiquette, I dove and snatched the bread up, shoving it into my mouth. I had no idea what was on it, and frankly I didn't care. It was food. I was not going to turn my nose up at anything edible.

When half the sandwich was gone, I took a drink of water from the glass on my bedside. It had been set there with a little note propped next to it. I wasn't surprised that it was Star who had brought me the food. That made much more sense than Lexen.

I didn't quite finish the sandwich, my stomach protesting. I set it aside on the bench and climbed into bed. I had planned on lying there with the lamp on for a while so I could run over everything that had happened today. Just before falling asleep was always my favorite time to process my life, when there were no other distractions around. It helped me see clearly, pick up details I would have normally missed.

But my eyelids kept fluttering closed, my blinks getting far less frequent, so I switched the lamp off. I would think everything over in the morning.

It's so hot. I can't breathe. Why can't I breathe? The smoke is everywhere. It's choking me. Slithering into every part of my body. I'm dying. Crawling with desperation, unable to see, unable to breathe. Searching for them. Hissing as embers bit into my exposed flesh. As smoke and heat charred my throat and lungs.

It had been a long time since I'd had the dream, the one that had consumed me for weeks after the fire. In it, I was always battling the heat and smoke. It choked me. I fought to escape. But unlike real life I never made it out of the dream fire.

With a muffled yelp I managed to wrench myself awake, sitting upright, my heart hammering hard in my chest. I had probably been yelling. Sara and Michael used to tell me I made a real racket when I was in the fire dream. I'd always awoken to find them standing at my bedside, worried faces staring down at me. I got hugs after that though; it was the one time I really craved the touch of another human.

Anything to wipe away the taste, smell, and feel of smoke choking me to death.

I was disoriented for a beat as I stared around the dark room. *The Darkens.* Right. I was at their house. No wonder the dream had returned; my stress levels were at an all-time high. Pulling myself out of the bed, I started to pace the room. I could never stay still after the dream.

I wondered what time it was. If it was almost morning I'd just stay up, but there was no way to tell from this room. I switched on the lamp to double check there wasn't a clock in the room. *Nope.* Creeping toward the door, I slowly eased it open, and then ducked through before shutting it just as quickly. I didn't want the light to wake Lexen.

His room wasn't that dark; there were beads of illumination coming in from a few different places, which helped in not tripping over anything. From memory there was a window near the bathroom door, so I headed in that direction, trying my best not to focus on the bed and the supernatural sleeping there.

Surprised to make it to the window undetected, I wondered where the "I don't need much sleep" asshole was now. Reaching out, I gripped the curtain, pulling them apart.

Oh. Instead of the window I'd expected, there was a double set of doors behind the heavy material, and the wood and glass doors were ajar. I noticed Lexen a beat before he said, "Nice to see you weren't murdered in your sleep. For a moment there I wasn't sure."

"Thanks for checking on me," I said drily, slipping out onto the wide balcony.

I immediately felt better being outside, breathing in the fresh air.

Lexen, who was still shirtless, had his shoulder propped against a nearby wall, staring out into the ocean. I had never realized quite how loud it was being near the water as it crashed against the cliffs.

"My job is to keep you alive," he said softly. "The rest ... you're going to have to look to Marsil, Jero, and Star."

I found myself leaning against the glass railing. "They seem to defer to you as their fearless leader ... or whatever. Why are you the boss?"

In this dull light I couldn't really make out his face. "It was the position I was born into." His voice was emotionless. "It's not something I chose."

I realized then that we were having an actual conversation that didn't involve yelling or insults.

"What did you dream about?" He straightened as he asked, and even though most of my attention was focused out into the world, I sensed his eyes on me.

The smell of smoke was still in my nose; his question brought back the choking sensation. It was so clear in my mind.

"I dream of my death."

I didn't want to talk about my parents – I couldn't talk about them. Not with the dream still filling my mind. Even worse, I didn't wake to a warm hug and smiles. I woke to this cold, mysterious guy. I woke to remember that what remained of my family was missing.

My chest clenched; the hot pressure behind my eyes told me I was going to have one of my moments. I was going to lose it. It didn't happen much anymore, but if I suppressed it for too long the breakdown would be so much worse.

"Ex ...cuse me," I choked out, before I stumbled back across the balcony, aiming for the doors. I needed to get back to my room so I could cry in peace. Without judgment.

I was trying to be kind to myself lately. If I needed to cry, I let myself. I didn't beat myself up for it. Not anymore. When I did that in the early days I almost sent myself to a mental-health facility.

Just as I was slipping through the doors, a warm hand wrapped around my forearm. "What's wrong?" Lexen asked sharply.

There was a note of concern in his voice and my throat tightened to the point where it was no longer possible for me to talk.

I tried anyway, because he wasn't letting go.

"My parents ... I dream of the fire." My voice was barely a squeak. The first tear slipped free from my eyes, trailing across my cheek in a hot line.

No more words were coming. A sob escaped, and I tried to yank myself free from Lexen. He wouldn't let me go. I wanted to beg, but I couldn't say anything. I decided to stop fighting. Why did I care if he saw me break? This wasn't me being weak, this was me hurting, and I was allowed to express that.

Sobs started ripping from my chest. I raised my free hand to cover my face. The tears were never-ending salty streams that filled my eyes and overflowed down my face. I caved in on myself, the pain in my chest so intense that if I hadn't done this plenty of times over the past eight months I might have wondered if I was having a heart attack.

Lexen didn't say anything, but he also didn't leave. He stayed right by my side, holding my arm and letting me cry.

"I miss them," I whispered, my voice a broken crackle. "Why did they have to die? Why did they have to leave me?"

I was so alone. Always alone.

He let out a low curse and dropped my arm. I expected him to run away – hello, crying teenage girl was boy kryptonite – but he didn't. He stepped forward and wrapped me up in both of his arms, pulling me close to his body. *Holy crap.* He might be an asshole, but he gave good hugs. His warmth surrounded me as my face buried into his bare chest. I flinched slightly as he pressed on my still tender skin. His grip loosened, but he didn't let me go.

"You're going to be okay. I'll make sure they find your family."

He was murmuring, and it was like I didn't know who the hell this guy was.

I was so astonished by Lexen's actions that I was able to push my grief back down. The sobs died off, the pressure in my chest easing again. This cry would relieve the aching for some time. In truth, the breakdowns were getting further apart. Maybe soon I'd even start to function like a normal, non-devastated person.

As I straightened, he stepped back and gave me space. I wiped at my cheeks, my breathing evening out. I felt hugely awkward. This was more emotion than I had expressed in a long time, and doing it in front of a stranger was not the most fun.

"I'm really tired," I lied. "Going to try get some more sleep." I could tell from the darkness and moon that it was still the middle of the night.

Lexen didn't argue. He nodded and propped himself back against the wall. "I'll wake you in time for school," was all he said as I slipped back into his bedroom.

By the time I got back into my box my head was spinning. *Stockholm syndrome ... screw off. You are not welcome here.*

9

I managed to drift off for a few more hours, which were thankfully dream free. Lexen kept his word, waking me by dropping a school uniform on my chest, along with a new toothbrush. Rubbing my tired, slightly swollen eyes, I stumbled off to the shower. By the time I got downstairs – without the help of my jailer, surprisingly – everyone was already standing around the kitchen island bench.

"Good morning!" Star sang. She looked beautiful, her long hair straight and shiny; her uniform fit her perfectly. She had on high black knee socks and heels to finish the ensemble.

Meanwhile I looked like someone who'd slept only a few hours and had been crying all over a dude who hated me. Lexen didn't even glance my way. Pretty sure we both just wanted to forget last night even happened.

"Morning. Thanks for the uniform." I returned her smile, before I turned toward Lexen. "I'll need to grab my bag before we go. My Daelight security card and school identification are in it."

Lexen flicked a look at Jero. "Go with her. We'll meet you by the gate. Everyone in one car today."

Jero held out a hand for me. I didn't even think twice before placing my palm into his. "Let's walk, pretty girl."

I snorted. "It's Em-ma..."

He just winked at me, completely unfazed. Our silence was comfortable as we walked along their long drive. When we closed in on the imposing fence, I asked him: "How come you get to bastardize the uniform and not get into trouble? I got slapped with a pretty hardcore set of rules when I enrolled."

He wore part of the uniform, the dress shirt and slacks, but he had his own suit jacket on, a different tie, and of course, expensive dress shoes.

"Rules don't apply to us," he replied simply.

"Is that why none of you take books to class?" I shot back. "Do you pay for grades?"

He shook his head, a half-smile tilting up the corner of his mouth. The scar was very visible in the light, but it really didn't detract from his devastatingly handsome face at all. Maybe he was right last night: chicks dig scars. Those crystal blue eyes locked on me.

"We don't pay for grades. We're just really fucking smart."

I hadn't heard them curse much. For some reason, in their accent it kind of made me want to laugh. Normally they sounded so cultured, European or something. Drop a swear word in there and the culture disappeared. Kind of. They pulled it off anyway.

As we crossed the road, my eyes immediately zoomed in on my driveway, hoping like anything that our old clunker would be there. That my guardians were just lost and had somehow found their way home last night.

It was empty. My throat got tight; my heart clenched. They had to be okay. I couldn't lose another family. I wouldn't survive it.

I must have made a distressed sound because Jero slung an arm around me. "I'd cry too if I lived in a dump like this. You should probably just move in with us."

His arrogance was enough to snap me out of my sadness. "Yeah, right. Lexen would absolutely love me being around permanently. And ... it's not too bad."

Total lie, but I felt the need to defend our little shack. It did the job it was required to do. For the most part. We were dry, and warm ... ish.

I'd run out last night without locking the door. When we stepped inside it looked like everything was exactly as I left it. "Wait here," I said to Jero. He was looking around our dingy kitchen and lounge room. It all seemed that much smaller and shabbier after being in the beautiful mansion across the street.

It is fine!

I couldn't afford to start acting like a snob. Literally couldn't afford it.

Crossing the five steps to my room, I shut the door behind me. I quickly changed my underwear, putting the borrowed ones into my laundry basket. I'd wash them and give them back to Star whenever I was released from the kidnapping program I was currently in. I also grabbed my makeup bag, and using the mirror above my dresser added a bit of powder, mascara, and lipstick to try to brighten my drawn face. I looked stressed, my eyes surrounded by dark circles. My hair went into a bun; it would keep it out of my way for most of the day. And that was as good as it was getting today. I picked up my mom's necklace, slipping it on over my head, feeling like I needed her support.

Snatching up my backpack from where I had thrown it last night, I checked inside to find my wallet and cards all accounted for. I slipped the provided dress shoes on, and then left to join Jero.

"You can't live here," was the first thing he said to me. "There's no coffee maker. There's no food in the cupboards."

I shrugged. "We manage. I'm sure this is going to come as a surprise to you, but a coffee maker is not an actual requirement of survival. Oxygen, water, food, coffee maker ... one of these things is not like the others."

He narrowed his eyes on me, brow furrowing. "Are you sure? That doesn't sound right to me."

I chuckled, pushing him toward the door. "Come on, let's get out of here. You don't want to catch poor."

He shuddered, like the very thought was horrifying.

Stepping outside, I locked the front door, ignoring Jero's snort. I was going to lock up, no matter how crappy our stuff was. An SUV was idling out the front of the quiet street. I knew it well since I had watched it drive past for days. The dark tint now was a relief. I'd be hidden from prying eyes once I was inside.

Jero opened the front passenger door. I expected him to climb in, so I was already moving to the back. He caught my arm. "You're in the front."

I tripped over my feet as I tried to change direction. "Are you sure? I'm happy to get in back. I'd actually prefer it."

"Get in the car, Emma." The growled command came from the darkened interior.

With a sigh, I stepped around Jero, and grabbing the handle pulled myself into the seat. My bag was dropped on the floor and seatbelt clicked on before I allowed myself to relax into the plush leather. For once the sun was out and actually hot, but I still felt the chill coming from the driver's side of the car. I didn't glance Lexen's way. Part of me was still annoyed that I'd cried on him last night. He was the absolute last person I wanted to show my vulnerabilities to.

Something landed on my lap, and since I had been so determinedly staring out the window I jumped about a foot. Glancing down, my heart beating slightly faster than normal, I gasped at the wrapped sandwich.

"You didn't eat."

My eyes moved to Lexen, and I had to stop myself from

reaching out and touching him. "Thank you," I whispered, my voice almost failing me.

He turned back to watch the road, but it almost felt like a little of the awkward between us was gone.

Star leaned forward, her face lit up. "Lexen got one of us into each of your classes! We're going to keep an eye on you, you don't have to worry."

I smiled back, my fingers already busy unwrapping the food. "Have you ever been to school before?"

She actually bounced in her seat and my smile turned into a chuckle. "Never. I can't wait. I watched a few movies about it last night."

"It's not really like the movies..." I started to say, but cut myself off. It wasn't my place to burst her school bubble; she'd learn soon enough. And, really, what did I know? For the elite, it might be exactly like the movies, with them playing the role of the popular clique. "I'm really glad you'll be in my classes," I said instead.

Star surprised me by leaning forward and giving me a hug.

I didn't even flinch. I relaxed into her embrace and let myself enjoy her warmth. It was funny. I had no idea where she was from, what race she was, or how she'd stepped through a doorway of light. But I liked her. I actually liked all of the Darkens. Except Lexen. He was staying under the category of asshole.

Who provided food. And occasional comfort.

On the drive to school I wolfed my sandwich down. It was delicious: fresh bread, chicken breast, sundried tomatoes, and some creamy pesto sauce.

That was it, it was decided ... I wanted to be rich. Just for the food and clothes.

We passed one of the school buses and I wondered if Cara was on there. She was probably wondering where the hell I was. I had no idea how I was going to explain this to her today, showing up with the Darkens.

I decided to ask the ones used to keeping secrets.

Marsil answered first: "You can't tell her the truth. Our council takes security very seriously. There are humans who know about us, of course – quite a lot, but it's not general knowledge. They want to keep it that way."

"How is that possible?" I asked, my thoughts from last night returning with full force. "In this day of technology, it's hard to keep a small secret, let alone something of this scale."

Jero let out one of those drawling laughs. "Trust me, there's not a piece of technology we can't manipulate. Any information to hit the net about us is destroyed before it can be viewed."

And yet, somehow, things got through to Michael. Definitely a setup.

"So what do I tell my friends when they ask?" Because they were totally going to ask.

There was a beat of silence. "Tell them we met on Daelight Crescent, that we hit it off and are now best friends," Star suggested, shrugging. "That's true, as far as I'm concerned."

I nodded. "They're going to grill me hard about you four. The elite are a big topic of conversation among the lower class."

"Lower class?" Star sounded astonished.

"We've been segregated," I told her, my voice flat. "We even have different colored cards so that no one can miss it." I whipped out my scholarship ID.

I heard her huff, and turned in my seat to see her glaring at Lexen. "That better not be your idea, Lex."

He indulged her in one of his rare, slow smiles, and I almost died. Legit, it was touch and go there for a second as my heart went into some sort of tachycardia rhythm.

"Humans like to know their place. It gives them a sense of purpose to understand how everything works. There are only a few who don't follow the path of the rest. We don't segregate them. They do that all on their own."

I translated that to "humans were sheep." The school was

probably run by humans, and these supernaturals reaped the benefits of their stupidity. We were always the makers of our own destruction. History showed that, over and over again.

Pulling into the parking lot now, I wished there was a way for me to sneak inside without the full attention that was going to come from a scholarship kid hanging with the elite. They had rules. I had broken one of them last night when I crossed the street, and now the entire balance was thrown off.

I was probably going to destroy the school somehow.

Lexen pulled into the same spot as yesterday. His spot, no doubt. Which, by the way, did not have his name written on it, but I would bet it was always free for him. When the car was off, he turned to address everyone: "Emma is our mission today. We do not let her out of our sight. One of us must be with her at all times. The council was adamant that we keep her safe until we find the guardians. Am I clear?"

Three heads gave a single nod. I crossed my arms, trying not to let my annoyance rise to my face. I knew I didn't have a say, but that didn't make me any less frustrated by the babysitting duties. Plus, part of me was kinda relieved that I had backup in these uncertain times. Something *had* happened to my family, and I was in no position to deal with these "bad" supernaturals. Whoever they were.

Truthfully, I had no reason to complain about being stuck with the Darkens. My belly was full, my clothes were clean, and I had a ride to school for once. If they could find Sara and Michael, then my life would be pretty darn awesome.

When Lexen opened his door, the rest of us followed. Eyes were on us immediately – eyes were always on the Darkens. The moment students realized I was in their midst, I felt the shock ripple through the crowd. Even avoiding their gazes, I couldn't unhear the gasps.

I kept my head down, staring at my feet as we walked along the front path and into the main building. I didn't notice at first, because my feet were so fascinating, but Marsil and Jero had closed in on either side of me, protecting me with their bodies. Lexen was behind, and I could *feel* him there at my back. Star was chatting away, walking a little in front of me.

"Humans are fascinating," she chirped. "Lexen was so right. Look at the way they congregate in their little groups. They even look alike."

She was pointing at a small group of kids who, despite the uniform, still managed to show their emo slash goth fashion tendencies with thick eyeliner, black nails, and somber attitudes. I quickly reached out and grabbed her forearm, pulling it down to her side. "Maybe ... don't point straight at them. *Humans...*" I lowered my voice dramatically, "don't like being pointed at like that."

Marsil chimed in then, his voice tinged with humor: "They also don't like being referred to as *humans*."

"Yeah, it kinda gives away your otherness—"

Lexen interrupted me. "Enough talking about this now. We need to blend."

Good luck with that, giant model-type dude.

There were a lot fewer students inside, which was to be expected since the first bell wouldn't ring for another twenty minutes. It was nice not to have so many eyes burning a hole in my face.

"I need to go to my locker," I told them all. "Since, you know, I require textbooks to pass classes."

Jero grinned at me, and I just shook my head.

"Star needs to check in officially," Lexen said, looking between his brothers. "So we might have to split up for now."

"We'll go with Emma," Marsil replied. "Meet back here in ten."

For the first time since I'd cried in his arms, Lexen met my gaze fully. "Is that okay with you?"

I blinked a few times, momentarily stunned by the fact he

seemed to be giving me a choice. And was looking right at me, which was always disconcerting.

I ended up blurting out, "That's fine. I'm happy to go along with whatever is easiest." One day I would act like less of an idiot. But seriously, for a bookworm, homebody, loner sort of human – as the Darkens would say – this was a lot. All at once.

You're doing it for the Finnegans, I reminded myself.

Lexen and Star turned to enter the main office and I jumped on the moving sidewalk with the remaining Darkens. No one spoke as we rushed along the arterial that would lead to my locker area. I remained grateful for the lack of students in here. Gawking was definitely to a minimum.

"I thought this was the storage facility," Jero said, staring around in confusion as the sections flashed past us. "Are you telling me there are student things back here?"

Raising one eyebrow in his direction, I didn't bother to answer him.

"My stop is next," I warned them, preparing myself to dismount.

This time I landed somewhat cleanly. *Improvement!* The boys waited silently on either side of me while I opened my locker and rifled through for the books I'd need that morning. I had to check it off against my schedule, which I hadn't memorized yet.

"Okay, I'm good to go now."

I hefted the heavy pack onto my back, hoping my old bag would survive the weight. Why did they need to make textbooks so freaking heavy? Yeah, yeah, lots of information to teach. Surely it wasn't all important. Learn to condense it down or something.

I must have been muttering as we jumped on the sidewalk, because Marsil gave me a look, his eyebrow raised as he smiled. "I thought you liked to read. What's with all the textbook hate?"

"How did you know I liked to read?"

He shrugged. "Jero mentioned that you had a lot of books

lying around your house. We managed to deduce the rest from there."

I looked between the two of them, confusion creasing my forehead. Must have been part of a whispered conversation in the back that I missed.

"The only school-type books I enjoy reading are history and archaeology. I love diving into stories of the past, hoping we can learn things from it. Otherwise I read sci-fi and fantasy."

"Like ... aliens?" Jero let out a low chuckle, and I zeroed right in on that.

"Exactly like aliens. So are you guys ali—?"

My question was cut off by Marsil wrapping his hand across my face and mouth. I swallowed hard, and winced a little at my mistake. I had almost said that out loud, and we were back in the main part of the school now, the bell about to ring; a lot of students were around.

"Sorry," I whispered, when he removed his hand.

He winked at me. "No worries. Just ... watch it around Lexen."

They acted like their brother was a big bad scary dude. Which he was. But for some reason he just didn't really scare me. Frustrated, for sure. Intrigued, oh yeah. But there was no fear. Maybe I was just too stupid and naïve to see it.

We had to wait a few minutes out front of the office, which was a fun experience. The three of us leaned against the wall and watched the numerous students trip over their own feet when they caught sight of me between the two Darkens.

"Knees," Jero said, as a leggy blonde walked past. "Definitely knees."

I elbowed him, and he laughed. "What? I meant she was going to land on her knees when she tripped."

Seeing his cocky grin reminded me of yesterday in class, and the redhead who had been glued to his side. "So ... who is Aria?"

He tilted his head in my direction, a smirk creasing his lips. "She's a Royale. Old family friends."

I laughed. It burst out before I could stop it. "Are all of you elites 'old friends?'"

He sobered up a little then, his expression falling into more neutral lines. "No, we aren't. Royale and Darkens are allies. Leights are generally a neutral third party. The Imperials ... they're mostly the enemy."

As if he had summoned them with those words alone, a group entered the front entrance. Two males and two females. I knew immediately that they were elites. Expensive clothes ... check. Arrogance exuding from every pore ... check. Dismissive way of treating humans ... check.

The girls wore their hair very short, pixie-style cuts flicking out in styled disarray. One was golden blond, the other a white blond. Both of them had very pale skin, almost to the point where they looked sick. But they were still somehow beautiful, like all of these ... beings.

The guys who strode in behind them were around six foot tall, their hair also a mix of blonds, but cut very short to their heads. Almost shaved bald.

The moment their group saw Jero and Marsil, they halted just in front of us. I could feel the tension coming from the two guys at my side, and I found myself straightening and going into some sort of panic alert situation.

"Thought you had petitioned the council to not come back this year," one of the males sneered. I kept my gaze off to the side, in the hope they wouldn't notice me.

Jero didn't say anything, and from the corner of my eye it looked like he was glaring, ferocity carving his face into hard lines. Gone was the relaxed playboy; in its place was a being who was actually a little scary.

"You know we have to be here, House of Imperial," Marsil said, his voice neutral. "There is no petitioning against an order from the entire council."

JAYMIN EVE

I should have guessed these were the enemies. They certainly had an "enemy" attitude going on.

The white-blond girl stepped forward then. "We've heard whispers that the council is looking into the Darken House." She popped her lip out in a fake pout. I was pretty sure that was supposed to be a sad face, but done by someone who was unsure how that emotion worked. I was instantly reminded of *The Princess Bride*, "*I do not think it means what you think it means.*" Classic movie, I needed to get another copy one day. I would eventually replace my collec—

My thoughts dried up as the Imperial chick locked eyes on me. I hurried to school my face back into a neutral expression. I didn't have to bother though, because in the same instant Marsil and Jero both shifted their bulk to block me. All I could see were the tense lines of their backs.

"Don't be worrying about our business," I heard Jero say. "You have more than enough trouble in your own house."

There were a few more words, but so low that I missed most of them. By the time I pushed my way through the barrier of Darkens, the Imperials had disappeared. I reached out and grabbed onto both of the guys' forearms, yanking them closer to me. "I think you all need to explain to me exactly what is going on here. How many of you elites are in this school?"

If I was to navigate this new world I found myself in, I needed to know what I was dealing with. There was a lot going on here. A lot of history. So much I didn't know, and nothing I was going to be able to infer from terse exchanges.

Marsil leaned in close to me. "We will tell you what we can, but the council has final say on what information we are allowed to release to a human."

"Sometimes ignorance is the best, especially when you're trying to stay under the radar," Jero added.

"Like ... the council might kill me if I know too much?" I said slowly.

They both shrugged, but neither disagreed. I shut my mouth, swallowing roughly to try to clear the ball of nerves in my throat.

"What happened?" Lexen's voice had us all spinning around; he was standing there with Star at his side, staring above my head at his brothers, but it felt like some of his attention was also on me. A few times his eyes flicked to mine.

"The Imperials. Laous' side of the family," Jero told him.

Lexen's expression morphed from concern into something I couldn't read. Maybe annoyance. Possibly anger. Definitely a sliver of worry.

"So they saw Emma?"

All of us nodded, and his jaw clenched. "Nothing has changed," he finally said. "They're no match for us. We continue to do our job and protect Emma. The council will tell us what step to take next."

Star, who was quiet and somber for once, stepped to my side and wrapped her arms around me. I patted her back a few times, not hating the close contact as much as I used to.

She pulled back. "What happens if the council tells us to forget about Emma?" she asked her brothers. "The Imperials have seen her now. They're going to try and find out why she's with us. They might hurt her."

Well, none of that sounded good.

Lexen stopped his sister's half hysterical rant by grabbing her hand. "It's going to be okay, Star. I won't let your first Earthside friend be murdered by our enemies, even if the council washes their hands of her."

Excellent news. Best news I had heard all day. *Wait a minute ...* I soooo wasn't ready to hear them admit they weren't from Earth – I was definitely ignoring that *Earthside* comment.

The bell rang before I could push for more information. My first class today was AP English, and I wondered which of my new group of protectors was with me.

"I've got Emma for this class," Lexen answered my unspoken question. "Star, you're with Jero and Marsil in chemistry."

I shuddered, and she jerked her head back. "What? Is chemistry ... bad?"

Another shudder rocked me. "The worst. Just ... good luck."

She blinked her wide pretty eyes at me and I couldn't stop the smile any longer. "I'm kidding ... kinda. I'm pretty good at science and math, but chem is not my favorite."

Star brightened then. "I'm really good with numbers. This is exciting."

She linked her arms through her brother's, and started chatting loudly as they moved over to jump on a moving path. I found myself staring after them. I was a little enchanted by the sweetness of Star. She somehow made the world seem a little brighter than usual. Her innocent joy in simple things was ... nice. I was going to try to learn from her example.

"Ready to go?" Lexen's low voice sent a brush of tingles down my spine. I took a second to calm my rapid heartbeat.

"Ready when you are," I said.

He started to walk and I fell in step beside him. When we reached the door, I waited for him to step through, but he hesitated.

"I need to speak with someone," he said, before he peered inside the classroom. "You should be safe for a minute. I'm only going to be right there." He pointed across to the far wall, where a few students were lingering.

I nodded. "It's fine. I'm not a baby. You don't have to worry about me eating food off the floor."

His lips twitched but he didn't reply. He just turned and walked away. I sucked in a deep breath, and then forced myself to stop staring at him and step into the classroom. Luckily, English was one of my favorite subjects, and I had read ahead in most of the assigned books. Because something told me I was not going to learn much today with Lexen at my side.

10

The classroom was empty, those fancy desks clean and shiny, waiting for students to arrive. I hesitated just inside the doorway, unsure about seating arrangements. Was I supposed to stick really close to Lexen? As in, sit in the elite area?

After a few moments of deliberation, I decided to sit in the same front desk I'd chosen yesterday. Lexen would no doubt be happy as long as he could see me. He might even prefer I didn't confuse the *humans* even more by breaking social rules and jumping twenty levels to elite.

When I took my seat I slumped forward and felt some of the tension I'd been carrying for days ease. I had no idea why; nothing much had changed, but it felt like as I sat down I physically couldn't hold on to that much stress any longer. I had to let some of it go.

"Oh. Em. Gee." The excited exclamation jolted me out of my thoughts. I turned to find Cara sliding in to sit at the desk next to me. "So, I was freaking out on the bus thinking you were going to miss school, and then I get here and the rumors are flying." She was waving her hands in the air, fifty-plus silver bracelets she wore jingling like chimes. "You arrived with the Darkens. Like in their car. Stepped out, walked between them. Didn't get murdered for getting too close. Oh. Em. Gee."

She collapsed into her chair, looking exhausted. Her face was still turned in my direction, her expression a mix of confusion, awe, and shock.

I cracked up. I couldn't help it. She joined my laughter, her eyes – which were a very pale green today – filled with tears of mirth as she held her stomach.

"Oh. Em. Gee." Another voice burst in from the side and Cara and I laughed harder. Ben looked more than a little confused as he glanced between the two of us. "I have no idea what you bitches are laughing about, but seriously, I need all the gossip."

His eyes were locked on me, that mop of curls flying in all directions as he wiggled on the spot.

More students were entering, but no Lexen, so I leaned in closer. "I met them, last night on our street. Their sister has just arrived to start school. She was living ... back with their other family. We hit it off, and they gave me a ride to school today." The fact that most of that was true helped me keep to the story. I wasn't the best liar.

Ben and Cara stared at me, wide-eyed and slack-jawed. It was like they had no idea how to process this information. Ben finally spluttered, "Touch this girl, she's freaking blessed." He then took me completely by surprise when he reached out and wrapped his arms around me, pulling me up and out of my seat into a bear hug. I knew from my brief time with Ben yesterday that he loved to give hugs, and again it didn't bother me very much. I was getting hugs all over the place at the moment.

Was I actually starting to heal?

Before I could delve too deep into whatever was my next psychological step of healing, a shadow fell over us. Everything inside my body tightened – I knew exactly who it was.

"Put her down." Lexen's voice was a low caress across my

nerves. There was an undercurrent there I didn't understand, but the look on his face was calm.

Ben very slowly dropped me to my feet, holding both of his hands up in the air. "Just friends," he said, eyes locked on the imposing supernatural standing close to us.

Lexen ignored him, turning to me. "You're sitting with me."

Some of my normal annoyance with him reared its head. I fought the urge to salute him. "Am I now? I didn't realize that order had been given."

I heard the gasps from all around us. Ben's was the loudest as he dramatically slapped a hand across his mouth. Lexen's attention flickered toward the many eyes on us. He leaned in closer. "Will you please sit near me?" Those words were forced out through clenched teeth.

I smiled brightly. "Much better. And, while I appreciate your offer, I think I'm going to stay with my friends."

I had no idea why I wanted to piss him off; something inside of me liked to rile Lexen, and then keep riling him over and over. His lips brushed my ear as he moved even closer. "I know what you're doing," he murmured. "It's not going to work."

He spun then and with ease stepped between the desks to take a seat near the back. I realized that a few other elites had arrived; most I didn't know. One of the Royales was there. I recognized the blond guy. Also the gorgeous, tiny brunette chick was already sitting. She was the girl I'd seen with Lexen yesterday; her almond-shaped eyes were locked on me. She did not look happy. I tried not to stare at the pair of them, especially as he tilted his body in her direction, his lips moving as they chatted.

I'd stood my ground for a reason, but there would be no point to that if I spent the entire time staring at him in class. Dropping back into my desk, I fought the urge to turn and check if he was looking at me.

I did feel eyes on me. Two set of eyes, to be exact. "What?" I finally said, a snort of laughter in my tone.

"Who are you?" Cara whisper-shouted. "The first day I met you on the bus, you barely spoke at all, and now ... you just stood up to Lexen Darken. Lexen. Darken."

She was getting louder and louder, so I quickly shushed her. "I just don't like being told what to do."

I sensed she wanted to ask me why he was even in a position to tell me what to do, but the teacher entered then and there was no more chance to talk. I struggled to pay attention in class, and as someone who prided herself on meticulous note taking, mostly because I was gunning for a scholarship, I was bothered by my lack of focus.

"We still have to join a group, or some sort of extra-curricular activity," Cara reminded me as we were packing up our books.

I groaned. "Did you have any thoughts about which one?"

She shrugged as she threw her bag over one arm. "Drama? Debate? The newspaper? Prom committee?"

I visibly flinched at the last suggestion. Prom ... I'd gone with my ex-boyfriend; it hadn't really been my thing. The new shoes were nice, I supposed.

"Chess club? Mathletes?"

I shook my head. I liked math, but not every day after school. And I'd never played a game of chess in my life. I was a checkers girl. Checkers all the way.

Ben joined us. "I'm thinking about running for student body president." He straightened his spine. "The top positions always go to the elites, but I figured it was worth a shot."

I met his gaze. "Maybe I can try for student government too. Lesser positions are fine by me."

There was a clearing of a throat, and a low laugh from my right side. I turned to find the exotic, dark-haired beauty standing there beside Lexen. She was the one who had laughed, so I locked my gaze on her. "Something funny?" I found myself asking, one eyebrow raised in her direction.

She shrugged. "I wouldn't bother trying out for *any* of the leadership roles. They're all reserved for..." She looked me over, wrinkling her nose. "Not people like you."

I blinked a few times, shaking my head. I was about to reply with something highly creative and snipingly witty, but Lexen interrupted before I could: "You need to get to your next class. Jero will meet you there. Kotar is going to show you the way."

I knew Cara and Ben were hanging on every word. No doubt their mouths would be wide open as they wondered why I suddenly had an elite escort everywhere. I didn't look at them to find out. I glared at Lexen. "Kotar?" I asked, my eyes flicking to the girl at his side. Was he talking about the snobby bitch?

She let out a breathy sigh. "Come on. I don't have all day to be a guide. Follow me."

She turned and flounced across the room, her shiny black hair cascading around her as she headed for the door.

I narrowed my eyes on Lexen, squinting hard enough to hurt myself. "Why are you doing this? I can walk to class on my own."

He just crossed his arms over his chest, staring me down with that formidable expression on his face.

"Okay, fine," I groaned. I sucked in a deep fortifying breath and followed Kotar from the room. She was already halfway down the hall, so I hurried to catch up. She looked forward, paying me no attention at all. I had a bunch of questions brewing in my mind, like, which house was she from? How did she know Lexen? How *well* did she know Lexen?

But there was no way to ask those questions without sounding like a pathetic human, and she clearly already hated my kind.

What do I have to lose, then? Before I could suck up the guts to open my mouth, we arrived at history class. Kotar waved at the door, which was her only form of communication, before she continued walking. I watched her tiny form as it disappeared around the corner.

Well, that went well.

Entering the classroom, there were a few students seated already. Jero was in his section. Aria, the leggy redhead, was nowhere in sight. I noticed Derek, the glasses-clad guy I'd met at lunch yesterday, already sitting front and center, a bunch of textbooks open in front of him. That was one serious-about-his-studies dude. No doubt he would be valedictorian of our year.

"Princess, over here..." Jero's loud call drew everyone's attention. I headed straight toward him. I had no problem sitting with this particular Darken.

He draped an arm around me and there was barely a sliver of discomfort. I had mixed emotions about this step forward. I didn't want to forget my parents – I would never be able to do that – but I wanted to hurt less. I'd survived, through some miracle. My psychiatrist told me I suffered from survivor's guilt. I didn't disagree. I had no idea why I had been the only one to make it out alive; we should have all gone as a family. But we hadn't. I knew my parents would not want me to beat myself up over my stroke of ... luck. I still wasn't sure if it was good or bad luck that I had lived, but it was luck nonetheless.

"Ready to learn about my illustrious family?" Jero hadn't removed his arm, and I got the distinct feeling he was leaving it there as a warning of some kind. Or maybe he was just a tactile kind of guy. He was certainly flirty enough.

"House of Darken today, right?" Mr. Perkins had mentioned that we were going to start on the founders straight away. "That should be illuminating. Do you get an instant A?"

He chuckled, both of us staring toward the door as the classroom started to fill. As more students stepped inside, more gaping faces were directed toward us.

Jero showed not an ounce of discomfort. "They have most of the facts incorrect," he said, picking up the conversation about today's topic. "But that's not the teacher's fault. Humans only know the history we allow them to know. You'll have to come to us for more accurate information."

"How long do you think I'll have to stay with you guys?" I asked. "Like glued to your sides?"

Some of his humor dried up. He leaned back in his chair, letting his arm finally fall off my shoulders. "By the end of the week we should have an answer. The council is full of ancient, powerful, think-they-know-everything bastards. The members are chosen from all four houses. They have been known to take a long time to reach decisions, but this has a sense of urgency about it. They won't screw around."

It was Tuesday, which meant I was stuck with them for five more days. I wasn't sure I could handle five more days of this. I needed answers. I needed them now.

I leaned in so as not to be overheard by the dozen or so students fixing their gazes on us: "Is there anything we can do? Places we can search? Surely there's a way to track my guardians' last movements."

The Darkens had been pretty confident in their abilities to keep information off computers and the internet. If they were that good, surely they could trace Michael's last online activities. He would kill me if he found out I let anyone touch his computer, but I'd deal with that. As long as he was alive, the rest was inconsequential. There was very little I wouldn't do to get my family back.

He patted my arm. "I'll talk to Lexen. We might be able to try something on our own."

I sensed Jero was just placating me. And ... it worked. For now.

"So ... what happened to your parents?" He blindsided me with *that* question.

I swallowed roughly, took a few deep breaths, and when the tears were under control, said, "They were killed in a fire ... last New Year's Eve." I kept it to basic facts, which was an additional help with the tears. "I must have crawled out into the yard, even though I don't remember a thing before waking up on the pavement out the front."

I had tried to go back in, screaming for my mom and dad, but some of my neighbors who had arrived to help held me back. They'd seen what I refused to: there was no way anyone was still alive in there. The house had been fully alight, and by the time the firefighters finished there was nothing but death and ash remaining.

"I'm really sorry, Emma." He used my name. He sounded sincere. My chest tightened. I pressed my hand to it to ease the ache.

"It's o—" I choked on the word. Because it wasn't okay. There was not a single okay thing about what had happened to me and my family.

"I'm dealing," I finally managed.

Jero sat a little straighter in his chair as he whipped his phone from his pocket and slammed his fingers against the keys. "We're going to find your guardians. You've lost enough."

It was still hard to talk around the lump in my throat. "Why are you being so nice to me?" My words were shaky. "I'm not ... one of you."

He dropped his phone back into his pocket, shrugging. "I know what it's like to be dragged into a world you don't want to be part of. I know what it's like to lose someone. I understand the burning hellfire of pain and regret which are no doubt churning within you right now. We're not as different as you think."

All conversations around us died off then as Mr. Perkins entered the room. Jero and I both faced the front, but my mind was roiling with everything he'd just said. Before I could stop myself, I reached out and grabbed his hand, squeezing it firmly and quick. I wanted him to know that I appreciated his kindness, his support. I was probably only dealing as well as I was because of the Darkens. All of them, even Lexen. Last night he had offered me comfort I'd sorely needed.

Something I never expected from the elite. In fact, most humans I met were far less kind than these ... supernaturals or whatever they were.

Mr. Perkins drew my attention then. "Today is a very exciting day. It's one of my favorite parts of the curriculum. House of Darken."

I heard the low exhalation of breath from Jero, but I was too busy listening to turn to him.

"We will learn much about this magnanimous house, about its illustrious leaders, and the generosity of their family. We will spend the rest of this week, and some of next week, on Darkens, and then you'll have a small assignment to complete, a paper summarizing your thoughts on their lives, charitable works and such."

A lot of the class was looking at Jero now, and it hit me that he was really a Darken. Literally part of this legacy that we were learning of. That was more than a little cool.

"Don't go painting me with a halo yet, sweetheart," he whispered to me from the corner of his mouth. "This is history, not current events."

I was still trying to figure out how it all worked. Why were these supernaturals here at all? I mean, why would non-humans want to draw attention to themselves? Did they want people on the ground, so to speak, to curtail any rumors before they even started? I mean ... did they get rid of humans who stumbled onto the secret? Was that still an option the council might decide on for me?

I had so many questions, and I was almost too impatient in my quest to find the answers.

Mr. Perkins moved to the board then and wrote "1875" at the top, underlining it multiple times. "This is the year the first Darkens immigrated to America. Tatina and Gregori Darken were the clan leaders. They brought across their people. They were extremely private, even back then, so information on those early days is scarce, but many believe they were part of a pilgrimage from Norway. They brought with them riches, and knowledge beyond anything anyone had seen in this area, and Astoria was extremely blessed to be chosen as their original settlement site. Our tiny fishing village found itself under the care and protection of these early settlers.

"You have a fan," I side-whispered to Jero. His lips twitched into a half-smile, but he didn't comment.

One of the girls at the front raised her hand. "Why did they choose Astoria?" she asked.

There was a slight pause, as if the teacher was surprised by this question, but his answer came readily enough: "It was a great area for northern trade."

"Wrong," Jero muttered. I knew he hadn't been talking to me, but I was still desperate to ask him to explain. Of all the places in the world, why had they chosen Astoria?

"What about the other houses?" another student asked. "How do they work with Darken?"

Mr. Perkins grinned so broadly that his ruddy cheeks were practically around his eyebrows. "I'm so glad you asked this. We will of course go more into the Houses of Royale, Imperial, and Leights at another time, but in general reference to Darken, they arrived almost twelve months to the day after the original founders. The history books tell us that they were allies, families who had ties back in Norway. This was the reason for their settlement here also."

"Wrong again," Jero said, his voice still no louder than a whisper. "And we're certainly not all allies."

I leaned in closer to him, keeping my eyes locked on the teacher so he wouldn't catch on to our conversation. "Imperials are your only enemies, right? What about Leights? How can they be neutral?"

Jero shrugged. "They choose sides as they see fit. Royale are our only true allies."

If my math was correct, and since I was a senior one would hope it was, the Darkens were still the strongest house. They had a solid ally. Two of them together versus two lone wolves.

I was of course telling myself this to make this new world I'd fallen into seem less dangerous for me. Because I was on the stronger side.

Yeah, right. As if life was nice and simple like that. Good. Bad. Right. Wrong. Strong. Weak. Nothing was ever that black and white.

The teacher was back at the board now. He had drawn three columns; above each he wrote, Starslight Prep, Darken Exports, and Daelight Crescent.

When he turned around, he clapped his hands together. "For the rest of the week we'll look at this house's initial contributions to Astoria. Firstly, they started a world-leading education institute, making sure our young folks received the very best learning they could. A vast majority of government leaders, business people, scientists, and revolutionaries in modern America did their schooling right here. We have ties to the top colleges – as most of you know."

I found my hand in the air before I could stop it. Mr. Perkins called on me.

"Have there been students in this school from these four houses since 1875?" I asked, deliberately not looking at Jero.

"Yes, more or less," he replied, "there have always been representatives from the four houses in Starslight. They're very proud of this school. There's no other place they would send their children."

I knew Jero was staring at me, but I didn't look his way. I had no idea why I asked that question. It slipped out, but I just had this weird feeling that the Darkens I knew were fairly new to this world. Like Star only coming across yesterday. From wherever.

I hadn't been sure if "supernaturals" being here was a new

thing or not. Apparently not new in general, just for the few I'd met only.

The rest of the lesson was spent on the many ways Darkens now ruled this world. Their exports business seemed to have interests in multiple industries, and I was amazed at how many of their products I had heard of.

When the bell rang, students jumped to their feet as conversations sprang up around us. "We'll continue on with House of Darken tomorrow," Mr. Perkins yelled over the departing students.

Jero followed me from the room, his giant frame towering over me. An added benefit of him as security detail was that students tended to get out of our way as we walked along. It made getting to class so much easier.

"What's next for you?" he asked when we were standing near one of the moving sidewalks.

I glanced at my schedule and let out a groan. "Gym. Seriously?"

"Not a fan?" he asked, watching me closely.

I shrugged. "Honestly, I suck at physical activities. I'm great at knitting, reading, sewing. Cooking, even. I make a mean apple crumble and double-choc brownie. I also jigsaw puzzle like a pro. And I'm great at shopping ... for shoes and clothes. But never ... I repeat never have I *chosen* to exercise."

"No sports? Jogging? What about ... gymnastics?"

I snort-laughed. "Almost broke my cheek on the balance beam. After that my parents finally started accepting me as an indoors kid. Puzzles and books showed up in my room the next day."

His laughter boomed out around us and we drew even more attention than we already had. "Of course you would like puzzles." He continued to chuckle. "Think I might just call you the crazy cat lady from now on. Get in early."

I nodded with all the seriousness I could muster. "Oh, definitely, that's in my ten year plan."

"I'll bet it is." He grinned. "Well, I don't have gym, but I can walk you to that section of the school. Lexen will be in that class with you."

Well, that's just great. He was definitely the one guy I wanted to make an absolute fool of myself in front of. Because he didn't already think humans were stupid and pathetic enough.

"Why does Lexen hate me ... or humans?" I lowered my voice on the human part. "I mean, the rest of you don't seem to feel the same way."

Jero's face closed off; all of the open happiness he had been showing faded in an instant. I sucked in a deep breath, wondering if I had hit on a sore point. "Never mind," I said, forcing fake cheer into my tone. "Not my business."

I turned and jumped on the closest moving path, not even caring if it was going in the right direction. I didn't look back to see if Jero had followed me. *Why did I ask that?* Why was I allowing my emotions to get involved, allowing myself to get attached to these Darkens? I mean, I didn't know them at all, and I no doubt meant nothing to any of them.

Plus, I had an actual family to find, so it was time for me to pull myself together and stop acting stupid.

"He doesn't hate you." Jero's voice startled me, and I spun around to find him right behind me. Dammit, did they have to be so much more stealthy than me too? "Mostly he's not happy about being forced to come here. And your question in class ... there have always been representatives from all four houses here, but it was voluntary. Usually those from the lower echelons of our society, those wanting to enjoy the treaty between our people. Now there are some new laws ... let's just say he disagreed with the council on this new order. His future is not working out how he expected. He's trying to deal with it in his own way."

I turned back to face forward. "I know how that feels," I

murmured. My entire world went up in a ball of flames. The future I'd imagined, gone in an instant.

We were silent for the rest of the journey, Jero only grabbing my elbow to assist me on exit. He already knew I was never going to nail one of these dismounts. He left me at the gym door and I reluctantly made my way into the girls' locker rooms to get changed. Ignoring the stares from the others who were already inside, I focused on dressing in the provided uniform of white shirt, black shorts, white knee socks and tennis shoes, before slinking my way out into the huge gym facility – cursing under my breath the entire time.

It was a circular room, mostly indoors, and there was a running track, courts for a variety of sports, including tennis and volleyball, an Olympic-size pool, weight area ... and the list went on and on. It was like I'd stumbled into a multi-billion dollar professional athletes training area. A shit-ton of money that was completely wasted on someone like me.

Joining the back of my class, I attempted to stay out of sight, knowing Lexen was somewhere here. The teacher stepped to the front of the group. I caught glimpses of his white cotton shirt, a whistle hanging against it.

"Today I'm splitting you into two groups." The whistle jumped up and down in time to his shouting. "One will be on volleyball, the other soccer. First, though, everyone jogs to warm up."

He blew the whistle, and while I heard a few groans, all of the students started running without much complaint. I wiggled on the spot, contemplating what excuse might work to get me out of this class. I really felt like forced gym classes were a form of discrimination against the eternally uncoordinated.

Was there a protest group against this? I needed to look into that.

"You're supposed to be running." The low voice had my chest

clenching tightly, goosebumps already sprinkling across my body. How did his voice do that to me? Every single time.

He had at least distracted me from my panic of running, so I pasted a smile on my face when I turned to him. *Holy shit, why? Just, why?* As if Lexen wasn't already far too lethal on my hormones, someone had to put him in a gym uniform. The shirt was fitted across his broad shoulders, powerful muscles in his arms and upper body very visible. I forced myself not to stare at his ass, which I already knew was amazing, and would no doubt be clearly defined in those pants.

"I don't run," I finally squeaked out, crossing my arms over my chest, goosebumps and nipples saluting the world. Stupid disloyal body. "And aren't you on the football team?"

He nodded, his eyes never leaving mine. God, he was intense, but not in an overwhelming way. More like a throw him on the ground and tear his clothes off kind of way.

No, Emma! Not human, remember? Why was it so hard for me to readily recall that?

"Yep, but Coach likes us to partake in other sports to keep up flexibility and fitness," he said, reminding me that I'd asked him a question. "We start football training in the second half of the class."

I nodded like an idiot. Almost all of the students were on the track now, which made Lexen and me very obvious, standing there, chatting. A lot of them were looking at us, tripping over themselves gossiping. I could see the hard, angry faces of a few of the queen bee type girls at the front of the pack. The last thing I needed was to draw their ire.

Dammit. I started to run. Ten steps in and my chest started to hurt, my breathing already heavy and erratic. This couldn't be good for you! I didn't care what anyone said.

Lexen fell in at my side, jogging easily. Actually, he seemed to be mostly walking really fast to keep pace with me. His legs were like twice the size of mine, so ... I wasn't slow. When I was halfway around the first loop, I wrapped an arm around my side to ease the stitch that had already started to dully thud there.

"I think we need to work on your fitness." Lexen sounded amused.

I, on the other hand, was not amused. And if I'd had even an extra eighth of a breath in my lungs, I would have yelled at him.

I settled for flipping him off.

He blinked at my middle finger a few times, shaking his head. Turning forward, he ignored me and I went back to focusing on not dying. By the time I hit the second lap I was walking. Lexen went on ahead, but I could feel his eyes on me, always keeping watch.

Someone fell into step beside me and I turned to find Kotar there.

"You need to back off the Darkens," she said without preamble.

Oh, goodie, I had been waiting for the cliché mean girl warning.

"I don't know you," she continued. "And while I don't care if you warm all three of their beds and then move on to Star in the morning, you'd better never forget that you're not one of us. You'll never be one of us. If you don't learn your place, someone is going to teach you."

I tilted my head to the side. "What house are you from?"

She turned her nose up at me like I was a fly that had flown a little too close. "I'm a Darken. And trust me, I'm not even in Lexen's league."

I was confused. "You're a Darken? So ... you're related to Lexen."

She smirked, shaking her head. "We aren't all blood related. When they say House of Darken, they literally meant that. Like a banner title. I am not related to any of the Darkens that you've been hanging around, but they're my house. My clan. I protect what is mine."

I. Was. So. Confused.

"Look, I'm not going to be a problem," I told her. "I'll be out of the Darkens' lives as soon as we solve a little issue which involves my family. Your warning is not needed."

Bitch, I silently added.

Her dark eyes narrowed on me, like she'd heard that last part.

"I'll be watching you, human," she finally spat, before she picked up the pace, jogging away, flaunting her ability to run and breathe.

"I'd listen to her." The smug voice sent a chill down my spine.

I stopped my lame attempt at power walking and turned to find an Imperial glaring at me, one of the blond, pixie-haired females.

"You're in way above your head," she continued. "I have no love for humans, but you should get out now while you still can. You should get out..." She leaned in closer, her weird smoky scent washing over me. "Before you get hurt."

"Back off." Lexen's voice was like a whip, and I felt his heat at my back. Without thought, I stepped back into his chest. His protection. I was usually all about fighting my own battles, but I knew this was above my grade. And not because I was female and Lexen was male – hell no – I didn't play ball with that kind of bullshit. It was because I was not a supernatural, and I was not stupid. No point throwing myself into a fight I couldn't win.

Lexen let me rest against him.

"She's human ... and under my protection," he added, voice deceptively calm. "Walk away now before you violate our treaty and start something your house can't win."

Her joking demeanor disappeared. "I'm really going to enjoy wiping your house out of both worlds. You think you have all the control ... you just wait. Change is coming, and no power is going to be able to stop the decimation of your people."

Part of me wanted to grab some popcorn, pull up a squishy arm chair, and watch the drama. This was better than the

Spanish soap operas I occasionally caught on television. She left before I could get too involved, and as she walked away I remembered that there were lives at stake. Many lives. My family's lives.

I spun around, only realizing just how close I was to Lexen when I brushed his chest. I knew I should step away, but in my panic I couldn't. I just tilted my head up to see his expression better. "Could the Imperials have Sara and Michael?"

If they were the bad guys, and I was already painting them with that brush in my story, then it made sense.

"I don't know." He sounded frustrated. "I can't think of a reason for them to orchestrate the situation to get your family here. But ... they're up to something. They've only recently come into new leadership, and Laous is not someone I trust. I'll talk to Father about investigating him."

Vulnerability rocked through me. It was on the tip of my tongue to admit I was scared, but I couldn't say the words. I refused to let the fear win. I had made it through bad things before. I was still alive, still functioning. I could beat this too.

Lexen's phone made a chirping noise from his pocket. He took a small step away from me, pulling his phone out. As he lifted it, I heard a few other chirping sounds in the class and I turned to find the Imperial chick and Kotar both lifting their cells.

Well, that was an awfully weird coincidence.

I turned back to Lexen – he was wearing an unusual expression. Almost like ... worry. My stomach cramped tightly, fear spiking through me.

"What?" I said, reaching for his arm. "Is it my family?"

He shook his head. "They haven't found them yet. Father just sent a message – the council is calling a meeting. They want to discuss some findings with the four houses."

"And you have to be there for this meeting?" I asked.

He nodded, looking down at his phone again. I wondered again then where this "home" of his was. Was it on Earth or another world? Could I handle it if they weren't from Alaska or the Sahara?

"What do I do while you're gone?" I asked, resigned. "The danger should be minimal, right? If there are no ... supernaturals here."

Amusement creased the corner of his lips, only for a moment, before those hard, stressed lines reappeared. He leaned down and murmured the next part in my ear: "I think it's time to learn exactly what world you've stumbled into. We're not supernaturals. We're called Daelighters, and we're ... more like aliens ... if you want to classify us."

Aliens. I paused, waiting to see if I was about to lose my mind with this information. Definitely not from Earth ... but surprisingly enough it felt okay. It fit with everything I knew.

"Guess the street name makes sense now," I choked out. "You're really from another world?"

He nodded. "Overworld, and you're coming there with us."

11

I was hurrying to keep up with Lexen as he rushed through the school. "I don't understand," I said, breathlessly. *Why was I so bad at running?* "How can I come with you? I'm not a Daelighter or whatever. I can't go to another world. Can I even breathe the air there? Will the gravity kill me?"

I'd done enough science classes to know that humans were perfectly designed for Earth. We had evolved and developed as a species to suit this world, and we had very specific requirements to stay alive. Most other planets we'd discovered would not support our biology. I'd never heard of Overworld, of course, so no doubt it wasn't in our solar system. But the same principle applied.

Lexen grumbled down at me, his previously prickly personality returning in full swing. "Clearly we're compatible species. We're here on your world, aren't we?"

Way to not so subtly call me a moron. "Yes, but you all keep telling me how special you are. I assumed my inferior human genetics were going to hold me back." I sarcastically drawled the last part so he knew I really thought his species were a bunch of dickbags.

His chest swelled as he stopped suddenly. I slammed right into him, because I was just barely managing to run and breathe at the same time. Dude was built like a rock wall. Huge hands wrapped around my biceps and I was lifted up slightly off the ground as he dragged me closer, his voice dropping ominously low. "Listen up, human. You're going to have to get with the picture, and fast. There is no time for you to freak out, or need a period of adjustment. Suck it up, deal with it, and maybe all of us will get out of this mess alive. Do you understand?"

"Lex!" Star's shocked voice washed over us. "What are you doing? You're hurting her."

It was possible it looked like that from her angle, but despite the steel-like strength I could feel in his hands he wasn't hurting me – unless you counted the way my heart was racing, and that dull ache low in my traitorous body. I was attracted to Lexen. I couldn't deny it any longer. But it was all chemical, because he was not good for me in so many ways, no matter how compatible our species were.

Lexen's dark eyes bored into mine and he released me. I swallowed hard, turning as Star wrapped her arms around me. Looked like I was pretty much cured of my aversion to touch, since I let these four Darkens handle me in whatever way they saw fit.

"Are you okay?" Her beautiful face was creased in concern, her gaze sliding down my arms.

I shook my head. "I'm fine. Thanks for looking out. Lexen didn't hurt me, though."

I found my eyes locked on his for a brief moment. His expression was unreadable, but the look felt different. Heated somehow.

Jero and Marsil sprinted up then, distracting us. "What happened?" Marsil asked, his gentle voice still taking me by surprise. His nature was so soft, and yet he was built like a linebacker. The contrast was odd, but ... I liked it.

Lexen straightened fully as he went into some sort of

command mode: "Father wants us home for this council meeting. It's called for all four houses. We will be gathering at the white field."

I expected the boys to salute at the end, but they just nodded their heads. "We should head there now." Jero already had his phone out, typing into it. When he was done, he seemed to notice I was still standing in his sister's half-hug.

"Hey there, pretty girl! What are you doing here?"

I snorted. "Apparently I'm coming home with you four to ... *Overworld*." My calm from before was starting to disappear under the reality of how freaking weird this was. What would happen once I was on their world? I'd be stuck there. What if the Darkens forgot about me and I couldn't get home?

While I was having my internal existential crisis, the others turned toward Lexen and he gave a single nod. "Council's orders. She's going to be under Darken protection. We're to remain at her side at all times."

I was shaking my head, mind made up. "I'm not going with you," I decided. "It's too risky. I don't even know anything about you!" My voice rose at the end, and when students turned to see what was happening, Lexen stepped in close, dropping his head closer to mine.

"You don't have a choice." His voice was low, and soothing somehow. "If you don't come with us now, the council will send someone for you. And they'll be far less interested in your cooperation."

I backed up a little, fear rattling through me. I had grown complacent ... fell into the trap of trusting beings who were not of this world, allowed myself to think for a brief moment that they were friends, that there was a bond between us. But what did I really know about them? They were ... *aliens*.

Jero nudged his brother out of the way. "Lex, man, you're scaring her." He held a hand out to me, not demanding, just palm open. "Listen up, sweetheart. Lexen is not lying. If the council wants something, they get it. No matter what. We want you with us because we want to protect you. Our family has some influence in Overworld. You don't need to worry about your safety."

"I ... I could get trapped on your world. I can't take the risk."

Most of me knew it was stupid trying to fight this. There was no way for me to hide from their council. I was a teenager with no money and missing guardians. If the council always got their own way, then it was going to happen. But I still had to protest. That was all the control left to me.

"Sara and Michael," I choked out. "What happens to them if I don't go with you?"

Lexen wore a blank expression again, except for those fiery eyes. "Reading between the lines of Father's message, the council believes your guardians are being held in Overworld. If we want their help to find them, we need to cooperate."

Damn, if they were on Overworld I was going to be there too. "How do I know you're not lying?" I finally said, no longer backing away.

Marsil shot me his gentle grin; it put me at ease. "You're just going to have to trust that we are on your side."

Trusting was hard for me, but it seemed I really didn't have a choice. In all honesty, my gut instincts since first meeting these four had been to trust them. It was a weirdness I couldn't explain, but my gut was usually pretty good with those things, so I would go with it for now.

And hope it didn't bite me on the ass.

Star, who had been quietly watching, letting her brothers talk me off the ledge, stepped in then and linked our arms together. "If I could stay here with you, I would," she said, sincerity dripping from each word.

"You want to stay?" Marsil sounded surprised.

"I only just got here..." She stamped her foot. "Literally just got here and already I have to go home. It took me almost a year to get Father to agree. A year!"

Her voice wobbled slightly. I squeezed her hand.

Marsil patted his sister's shoulder. "Don't worry, we won't let the overlord keep you there. When this council meeting is done, we will *all* be coming back to our own little slice of Earth."

"Don't make any promises," Lexen growled. "I think this little experiment has failed. It was one thing when it was voluntary, but the moment they started to force compliance, everything fell apart."

No one said anything more, and I tried to ignore the small stab of pain I felt at his need to get away from Earth and ... us humans. *Whatever.* I shouldn't be surprised, Lexen had never made it a secret. There was a lot of background story I didn't know, and a part of me was excited to be going to Overworld. Terrified, of course. But excited at the same time. An emotion I was more than a little happy to feel again. When my parents died, a part of me died also, the part that cared about the world going on around me. But ... this felt different. For once I was not apathetic. I wanted to know everything. Hopefully I would get all of the answers soon.

Our first stop before leaving Starslight was a set of lockers near the entrance. Huge and shiny, they were at least twice the size and depth of mine. When Lexen pressed his thumb to the scanner, I realized it was his. I had no idea what they needed lockers for; they never carried books or bags.

"Dump your stuff in here. You won't need it."

Oh, right. The locker was for me. I thought briefly of grabbing my wallet, but no doubt the student identification and Daelight Crescent card were not going to be useful on Overworld, so I didn't bother to take anything.

"We have everything you need in our territory," Star told me. "Don't worry about a thing."

Did they have to be so nice all the time? The lines were blurring for me.

Meh, who the hell was I kidding? They had been blurred

almost from the first second I moved onto their street and was told not to cross to the rich side. My fascination with these Daelighters was worrisome, but at least I understood what Cara was talking about. It was impossible to stay away once you'd tasted their world.

We left the school without a word to any teachers, and we weren't the only ones. I was about to see the full scale of these Daelighters here on Earth. Well, at least here in Stars High. There were at least fifty students trailing out and climbing into their cars – all of which were worth more than the last three houses I had lived in put together.

"So ... all of you are rich?" I said, half envious, half impressed with their setup here on Earth. "Couldn't you have just gotten by with your exceptional good looks and photographic memories?"

Jero chuckled. "I'll take the good looks, but photographic memory is not one of our gifts."

"So the no books thing...?" I'd asked him before, but I wanted more explanation.

Lexen opened the door for me, which had me a little stunned, but ... I also liked that he'd done something thoughtful.

"We have already completed all of our schooling," he said as I climbed into the passenger seat. "We're older than you, in a way. Therefore we're not learning anything new. This is just to keep up appearances."

"How are you older in a way?" I asked, when all of the Darkens were inside the vehicle.

They exchanged a smile like I was missing out on an inside joke. I hated when people did that. So freaking rude.

"We're ... older than you, that's all you need to know."

Fact of the day: Lexen was a dick.

"Why would your age be a secret?" I said, my tone filled with derision. "I mean, seriously, why the hell would I care if you're old?"

Lexen tilted his head, flashing me one of his very rare grins. "Why are you asking if you don't care?"

I bit back my frustrated scream.

"I'm fifty-five in human years," Star cut in, shooting her brother a narrow-eyed look. "I'm the youngest."

What. The. Freak?

"Fifty-five?" I repeated, trying to wrap my head around what she was saying. She looked younger than me. "So, I'm going to guess that Daelighters age differently to humans?"

Four head nods. Marsil filled me in: "We stop aging once we reach maturity."

"You don't age?" I almost collapsed against the shiny door of Lexen's car. "My human brain can't compute that sort of information." I mean, did they die? Or were they immortal?

"Hence why we don't talk about our age," Lexen said with a shake of his head, starting the car.

I could sense Lexen's urgency to get going, so I wasted no more time on questions. I buckled myself in. As soon as my belt clicked, we took off in a squeal of tires. I gripped the door, because Lexen was channeling a racecar driver on the way home, foot flat to floor, weaving in and out of traffic.

"Please remember that one of us is human," I griped, my knuckles aching from the death grip I had on my handhold.

Lexen just laughed, the carefree sound mildly distracting me from my fear. "You're safe, little human. I can handle her."

I muttered about boys and their toys, closing my eyes for the rest of the way. Lucky there weren't a lot of cars on the road. Well, except for all of the aliens following us. When we reached Daelight Crescent, the huge gates were already open and Lexen flew down the road, pulling into his driveway. We all piled out, and I realized that we weren't going inside at all. *Great,* I was going to be stuck in my gym uniform.

Even worse, I would have to use that swirly light thing that Star had emerged from.

As though she had heard my worries, Star popped up beside me. "Don't be nervous," she told me. "It doesn't hurt. The portal between our worlds is linked strongly at this gateway. You just need to step through and you'll be on the other side."

"More or less," Marsil said, patting me on the shoulder.

I looked between the two of them. "Well, is it more or is it less? Because I'm not feeling very confident with that answer."

They both shrugged and I bit back an angry retort. When I got nervous, I turned into an asshole. I was working on it. Among my many other faults.

"House of Darken takes the first light beam home, so we need to hurry." Lexen was already walking, his words drifting back to us.

Star moved then, dragging me along; she was surprisingly strong. Then we were all hurrying. A glance back told me the street was filling with teenage-looking Daelighters, all of them ditching their cars in front of their mansions. There was not one person on this street who looked older then late teens, early twenties.

"Do you die?" I whispered to Star.

She looked astonished for a moment, and I realized that my blurted question might have sounded vaguely threatening. She recovered smoothly. "Yes, of course we do. We're very long-lived but not immortal. We really do just age differently to humans."

I sensed that was the best answer I was getting for a while, so I shelved any further questions and focused on the simple – and hideous – task of running to keep up with all the long legs around me. In the bright light of day, streets usually showed their grimier side, trash, graffiti, potholes. Not Daelight. It was pristine, not a leaf out of place in the hedges. Not a dead flower in the gardens. The asphalt was untouched. The lines were bright white.

There had been a reason my spidey senses went off the first moment we drove up to the gates. It was actually the only time I had ever given true thought to Sara and Michael's crazy theories. A sense of something unnatural was laced into this street, making it impossible for me to continue to insist my guardians' theories were pure insanity.

Damn, I really owed them an apology.

I have to find them.

I couldn't consider any other possibility. My sanity could not handle another loss.

When we turned down the rose-covered lane, nerves kicked in again and wiped all other thoughts from my mind. Star was half dragging me; my feet were slowing on their own accord apparently.

"I'll take her from here." Lexen's deep voice cracked through some of my nerves and I was able to recover enough to glare at him. "Don't make me carry you," he warned, before he reached out and pulled me away from his sister.

My eyes were no doubt wide and panicky as I turned to Star, silently begging her not to leave me. She just shrugged and hurried forward. Traitor.

"I don't need your help," I snapped at Lexen, hating the way he made me feel like a burden.

"I'm the only one you should trust to bring you to Overworld safely. But hey, feel free to try and make it on your own if you want."

I growled at him. Like an actual growl rocked out of my chest. He blinked once, before one corner of his lips lifted slightly, like he was fighting a grin and had lost. Before I could growl at him again, because I was tempted to, a flash of light stole all of my attention and I found myself shuffling closer to the grumpy Daelighter without even thinking about it. The ball of light had been scary enough before I knew it was dangerous to cross. I was even less keen now to step into it.

I reached out and grabbed Lexen's hand. "You won't let me die, right? I know you hate humans, and I'm a human, so therefore you must hate me. And when you hate someone you give zero shits about them dying. Sometimes you even wish they would die." I sucked in a few deep breaths, leaning forward and bracing my free hand on my knee like I was winded.

His strong hand wrapped around mine as he pulled me back up. I tilted my head all the way back to see his face better.

"I won't let you die, Emma. You're safe with me." His voice was a low caress across my senses.

I swallowed hard. "You didn't say if you hated me or not," I whispered.

He shook his head, that half-smile back on his face. "Don't push your luck, little human. Now come on."

I silently followed, blinking rapidly as the light blinded me. It seemed larger than I remembered – more intense – and as we got closer I noticed details I had missed last time. Understandable ... I had been a little shocked and panicked yesterday. Seriously, had it only been a day? Time was doing very strange things at the moment.

Focusing again on the light, I saw it wasn't actually a huge ball. It appeared to be made up of thousands of thick strings of illumination, all intertwined and meshing together. Strands randomly flicked off from the main group and I let out a gasping shriek when Lexen grabbed my hand and reached out to capture a strand.

"Hold on."

His warning registered just as I opened my mouth and started screaming. Loud, gulping sounds of panic continued to tear up from my chest and out through my lips. My brain couldn't quite compute what was happening. It was too far beyond my understanding of travel and physics. Somehow we were being yanked along a string of light, through darkness and light, fire and ice. Lexen's hand firmly wrapped around mine was the only thing keeping me together.

The end of the string appeared in the distance. We hurtled

toward it and I had to close my eyes because it felt a lot like this was the last moment of my life. At the speed we were travelling, there was no way to survive. We would either hurtle off into space, off into the darkness of this wormhole we traveled in, or we would splat against the end. Whatever was at the end.

So eyes closed it was.

I waited. And waited. Finally, when it was clear that I hadn't squished into a wall, I slowly popped one eye open and looked around. We were no longer in the darkness. We now stood on a well-lit platform, a few feet from another ball of light.

Eyes so wide that I no doubt looked ridiculous, I took a moment to take it all in. *Toto, I've a feeling we're not in Kansas anymore.*

We stood near the center of a huge circular metal platform. Well, it looked like metal – gold and shimmery – with lots of symbols carved across it. The symbols seemed vaguely familiar, but as I ran my gaze across the ones near me, I couldn't quite place them. They definitely weren't hieroglyphics or Mayan.

"This is the point where Earth and Overworld intercept," Lexen explained, distracting me as he pulled me further away from the light. "Our worlds exist parallel to each other, in alternate universes. There are these scattered points where the energy of the two overlap. We use our network to create portals in those spots."

"That's why Astoria was the place you first emerged, not because of trade with the north."

He grinned. "Yeah, trade with the north was not exactly a priority."

"So ... why did you come to Earth at all?"

A beam of light shot out from the ball then and Jero appeared, stepping out gracefully. I figured I wouldn't get any more answers from Lexen now, but he surprised me when he said, "Daelighters have been crossing to Earth for thousands of years. That network I mentioned, it's linked to the energy of multiple universes and worlds. Earth is one of the few we are totally compatible with." He was staring out across the platform now. I didn't know what he was looking at though, because I was too busy watching him.

"About a hundred and twenty years or so ago, our network started to fail. The energy was disappearing, and our world was on the brink of total annihilation. Without the network, we wouldn't be able to power our land, or the beings living within it. There was a possibility we would all fade away." *Holy crap, we were getting to the serious part of the story.* "It was someone from my house who noticed that every time he opened a transporter there was a surge in the power in the network ..." At my blank look he explained. "The balls of light are called transporters."

"So you formed the treaty," I guessed.

He nodded. "Yes, we had no choice because we needed a permanent transporter, one much larger than the random ones we had been creating before. It was time for humans to know about us." He waved an arm in front of him. "We decided to create this platform. It's mixed with elements from the four houses, etched with our ancient language, and with a permanent transporter to Earth. Almost immediately our network resumed its full functions."

Jero and Star were through now, and I knew I only had a few more moments alone with Lexen, so I quickly asked: "The treaty allows your network to be powered from Earth's energy, or from something to do with Earth. But what do they get in return? I assume there has to be a return, if they decided to take you up on the treaty."

He inclined his head. "You assume correctly. The leaders of America, at the time, were gifted a very special piece of Starslight stone. This is a sacred rock to us, very powerful. It's a one-off, its size unrivaled by any other in our world. It turned out that Earth needed help at the time too. It was having some very serious weather occurrences. Earthquakes, tsunamis, tropical storms.

This stone was buried near your equator, and it calmed the tectonic plate movements. Halted much of the dangerous weather."

No freaking way. "Starslight, like the school?"

He nodded again. "Yes, exactly like the school, and it's also where Star gets her name."

Our conversation dried up as the other Darkens approached us. They were all through the transporter now. Jero swept me up in a hug. "How was the trip across, angel face? Any turbulence?"

I smacked him on the arm. "Put me down, you weirdo."

It was at that point my reality registered with me. Like actually registered. Despite my *Wizard of Oz* thoughts before, I hadn't quite comprehended the truth. Mostly because I was too busy focusing on Lexen. But I was not on Earth any longer. *I was not on Earth...*

As Jero set me on my feet, I spun around and sucked in a deep breath. The air was cool and crisp; my lungs seemed to expand more than I'd ever felt before; my head swam at the overload of oxygen. The platform they'd created for the transporter was high, almost like it was perched on a mountain, and stretched out below it, as far as I could see, was their world.

As I spun, more of Overworld came into focus. If I had to explain the layout, I'd call it segments, like gigantic slices of cake – three at least. A green, mountainous landscape was a segment to my right. It was the largest, taking up approximately twice as much space as the other two. It looked cold there, white topping many of the mountains.

The next segment was the smallest, but by no means was it actually small. The flat land was filled with billions of trees, spanning off into the distance, with almost no break at all in the forest. And the last was one continuous unbroken mass of water.

Marsil and Star stood on either side of me. "This is incredible," I spluttered out. "But there are only three segments and four houses?"

A sneer from nearby drew all of our attention and I found myself staring at the Imperials, the same ones who had been in the hall that day. Jero had said they were from Laous' side. "House of Imperial does not have to share their territory," one of them said. "We have it all. We control you all."

Say what? Where was their territory if they didn't share?

Jero slung an arm around me, turning us away from them. No one bothered to reply and I could feel eyes burning into the back of my head.

"So where is their territory?" I whispered, unable to keep my curiosity any longer.

Jero leaned his head down. "Our transport should be here soon. We'll talk more when we are back in our land."

I stifled a sigh, forcing myself to simply enjoy this new experience. It was like I had stepped into one of my novels, the ones where the females who found themselves abducted by aliens usually fell for their captors and ended up with a happily-ever-after on some strange world.

I loved reading those stories, and so far living it was interesting, but I wasn't sure I wanted the same ending. I was just hoping to find Sara and Michael and make it out alive.

More students from our school – everyone still in uniform – joined us as we moved toward the edge of the platform facing the mountains. I twisted my head, peeking out from under Jero's arm. Looked like these were the House of Darken members. Kotar's dark eyes flashed at me as our gazes met and I quickly looked away. At least fifty or more students were now through the portal, separated out, each standing in front of the territories. The Imperials were the only ones not moving, remaining right near the ball of light.

A swift breeze caught my attention, and since we were standing on the edge staring out into the stunning mountain world beyond, I had an uninterrupted view of what was coming for us.

Ohmyfreakinggods. Holy ... sweet ... baby ... Jesus.

Two beasts rose into the air, their powerful wings sending gusts of air in our direction. Dragons. There were dragons here. Okay, most probably they called them another name, but they definitely resembled dragons.

I took a step back, followed by another and another, only halting when I slammed into a Daelighter who had been standing behind us. I spun to find an angry looking male, a few inches taller than me, with orange hair. Not ginger so much, but pumpkin orange.

"Watch where you're going, *grubber*," he growled.

A hand whipped out from over my head and smacked him in the face. I turned, expecting it to be Jero – Marsil was too gentle, and Lexen didn't give a shit – but surprisingly enough it was Star.

"Don't ever talk to her like that," she snapped at him. "We're no better than humans, just different."

He sneered, reaching up to rub his jaw. I mentally gave her a high five. Nice work, girlfriend! There was a red print already forming across his cheek.

"She shouldn't be here," he tried again. "It's bad enough we have to go to their world, but now we're bringing grubbers back here. Where does it all end?"

Okay, so *grubbers* was definitely some sort of mean slur for humans. Still, considering it was a *grubber* planet which was keeping theirs alive, they could be a little more grateful.

"Enough." That one word from Lexen finally shut orange-hair up.

His eyes shot daggers into me, but when he lifted them to the huge Darken there was nothing but blankness in his blue irises. "As you wish, Overlord."

I blinked a few times, swinging my head up to Lexen, staring at him like he had two heads. *Overlord?* I had heard that before, when they were talking about their father.

I was distracted from this as another strong gust of wind

slammed against me and I almost lost my footing. Marsil wrapped an arm around me, pulling me closer to him.

The two dragons were hovering at the edge, and I hadn't noticed before, because dragons pretty much took up all of my attention, but they were tethered together.

And there was something attached to the back of them.

Was that a freakin' flying carpet?

12

y heart was pounding so hard that it felt like an actual drumbeat in my chest, but I couldn't tear my eyes away from the fascinating – and terrifying – beasts. They looked exactly the way I imagined a dragon would, minus a few little details: as tall and wide as a house, with four powerful legs, a long spiked tail, huge head, and sharp teeth-filled jaws. One was dark, a shiny, shimmery black, like oil spilled across the top of water. I could see other colors within the inky coat of scales, but for the most part it was darkness. If darkness had thick wings lazily flapping behind to keep it aloft.

The other dragon was white, its coat almost blinding in its intensity, reflecting the light of this world. I couldn't see a sun in the sky, which was a deep, rich emerald color, but something was definitely illuminating Overworld. I was distracted from my stunned observations by Lexen stepping forward, balancing precariously on the edge of the platform.

The drop below would have to be miles, and I fought the urge to reach out and pull him back. Surely he knew what he was doing, being this *overlord* and all. Whatever the hell that was.

The white dragon popped its huge head up right before him,

and I managed to swallow my gasp, too petrified to do anything except stare. Its head alone was bigger than Lexen's body. Shit, it probably had teeth bigger than his body. He didn't seem worried, holding out a hand and waiting for the dragon to press its snout into it.

"Hey there, beautiful." His voice was low and lilting, emotion resonating on each word. He then switched to another language, one that was musical and so damn beautiful that for a moment all of my fear calmed. I was entranced, focusing only on Lexen and his voice.

"*Lotera muschin roatina, Qenita.*"

"It's a dragon," I breathed, needing to say it out loud.

"Her name is Qenita. She's bonded to Lexen," Star whispered in my ear, her eyes lit up.

Ohmygod. Bonded to Lexen. What was happening? How was this my life?

Darkens around us started to move, all of them striding over to the carpet, which was twenty feet wide and the same deep. It was a shimmery white, looking like ... well, a magic carpet, right down to the tassels which hung off the very end.

One by one the members of House of Darken leapt across – none of them afraid they were going to fall to their death – landing on the white rug. Lexen, finished greeting his dragon, turned to hurry the stragglers along.

Star used that superior strength to haul me over, letting me go when we neared the carpet. "We're all taking the oblong sphere home. Don't be afraid. Once you're on, your feet will lock in place."

I flailed my arms and dragged my feet. "I can't jump down," I gasped out, sucking in deep breaths. "Learn this about me immediately! No jumping or running. If you need to discuss literature, or help with dinner, I'm your girl, but athletic ability ... look elsewhere." I was rambling, my head feeling light again. Maybe the overload of oxygen here was too much.

"Go on," Lexen told his family. "I'll get Emma across."

Jero winked at me, before he turned and gracefully leapt. As Star had said, the moment his feet hit the ... oblong sphere ... he didn't move again, except to cross his arms.

Marsil and Star followed, each of them landing right beside their brothers. Unfair. Not only could they jump the five feet to reach the sphere, they could also aim where they landed.

"I won't let you fall." Lexen's voice distracted me, and I crossed my shaking arms over my body, trying to hide my nerves. "Trust me."

I snorted, glad when some of my spark returned. But before I could say anything I was being lifted up and tossed over his shoulder like a bag of potatoes. I wanted to scream and smack him in the head, seeing I could finally reach it, but he was moving and I really didn't want to die today. I closed my eyes when he jumped, opening them again as I felt the landing. I was dropped to my feet almost immediately, and as promised, my tennis shoes suctioned to the rug. Looking down, it wasn't obvious what was holding them. Clearly magic, because why not?

I knew I was focusing on something small, like the foot suction, so I didn't have to deal with the fact I was on an alien world ... riding a magic carp ... oblong sphere, and dragons were pulling said sphere like a carriage.

There was a small jolt; breezes blew up as the carpet moved. I had never been particularly great at keeping my balance, something that contributed to my hatred of physical activity, but as the dragons flapped and we rose up above the height of the platform with its light ball in the center, I wasn't thrown off at all. I had a very good view then of the other houses. Imperial still remained near the center, but it looked like a whirling mass of light – similar but not the same as the one we just took from Daelight Crescent – had appeared in the floor before them. I gasped as one by one they stepped forward onto the whirl of gold and then disappeared.

Where was their territory?

As the dragons surged forward, we crossed closer to the water world, which was … House of Royale – I recognized some of those blond students, some with hair so white it was a blinding beacon on top of their heads. They were taking turns to dive into the water, graceful despite the fact the platform was quite a ways up from the water. I blinked a few times, then more rapidly as I caught glimpses of scales as they disappeared below the surface. Jero must have caught my fiftieth gasp for the day.

"They're mermaids," I said.

He tweaked my nose. "Good try, doll, but we call them *Caramina*. Cara means 'tail' or 'appendage' in our original language. Which roughly translates to 'tailed folk.'"

Sounded like a mermaid to me.

I tried to see the final house, the one made up of the sector of trees. That had to be the Leights. There were only a few of them left on the platform. I hadn't seen their house at school before, so I tried to catch all the details I could. They had dark skin, varying in shades from light brown to a beautiful ebony. They also had long hair, most calf-length or longer, thick and wavy. I was immediately envious. There didn't look to be a single strand of frizz or fuzz, despite their waves.

So unfair.

I strained to see what their special gifts were, but just as one stepped toward the end of the platform, the dragons changed direction, and then all I could see were the billion-plus trees that made up their land. The dragons moved fast, their powerful wings pulling us with great speed through the sky. I lost sight of the platform completely, focusing on the world below. The mountain ranges were vast, rising and climbing in no discernible pattern. The weather was quite mild, but it looked cold in some areas below.

"You don't have clouds?" I asked, keeping my voice low. I had not missed all the questioning looks I was getting from the *other*

House of Darken members, some of them downright hostile, but I was too busy enjoying my first ever trip to an alternate world to really care.

Star let out a light giggle, the sweet sound drifting along the air. "Clouds are fascinating. I really enjoyed seeing them."

I couldn't help but snort, a far less sweet a sound. "Astoria is the perfect place to see clouds, although not really the fluffy white variety. More mean and stormy."

She hadn't answered my question, and even though I really wanted to know – the emerald sky was untouched by no other color or object that I could see – I didn't want to ask again.

Jero came to my rescue. "No clouds. It doesn't rain here. Water comes from other sources."

The way he stumbled over the word *water*, I wondered if it was different here, maybe called something else.

So I asked him.

He shook his head, that caramel-streaked hair tumbling across his forehead. Piercing blue eyes locked on me, eyes I could no longer call sky blue, since their sky was emerald. "It has the same sort of properties as water, but it doesn't exactly taste the same. It will keep you healthy, though, so don't worry."

"What do you call it?" I knew it wasn't going to be water.

"Water," he said drily.

I snorted again, so ladylike. "Well ... I did not see that coming."

Jero cracked up then. He might not have been able to move his feet, but his hands worked fine as he alternated between laughing at me and ruffling my hair. "I'm just messing with you, pumpkin. We call it *legreto*, liquid life." Their accent was so beautiful that even English resembled poetry when they spoke it. Then they had to up it by using their native language, which literally sounded like music on their lips.

Damn them.

Legreto. I let the word roll around my mind; it rolled so

smoothly off Jero's tongue that part of me wanted to speak it out loud. I was just opening my mouth when a set of dark eyes met mine, dark eyes with twilight twinkling strongly within them. Lexen had been quiet since greeting his dragon ... friend. I hadn't forgotten that he was an overlord, whatever that was here, and all of the reverent looks that he received made a lot more sense. He was important.

"Your hair!" I had a sudden realization. "The symbols are the same that were on the platform."

I knew they had seemed familiar. I found myself staring at the intricate symbols etched into the side of his hair, just the one side, which somehow suited him perfectly. "What do they mean?"

He grimaced, reaching up to touch them. "They're a cage of my position. Unique messages, written in the old language. All of the overlords have them. Mine formed at birth, so I'm next in line for whenever my father steps down."

"Can a woman be an overlord?" I asked, wondering if this was a patriarchal society.

All of them nodded. "Yep," Star said, sounding proud. "Sometimes there are multiple children born with the marks. Sometimes there are none and then the houses will vote for their next overlord."

"Those who are voted in, rather than born to the position, get their symbols after their initiation," Jero told me.

I really wanted to know what Lexen's symbols said, but I was a little afraid it was like asking someone their weight: personal, and none of my business.

"So ... what do your symbols say?" Holy shit, where was my filter? I tensed, waiting for the slap down, but it never came. Lexen wasn't the one to answer though.

"'Draygone Lord, Ruler of Skies,'" Star trilled. "Lexen is the first to wear the draygone lord symbol in thousands of years. Father is so proud." She said *draygone* not dragon, but since they sounded similar, and no one had corrected me before, it must translate.

I thought it was a little odd that we would call the beasts something so similar, but maybe the myth of dragons on Earth actually originated from Daelighters.

Jero, Marsil, and Star all looked proud of their brother. Lexen just looked resigned, like he knew it wasn't something he'd earned, or probably even wanted, but he was stuck with the position. Kind of like being sent to Earth, another obligation. But what did Lexen truly want? What made him happy?

Before I could dig too deeply into his psyche, the dragons started to descend, swinging in close to one of the mountains. It had to be a hundred miles wide, and almost that tall. The huge creatures weaved expertly in and out, using air currents to glide toward the base. I lifted myself, standing as tall as I could to see everything. The mountain, while looking similar in structure and shape to ours on Earth, was made of a material other than rock, more like ... an opaque diamond, with swirls of color intersecting throughout. Snow caressed the top, cascading down in long stripes of white. Except...

"How do you have snow without rain?" I asked, not taking my eyes off the peak.

"The draygones," Marsil said simply. "The draygones are responsible for most things in Darken. Always look to them first."

"How is it you live with dragons and they don't eat you?"

The silence was long. I had to turn from the mountain to look between them. "They don't eat you, right?"

Jero shrugged. "It has been known to happen. I wouldn't suggest wandering off on your own."

I was waiting for him to laugh again, tell me he was joking. I mean, the white and black beasts pulling this carpet looked absolutely terrifyingly ferocious, but Lexen had walked right up to Qenita. 'Dragon lord' was making a lot more sense now.

The carpet did a huge drop then. I caught my shriek as it was about to burst from my lips. I pressed a hand to my chest; my heart thundered. We were really moving fast now, and a lot of the chatter from other Darkens died off.

"Do you think this council meeting is going to reveal anything new?" Marsil asked, his tone serious. "We haven't even been Earthside for half the allotted time. Seems odd that they would request our return so quickly."

I remained quiet, not wanting them to remember a stranger was in their midst. I wanted to hear this.

Lexen, who had been focused on the mountain we were approaching – we looked to be only halfway down its massive height – turned to his brother. "No doubt it's to do with Emma's guardians. If they have indeed been taken from Earth to Overworld, it's a direct violation of the treaty. The council is not going to sit on that."

Marsil growled, which was so odd that I had to look twice to make sure it had actually emerged from him. "This is about the Imperials." His voice was a low rumble. "Ever since Laous became overlord ... he's up to something."

Jero clenched his fists. "I can't believe no one interrupted the initiation ceremony. The council has been trying to keep Laous from taking that position for years."

"Laous was the one to propose that the overlord families send their children to Earth." Lexen's voice was hard. "Father only agreed because another war between the houses would be devastating. We've hardly started to recover from the last one."

I was following along with about half of what they were saying, but the definite vibe was just how bad news these Imperials were. Maybe they should get those munch-happy dragons on the case. Problem solved.

We dipped again, and this time, despite whatever amazing stability magic this carpet had going on, I didn't keep my balance. Falling forward when your feet are locked in place is not something I would recommend. For my hands to break my fall, I had to bend my knees, because flexible I am not, and then I almost ended up face-planting and snapping my ankles at the same time. Once I was down, it was impossible to get up, but at least the suction holding my feet released before my ankles actually broke off. I tumbled forward, this time landing on my face. The carpet was a thick, soft material – thank freak – so I didn't stress too much, deciding instead to have a nap.

A nap sounded really great, actually.

"The overlord is going to love you, poppet," Jero said, grinning broadly.

I rolled over to see him better, and also to free my arm so I could flip him off. I was surprised to find Marsil glaring at his brother. "Leave her alone. This must be a lot to take in. Remember when we first got to Earth. It was hard to adjust, and we were prepared for it."

Ah, always such a sweetheart. I was totally keeping him.

I joined him in staring Jero down. Okay, from my current flat-on-my-back position, I was staring him up, but the glare was the same. Lexen let out a low rumble of annoyance, leaned over, and in a swift motion pulled me up to my feet. I expected him to drop me down as soon as I was vertical, but he kept me in a tight hold pressed to his body. My feet were almost on the ground but he was pretty much holding me up. Tingles raced along my skin and it was all of a sudden very hot.

His next words barely registered: "The oblong will not engage your feet again," he said, his voice rumbly in my ear. "Not while we are in motion. I sense that you'll not be safe standing alone."

In an ironic twist, I actually felt safe. I hadn't felt like this since my parents died. Despite his prickly nature, there was something solid about Lexen. About all of the Darkens. Like ... I could rely on them. Which was weird considering they had kidnapped me and I had only known them for a couple of days. Even Lexen ... he might hate me, but I sensed he wouldn't let his dragons eat me.

I'd never had that sort of connection before, a bond that seemed to supersede the normal time required for trust and comfort to develop in a friendship. I mean, maybe this was a very complex form of Stockholm syndrome – I had been alone and hungry, no way to find my guardians, when the Darkens had snatched me up and deposited me in their lives, giving me the essentials I had lacked.

Don't get attached, Emma! A last-ditch, desperate attempt to convince myself.

I had to try, because if everything went according to plan, I would find my guardians, return to Earth, and never see any of them again. It would truly be like the last page of a book. *The End* before I was ready for one.

Lexen continued chatting to his brother about the council and this meeting. My head was spinning a little, so in a bid to calm my mind I pressed my face into the firm chest I was being held against, breathing in the scent that clung to Lexen. It was not a smell I could give a name to, a mix of that first snow, a crisp, outdoor smell and smoky fire. I was immediately transported back to my last Christmas with my family. We always put up the tree, sang carols, had hot cocoa around the fire...

So much pain shot through my chest that I gasped, hopefully low enough that it was lost in the shirt beneath my face. I choked, holding in my next gasp, my head spinning even more than it had been. Before I could freak out, or cry, or faint – all three were possibilities – a warm hand pressed into my spine. The firmness of that touch grounded me for a second, brought me out of the horrific memories threatening to drown me. Lexen moved his hand up and down so minutely I doubted anyone else even noticed, but it was enough for my breathing to even out, syncing to the strokes.

My heartbeat slowed to a normal rate. I swallowed down the tears. No doubt we looked quite intimate, but Lexen's bulk was hiding me from the rest of the Darkens. Only his family could see us, and they were still talking away like this was normal.

"Is she okay?" I heard Star whisper in a lull of conversation.

Okay, so they *had* noticed.

"She has flashbacks," was Lexen's short reply.

Sucking in a deep breath, I turned my head, that bittersweet scent clinging to me now. "She can talk for herself. I'm fine. Thanks, Star."

She gave me an awkward hug, considering she couldn't step any closer and Lexen was still holding me steady. I felt heat tinge my cheeks and ears. My blushes were usually more than a little obvious, despite my skin tone. Hopefully no one noticed, because it looked like we were about to land.

I had been expecting to land at the base of the mountain, but we actually stopped about twenty feet above the rolling green land. Then the dragons spun us three-sixty degrees so we were facing what looked like a reinforced, shimmery golden doorway carved into the side of the marbled mountain. Well, not so much a doorway as a huge barrier. Lexen, who could apparently move his feet again, handed me off to Jero and stepped to the edge of the oblong. I untangled myself since the carpet was no longer moving and I didn't need to be carried like a child. Jero grinned down at me, ruffling my hair.

Ass.

Lexen murmured something that was not English and waved his hand. There was a grating sound and then the metallic door opened, dropping down onto the edge of the carpet. Lexen and his family stepped to the side – dragging me with them – letting everyone else leave first. The chatting Daelighters stepped into the mouth of the mountain and disappeared into the darkness.

"Do you need help?" Jero asked, donning his arrogant smile.

Unlike Lexen and me, who were stuck in our gym clothes, this particular Darken was wearing his suit and thousand dollar shoes.

"No thank you," I said primly.

No jumping was required; the platform was at least six feet wide, so I should be safe to walk across. As long as I didn't look down. There was a decent drop on either side. Sucking in deeply, filling my lungs with the sharp, slightly smoky air, I picked up my feet and moved. I was one of the last to cross, and my pulse rate only calmed when I was standing safely on solid mountain.

The entire student body of Darkens was moving into the cavern, which opened up into a large tunnel. I wasn't a huge fan of tunnels, what with the chance that a billion, trillion tons of rock could fall on my head at any moment, but this one at least was wide and well ventilated. There were also plenty of lights scattered along the wall, just above my head height. I had no idea how there were lights attached to a mountain, but like everything else I didn't understand, I was putting it in the alien technology category.

Lexen pushed through the crowd, making his way to the front. When he spoke, everyone paid attention. "When we reach the silver city, go and find your families. They will let you know the date and time for the council meeting."

"What's the Silver City?" I asked Star, who was leaning close to me, her arms crossed and a slightly bored expression on her face.

"It's the main city in Mount Draygone. There are multiple cities, situated across multiple mounts. This is the largest, and our home."

"So this mountain is called Mount Dragon?" I clarified. "The city within it is the Silver City? And what are those lights made from?" My curiosity was apparently unsatisfied with "alien technologies."

She chuckled, and then nudged me forward. The group had started to walk; she made sure I kept up. "To answer, yes, yes, and they are flames from the draygones. They can shoot and place a flame anywhere and it will burn forever without need of fuel or energy source. We have been blessed with many great conveniences through our bond with the majestic rulers of this land."

Note to self: do not insult the dragons while here. They were a big deal, a very big deal.

The stone surrounding us did not change color or texture as we walked. It appeared someone had carved and polished this path, bringing the multifaceted mineral on either side to shine like the most precious of diamonds.

"How big is Overworld?" I found myself asking as I tried to map the planet in my head.

I knew there were sections, at least three, with the Imperials somewhere else, and while the land of Darken seemed vast, could it really rival Earth in size?

Jero, who had been slightly in front, dropped back. "Overworld is huge," he said, his Discovery Channel voice kicking in. "Larger than Earth actually. Our four houses – and their lands – are part of a small sector ... what you would call a country. There are lots of these sectors. Ours is called Dae. They're all vastly different, and for the most part none of us interact. It's forbidden to travel outside your sector."

"So your sector is the only one who has dealings with Earth?" I asked.

Star and Jero both nodded. "Yep," he answered. "We're the only ones with the ability to cross to Earth, or for humans to cross to us. None of the other sectors even know about the treaty."

The tunnel was widening now, the lights growing brighter, and I had to stifle my gasp when we finally stepped out into the open.

"I ... how ... *holy shit.*"

My stuttered exclamation would make no sense to anyone, mostly because the jumbled thoughts in my head made no sense to me.

"How is this possible?" I finally got a semblance of a sentence out.

Jero, Marsil, and Star just laughed at me, no doubt enjoying my wide eyes and even wider mouth. But, seriously, it was like something out of a dream. The inside of the mountain had been carved into a city. Silver City, apparently. It was spectacular, spreading out much further than I could see, the roof high enough to seem like a flaming speck above us. Despite its distance, that light was illuminating the entire city. Dragon fire again...

The city itself was carved from something silver, but not like the metal on Earth. The only thing I could liken it to was a silver diamond: translucent, faceted, with a shimmery color unlike any gem I'd seen. We were standing high on a ledge, before a path that wound down the side and into the city. I was ushered along, Marsil taking pity on me and wrapping an arm around me so I didn't stumble off the side. It was a very real possibility, because there was so much to look at.

It was beautiful, like a Christmas village, everything lit up with tiny lights. Some other colors broke up the silver, golds and mauves being the most prominent.

"How long did it take to carve this city?" I turned my wide eyes on the three Darkens with me, looking between each of them, desperate for answers.

Jero turned back to his city, tilting his head as though seeing it for the first time. "Legend says this city was carved a million years ago by the Draygo, the first draygone people. They could change their shape between what you see now and the beasts who rule the skies. Their magic could bring the land to life. They would sing it into the shape they desired."

A shiver went down my spine as I thought about the insanity of my life. It was almost too farfetched to believe. I kept waiting for someone to jump out and tell me it was all a joke. Or for me to wake from the coma I'd been in since the fire.

Somehow, it felt real. Maybe the Finnegans had rubbed off on me over the last eight months, or maybe my mind was finally gone. Either way, I was going to enjoy this new experience.

"Are there still dragon people?" I asked, keeping my voice quiet on instinct. I thought Lexen glanced back at me then, but he was far enough away – still leading the group – that I was probably imagining that too.

Marsil spared a quick glance at his brother. "There are a few," he said briefly. "Secretive and powerful. They live with the draygones, not with Daelighters. You would do well not to speak of them again."

In. Sane. This was all just insane.

13

*B*y the time we reached the base of the city I was feeling quite overwhelmed. The excitement was still there, but it had waned because there was no way to maintain that level of euphoria for an extended period of time. I was the equivalent of a three-year-old halfway through a birthday party. I'd worn myself out.

My lack of sleep was also catching up to me, the slightest of tension headaches pounding in my temples. I should have expected this though. This entire little excursion into another world was a huge deal. I'd avoided strong emotions for almost a year now, because feeling anything was painful, so today was definitely going to affect me.

Despite my fatigue, I was still cataloguing and learning as much as I could. Fascinatingly enough, this city was set out in the same block formation like big cities back home. There were even signs – not that I could read them as they were not in English, but I recognized them all the same.

"Are you okay?" Star asked, no doubt noticing my sudden quietness. Not five minutes earlier I'd been going on and on about how amazing this place was, so my silence now was kind of obvious.

"Just ... tired." That was mostly the truth.

She was opening her mouth to reply when Lexen said something and the rest of the other Darken students hurried off to find their families. We were pretty far into the city now, and it was hard to not feel overwhelmed by the shimmering silver surrounding us.

Star ignored her brothers, focusing on me. "Come on, let's get you to our home. There should be some time to rest. I expect the council meeting won't be until tomorrow."

Lexen joined us then, seeming more relaxed now that he wasn't wearing his leader hat. "We don't know the timeframe yet," he reminded his sister. He stood taller, looking right at home among the opulence of this world.

I would never have guessed from what I saw of him on Earth, but here it was abundantly clear: Lexen was trained and groomed to lead. The way he took charge, carried himself, spoke to the other Darken members...

I kind of missed his bastard side. He had been real. Here ... I got the mask. I wasn't sure I liked it. *Nothing to do with you*, my inner voice tried to remind me, but it didn't change my feelings.

Our group was silent as we continued through the town. A lot of inhabitants were scurrying around, still surprising me with how similar our species were. The Daelighters were like Hollywood-spec humans, tall and beautiful.

I got a few glances from the locals, but my companions were the ones receiving the majority of attention. Also salutes – or a version similar enough that I was going with it. Lexen got bowed to. A lot. The Daelighters who crossed his path would place both of their palms flat on their forehead, one hand overlapping the other, and then they would bow very low to him.

Lexen would return the gesture with a simple head nod.

This process continued on and on. I was so fascinated that I missed the rest of the town. By the time I noticed my surroundings again we had reached their home. Well, the large gates outside it, carved from a different material, one which looked more like the outside of this mountain: a smoky, opal-colored crystal.

Lexen pressed his hand to the gate – the entire property was fenced – and said something in their language. The barrier opened immediately and we all stepped inside. I was surprised by the lack of security, especially after the overkill in Astoria.

"Does everyone speak English here?" I asked as we stepped inside, the crystal barrier silently closing behind us.

"Ever since the first signing of the treaty," Lexen said, disarming me with his full attention again.

"Does anyone on Earth know ... your language?" How intertwined were our worlds? How could no one know about this?

"Dray," Lexen filled in the blank. "All houses use the original language of the Draygo people. There are a few representatives on Earth that understand it, but since, for the most part, we're not known about by humans, there's no reason for them to learn."

I kind of wanted to learn it, but no doubt my mouth and vocal cords would struggle to form the melodic Dray words. I couldn't sing for crap, and it sounded musical to me.

Lexen was the first to walk again, leading us along a path toward a white building.

Okay, building was a vast understatement. It was more like a resort, widely spread, square-shaped, with towering wings and lots of windows. The details were hazy from this distance, so I focused instead on the gardens surrounding us on either side. There were so many plants, huge trees, flower-filled garden beds. It could have been cluttered, having so much crammed in, but it just seemed cozy and tranquil. The scents ... they were almost overwhelming, their sweet natural perfume filling the air.

It seemed a miracle to see an area so lush and natural on the inside of a mountain, but considering I flew here on a dragon carpet, anything was possible. The energy of the dragons kept things powered here. The warmth and light from that burning dragon fire, so high above us, did have a sun feel to it.

It took a long time to reach their home. Unlike a lot of the other structures under here, it was not made of the silver-diamond stone. It looked like ... I reached for my necklace, pulling it free from where it had been tucked in my shirt. I rarely took it off, not even for tortu ... gym class.

"What is this stone?" I asked, my voice low. "The one your house is made of?"

Star's hand zipped out and grabbed my pendant, bringing it closer and almost strangling me in the process. "How do you have starslight stone? It's a rare mineral which falls from our sky—"

She looked to her brothers for help.

"Like a meteorite, falling from space," Marsil filled in for her. "This stone is not natural to our land, but we collect it every time it falls from above. It has a strong natural energy and can be used to power many things."

"Like the stone in the treaty with Earth?" I confirmed what Lexen had told me earlier. The others looked surprised, but recovered quickly.

"Yes," Star exclaimed, as she finally released me. "The exact same one."

I shook my head, trying to piece all the information together. "How would my mother possess a necklace made from this stone?" Could it have fallen to Earth as well? Even if it did, why would my parents have it? They were definitely not into anything space-like.

Part of me was freaking out at what possible answers I was going to get. I adored my parents more than anything else in the world. Could I handle having their memories tainted by learning they had kept some huge truth from me.

Jero, uncharacteristically somber, reached out and lifted the chain too, gentler than his sister had. "This rock has never landed on Earth. I can tell you that for a fact. The only piece there is the one gifted as part of our treaty. It's extra special. It has a literal beating heart which calms your world."

"What did you say your parents did again?" Lexen interrupted.

"Accountant and school teacher," I replied without hesitation.

"Did you ever go to their work?" Lexen pressed. "See them do these jobs?"

My reply died on my tongue as I thought about his question. I hadn't actually ever gone to their work, but Mom had shown me tests from her class, and pictures of students.

"They did not lie to me," I finally said. "They wouldn't lie to me about something as huge as that."

A darkness flittered across Lexen's face. I couldn't pull my gaze from his, locked on to the intensity. "Humans lie all the time, Emma. It is something we noticed from our very first interactions. They lie for a multitude of reasons, mostly to protect themselves, or to protect others."

My breathing was harsh as I tried to calm my racing pulse. "Are you saying my family was involved in this treaty? That they hid everything from me in a bid to protect me? And that your world might have something to do with why they died?" My rushed words were just below a shout by the time I finished, chest heaving.

Star stepped forward and I could finally look away from the harsh planes of Lexen's face. "I'm so sorry, Emma. I promise we'll find out everything we can," she said, her usual hug coming my way.

I squeezed my eyes as tightly as I could, not wanting to break down. I had been holding it together, but the moment her arms wrapped me up so firmly, the sympathy in her words cracked through my control.

"Star, let her go," Lexen said, softer than he usually spoke.

I was released a beat later. Star's eyes were glassy as if

she'd been trying not to cry too. I was waiting for Lexen to pretend that my emotional breakdown wasn't happening, but he surprised me. "Star is right, I *will* find out what happened to your family. There's a reason the council is so interested in keeping you safe. A reason they've let you into our world – insisted on it actually. We'll find out exactly what's going on."

I swallowed roughly, my throat seizing up. "Thank you," I managed to get out. "Nothing can bring my parents back, I know that, but I've been struggling with closure. Acceptance. Maybe more information will help."

I had never been able to let it rest, the fire continuing to haunt me. I figured it was a timing thing, as in I needed more time to heal, but maybe there was something more.

"My babies!"

We all turned toward the large, white, double doors we had been standing a few feet from. They were half open and a tall, slender brunette woman was dashing through them. Her face was lit up and I felt the love pouring from her as she threw her arms around Lexen. He hugged her back tightly, looking younger and more relaxed than usual.

"We missed you too, Mom," he said with a chuckle as she finally let him go.

"I have missed you all so much. I've argued with your father about sending you to Earth, but he *continues* to say that we have no choice."

It was hard to believe she was their mother. She looked only a few years older than me. Her hair was long and thick, hanging in a silky sheet to her waist. Her eyes were blue, just like Jero's, her skin darkly tanned.

She was beautiful and regal. Wearing white linen pants and a tunic top, also white, everything about her screamed money and class, just like her children. As she hugged each of them, holding so tightly, a look of absolute joy on her face, I was starting to understand where the pure kindness from each of the Darkens came from.

Star snorted as she was squished tightly. "Mother, I have been gone for two days."

The woman pulled back, holding her daughter at arm's length. "Longest two days of my life, sweetheart."

Finally, after greeting each of the Darkens, she noticed me standing there. Awkwardly. I wasn't sure how I would be received. I half expected her to treat me like an interloper in their lives, but she took me completely by surprise when she wrapped her arms around me. I was stiff at first, but this lady held the same power as the rest of her family, and eventually I relaxed enough to lean in to her, the flowery scent she wore wrapping around me.

Thankfully she didn't hug me too long, or I might have done something embarrassing like cry. She was so loving and motherly, and after just speaking of my parents, my heart was raw.

"Welcome to the House of Darken, Emma," she said when she pulled away. "I have heard a lot about you. Oh, and please call me Ambra. We don't stand on formality here."

I was grateful for that, because I'd had no idea what title to call her.

"Thanks so much for allowing me to stay with you, for offering your protection," I said, a smile forming on my face. Why did I continue liking this family so much? I was turning into a mini Darken-stalker.

She waved her hand at me. "Anytime, darling. Think of us as family while you stay here. I can't even imagine how you must be feeling, venturing to a new world."

"I'm loving it actually." I was practically grinning now. "Once in a lifetime chance to see something as spectacular as your world. I consider myself lucky."

"Ambra, *melerde*," said a man's voice, "bring them all inside. We have much to discuss, and very little time."

The tall, imposing male was perched in the doorway. I had no idea how long he had been there watching our exchange, but I immediately brushed my hair back and tried to make myself look a little more presentable. I had absolutely no doubt who he was – the overlord.

"Come, your father has been anxiously awaiting your return," Ambra chimed, as she stepped forward into her husband's arms.

I took a moment to examine Daddy Darken. At the most, he looked to be in his late twenties, but his eyes, and the distinguished way he held himself, told me that he was much, much older than that. He had dark hair streaked with caramel tones like Jero, short on one side, symbols carved into the dark strands. His eyes were a very dark brown, close to Lexen's, but without the starlight sparkles of his son's.

The Darken parents were exceptionally beautiful, which explained why their children were all supermodel material. Amazing genetics. The overlord, whose name I learned was Roland, greeted each of his kids in the same way Ambra had, with hugs and soft words.

The Darkens were blessed in more ways than just exceptional looks and whatever powers this world provided them. They had something that could not be bought: unconditional love, support, and acceptance. It made me more than a little jealous. I was so often alone. Even when my parents were alive, they had been busy. So ... yeah, I had been alone a lot.

A pity party for another day.

"I've had some food prepared, so we should eat and catch up," Roland said as we followed him and Ambra into the first room of their home. The large, open entry had lots of thick dark rugs scattered about. There was also a sitting area surrounded by plants. It was warm and inviting.

Lexen caught my eye as I gazed around. "It's beautiful," I said, needing to express my awe. "Feels really homey, even being so ... huge."

"I have missed it here," he admitted. "There is nothing else to compare."

I let out a low snort of laughter. "Yeah. Guess I can kind of understand why you were such an assh—" I cut my curse off, glancing at his parents, who were leading us up a set of white stairs. "Why you don't particularly care for Earth. Our world is not like this."

"It has its positives, gorgeous," Jero added with a wink.

I pointed my finger at him. "No winking. No flirting. And for the last time, my name is Emma."

He grabbed that finger and used it to pull me closer. I was already teetering on the edge of a stair, and that action tipped me fully off balance. I would have fallen if Jero hadn't caught my arm.

"Whoops," he murmured. "Sorry about that. Overestimated my strength. Just wanted to pull you close enough to say you love it, my flirting that is." He didn't wink this time, but somehow it still felt like he had.

"Jero, leave the poor girl alone," Ambra scolded, standing on the first floor already, waiting for the rest of us to get upstairs.

"She loves it, *Ma*. I promise."

Ambra shook her head, an indulgent smile on her face. Poor thing, she couldn't see past her son's charm. I hit him with my elbow as I marched up the stairs. Lexen, Marsil, and Star were already a few steps above. Jero was last up but somehow first into the room with the long, food-laden table.

I ended up next to Lexen, who sat on the right side of his father. I still had not seen any guards, which I made a comment about. Roland flashed a broad smile at me, and it was just like Lexen's. When he bothered to smile that was. "The draygones protect the overlords. No one messes with the draygones."

Fair point. I wouldn't be messing with a dragon anytime soon.

Daelighters entered the room dressed in simple white tunics. They were carrying platters of food. I didn't recognize anything, but I did notice there were a lot of fruit and vegetable looking items, and very little meat. I spent a lot of time looking over the selection before carefully selecting a few berries. In appearance and taste they were a mix between a strawberry and a blackberry. I also tried something in a pastry shell filled with a white creamy sauce.

"Meat is a rare luxury here on Overworld, or at least in our sector," Marsil said between mouthfuls. "For the most part, we eat what we can grow."

I swallowed down another berry, enjoying the mix of tart and sweet. "I'm not a huge fan of meat," I told them when my mouth was empty. "I've learned recently that when I'm hungry I'll eat anything, but if I had a choice ... meat would be last."

Ambra looked concerned then, her brow crinkling as she reached across from the other side of the table and grasped my hand. "You've been hungry? Why? Is Earth running out of food?" She swung her head toward Roland. "The stone is supposed to stabilize their world, stop the destruction of crops and other food sources."

I rushed to the poor overlord's defense. "Oh no, it is nothing to do with that. My parents were ... they ... I..." My breathing got rapid I tried to choke out the words. It was going to be one of those days where I could not talk about it, could not even think about it without the intensity of the pain threatening to rip me apart.

"Her family was killed in a house fire," Lexen finished, his voice rumbling in a low octave. Somehow he knew my story without me even telling him it all. "Her file was quite extensive."

Okay, then, bastard read my school file. I glared as hard as I could at him, unable to speak still, but thankful the anger was washing away the pain.

"She wears a piece of starslight," he continued in a matter of fact tone. "Now her guardians are missing after being called to Astoria through suspicious means. Emma is more involved in our world than any of us realized."

Roland dropped his half-eaten green-apple-looking-fruit on the table. He didn't seem surprised by Lexen's revelation, and I leaned closer, my breath catching as I waited for him to speak.

"The council told me that Emma was a very important person in an investigation they're doing," he said, kind eyes locked on me. "Secret keepers are supposed to check in every two hundred and forty-four Earth days. The first family missed the last one."

No, please, God, no. "They think my parents were the ones who missed the check-in?" I asked, my voice flat. Panic and dread unfurled deep inside of my chest, like an insidious smoke filling my body and choking the breath from me. I knew I should probably ask what exactly a secret keeper was – or what secret it was they kept – but right now I could think of nothing but this new revelation.

Roland gave me a sad sort of smile. "Yes, they believe it was. Somehow they were tracked down, and we believe killed by a Daelighter who is trying to break the treaty between our worlds."

"How ... how did I survive?" I choked out. "The fire, I ended up outside somehow."

He shook his head. "If I had to guess ... possibly your life was what was threatened to reveal their secret." His eyes darted between his four children. "I know I would do a lot to protect my family."

My heart shattered, exploding in my chest like a glass-filled balloon. Sharp slivers sliced through me, ripping apart my insides. I caved forward, wrapping my arms around myself to try to stop the blood from pouring out. I mean, I knew there was no literal blood, but it felt like there should be. It felt like I should be bleeding from a thousand wounds.

"Enough," Lexen said sharply to his father. I hadn't even realized Roland was still talking. I'd missed whatever he'd said next.

Unable to hold it in any longer, I jumped to my feet, sending my chair flying out behind me. I didn't know where to go, so I hurried back the way we'd just come, down the stairs and through those front doors. When I was outside, that warm dray-gone light shining down on me, I took a sharp left into the nearest garden. My mind was desperately searching for something to distract me from the fact that the fire wasn't just a random bad accident. It wasn't bad luck.

It was murder.

My parents – who had apparently been lying to me my entire life – were cold-bloodedly murdered. I survived because they protected me, like they had always done. I might not have known everything about them, like their connection to this world, but I always knew they loved me. They proved that with the ultimate sacrifice. A sacrifice I would never have asked from them.

"Why?" I cried, falling to my knees, my legs unable to hold me up any longer. "Why did you save me? I would have preferred to go with you."

Sobs shook my entire frame, hands covering my face as I mourned all over again. I had no idea how long I cried, but eventually strong arms picked me up and set me on my feet. Just like the time in his room, Lexen did nothing more than hold me while I fell apart on him.

"Why did they save me?" I was still murmuring, unable to stop the tears, unable to stem the pain.

His hand went to my spine, rubbing up and down slowly. This was becoming his signature move, and there was no denying it: Lexen Darken was an amazing comforter, despite his normal attitude problem.

"They saved you because you were singularly the most important thing in their world, Emma Walters. Your life is their gift, and they would be so proud of how strong you are."

Surprise had me pulling back as I wiped away my tears. "You think I'm strong? Even though I cry on you all the time?"

His dark eyes flashed, that sprinkle of light almost mesmerizing as it moved about his irises. "You have fought me from the first moment we met. You have fought for your guardians. You're fierce and annoyingly stubborn. I don't know you that well yet, but ... I sense you're worthy to wear the starslight stone."

Did that just happen? Did Lexen just pay me a compliment? Me ... a human.

"Thank you," I said, my voice hoarse. "It just hit me hard, hearing the truth about their sacrifice. I didn't know about this *huge* part of their life ... what exactly is a secret keeper?"

I got the general concept, but not how it specifically referred to my parents and Overworld.

Lexen remained close, although we weren't touching anymore. "When the treaty was formed," he started slowly, "the human government was worried that one day we would decide to take our stone back. They knew we were more powerful, if it came down to a war, so they wanted some reassurance. In the treaty, it was stated that a Draygo would be the one to bury the stone, but there would also be a secret sect of humans that would know the location also.

"A hundred or so humans were hand-selected to be told about the treaty. Ones who were educated enough to understand the complexity of this agreement between our two worlds. From those hundred, four who were pregnant at the time, were given an additional task. Their soon-to-be-born offspring would become the secret keepers of the stone's location. They birthed their children in our world, one in each of the houses – all had to be born in the same year – so they would be bonded to each other and to our lands. Together these four can lead someone to the location of the stone."

"How?" I asked. "That sounds next to impossible."

Lexen shrugged. "I don't understand everything, the treaty was before my time and information is scarce because it's supposed to all be secret. But from what Father told me, the first family held a clue which would lead to the second family."

"Who would lead to the third..." I guessed.

He nodded. "Yes, and the fourth had a map to the location of the stone. This map is connected directly to the Draygo, so if they moved the stone, the map would change. It meant that there was no way for the stone to ever disappear without humans knowing."

"My parents were killed because someone wants to find the stone?" It was all starting to make perfect, horrifying sense now.

"This is what the council believes."

"Which of my parents was birthed in Overworld?"

Lexen's broad shoulders lifted in a half-shrug. "No way for us to know now, but it seems that whichever it was, they might have revealed the location of the second family. Which means we could very well be facing a serious problem."

A memory flickered on the edge of my mind then, something I had not thought about in years, and I fought to recall even more. "My mom used to tell me this bedtime story," I said, my voice catching again as the memories grew stronger. "Every night for years. She stopped when I was about six or seven, which is why my recollections are so vague, but I'm sure she told me about a boy who would ride on the back of dragons. She called him 'the one.' No ... 'the chosen one.' I can't really remember, but he was best friends with a merboy. The three of them, dragon included, would swim in the lake."

When I focused on Lexen again, he was still wearing a solemn expression. "It sounds like she was quite well acquainted with our world," he said.

"It was you, wasn't it? The chosen one, the boy who rode dragons?"

He reached out and brushed his hand against my cheek, pulling away with droplets of moisture on his fingers. The last of my tears.

"When I was younger," he said, "before my metamorphosis, Qenita and I would travel across the sectors. Xander Royale is one of my oldest friends. He's the caramina she spoke of, the merboy."

"So you're how old?"

"Sixty-five," he said quickly.

Whoa. "You are old as shit," I said with a snort of laughter. "But ... you were still a boy when my parents were here." How was that possible? My parents had been in their early forties when they died. Again, the math was not adding up here.

Lexen crossed his arms, leaning back against a nearby garden pillar. I noticed then that I'd actually run into a maze of sorts, large hedges surrounding us. An area which could have kept me lost for hours.

"In Overworld we age ... differently," he said, hesitating minutely over the last word. "We're children for a long time. Much longer than Earthlings. We mature slowly, and then, when our bodies decide that we are ready to grow, we do, in a large 'metamorphosis' burst. We don't age year by year."

"Have you stopped now?" I was impressed by how well I was handling these obvious differences between us.

He shrugged. "More or less. My father is hundreds of years old and no longer has growth spurts, as my mother so eloquently puts it. Not physical ones, at least, but mentally we never stop advancing. Unlike humans, our minds do not deteriorate."

Lexen held out a hand for me. "Come on, let's go get some rest. Father said the meeting is to take place early in the morning. This is where we'll put pressure on the council to give us more information on your parents and your guardians."

I took his hand without hesitation, craving the safe way he made me feel. I expected him to let go as I followed his steps. But he didn't. If anything, his grip tightened and he pulled me even closer, his huge bulk towering over me. We were silent, traversing the twists and turns in and out of hedges. How far had I run in my grief? I didn't even remember coming this way.

"Thanks for finding me," I whispered when we neared the front door. "I would never have gotten out of that maze on my own."

He didn't say anything, but it felt like he gave my hand a gentle squeeze. When we reached the third landing we walked down a long hallway until we finally reached a wing of bedrooms.

"Mother will have had a room made up for you," Lexen said, stopping before a door. He let my hand go and I tried not to feel bereft about it. Stockholm syndrome or not, Lexen was fast becoming my comfort in this crazy world.

When he swung the door open, he stepped aside so I could enter first. Peering inside, I was taken aback by the beauty. The flooring was white, carpet style, but somehow fluffier. There were billowy curtains, a lilac-colored bed, and off-white walls. Just enough purple accents to give the room a pretty tint. It appeared that a lot of their décor was styled off the colors of the stones and crystals of this mountain.

"Thanks ... for everything," I said again, stepping inside. My heart sank as I stared at the bed, knowing that my dreams would be haunted tonight. I was too close to the tragedy again, to my parents' deaths. To these new revelations about them being born in Overworld and possible secret keepers. There was no way I was getting any sleep tonight.

But I would bite my tongue off before showing any more weakness this day. So I gave Lexen a wave, and as he turned away I shut the door.

Leaning back against the door, I let out a deep sigh, straightening to explore the room. That would kill some time. Hopefully their sleeping hours were shorter here than on Earth. Maybe I wouldn't have to keep myself occupied for long.

14

*T*here didn't turn out to be much in the bedroom, just the bed, two side tables, and an empty armoire. A pretty white door, with ornate carvings of roses and symbols across it, led me into a bathroom with a huge round tub built into the floor. It was almost like a mini-pool, with tiled steps leading into it. *Here is the perfect time killer.* I hadn't had a bath in almost a year. None of my rentals with the Finnegans had tubs, only showers.

It took me three attempts to figure out how to fill it; it turned out to be pretty simple once I got the hang of the levers that adjusted the hot and cold water flow. As I ran my hands across the surface of the rapidly filling tub, I understood what Jero had meant about their legreto not being quite the same as water. It was thicker, encasing my hand, and sticking there for longer than a water droplet would. When it dripped from my fingertips, it felt like they were left extra-clean as it absorbed whatever was on my skin.

Once the tub filled all the way up, I removed my clothes and stepped down. There were inbuilt seats along both sides, so I settled back into one, the liquid coating me almost to my neck. It cocooned me, sending warmth through my body and into my bones. It was like being surrounded by my favorite blanket while drinking hot cocoa at the same time.

Closing my eyes, I laid my head back to rest in a perfectly-shaped groove behind my seat. This was seriously the best thing I had ever experienced in my life. It could only be improved by something to wash my hair and shave my legs, since both were in desperate need.

"How're you doing in there?"

I let out a scream, eyes flying open as I wrapped my arms across my chest. With a huff, I relaxed, realizing it was just Star. She was dressed in what looked like very comfortable sleep clothes: a pale pink pair of short shorts and tank-top.

"Sorry," she giggled. "I didn't mean to scare you, but I thought you might need some toiletries."

She gestured to a pile sitting on a small bench beside the bath. "These are to wash your hair," she said as she picked up the two clear bottles, orange liquid inside swishing. She then dropped them and grabbed a long white tube and a small bristled brush. "Use these two to clean your teeth." Next was a small dark tub. She tapped the lid. "The gel inside removes hair from your body. Just smooth it across, leave for about fifteen seconds, and wipe clean."

She flashed me her broad smile, before shuffling all of those items closer to me.

I returned her smile, already reaching out for them. "You read my mind," I exclaimed. "Thanks so much. I really appreciate you bringing these to me."

"I also brought you something to sleep in." Star lifted a set of clothes very similar to the ones she was wearing, but in black.

I blew her a kiss. "You're the best, Star. I'm so glad we met."

"I'm so glad we met too!" she exclaimed, surprising me with a hug. "It was the best day of my life."

I snorted. "Thank you, but if we could have less naked hugging in the future, that would be great."

"Oh!" she pulled back, droplets of wate ... legreto flinging off her. "I'm so sorry, I didn't think." There was no awkwardness as we laughed, and then she jumped to her feet. "I'll leave you to your nightly routine now. See you in the morning."

"See you in the morning," I called after her as she scurried away.

I laughed again, thinking how weird this entire day had been. Weird, emotional, but kind of amazing.

Twenty minutes later I was clean, hairless – in the places I liked to be hairless – and dressed in Star's clothes. The top had an inbuilt bra and I had new underwear, because apparently Star's wardrobes on both worlds were filled with many items of clothing that she had never used before.

Weariness pressed on me, but I didn't want to sleep, so I stared around for another distraction. A basket on the end of the bed caught my eye. Before I could reach out and touch the contents, there was a knock. With a shake of my head, I hurried over to open the door. On the other side were Jero and Marsil.

"Well, hello there, lollipop," Jero said, leaning against the doorframe. Like Star, he looked to be dressed for bed. Unlike Star he was bare-chested, wearing just a pair of dark gray shorts.

I narrowed my eyes on him, trying not to stare at the wide expanse of skin he had on display. Jero was not as heavily muscled as Lexen, but he still had more than his fair share. Broad shoulders, tapering down to slim hips; the shorts looked to barely be staying up. His hair was damp, the scar visible as the strands were pushed back in messy disarray.

No wonder he could get away with treating women like crap; he was so pretty they probably didn't even notice. Marsil was thankfully still dressed in the same clothes he'd been wearing earlier, which was a relief. I wasn't sure I could take any more perfect chests.

"We just wanted to check in on you," Marsil said, distracting me from my ogling. "Do you have everything you need?"

Warmth filled my chest. It had been a long time since anyone had checked in on me like this. I was finding I could grow quite accustomed to the caring this family showed me.

"Thanks, I'm all good. Uh…" I flicked my head back toward the bed. "Someone left what looks like a knitting kit on my bed, and some books." Truly the perfect things to keep me occupied.

The brothers exchanged a look, returning their gaze to me. "Wasn't us," Jero said. "And Star didn't mention that when she said she was bringing you clothes and bathroom stuff."

Which left only one other Daelighter, one who no doubt knew I was going to struggle to sleep tonight and had provided me with something to occupy my mind. Damn Lexen. Damn him being so thoughtful. The asshole box that I had been stubbornly keeping him in was slipping away. No longer could I hold on to those feelings of animosity toward him. But I needed to … I couldn't fall for him. We were from different worlds. He was going to be the leader of his house. He was an entire universe out of my league.

"Well, well, well, looks like Lexen might just be on team human now," Jero said, amusement crinkling his eyes. He had deduced the same thing as me. Lexen was the only one who could have left that basket.

"It can't work, and … and I don't even care." The words slipped out, my thoughts unable to be contained any longer.

A blush stole across my cheeks. I could feel the heat, and as my embarrassment grew, so did Marsil and Jero's grins.

"Shut up," I snarled, sticking my tongue out at them and stepping back to firmly shut the door. I dropped my head against the wood panel as their laughter echoed through to me. I stayed like that until I felt the warmth leave my cheeks, then I slowly made my way back to the bed. I crawled up onto it, the thick pillow-top of the mattress cushioning me fully.

I was going to struggle to stay awake, but the thought of my dreams ... of reliving the smell and feel of the fire ... of reliving my parents' death ... I couldn't go through that tonight. I just couldn't.

Hooking a hand into a handle on the basket, I dragged it closer. Inside were a few different knitting needles. They had a slight curve to both ends, but I was pretty sure with a little practice I could use them. The wool was ... not wool, but seemed to knit similarly. I didn't have any great plan in mind, I just wanted to keep occupied, so I started with a square pattern.

There was no way for me to tell time here. I couldn't see anything that resembled a clock in the room – no doubt they used something different to measure their days anyway – so I guessed I'd been knitting for an hour when I ran out of the blue thread.

Needing a break, I dropped my half-finished project into the basket, picking up the three paperbacks that were in there too. I didn't recognize any of the stories, so I chose the one with the cover that appealed to me the most. I was a bit of a cover snob; the "not judging a book by its cover" thing was not something I'd ever been good at.

I chose a fantasy story, with bright imagery of dragons, fire, and waterfalls.

Laying my head back, I got comfortable and started to read. I was five chapters in before I realized it, and when that fact registered I took a second to be grateful for books. They were a magic that could not be replicated, even when I was actually in a fantasy world. The escape they offered, it was priceless. It had saved me so many times, and I knew I wasn't the only one. When my parents died, most of my friends handed me suicide-crisis-line numbers. The rest ignored me, preferring not to deal with it. Not one had told me to pick up a book. That should have been their first piece of advice.

I managed to make it another few chapters before my heavy eyes won, and...

It's so hot. I can't breathe. Why can't I breathe? The smoke chokes me. Slithering into every part of my body until I feel like I'm dying. I crawled with desperation, unable to see, unable to breathe. Searching for them. Hissing as embers bit into my exposed flesh. As smoke and heat charred my throat and lungs.

I rolled across my bedroom floor, crying out again as more flickers of fire bubbled my skin. Coughs rocked through me, my lungs screaming for air. I dragged myself, busting through the door to my room, ending up in the hallway of the upper level.

The sound of a fight registered in my hazy mind. I was only just aware enough to know that the sobs belonged to my mother. She always gasped like that when she was devastated.

Dad! Something must have happened to Dad. But who was she arguing with?

My crawl slowed, then a scream ripped through the air, jolting me, and I found myself screaming with it. That scream had been my mom, a call of pain, a cry of death.

I jolted upright, my own screams dying on my lips as tears relentlessly fell down my cheeks. I attempted to lift my hands to scrub at my face and throat, trying to dispel the smoke that always seemed to linger. But I couldn't move them. I was being held in someone's arms, and as soon as I felt that firm hand stroking up and down my spine, I relaxed into him.

"The fire again?" Lexen said, his voice low and rough.

I pressed my face harder into his chest, trying to stem the tears and calm my heart.

"Yes," I mumbled. "But there was more this time. It's like ... an extra memory unlocked. My mom, she was crying and arguing with someone. Then she screamed." I pulled back to stare up into his dark eyes. "I was on the top floor. The building was completely ablaze. There was no way I could have survived without help. No way."

His grip tightened on me, that hand on my spine pulling me closer.

My chest heaved and I fought against the nausea rising within me. I really didn't want to vomit on Lexen. "Someone murdered them. The fire ... it wasn't natural. Which of the houses can control fire?"

Darkness fell like a heavy sheen across his face. "Darken – but not all of us. I'm the only one at the moment who can control draygone fire, and I promise you it wasn't me. Not to mention that sort of flame would have incinerated your house instantly." Before I could assure him that I'd never suspected his family – they were far too nice – he continued, "The other house with ties to fire is Imperial. They control the land beneath. The underworld. Their domain is the land of death, and they can control the eternal fire."

I blinked a few times, wrinkling my nose. "The underworld? Like hell?"

Lexen shook his head, the slightest of smiles curving his full lips, although he didn't exactly look happy. "It's not as you're probably imagining. This is a land of judgment. Your soul will be judged at death, and depending on what is found, you can be reborn, or you go into the Cascading Justices. Where you end up after that is up to you."

"How do the living go there?" I asked, trying to wrap my head around this place he was describing. My family was not religious, but I still understood the concept of heaven and hell. This underworld business was a little more outside of my knowledge base.

"Think of the Greek underworld," Lexen started to explain. "River Styx and the ferryman. House of Imperial are the ferrymen. They hold the key to entering, and they can do so without having to die. They control the gates and the transporter. They use these powers to keep the souls from doing what they are not supposed to. Going where they are not allowed. From—"

"Escaping?" I supplied.

He nodded. "Yes, there are some who know they're not going to fare well in the justices, so they try to escape."

My body brushed against his and I realized how close we were lying together on the bed. Lexen had a shirt on, but I could still feel every one of his rigid chest muscles pressing into my chest. My nipples, which were only secured in this thin sleep shirt, were saluting the world and letting all of us know they were happy with their current position.

I couldn't bring myself to pull away, choosing to remain wrapped all cozy-like in the darkness. "I was afraid to go to sleep." My voice was a low whisper. "I knew the dream would—" All that emerged after that was a croak, so I swallowed roughly.

Lexen surprised me when he brushed one of my long strands of hair out of my face. "I tried to wake you." The low rumble of his voice had my disloyal body reacting even further. "But there was no way to bring you out of the dream. You only calmed down when I climbed in and held you." He shrugged like it was no big deal. "I was worried you would hurt yourself. You were thrashing around a lot."

Rational thought dropped away and instinct took over. I wrapped my arms around him, needing to show how grateful I was. "Thank you. I don't know why you're the one who keeps getting stuck with me during these moments, but I promise I'm not normally this broken." I pulled away before things got uncomfortable. "It's just been a long week. I'm not handling it very well."

He pressed his hand into my spine one more time, sending flashes of heat low in my body. I almost rocked forward to try and relieve the pressure building inside of me. I managed to stop myself only because he released me and swung his long legs over the side of the bed. I watched, unable to look away. When he was standing, he met my gaze. "You're handling it better than most humans," he said, sounding much more serious than he had before. "You're actually making a pretty compelling case for the treaty at this point in time. Your government should thank you."

I swallowed roughly, knowing he was going to leave, but unable to think of anything to say that might keep him here. "Well," I began awkwardly, "thanks again. I'll see you in the morning."

He held out a hand and I stared at it stupidly, wondering what he wanted me to do. He didn't move, standing there hand out before him. I tentatively reached out, placing my palm against his. When his fingers wrapped around mine, I was pulled up and off the bed in a flash, Lexen catching me when I would have fallen, before he set me on my feet.

He wrapped one arm around me. "Come on, I need sleep. I have to be overlord minor tomorrow. You're coming with me. I can keep a closer eye on you if we're in the same room."

My rapid blinking probably made it look like I was having a seizure, but I couldn't understand exactly what he was saying. "You have another bed in your room here too?" I wheezed out.

Lexen shook his head, starting to walk and half dragging me along with him. "No, we're going to have to share. I'll figure something out for tomorrow night."

"Share!" I tried to ground to a halt, but he was much stronger than me. When he realized I wasn't walking, he let me go. We faced each other in the hallway.

"Yes, we're going to share. I don't bite or snore. Even better, I don't have dreams to scare the shit out of you, dragging you from a deep sleep."

Ah, there he was, my ... *the* arrogant alien. "Apologies, Overlord Minor, I didn't mean to disturb you."

He laughed, confusing me with his mood. Was he upset or happy that my screaming woke him?

"Overlord minor is my official title, and I hate it. I'll be the overlord major one day, when my father is ready to step down. It's not a position I want. It's not one I asked for. But there's very little choice in the matter for me."

"Do Jero, Marsil, and Star have titles?" It was fascinating learning of this new form of monarchy.

He gave me a little nudge and my feet automatically started moving, following him along the hall again.

He answered me as we walked: "Marsil is next in line after me. He's admiral major. Jero is admiral minor. Both of these positions have official duties, mostly to do with the warriors and the war between the houses. We've had peace for only just over a hundred years – since the treaty. It was part of the reason we formed a bond with Earth.

"Star is the youngest, so she doesn't have an official title. Fourth in line has no title, but if she had been first in line, born with the marks, she would be the overlord minor. It has nothing to do with male and female here, and everything to do with order of birth." I was extra glad to hear that. "Mother is the matriarch. An overlord rules with his matriarch. Together. A true partnership."

I was so caught up in learning about his world that I didn't even notice that we'd left the hallway and were now standing in his room. Beside his bed. Which was even larger and more comfortable looking than mine. The ivory blanket was rumpled from where Lexen had no doubt jumped up when I screamed. He dropped down onto his side and I remained standing there, staring down at the wide expanse he had left for me.

"Get in the bed, Emma," he all but growled. "Don't make me throw you in here."

I snorted, glad his normal attitude was back. It helped me move past the nerves of sleeping next to a guy. I'd never slept in the same bed as anyone before, except my parents when I was a young child.

He might not snore, but I had no idea if I did. Shit. With my luck ... I definitely snored.

"Emma..." he growled again.

Straightening my shoulders, I was about to gingerly slide into the bed when Lexen froze, his body going unnaturally rigid, eyes focusing on something behind me. I wasn't sure whether I should say something or not – I quickly glanced behind to make sure there were no bugs – and thankfully he snapped out of it before I had to decide what to do. Leaping from the bed, he quickly crossed toward a nearby door, and when he opened it I got a glimpse of rows of clothing. He disappeared inside. Meanwhile, I was still in my position at the side of his bed, wondering what the hell had just happened.

Just as quickly as he'd disappeared into his huge cupboard, he reemerged fully dressed in worn, dark-denim jeans, and what looked like a ribbed, black, fitted Henley-style shirt. He also wore boots.

"Uh, going somewhere?" I asked, my forehead wrinkling as I took in his fully clothed form.

He had a thick dark garment in his hands, and when he tossed it my way I managed to catch it.

"Put that on, we have to go out for a bit," he said, running a hand through his hair, leaving it in a messy disarray on top, sexy and tousled without even trying. Mine probably looked like someone had dragged me backwards through a hedge.

"Where are we going?" I asked, my voice muffled as I pulled the thick sweater down over my head. It was miles too big for me, hanging almost to mid-thigh, and it smelled delicious, like the combination of whatever they washed their clothes in here, and Lexen.

No answer, and by the time I had vision of the room again I realized I was alone. Lexen's door was open. Did he just leave me? What the hell was the point of the sweater, then?

Just as my temper started to make itself known, along with some worry because whatever was going on was random and had taken him by surprise, he reappeared in his doorway, my tennis shoes in his hands. Every ounce of annoyance inside of me disappeared and I felt like an idiot.

But seriously, that was way more thoughtful than I'd expected.

"Thank you," I murmured when he handed them to me. "Now can you tell me where we're going? Remember the dog conversation...?"

The starlight in his eyes glowed as he said, "I just got a message from friends of mine. I need to meet them, and I don't want to leave you alone here."

I paused, halfway through pulling a shoe on. "Is everything okay?"

Lexen nodded. "Yeah, we just have to be careful with our communications. Better to meet in person."

All very cloak and dagger in the world of the Daelighters. I was intrigued, and glad he wasn't going to leave me behind.

Lexen led me out the bedroom door and along the hallway. We ended up going down multiple flights of stairs, until we ended up in a small basement-style room. It was freezing down here, and I snuggled into the sweater, keeping my hands in the wool-lined pockets.

"This is one of the older transporters," Lexen explained as he closed the door, turning me toward the flickering ball of light near the back, a duplicate of the one we had taken from Earth to Overworld. "We don't have many permanent transporters left, just this one and the one on the main platform between the four lands. Generally, if we need to travel, we just engage the network for a temporary transport. I only use these permanent ones when I need to hide my movements, since tapping into the network leaves a trace behind."

I blinked a few times as I said, "Twelve percent of what you just said made sense to me. But do whatever you need to."

He stared at me for an extended moment, the light of the nearby transporter flickering over his face. Then he stepped into me; all breath halted in my chest, rattling around in there, unable to be released because my lungs weren't functioning.

"You ready?" he murmured, those dark as sin eyes burning through me.

I managed to nod. He took my hand, reaching out for one of the glowing strands of light. Just like last time, we were sucked through, hurtling along time and space ... or whatever. I still had to close my eyes at the end, almost definitely sure this time I was going to end up dead by slamming into a wall.

We survived, and the moment my eyelids popped open I sucked in a breath. We were back on the platform, the one we had arrived on earlier this day. The sky was now lit in a twilight glow, bright enough to still see the three large shadows waiting off to the side for us. As Lexen released my hand, he leaned down. "Stay by my side," he murmured in my ear. "This should be a quick meeting."

A sense of déjà vu struck me as we walked closer, and it didn't take me long to figure out where it came from. The entire scene here reminded me of my first night with the Darkens, when Lexen had had his clandestine meeting with three hulking, shadowy dudes. A spike of fear hit me as my mind went back to that night. It was still odd that I'd been so worried about my kidnapper, but Lexen had been under my skin even then.

He was relaxed at the moment, so I took a cue from him and pushed my unease to the side. I was interested to see who he'd been meeting with. As we got closer I recognized the blond-headed male standing with his arms crossed. His very impressive arms, muscles bulging out. He rivaled Lexen in size, and I could see every one of his muscles because he wore no clothes except a pair of soft looking shorts.

Xander Royale was definitely striking. And ... he was a merman ... caramina ... which no doubt explained all of that golden skin on display. I didn't know the other two men, and as Lexen stepped into the space left in their circle, keeping me close to his side, I took a second to observe them. All four of the Daelighters were around the same height, well over six foot – towering over me. Unnaturally tall. Unnaturally muscled. Unnaturally broody.

Not one cracked a smile. I sensed they were wondering why the hell there was an interloper in their midst. Small glances kept going my way but no one questioned Lexen. Xander just reached out and slapped his best friend on the shoulder, the two doing some sort of bro-hug. After this everyone seemed to relax.

The first thing I noticed was that all of them had symbols carved into their hair, just like Lexen, which meant they each were overlords. Minor or major, there was no way for me to tell at the moment. But I was literally standing in the midst of Daelighter royalty. When had this become my life?

I found my gaze lingering on the House of Leight's overlord, fascinated by his beauty. He was slightly more slender than the other three – who were built like linebackers – his muscle was hard and lean, like a swimmer's. His skin was dark, not quite as dark as his hair but the same tone. His hair was almost black, and most of it was short, especially where his symbols were marked. On the opposite side to those, he wore a few long braids, some of which fell to his thighs. Golden rope was threaded through those braids, glittering whenever he moved his head.

His shimmery green eyes met mine; their color was so light and intense that it was startling against his beautiful rich skin tone. Like Lexen and the other two, he was intensely beautiful. Hot dudes club, clearly.

Leights smiled and inclined his head toward me. I returned the nod, my smile genuine. There was something about him that immediately made me feel at ease. He oozed tranquility ... and strength ... and stability. Being a damaged human, I craved stability now. It drew me in.

"This is Emma," Lexen said bluntly. "She's under my protection. It's safe to speak in front of her."

He then went on to introduce the others to me. Xander of House of Royale, Chase of House of Leight, and Daniel of House of Imperial – overlord minors.

My head snapped up at that last name. I stared at the male who was from the house that had probably killed my parents. I wanted to hate him on sight. He even outdid Lexen in the badass vibe: bronze skin with a shaved head; his dark symbolic marks must have been actual tattoos. They peeked out of the neck of his dark, fitted shirt, before curving up along the back of his neck and into the side of his head. It seemed he had more marks than the other three. I wondered how many more were beneath his shirt.

He met my gaze without flinching, and I realized that despite my messy emotions there was no hate there. Daniel might have looked scary – gorgeous but scary – but his eyes, the color of cinnamon, rich and deep, with actual rings of gold in them – were sad. I recognized sad eyes. I'd stared at mine every time I looked in the mirror in the last eight months. His sad eyes, full lips, and almost-too-pretty-for-a-boy face offset the tattoos and shaved head enough to make him intriguing instead of scary.

"What's so urgent that we needed to drop everything and get here?" Xander asked, relaxing his arms to his sides as he stared at Daniel.

I caught a glimpse of something strange across his stomach then – not the abnormal amount of abdominal muscles – but a flash of what looked like shiny scales. It disappeared quickly, but it had definitely been there. *Fantasy world, Emma.* I was in a damn fantasy world.

Somehow my childhood wish had come true and I'd stumbled into a fantasy book world. I told my parents all that reading was going to come in handy one day.

Look how prepared I was for this situation...

"Laous is up to something," Daniel started without preamble, his voice a low, rich rumble. The voice of a whiskey-drinking singer; that low tenor sent shivers down my spine. "He was the one to suggest to the council it was time for a meeting, and that all four houses needed to be in attendance. Watch your backs, and your families tomorrow."

His eyes rested on me again, and I fought the urge to give him a hug. It might have been a strange urge, but sad eyes did that to me every single time.

"I heard talk of an Earthling," he added. "One who interests House of Imperial, and then you show up here." I swallowed roughly. "Don't let her out of your sight, Lex." Daniel lifted his gaze to the male standing next to me.

I'm not sure Lexen even realized he did it, but as soon as Daniel finished he angled his body to partially block me from sight. Shielding me. He then lifted his right arm, wrapping it around my shoulders, pulling me closer into his side.

Everyone was staring at me now, fully staring, and I was amazed by the shock in their wide eyes. Did Lexen not usually act like this? Or was there something else surprising them? Was it because I was a human?

With a rumble of annoyance, Lexen pulled me even further behind him. "Emma is here because her family has something to do with the treaty. Keep an ear out for me. Let me know if you hear anything more which might affect her."

I pushed Lexen to the side, glaring at him when he looked in my direction. I wasn't a doll he could put on a shelf to keep me safe. I mean, don't get me wrong, I knew I was way out of my league here, and would not be rushing out to play the hero. But it went against my nature not to stand up for myself. I had a quiet confidence, as was confirmed by multiple teachers over the years. I did not seek out conflict, but I never backed down.

When I nudged the huge Darken to the side again, stepping out from under his arm, I heard a chuckle. I swung around to find Chase laughing, his braids swinging wildly. Even Daniel had a smile on his face.

"Nice to see someone can put Lex in his place," Xander joked. "I think I like you already, Emma."

He winked at me and I set my best scowl on him. Unfortunately my scowl only made him laugh harder, and he looked like he was going to ruffle my hair, but his eyes flicked to Lexen for a moment and he dropped his hand. I didn't even want to turn and see what Lexen had done over my head. Not worth my time.

Daniel straightened. "I've got to get back now. I don't want Laous to be suspicious. Whatever game he's been playing since he killed my father ... he's moving into the next phase, but if you stay on guard you should be fine." He looked toward the transporter. "Time to ensure the daily assassination attempts are thwarted. See you all tomorrow."

The four exchanged farewells and then the other three disappeared back to their lands. When it was just Lexen and me remaining, I turned to him. "Why are you guys hiding your friendship?" It was the only thing that made sense to me. All these secret meetings. Not wanting to use their network.

Lexen shook his head. "The four houses have been enemies forever. Even with the current peace, old tensions always remain. For some reason though, the four of us have been best friends since we were very young. Overlord families do spend a lot of time together while our parents are working."

"You care about them," I said, watching the play of emotions on his face.

He didn't even try and deny it. "They're annoying as hell, but they're my family. My brothers. We formed an alliance in our youth and we have stuck together ever since. But if Laous found out about this friendship he would up his game trying to kill Daniel. Even my father wouldn't really approve."

I guessed he even kept it a secret from Jero and Marsil, since neither of them were that excited about the last meeting.

"How did they communicate with you for this meeting?" I asked, remembering his weird freezing thing in the bedroom.

"We can't talk to each other through the network, but it's easy to send signals. Over the years we've worked out a basic code. We try never to divulge sensitive information through any of our networks. It's too easy to be overheard."

He started leading me toward the transporter.

"So the four of you keep each other updated about the overlord majors' actions in the houses, and one day you'll all be the rulers?" I surmised.

He nodded, reaching out to take my hand. "Yes, for now we bide our time. One day we will rule and the houses will no longer be divided. It's time to change. Old prejudices will no longer be welcome in Overworld."

My mind was a frenzy as we caught the golden strand back to Lexen's home. I felt young and naïve thinking about the responsibilities on the four overlord minors' shoulders. Especially Daniel. Assassination attempts, seriously. Laous needed to be stopped.

I barely noticed the trip back to Lexen's room, and before I knew it I was crawling into his bed and snuggling down under the covers. For some reason my nerves from before about sharing his bed were gone, possibly because I was too tired now to care.

It was chilly still, but I had to sit up and take the sweater off. I couldn't sleep in a lot of clothes; I got claustrophobic when they wrapped around me. When I was comfortable again, I took a moment to marvel about the dragon fire high up in this mountain. I wasn't sure when it had happened, but I'd noticed through Lexen's window that it was dark outside. It was like they had an artificial sun under this mountain that they could dim and brighten. It was literally the power of a god – both amazing and scary.

Lexen's shoulders were so broad his bulk filled half the bed. He was clearly way too ripped to be a teenage boy. It was amazing no one had called him on it back on Earth.

"You're thinking very loud," he said with a low rumble in his voice. "Go to sleep."

I rolled on my side to face him, but before I could bestow my very best glare on him, he murmured something and the light at his bedside turned off, leaving the room in semi darkness.

"You can control the dragon fire?" I accused. "Are you the one who dims the huge one above Silver City?"

He chuckled, the deep sound filling my head and sending trills of tingles down my spine. "Qenita controls that one. She's asleep high in the caves. I could, technically, control it also. I'm the draygone lord. I was born at the exact same moment as Qenita. We bonded, despite the fact that we were nowhere near each other. I have ... some similar abilities as the draygones. I can do much more than a regular Daelighter."

There was an openness between us that had not been there before tonight. It lowered my guard and I found myself whispering, "Do you think my guardians are alive?" I'd been too afraid to voice this question before now, but I needed to prepare myself. Otherwise the reality might completely kill me.

He shifted closer, half rolling to face me. "I believe there are two options. Either your guardians were simply in the wrong place at the wrong time, dug their nose into something they shouldn't, and if that is the case, then yes, I think they will have been killed..."

My inhalation of breath was loud, cutting him off for a second. Breathing became harsh and ragged as I fought to contain my grief. After a few seconds Lexen continued, his voice low and gentle: "The second option is that they were specifically targeted for some reason. That they are being held hostage because the Imperials want something to do with them, or with..."

"Me," I finished for him.

I felt him nod, close to my shoulder. "It's a possibility. The pieces aren't quite adding up, though, because your parents were the secret keepers, not you. But maybe there are some important facts that we're missing."

I quickly wiped away the few stray tears that had escaped. "I'm really praying for the second option. I don't even care if they want something from me. I need Sara and Michael to be alive."

I startled as Lexen reached out and took my hand. I expected a quick squeeze, but he held it, silently supporting me. His thumb was even doing this slow glide up and down, unhurried and smooth. It was so ver...

I DIDN'T RECALL one moment of my sleep for the rest of the night. No more nightmares, no tossing and turning in restless slumber. I simply passed out and did not wake until the dragon fire in the mountain was burning brightly. A cool breeze brushed across my face and I struggled to get my eyes open. When I finally did, I was amazed to see that there was a panel of doors along the back wall of Lexen's room. All of them had been pushed back to leave an entire wall open, showcasing the city and the stunning stone that made up this mountain.

I lay there for many moments, snuggled and warm under the thick covers, just breathing it all in. It was so peaceful. I knew Lexen wasn't in the bed any longer. He emitted so much heat that it was immediately obvious when he was close. I was just wondering where he'd gotten to when another whoosh of cold air hit me. I bolted upright as a dragon appeared in that open wall. Qenita's huge white head wiggled inside and a gust of breath left her, sending icy particles through the room to slap me in the face.

"Um, hi," I squeaked, holding the covers up to my chest as I wiped the icicles off my face. "Lexen is not here, sorry. Please don't eat me, I'll probably taste terrible. I've literally been living on Fruit Loops for months."

Who was I kidding? Fruit Loops were delicious. She was going to love chomping down on me.

We silently stared at each other from across the room, and I wondered if she understood English. I also wondered where the freak Lexen was. It was his job to stop Qenita from eating me. As if she'd heard that thought, the dragon let out another snort of air. This time I ducked before more ice could hit me. A soft thud had me flinging my head up again in time to see Lexen walk across her back and drop down into the room.

He looked wild and forbidden in that moment, his hair tousled, eyes lit up with so much white light it was almost eclipsing the dark. My mouth suddenly went dry as a desert, my body doing that thing again where it ached for him. *Traitor.* My body was a freaking traitor.

"She's not going to eat you, and what the hell is a Fruit Loop?"

His words returned some of my clarity, and I focused on how amazing it must be to fly on a dragon. Sure, I'd gone on the magic carpet thing, but that wasn't the same. To ride on the back of such a powerful beast as it ducked and dived between the mountains ... I couldn't even imagine.

Lexen ran a hand through his sexy disarray of hair, pushing the longer side over, leaving the symbols standing out starkly. Despite the chill in the air, and the chill from his dragon, he wore only a black fitted shirt and black pants with heavy boots. As I stared, he tilted his head to the side, observing me much closer than usual.

"Would you like to meet her?" he asked, holding his hand out to me again.

Without a thought of hesitation, I placed my palm in his, already moving before he could help me.

"Slow down," he warned me. "Qenita might seem domesticated, but I assure you she's anything but. The draygones are wild, magnificent beasts. I'm honored to call her a friend." He started leading me closer to where Qenita had her head resting. Most of her massive body was out of the room, her wings slowly flapping to keep her from dropping lower.

Lexen stopped near her right eye. "This is Emma," he said, placing his free hand onto her snout. "She's my friend."

He eyed me and I chuckled, low, so as not to startle Qenita and get eaten by accident. "Bet you never thought you'd say that about a human," I murmured, leaning in close to him.

Before he could voice whatever smartass reply was coming, Qenita sent out a ring of icy moisture; it swirled in the air, crashing against my chest. The sudden blast of cold filled my veins and I gasped a few times.

Lexen laughed. "She likes you."

I rubbed my hand across my collarbone, trying to bring some warmth back. "Hate to see what she does if she doesn't like someone," I grumbled.

"Usually she smashes them with her tail," was his prompt reply.

I almost took a step back, but I didn't want either of them to realize how much of a scaredy human I was right now. Being this close to a dragon, it was the way I felt when I went to the zoo and stared into the eyes of the lions and tigers. There was something so predatory in their gazes; the lazy way they watched told me they knew exactly what I was doing, cataloguing every one of my movements, waiting for the right moment to attack. Yep, it was that feeling, just times a thousand.

With Lexen at my back, Qenita didn't feel like a threat, but I also wasn't going to be comfortable in her presence anytime soon. I was relieved and disappointed when Lexen released my hand, pressing both of his palms into her long snout and leaning in close to whisper to her. As the breezes picked up around us, we backed away and she flapped harder, wiggling out of the room. Lexen and I watched as her huge body gracefully soared away.

Everything in my body was thrumming. I felt alive in a way I could never remember feeling.

A real dragon.

I opened and closed my mouth, blurting out, "Most human guys have a dog, maybe two. A snake if they are particularly daredevil. You have a dragon as a ... a friend." I could never call

Qenita a pet. She was about as far from a pet as any being could be.

"I'm not human, Emma Walters. Do you need a demonstration?"

Before I could tell him I definitely didn't need a demonstration, twin balls of fire rose from his hands. The heat was immediate and intense and I took a step back, ending up on the small balcony area. A balcony without a railing, because it was clearly used as landing pad for a dragon.

The fire winked out in an instant and Lexen reached out for me before I could fall to my death. He hauled me inside and left me to stand there like a clumsy idiot while he shut those sliding doors.

"Guess I know why you like your showers so hot," I said. "You're like fire ... and Qenita is ice?"

He nodded just as there was a hard knock on the door, followed by another almost immediately. The door was then slammed open and a harried-looking Jero rushed inside. "Emma is not in her roo—"

His words died off when he caught sight of me standing there shivering in the cool air. I shook off some of my chill, narrowing my eyes on him. "Good job on the name."

He relaxed, his signature smirk crossing his face. He seemed so much more approachable not wearing his normal suit. There was no denying it, Jero was intimidating dressed in all of his finery. Without his suit there was a little more vulnerability about him, and I liked seeing that part of him. Of all the Darkens. They had let me into their inner sanctum. I was one of the lucky few to see the real beings.

As I strolled a little closer to Jero, I tilted my head to the side and smiled broadly. "Looks like someone was worried about me. You even remembered my name. Come on, Jero, admit it, you like humans."

He chuckled, reaching out and ruffling my hair. "Never said I didn't. Lex here is the one who thinks he's allergic to humanity."

The man in question didn't agree or disagree with that statement. He just pointed at the door and told us both to get out. Apparently it was time for us to dress, grab some food, and make it to the meeting of the houses. I was nervous. Soon I would meet this council and find out everything. Find out about my guardians.

Find out if my life was going to end all over again.

15

Star loaned me clothes. Ambra handed all of us delicious crunchy bread rolls filled with a creamy cheese-like spread, and then we were ready to go. Setting out from the overlord's home, back through Silver City, it was a long progression, Daelighters joining behind us as we travelled.

The Darkens were dressed far more formally than they had been the day before. Roland and Lexen, who led the way, wore floor-length maroon robes covered in silver symbols like those in their hair. The robes had hoods – which were down at the moment. They had jewels embedded in their hair, almost like a small crown, intertwining among the dark strands. They also wore a sword-shaped weapon down their spine, in a sheath.

I tried not to take that as a bad sign. It was just part of their uniform, right?

Jero and Marsil wore robes as well, theirs blue, with only a few swirling symbols. Ambra and Star looked stunning, like true royalty. They were decked out in formal gowns, floor length. The material was a shimmering maroon, in the same shade as the overlord's.

Glancing down, I shook my head at what was probably the nicest dress I'd ever put on, black velvet, with a scooped neckline and long fitted sleeves. The design hugged my body, ending in a soft swish around my ankles. It was comfortable, as dresses go. I'd even let Star pile my hair in messy curls and pin it to the top of my head, along with some sparkling gems pinned in amongst the disarray. The only other jewelry I wore was my necklace, which somehow perfectly set off the entire outfit.

For a few moments after Star finished my makeup, I pretended to be as royal as the family I had temporarily found myself part of. But I got over that pretty quickly. If the dirty looks from the fellow House of Darken members were anything to go by, I was not going to find myself very welcome in this world. I was certainly never going to be accepted as a Darken.

"A grubber is equivalent to 'piece of crap,' right?" I asked Star as we made our way through the mountain city.

Her lower lip popped out as her face fell. "I really wish Daelighters would stop using that word. It's rare now. Mostly from those who are too limited to see that both worlds need each other. Those who believe we have weakened ourselves by sharing power."

"We're not very tolerant of those who use it," Jero added, from where he was trailing behind us. "It's the name of a bug which lives in the dirt of the underworld, a creature which survives from eating the essence of those who don't make it out of the cascades. Like a bottom feeder."

I shuddered, trying not to think about what sort of bug this grubber might actually be. Safe to say, it was probably gross and scary. I wasn't really offended by being called that, mostly because the word didn't mean anything to me, so there was no connotation to hurt me. But it was nice that some Daelighters were insulted on my behalf.

Lexen, a dozen or more feet in front of us, caught my eye. I couldn't read anything in his dark gaze; he was back to being aloof and uninterested, but I was too nervous about where we were heading and what information I might learn to feel upset by it.

I wasn't so far gone though that I couldn't admire how good he looked as a prince. The robes. The stance. There was no missing how important he was. Far more important than anyone at Starslight Prep could have imagined. They thought he was out of their league because he was rich and gorgeous and a member of the founding family. They had no idea.

No. Freaking. Idea.

I had to keep reminding myself that Lexen was so far out of my league we weren't even the same species.

By the time we reached the cave entrance there were a few thousand Darkens behind us. Star had explained to me that not everyone would attend, only those who were willing, able, and interested. Apparently the Silver City alone held over a hundred thousand inhabitants – it was a big-ass cave. There were also many other cities within the Darken territory of Overworld, but, still, only a few thousand total would attend.

I knew they were planning on creating a temporary transporter, but I still expected the dragons to be outside when we emerged.

"No dragons?" I asked, not seeing any.

Star shook her head. "No, the only reason they met us yesterday was because of Lex. The draygones do not usually lower themselves to pull the oblong sphere. Qenita and her mate do that for Lex and only Lex."

No wonder he was such an arrogant bastard. I wanted to hate him, mostly because it was easier than admitting he stirred other feelings inside of me, but after his comfort last night I couldn't say that any longer and not be a straight-up liar. Something had shifted between us; there had been a wall up, a wall he had continued to reinforce by being such a dick all the time, but it was crumbling. He'd let me see some of the real Lexen and now I couldn't unsee it.

As if he'd sensed the heavy thoughts I was having, Lexen shifted those broad shoulders so that they were angled in my direction. He held out a hand, and just as I was wondering what he wanted, Star hurried over to join her brother. *Okay, then, not for me.* Sometimes I was an idiot.

All of the feelings stirring inside of me had me acting like a lovesick fool. I'd never done that before, not even with my one serious boyfriend, Jake. We had broken up because he couldn't handle me being an emotional wreck any longer. He would never admit that of course, but there was no doubt in my mind. I couldn't really blame him either. I had been a mess. With no sign of ever recovering.

I eventually realized it was for the best. A long-distance relationship wasn't something either of us were particularly interested in. He had been the first and only boy I'd loved – or thought I loved. He was my first in all ways, but whatever feelings I'd had had faded very quickly when he declared – two weeks after my parents' death – that I was no fun anymore.

Apparently, according to him, sex heals all wounds, and I was just being selfish not indulging that truth. Funnily enough, "sex" had not been listed as one of the stages of grieving my therapist gave me, but apparently Jake Mcloughlin subscribed to a different theory.

Thinking back, I'd barely even noticed when he walked away. Compared to everything I'd lost, it was such a minuscule sliver of pain. I had a terrible feeling that it wouldn't be that way with Lexen. That if I let myself care about him, and then lost him, it could destroy me. Which was exactly why I was going to step back. No more sleepovers. I would share with Star tonight.

"Emma?"

My head shot up as the girl in question called my name. I realized everyone was waiting for me; I was holding the line up. Fiery heat shot through my body. I lowered my head to dash forward, trying not to trip over the long gown. I wasn't used to wearing something like this dress, especially with the black low-heeled ankle boots I had on underneath.

When I reached the gathered royal-Darkens, Ambra held out a hand for me. "We all go together," she said. "Overlord's family first, so we can protect our people from dangers on the other side."

I blinked a few times before placing my hand into hers. I was feeling a little choked up at their continued acceptance. It wasn't like parents hated me or anything. On the contrary, I was actually pretty good at dealing with my friends' parents, even when they were difficult. But these were monarchs ... surely royal people were much fussier. Snobby.

This theory was based off books and movies of course, because the Darkens were my first real-life royalty meeting. So far they were blowing all of my theories out of the water.

As soon as my hand was in Ambra's, she reached out and snagged a string of light. The others did the same, and then we were yanked along. I closed my eyes again for that final hurtle-at-the-wall thing, because I was never going to convince my mind that I wasn't about to die.

When Ambra squeezed my hand, I figured it was safe to reopen my eyes. She released me just as I got my first glimpse of where we were. I blinked a few times before spinning in a circle. How in the ... were we floating in the sky?

As far as I could see, surrounding us in all directions, were clouds, fluffy and stereotypical. Except they weren't white ... they were a deep, rich, dark gray. I couldn't see any sky above or below; it was as if this entire world was gray clouds. Walls, floors, ceiling. Wherever we were, I officially dubbed it "Cloudland."

I took a tentative step forward, surprised by the firm and slightly buoyant surface. My heels didn't sink in or anything. Jero chuckled when he caught sight of my face. No doubt I was looking a tad shocked.

"What's got you all confused, little petal?"

I wrinkled my nose at him. "I thought there were no clouds here? In Overworld."

"There aren't," he replied. "This isn't Overworld. It's a land between. A neutral zone we use for meetings. Daelighters couldn't survive here for long. There's no food or sustenance, so we only use it for mass gatherings of the four houses. Works well because we don't tend to cross into each others' territory. All the wars and fighting and such ... we're suspicious aliens."

He shuffled me along, keeping us with his family, who were moving away from the golden ball of light. I noticed then something I'd missed earlier. A few hundred feet away were five raised platforms, shiny and metallic; one sat a little in front of the other four. The Darkens were heading toward one of the middle ones in the back four.

"Overlord families stand on the platforms," Jero told me as we caught up to Marsil.

Marsil reached out and placed a firm hand on my shoulder, giving it a brief squeeze. "Are you doing okay, Emma?" His gentle voice soothed some of the nerves inside. "You're handling all of these new experiences really well."

"Was it hard for you on Earth?" I counter-questioned him, knowing there was no way I could lie and say I was calm. It felt like I might only be one more "new experience" from a screaming breakdown.

He nodded, completely unashamed to admit he had struggled. "We know a lot about Earth. We have adopted customs and languages and many other practices from your world, while also sharing some of ours with you, but knowing and experiencing are two vastly different things. Even the smell of Earth was odd. It doesn't smell like home. It took me longer than I expected to adjust."

Funnily enough, I hadn't had the smell problem with this place. Which kept this niggling thought in my head that maybe I'd been here before. Could my parents have come back when I was really young?

Realizing Marsil had bared his soul and I was just standing there lost in thought, I cleared my throat. "I'm eternally grateful that I've had you guys to help me out. I'd definitely be less calm navigating on my own." I was hoping my true depth of my gratitude was clear.

I surprised Marsil – and myself – by leaning forward and giving him a quick hug. Jero was next. He chuckled and hauled me in. As I pulled away, I could feel a burning gaze on me, and I wasn't at all surprised to see it was the oldest Darken brother. He was standing beside Star, already up on the platform. His gaze lowered to my hands, which were still flat against Jero's chest.

I lifted one brow, narrowing my eyes on him. *What?* my expression said.

He opened his mouth, but at the same time Roland said something and Lexen had to turn away to answer his father. All breath rushed out of me.

Jero chuckled again. "As much as I enjoy your hands on me," he drawled, "making Lexen jealous is a bad idea. You're playing with fire."

I snorted out some laughter, dropping my hands off him as quickly as I'd put them on. "I'm not trying to make him jealous. That would be an absurd action."

"Whatever you say, pretty girl." He smirked and, turning away, gracefully vaulted up onto the platform.

Again I was last, and since I wasn't sure if I should be up there, I kind of just hovered near the edge. There were a lot of Daelighters around now. From my low vantage point I could not see the full scope of the numbers, but I saw enough to know this cloud land was filling up. Along with all of the platforms.

The noise was almost overwhelming. The acoustics in this place were perfect for bouncing sound around, making it appear that the thousands of Daelighters were really ten times that number.

As I remained standing at the edge of the raised platform, minding my own business, people-watching, a few young, overexcited boys bumped into me. They looked to be about fourteen, but I had no idea what their actual age was because of that metamorphosis aging they did here. I let out an *oomph* as they knocked me into the side of the platform, which was definitely not made from anything soft or cloud-like.

Pulling back, I grabbed my aching ribs, freezing at what sounded like a burst of thunder.

Before I could look up, there was a harsh command from above. "Don't move a damn muscle."

Every single Daelighter around me froze. Tilting my head back, I found Lexen standing right above me, his eyes a blaze of white lights. In fact, the blackness seemed to have faded away to be replaced completely by starlight. Everyone in the vicinity – myself included – was completely mesmerized.

When he spoke next, it was not in English, so I couldn't understand, but I definitely recognized the fear in the eyes of those around me. Especially the four teens who'd hit me.

Knowing it had been an accident, I straightened. "Lexen!" I demanded, hoping to break whatever tension was lacing the air.

Everyone gasped. Like a loud, dramatic hand slapped over their mouths kinda gasp.

Those blazing eyes locked on me and I had to force myself not to flinch. I reminded myself I had been through far worse than a pissed-off dragon lord, so I hurried on: "It was an accident. They're just kids." Kids who were probably twenty years older than me, but whatever. They looked like kids.

Some of the darkness flickered back into his eyes as he narrowed them on me. "They hurt you."

He pointedly looked at where I was still holding my ribs. I released them, swinging my arms as casually as I could without wincing. "It. Was. An. Accident," I repeated, getting a little annoyed now.

Cue another series of shocked gasps.

Jero and Marsil stepped up on either side of their brother. The overlord and his admirals. I had to admit it was an impressive sight. Scary. Intimidating. I was really feeling for the Daelighters around me. This was the Lexen from Starslight Prep, the enforcer, the one who everyone feared.

I'd never seen him that way though, so with almost no hesitation I turned and faced the small crowd, who were still frozen in place. "Go," I murmured to the boys. "You're not in trouble. I'll keep them occupied."

I winked at the closest boy to me, and he managed a shaky smile. "We are so sorry," he choked out, his accent heavy. "Thank you."

With a few final terrified glances at their overlord, they sprinted off into the crowd, and everyone else who had stopped to look did the same. I turned back to the Three Stooges.

"I have to join Father," Lexen said to no one in particular, even though his eyes were still blazing and focused on me. "Keep an eye on her."

"*Her* is standing right here," I muttered under my breath as he turned away.

Marsil dropped off the stage, and before I could stop him he pressed a hand to my side. I gasped, even though his touch had been gentle. My breath was coming in and out roughly as I fought through the dizzying pain. Holy crap, why did bruised ribs hurt so much?

"You need to see a healer," he said, lightening his touch even more. "We should go now."

I shook my head, still panting. "No, you all need to be here, in case there is trouble. I'll be fine. It's just a bruise."

He gave me a look that was far more like Lexen than his normally calm stare. "Okay, then, get up on the stage if it's just a bruise."

I sucked in deeply and straightened the best I could. "Okay ... I will."

I eyed the five-foot-tall structure, squaring my shoulders. I could deal with the pain long enough to not weaken the House of Darken by taking away some of their royal family at a time like this. Before I could do more than lift my arm, though, a loud voice boomed out. It sounded like it was amplified over a speaker.

I turned to see what was going on. All of the Daelighters appeared to be gathering before the front platform now – which held about two dozen beings. I was going to guess this was the council's stage, judging by the fact that I could see members of all four houses on there.

A male and female appeared to be the spokes-Daelighters for the council. They switched between English and another language, making it hard for me to follow along.

"They're talking about your guardians," Jero said, startling me.

I swung my head around to stare right at him.

"Saying that someone has violated the treaty by luring them to Astoria ... and then kidnapping them. That whoever is involved better release them now or there will be consequences."

I swallowed roughly. "How do they know they're here? And why do they care about humans so much?" I whispered back.

He shrugged. "It's not that they care so much, it's more that the treaty is important to them. Kidnapping humans ... huge violation. They will do everything to make sure this is rectified."

Every world was built on politics, apparently.

I listened harder now, wanting to know what information was

being released to the public, but it was impossible to follow the mixed language.

"...the fate of both worlds rests on this treaty," the male voice said.

"...*forestima judicia letins warnt death*," came from the more feminine tones.

Over and over they went on, apparently moving topics rapidly.

"You have one cycle of the moon-phase to release the Earth-lings," the male said in conclusion. "One more cycle before we enact a punishment of the highest order. Our secret keepers have been targeted, the four families who hold the key to the safety of the stone. This breach will not be tolerated."

The audience seemed to hold their breath, an unnatural silence filling the land. Then noise exploded around us, along with a mild level of mayhem. Fighting, curses, threats. Lexen, who had been lingering near the middle of his platform, stepped forward until he was right on the edge of the Darken area. I was only getting a glimpse of his side profile from where I stood, but his face was fierce, eyes locked out in the crowd.

Jero and Marsil jumped up to join their brother, both of them apparently forgetting they were supposed to be keeping an eye on me. Which was a relief, because I could finally clutch my ribs again as I leaned into the platform. The hot throb of pain was not going anywhere, and pretending I was fine was taking a toll.

Distraction came from Lexen when he shot sparks of fire and ice high into the air above all the Daelighters. Whatever dragon power he possessed was enough to distract and calm the crowd somewhat. All of the other houses were also using their partic-ular brand of power on the rowdy Daelighters. Royales sent out rain, because they could control water, apparently. *Made sense.* Roland, Lexen's father, added his power to the Royale rainstorm, wind and lightning whipping from him and across the cloud land. Darkens must control weather to some degree. Imperials' swirls of fire were so hot that even a few platforms across I could feel the hot gusts on my face. And the Leights, well ... they had turned into trees.

Trees?

My brain continued trying to refute what my eyes were seeing, but there was no denying it. The Leights' bodies had changed from human-looking supermodels into literal trees with trunks and branches and arm-shrub things. They didn't have branches out the top, with leaves, like a normal tree. Their heads were bald and barky, all that long hair turning to bark across the surface. Their bodies grew to six times their previous size, big and powerful, and much faster than I would have expected. I mean, I'd never actually imagined a redwood jogging along a path of course, but if I ever had I would have expected them to be kinda slow, cumbersome.

I swallowed a screech as a Leight got a little too close to some of the Imperials' flames, his barky skin catching alight in a whoosh. Luckily the Royale overlord sent a huge splash of water into the crowd, dispersing the lethal flames.

Rather quickly, considering how loud and out of control the Daelighters had been only a moment ago, the leaders of the four houses calmed their people. Apparently, when they did work together, there was a special sort of magic between them.

Pressing myself back out of sight, I waited for everything to finish moving back to order.

Trying to breathe through my pain, I thought about all the questions still unanswered. One of the main was Laous ... it felt important to know what plans he'd been trying to initiate since killing Daniel's father. More specifically, why had he decided to push for all the overlords and admirals of the four houses to go to Astoria? This was a new order, and the reason Lexen had been so pissed on Earth: the first "forced compliance" of the treaty terms. There had to be a reason Laous decided to make it happen now.

When did they first go there? Had Star said something about it being almost a year?

Which would make it just before Christmas and New Yea...

Everything inside of me froze and I struggled to suck air into my lungs. I recognized the panic attack I was having. It wasn't the first, that was for sure, but I couldn't recall any of my therapy techniques to calm myself.

Because I'd just had a realization.

My parents were killed eight months ago. The houses sent their royal leaders just before that. What if Laous somehow figured out a way to use these overlord minors to track down the secret keepers? What if the only ones who had a shot at finding us were ones who held the power of their houses? There was no way he could get the actual overlords to go, so he chose the next best thing.

My gaze locked on Lexen, grief tearing through me with enough force that it actually felt like my heart was being slashed by a blunt knife. He'd promised me he had nothing to do with the fire, and I'd believed him, but what if he'd helped without any knowledge, inadvertently killing the only two people I'd had in this world. My family.

A sob escaped before I could stop it. Followed by another.

I crumpled forward, the pain in my heart so much stronger than the pain in my ribs. Emotional pain eclipsed physical pain every time. I would take a million shattered bones over a broken heart, that was for sure.

Pushing through my pain, I worked hard to reassert my logic. It was wrong to blame Lexen. Whatever he had done had probably been outside of his control. I knew enough about him to know he would never deliberately hunt down and burn innocent humans to death. I had to keep my faith in him, because everyone deserved a chance to explain themselves.

This resolve calmed me. I managed to stand straight again and turn my attention back to the crowds. The inter-house fighting had fully abated. I felt eyes on me and somehow knew it was Lexen, but I couldn't bring myself to look in his direction, afraid I would break down again. The last thing I needed was him noticing I was upset and coming to ask me about it. I wanted to talk to him when I was calm and collected, not when I'd just had a terrible revelation and was processing. Right now I was likely to start screaming accusations at him, and that was unfair.

His gaze continued burning a hole in the side of my head, so I took a few steps back, and then a few more, hopefully slow enough to not look suspicious. The council had just started to speak again, and I used the distraction to hurry to the back of the Darken platform, out of their line of sight.

I was done with all Daelighters. Part of me was desperate to get back to Earth, back to what was familiar. But that wasn't going to happen until someone returned the Finnegans to me. No way was I going home without them.

"Are you okay?"

The soft words took me by surprise. I swung around to find Lexen standing at my side. His arms hung loosely and he looked relaxed – well, as relaxed as Lexen ever looked. The darkness of his eyes captured me as always, my fascination with those depthless pools growing every time I stared into them.

"I'm fine," I choked out. "Just ... this is a lot, you know."

His face was a hard cut of lines; his jaw looked clenched. "The council is going to find your guardians. They have assured us that this is the number one priority for them."

"When did you first arrive in Astoria?" The words burst from me before I could stop them. Damn it. So much for waiting until I was calmer.

If Lexen was surprised by my sudden change of topic, he didn't show it. "We started at the beginning of junior year."

"So you started August last year," I said slowly. "And my parents were killed in December." My voice broke as I tried to figure out how to phrase my next question. I needed to know, though, which is why I couldn't stop from asking.

His chest rumbled. "I didn't have anything directly to do with their deaths, Emma. I swear this to you."

Clearly my thoughts had been written all over my face.

"The timing was suspicious, I'll give you that," he continued. "But I believe everything which hurt you, the loss of your parents and missing guardians, it's to do with House of Imperial. With Laous."

"Daniel?" I asked tentatively. I wasn't sure of his position.

Lexen was already shaking his head. "No, it's not Daniel. I trust him with my life."

For some reason I believed him. Daniel seemed like someone who was reliable and fair, if not a little scary in a bad boy way.

"Emma..." That husky murmur of my name caught my attention. "You can trust me. I might have acted like an asshole when we first met – I will own that – but I had my reasons."

I didn't think he was going to tell me those reason, because he was usually reticent with information. So when he did, I ended up gaping like a freak at him.

"From the first moment you stumbled into my world, all fiery and beautiful and innocent, soaking wet but still defiant ... facing things which should have made you question your sanity, you never crumbled. You were so determined to save your family." He ran a hand through his hair. "Shit, I had to do something to try and deter you. To make sure you weren't dragged into the mess of my world. A human cannot fight a Daelighter, and there are too many politics at play, especially when you get involved with the overlord's family."

Beautiful? He'd called me beautiful, which was probably the least important thing he'd said. Still, it had my heart and stomach turning twirls.

"Turns out I'm already involved in your world," I managed to get out. "So there was no chance of protecting me from it."

His smile almost killed me. The rapid beating of my heart seemed to be increasing the pain in my ribs, but I didn't even care. Lexen leaned in closer. I wanted him to kiss me so badly I could barely stand it. I had no idea what had brought on this emotional side of him, but I had no defense against it. Against him. The kindness Jero, Marsil, and Star had shown me ... Lexen held equal amounts within himself. Tempered by dragon flame, of course.

A warm hand pressed into my side, and then a blast of cool air shot straight into my ribs. Relief from the pain was instant, like the area was numb now. "That will speed up the healing," he murmured, lowering his head so that his face was close to mine.

"How did you know I was in pain?" I asked, tilting my head back to stare directly into his eyes.

Lexen tensed, the masculine lines of his face deepening. "The heat from your injury," he finally said, dragging his fingers across my side. "It's inflamed. And you're also moving gingerly. I noticed it as you tried to escape back here."

Well, no doubt he could now sense the heat in my cheeks.

"Didn't realize anyone was watching me so closely," I choked out, half lying, because I had felt his eyes on me and I had been trying to escape him. "Sorry for suspecting you again," I added in a rush. "The timing of my parents' deaths and your arrival on Earth, it all just hit me. I knew it would not have been anything you did deliberately. I just wondered if it wasn't some sort of combination of all four overlord minors being in Astoria. Being on Earth."

Lexen stilled, his eyes locked on mine, his teeth partly bared as a fury stronger than I'd ever seen descended across his face. "Fuck," he bit out. "There's a way he might have used us. It's difficult but possible." He spun, his expression fierce. "Wait here. I have an overlord to kill."

He prowled away with a scary amount of speed. Okay, then, he was pissed. That made two of us.

"Lex—" I got partway through shouting out for him when a hand wrapped around my face and I was roughly yanked backwards. His name turned into a scream as agony crashed into my side, the numbness gone in a flash of twisting bodies and wrenched ribs.

Raging flames filled me, an intense heat that was impossible to fight against. No matter how much I struggled against the hands, the burning continued to grow. Right when I felt like my head was going to explode, the pressure and pain became too much, and everything went dark.

16

$\mathcal{T}$he dryness in my mouth woke me. I choked and it felt like I almost swallowed my tongue – an impossible feat – as I tried to find moisture.

What was going on?

My head pounded as I attempted to piece together my last memories. Why was my mouth as dry as a freaking desert right now? Had I gotten wasted with the Darkens? That didn't feel quite right.

I squinted as best I could, allowing small slivers of light to enter; while still struggling on the smooth, stone-like ground.

After a few minutes of flopping around like a fish, I managed to pry my lids all the way up, swaying as I pulled myself into a sitting position ... only to fall forward again. My brain was fried; this was definitely no hang-over. Or none like I'd ever experienced the entire two times I'd been drunk before.

Eventually I got my shaky hands down, using them as leverage. My eyes still didn't seem to be focusing, because there was no color around me at all. Everything was white, the floor, the walls, even the ceiling, so starkly white it was like being in a world without any pigment.

Memories of an intense heat slammed into me and I lurched to my feet. I waited for the burst of pain in my ribs, but only a dull tightness lingered there now. Had someone healed me? Or had I been here for a long time? That would explain the dying-of-thirst thing I seemed to be doing.

On wobbly legs I crossed to the closest wall. *Shit.* Everything was literally glowing white, but at least my eyes were fine. I pressed my hand up to touch the semi-transparent thin and flexible plastic that made up the wall. Almost like someone had used white wrap to cover this place.

Before my hand could make contact with the wall, it flexed out, swelling away from my touch. I took another step closer to it, and the same thing happened. What in the actual fu—?

"Hello!" I screamed. Or attempted to. My voice was a rasp, and no amount of throat clearing was going to help.

Again I attempted to slam my hands into the side – the wall swelled outwards. I tried a few more times; it continued to move, avoiding me, even when I pressed closer. The view I saw through the murky plastic never changed. My prison was not moving. Outside was a ton more egg-shaped structures, and within them were shadows. Other prisoners?

Was this some sort of egg prison?

Great. Unless they had the word Easter in front of them, I wasn't a fan of eggs. I started to pace back and forth, trying to work through my thoughts. My brain was coming back online slowly; clearly it had been fried by that burst of heat. I could remember talking with Lexen, discussing the possibilities that the overlord minors going to Earth might have had something to do with my parents' deaths. That was the last thing I remembered before the darkness.

I panicked at the thought that something might have happened to the Darkens, to a family I had grown quite fond of. All of them were kind, caring, never once making me feel like I didn't belong or was a burden to them.

And Lexen ... the most infuriating, frustrating, intriguing guy in two worlds. He had comforted me through more breakdowns than almost anyone else in the past eight months. He had kept me safe despite not wanting to involve me in his world, because I knew he trusted no one else to do it. A burst of clarity was enough for me to acknowledge that he had protected me fiercely from almost the first moment we met.

It was also clear that I was a complete idiot.

My breathing grew ragged as my mind filled with worries. Had I put the Darkens in danger? Lexen would be the biggest of all targets, especially since he'd never back away from an attack. He'd also been hell bent on "killing an overlord."

The sides of my egg prison swelled then; air whooshed past me. Every one of my muscles tensed as I waited to see what was happening. I hadn't moved, and nothing was touching the walls, but they kept on expanding out. Then, with a pop that left my ears ringing, my egg prison shattered.

I wasted no time in trying to escape, but before I could make it more than two steps, a line of men stepped into view, blocking my path. I didn't recognize any of them, but they had the same sort of look as Daniel: shaved heads, ink across their necks and arms – none on their heads.

House of Imperial.

Wait, the one in the center, who looked to be in his early thirties, had symbols across his head.

Laous. The overlord.

His eyes were small and mean, and they narrowed even further as he glared at me. He was around six foot tall, with a wide chest and skinny arms. Not to mention this dude had definitely skipped leg day. Bad move, barrel man. No one wants to look like a keg with spindly arms and legs.

"You were a hard one to get hold of, Earthling."

My insane mental blather died off.

"I'm the overlord of House of Imperial. You can call me Overlord," he said.

I crossed my arms over my chest, trying to stay calm.

Something twitched in Laous' jaw as he stared me down, but I had grown quite adept at dealing with Daelighter animosity, so I kept my cool.

"Do you know why you're here?" Laous broke the silence, and I gave myself a mental tick for winning that round.

"I have no idea. There's nothing I have that you could possibly want," I said evenly, clenching my fists, which were tucked under my armpits to hide their shaking. This bastard had already taken everything from me – meeting him more than cemented my belief that he was behind my parents' deaths – so what the hell did he want now?

His chuckle startled me. "Actually, that's quite far from the truth." He started to pace, his men remaining in a stoic line behind him. "It took me longer than I'd like to admit to figure it all out. How the secret keeping worked. The "information" which is scattered between all four members..."

He turned and took a step closer to me. Then another. I barely held my ground, wanting to turn and run, but as there was nowhere to go, I forced myself to remain calm.

"Did you know you were born here, in Overworld?" That casual question took me completely by surprise.

I sort of gasped, stifling the sound. It was enough, though, to let him know that I had been very unaware of that information.

"Born in the sacred legreto of the House of Darken, actually." His voice was a slimy coo. Barrel man was enjoying this. "This legreto was blessed by the starlight stone, the same one from the pact. The stone which was stolen by the humans. Its energy fills your blood. Blood that I need."

I swallowed roughly. "You killed my parents." *I was the secret keeper. It had been me all along. How was this possible?*

He nodded. "A Draygo stumbled into House of Imperial, not

the one who buried the stone, but one who knew a little about this secret keepers business. He told me that there are four humans, born in this world, one for each house. Darken first, then Imperial, Leight third, and last Royale. The four would lead me to the stone I sought. The hardest part was finding the first, but eventually I figured out a way by using the energy of the overlord minors." I knew he had sent them to Astoria for a reason. The piece of shit. "The power of the four houses led me to your parents. I thought one of them was the first, so I took his blood, and then disposed of him so he would not inform the council."

Disposed, like my father was trash that needed to be thrown away.

"Only it turned out I was wrong." Laous still sounded shocked, even though this event had been months ago. "His blood held no properties from Overworld. Nor the wife's, which I took as a precaution. That was when I figured out where I went wrong. It was you I needed. You and a key, apparently. Which that useless Draygo had neglected to tell me the first time I questioned him." His eyes were boring into me and I wanted to gouge them out. "He didn't make that mistake again." His chuckle was low and raspy. "Once I finally figured it all out, it was easy to lure you to Astoria. Then just as easy to get you here in Overworld. All without drawing any attention to myself."

Not exactly true. Daniel had noticed, and he had told the other overlord minors. They would be able to go to the council ... hopefully it wouldn't be too late for me by the time they convinced them.

"Now that I finally have the right blood..." Laous scowled at me, like it was my fault he screwed up. "It should lead me to the key, and then that will lead me right to the other three."

He flicked his fingers and two of the men in the middle of his line of defense stepped forward. I tensed, taking my first step back, arms falling from across my chest to rest at my sides, loosely held, ready to protect myself.

"It's in your best interest to help us, human."

Those words had me blinking at the overlord. "Oh yeah, I'm sure it's totally in my best interest," I replied, sarcasm strong.

A pop nearby blasted through us, my ears doing that weird ringing sound again. As the prisoners tumbled out of the egg about twelve feet from me, a single tear tracked down my cheek. Sara and Michael could barely drag themselves along the ground as they tried to move closer to each other, their emaciated forms weak, near dying.

"I will do whatever you need – please just help them," I said in a rush, never taking my eyes from my guardians.

Laous chuckled, another psycho switch of emotion. "Your parents' oldest friends, who've spent their lives trying to track down my world. Your parents caused that, you know, telling them stories that they shouldn't have, opening their eyes to the wonders beyond Earth."

Sara's dark eyes were pools of pain, locked on me. I returned that gaze with my own, barely able to stop myself from rushing toward them. I needed to be smarter than that. There were a bunch of assholes standing in the way who could knock me out with one blow. Now was not the time for rash actions. Whatever happened, I was determined that Sara and Michael would be safely returned to Earth.

"If you need my blood, then just take it," I demanded, my voice vibrating with emotion.

"Oh, I will." A bark of words in return. "But it would be much easier for me if you just told me where the key is, rather than the tedious task of tracking it down. It will be something very special to your family, something which you feel a tie to."

"Release my guardians first." For once there was not an ounce of fear in my voice. Mostly because I was very serious about rescuing Sara and Michael. I owed them so much.

Sara lifted her head as high as she could manage, her dark

curls matted and bunched on one side. "No," she called out in a reedy voice. "Don't ... Em ... no..."

My chest was hurting so badly, not the ribs this time, but right around my heart. I had to help them. I had to save them.

I eyed Laous again. "If you don't send them home, they're going to die, and I will never help you. You can torture me until I'm dead. I will never reveal where this key location is, and I will fight you for my blood. I will fight you the entire time." My threats were somewhat empty, because these guys could over-power me in a second. And I had no idea what this key was he talked about. My parents hadn't been precious about any of their things; they didn't care about stuff. Besides, if there had been anything, wouldn't it have burned up in the fire? Still I had to try to convince him it was better to let the Finnegans go.

"If you release them," I continued, my voice confident, "send them back to Earth, show me evidence of them safe, and then give your word that you will never touch them again, I will help you with whatever you need. I give my word, which is worth as much as yours."

He observed me for a few long moments. I was practically holding my breath, praying he would accept my terms. Finally he nodded. "I agree to your stipulations. You provide me with the key, and in return I will not harm your guardians. They'll go right back to Earth, free to go wherever they please."

"No..."

I ignored Sara and Michael's pleas. "Are you sending them back right now?"

His eyes flicked across to the Finnegans, coming back to rest on me. "I'm going to give you three a moment to catch up, a chance to say goodbye. I want you to remember how much they mean to you."

Lexen's face flashed through my mind. I was eternally grateful that it seemed like House of Imperial knew nothing about my fondness for the Darkens. This dickbag would no doubt threaten anyone I cared about.

I could protect them from this. All of them.

The line of guards parted and I realized I was allowed to go to Sara and Michael. I started to cry as I hurried toward their frail forms. Neither of them could do much besides hold their heads up off the ground. I had no idea how they were still alive. Panic was very much taking over my body as I worried it was already too late. "I'm so sorry," I whispered over and over as I knelt between them.

There was no way this was just starvation. They'd only been missing for a bit over a week. Laous had done much more than just starve them.

"Em..." Sara's low murmur caught my ear, and I leaned down so I was resting my head next to hers. Our eyes locked on each other.

"Escape. Can't ... gii-ve ... the key."

Every word was a struggle for her; her chest wheezed as air sucked in and out. Tears fell down my cheeks but I managed to hold my sobs inside, even though my throat ached like it was in a stranglehold.

"It's going to be okay," I whispered back, placing my hands on hers and Michael's. "I love you both so much. You saved my life this year. This is just a small thing I can do to return the favor. When you get back to Daelight Crescent, go straight to the guard and tell them you need to speak with a Darken. Make them contact Roland or Lexen. They will protect you."

I didn't know where this key was, so I had to hope they could get to safety before Laous decided to go after them again. I was giving them a chance; it was the best I had. I heard footsteps coming closer. My time with them was up.

I pressed a kiss to Sara's cheek first, and then to Michael's. "Please don't search for supernaturals any longer," I added as I pulled back. "Promise me that once this is all over, you will go and live normal lives."

Sara struggled, her eyes red as she sobbed. There were no tears, which probably meant she was too dehydrated to shed them.

I gave their hands one last squeeze before standing. "It's going to be okay. I will fix this. I have allies. You don't need to worry about me."

The empty promises I made crashed to the ground, shattering around us. No one believed me, that was clear, but it felt like the right thing to at least try to settle their concerns. I had to turn away then, away from their frantic eyes, away from the anguish of knowing this might be the last time I saw them. Laous knew exactly what he was doing giving me these few moments with my guardians. Motivation to provide him with everything he wanted.

Some of the Imperial guards brushed past me; I heard a mild struggle before an echoing silence descended. The air changed after Sara and Michael were gone. Everything felt darker, more painful. I was alone again ... always alone. But it was okay because I was keeping people I cared about safe. Sara and Michael. Lexen ... all of the Darkens.

Laous was waiting where I'd left him, right near my egg prison. "I will not give you one thing until I see evidence of Sara and Michael, free and healthy," I said, no inflection in my voice.

The healthy part was what had me most worried. Laous just nodded, a half-smirk on his face. I turned and marched myself into the egg. New walls immediately closed around me and I sank into the center, wrapping my arms across my legs. I felt sick, my stomach churning over and over until I felt like I would throw up. If I'd had anything to eat recently, it would definitely be making a reappearance. How could my parents not tell me I was the secret keeper? It was one thing to hide that information when it was about them, but if it was my burden to bear, then I really should have known about it. About Overworld and Daelighters. About everything.

I sat in that same huddled position for what felt like hours, my mind racing with everything that had happened to me in the last little while. Everything I could blame Laous for, all the ways he had ruined my life.

An ear-ringing pop signaled that my cage was open again. An unknown Imperial entered. He had red tattoos all the way up his face and across his neck. He held a small device out to me. It had a screen on one side and I grabbed it, pressing my face closer to watch my guardians. They were in our house on Daelight Crescent. My breath caught again as one of my hands lifted to brush against the screen. They both looked perfect. Healthy, strong ... alive.

"Prove to me that this is footage from right now," I demanded, knowing it would be easy to manipulate me with old footage.

As if he'd been expecting it, red tattoo pressed a small black button on the side, and then we had audio.

"We need to get her back!" Sara's voice sounded desperate as she paced across the tiny living room. "They're going to kill her, just like they did Chelsea and Chris."

Michael moved forward to comfort his wife, his normally jovial features tight and drawn. "There is no way for us to get back to Overworld. We can't use that transport light thing. We did as she asked. For now we have to wait."

I was relieved they were being circumspect about talking with the Darkens. Maybe they knew Laous would be watching the house. Michael's paranoia was coming in handy.

"How could Chelsea and Chris hide this from us?" Sara sounded desperate. "Tell us just enough to hook us but never reveal that Emma was so important. Even though we were always going to be the ones to care for her if they couldn't..."

I'd always wondered how a straight-laced teacher and accountant became such great friends with supernatural hunters, and now I knew. There was nothing normal about my parents, and whatever they had been involved in, it had influenced the Finnegans, causing them to jump into this crazy life of hunting down Daelighters. It got my family killed, and almost the Finnegans too.

Was I next?

"Are you satisfied?" His gruff, heavily-accented question was hard to understand, but I got the general idea.

I nodded. "Yes. I will help you in any way I can. But you need to tell Laous that I have been trying to think of a *key* my parents would have treated reverently and I'm drawing a blank."

Red tats smirked, and I was immediately wary, stepping back while keeping my guard high. Thankfully, he didn't move toward me. He just shut off the cameras and gave me a simple wink, which somehow felt as intrusive as if he'd touched me. "You better think harder, grubber. Laous does not take well to being denied what he wants."

Then he was gone, walking out of the egg; the walls snapped into place with a twang, like a rubber band flinging back into place. Some of the relief at seeing Sara and Michael returned to good health – through some sort of alien magic obviously – faded away as I realized that I could no longer stall Laous. He wanted to know where this key was, and apparently I was the only one who could help him. It might have been a little easier if I had an idea what sort of object it was. Was it a literal key, or something less obvious?

I could not remember a single time my mom had mentioned a key or secret keeping, or anything like that to me. *How could they do this?* A burst of anger had curses flying from my mouth, one after the other.

Energy boosted me to my feet, and using my temporary rush of emotion, I kicked out at the walls again. Again they shifted away so I couldn't touch them. "Come on!" I shouted. "You stupid piece of crap, open the hell up. Let me out!"

By this point I'd clearly lost all semblance of sanity, morphing into a screaming banshee. There was no real reason for it, I knew that, but it felt cathartic all the same. I'd had a really long, shitty in some ways – amazing in others – week, and I really needed a release.

When I got that out of my system, I decided to stand and glare at the walls for a good twenty or thirty minutes. Then I started to sing. I chose the most annoying, ear-piercing song I could think of, humming it at first, then breaking into a full-on ballad. High notes included.

The truth was, fear was eating me up inside. Fear. Worry. Pain. So I would just sing my songs and pretend I wasn't being held prisoner in hell.

Literally Overworld hell.

My song died off as the walls burst open. Laous stood on the other side, beady eyes drilling a hole through my face.

"Yes, can I help you?" I asked, like he'd just popped in for a chat.

"Do you have the location of the key?"

Sucking some air through my nose, I shook my head. "I'm trying to figure it out, but I'm almost positive that there was nothing like that in our house. We didn't collect things."

His face was going red, the tattoos blending into his skin tone. I wondered briefly why his marks were red while Daniel's were black. It didn't really matter, it just struck me in that moment as odd.

He took a step toward me, so I quickly said, "Is it a literal key? Did you check the house before you burned the damn thing down ... you probably destroyed it." That would be a nice sort of karma.

"This object would not burn." That was all he said, before he turned and flicked his head. A guard appeared at his side. Whatever joy I'd gathered from singing vanished in a puff of terror. The guard, again one I had never seen before, held chains in his hands. Before I could blink, or fight back, he was on me, trussing my hands behind my back.

"I'm telling you the truth!" I said to Laous.

He nodded. "I know you are. I'm very good at discerning truth from lie, but that doesn't change the fact that the information is within you ... somewhere. Trainer here is going to see if he can't give you a little incentive to figure it out."

Incentive? Everything clenched in my body; my legs seized up and wouldn't move. This didn't bother Trainer. He lifted me with one arm, half dragging my body out of the egg and across the room. I started struggling as hard as I could with my arms restrained.

I could not move him at all. I might as well have been fighting a rock. He was silent as he hauled me between what looked like hundreds of egg prisons. I kicked out, aiming for the back of his knees. He avoided the strike with ease. Shit, I really needed to work on my self-defense skills, even though something told me I wouldn't have much hope of beating this guy, even if I were the best trained fighter in Earth.

I tried to calm myself, tried to think again of what this key could possibly be. Keys were designed for locks, right? So it had to be something which could be used in that manner. Something metal, maybe...

Could the answer be hidden in the stories mom told me? Like the one about the boy and his dragon. Did they hide it here in Overworld? My frantic trip down memory lane was interrupted when we reached an arched doorway, stepping from the white egg room out into ... the underworld.

I had a perfect view from where we stood. The egg level, was sitting right above everything else. Then there were multiple ... platforms ... dropping down like a giant staircase, each step spanning off into the distance. I could barely see the ends of most of them, and yet somehow I could still see some detail from all the different levels.

Each level had a different version of hell on it. One was a land of fire and flame, red slashing across black, ringing with screams of pain and panic. Another was a land of monsters, giant beasts screeching in the air and on the land, ripping into each other and Daelighters. Right at the very bottom I was catching glimpses of an oasis, but it looked like you had to get through six or seven levels first before you had a shot at the oasis.

The Cascading Justices. It had to be.

Lexen had briefly explained it to me, but I couldn't remember if everyone who came here had to fight for their peaceful existence. Had he said something about good and bad deeds being weighed?

The guard startled me by growling in my ear: "Laous thinks you are our salvation, but you're our curse. The treaty cannot fall. I'm giving you a chance. If you make it through the justices, you will find escape."

He released me, and since I hadn't been prepared for it, I tumbled forward. Then a heavy boot into my back sent me flying right over the edge into the step below.

17

I couldn't tell you how long I fell for, my screams echoing in my ears. After an eternity, trees caught me, my body slamming into them with enough force to knock all breath from me. At some point the restraints holding my hands behind my back were torn free, almost taking my arms with them.

My body ended up wedged in the branches of a tree, my dress shredded, along with half my skin. I didn't move for many long moments, trembling, struggling to draw breath into my lungs. A branch had pierced my shoulder; the pain was muted as adrenalin coursed through me, but just trying to tug myself free was enough to send sharp jabs of agony through me.

Knowing I couldn't just hang there and starve or bleed to death, I sucked up every ounce of my bravery, gave myself multiple pep talks, and wrenched my arm off the branch with a loud scream. Panting breaths were my sole focus for a few moments as I waited for the stabbing sensations to die down. It didn't. Eventually I just sucked it up and dragged my pained and broken body further up the branch. My blood made everything slippery, and I was athletically challenged, so it took longer than it should have to reach the trunk. Once I was pressed against it, I wrapped my hand over the wound in my arm, applying pressure. I was losing way too much blood. There was no way I'd survive if I didn't get that under control.

A burst of hysterical laughter left my lips, followed by a sob. Who the hell was I kidding? There was no way I was making it out of here alive. Six lands of terror. *Six!* Before I would find freedom.

Still, I was never one to give up. I would fight until there was no more fight left.

I tore a strip off the bottom of my dress. It was pretty much in shreds at this point. I kept tearing until it was thigh level – the long dress would hamper my ability to run and climb. The heels would have to go too, but since I had no idea how my feet would hold up in this sort of terrain, I'd remove them when I had no other choice.

Searching for what looked like the cleanest part of the material, I pressed a bundle against my wound, and then used another long strip to wrap round and round my shoulder, compressing the blood flow the best I could. Once I had done everything I could to staunch the bleeding, I focused on the land I was in.

This hadn't been a level I'd seen much of when I looked across the justices, so I hadn't noticed what dangers were lurking within the trees. Logically I knew there had to be a ton, because ... it was hell. The first level of hell to be exact, which technically should be the worst.

The ground below my perch looked like what I'd expect to find in a forest. Undergrowth, leaves, shrubs. Perfectly normal. Lifting myself off the bough, I shuffled forward, ignoring the pull of rough bark-like material against my skin. The trees here were a lot like Earth's, except instead of wood they were made from porous-looking stone. Almost like ... coral. The leaves were also different, but not enough that you could tell until you got closer.

There was another thick branch just below mine. I lowered

myself down onto it, shuffling along again, before finding another lower one. I continued on this way, slowly, steadily, body fatigued but not letting me down yet.

When I was on the lowest branch before ground level, I slowly swung myself down. My lack of athletic ability was definitely going to be an issue here, but I was determined to survive. The skills needed would just have to be learned on the run. When my legs were dangling, my one good arm taking most of my weight as I lowered myself, my strength gave out and I tumbled the last few feet to the ground, landing with a solid thud.

There was a brief pause, like the land was confused about what had just happened, and then everything went to shit. The ground started to violently rock and buck like an angry bull trying to throw its rider off. I was tossed into a nearby tree, pain slashing my cheek and arm.

My body slid down to stop on a large bushy shrub and the land calmed. My heart was racing as I tried to figure out what had just happened, and how to prevent it from happening again. Deciding that the longer I sat still the worse it was going to get, I rolled off the plant and dropped almost gracefully to my feet.

The land bucked again, pitching me forward into the bushes. As soon as my feet left the ground, everything calmed. *Shit. Ass. Shit.* I'd figured out what made this level of the justices so dangerous. The moment you stepped foot on the land, it tried its best to get rid of you.

I needed to get back into the trees immediately. Of course I was now a good six feet from the closest tree. A tree which did not have a single branch I could reach.

Except ... if I was vaulted headfirst at it? As plans go, it was up there with the stupidest, but I couldn't think of any other way. Taking a deep breath, I jumped as far as I could, landing below the tree. Bending my knees as I dropped, I prepared myself for the bucking. The ground shot me up into the air, and then I was flying, shifting to try to reach the branch I'd been aiming for, and somehow I managed to grab on. My good arm shook as I used it to keep me steady while I hooked a leg over the bough and pulled myself up and across to rest on it.

The limb creaked; I felt it strain, too small to support my weight. I needed to move. Dragging myself toward the main trunk, a relieved breath left me as I ended up on a sturdier bough. Everything ached as I tried not to cry. This was no time for tears – even though it was starting to become painfully obvious that I was not going to survive this. Unless a miracle fell in my lap, there was almost zero possibility. I was tired, losing blood – the black cloth hid it, but I could feel how heavy and saturated it was getting. And this was only the first level.

Freaking Imperials. Hopefully Lexen would get Qenita to gut them the next time he saw them. "You better avenge me," I shouted, half delirious.

"You got it, gorgeous."

The low, deep voice should have startled me from the tree, but I was half passed out and only managed a gasp. My lashes fluttered as I tried to focus on the blurry person crouched in the tree across from me, a large shadow dressed all in black. The brief glimpse of face underneath his low cap was familiar, but I couldn't figure out how I knew him.

"I'm going to help you, Emma. But you have to trust me."

That voice too ... it was so familiar. And his eyes ... sad eyes.

I cried out, losing all thought as he lifted me up. Somehow he was able to hold me and step gracefully along the low branch. Everything after that was pretty blurry, walking through trees, jumping across bushy shrubs, until finally I couldn't hold on to consciousness any longer.

HEAT WOKE ME. My head was pounding as I struggled up from my hard resting place. Well, this was becoming a far too familiar sensation. Unlike last time in the egg, I immediately remembered everything that had just happened.

Swinging my head around, a few droplets of sweat flung off me. *Was I in a sauna?* At minimum I expected to see a roaring fire right at my side; it was that warm here. But there was nothing in the cave-like room. My skin felt tight as I lifted my right hand – the left was uselessly attached to my injured arm – to rub at the pounding in my temples, trying to relieve some of the pain there. Sharp agony burst behind my eyes, and before I could even move, my stomach roiled and I dry heaved over and over, nothing able to come out as I had not eaten or drank anything since I was taken.

Vomiting plus headache was a terrible combination, and I did briefly wonder if I was going to die in this cave.

Speaking of, how in all of this underworld did I get into a cave? I'd been in the trees. I definitely remembered some coral-trees, and a land that did not appreciate being walked on. The shadowy man ... he must have brought me here. Examining my surroundings – basic cave – I looked down to see that the wound in my arm had been rebandaged with a white stretchy-looking material. I still wore my tattered black dress, but there was more gauze along my arms and legs. The stupid heels were also gone, which would hopefully help me to stay upright.

I jumped to my feet – wincing at the increased pain in my head – as a broad-shouldered figure stepped into sight.

"Nice to see you're awake, badass. I was getting a little worried there."

I narrowed my eyes, face scrunching tightly as confusion hit me. "Daniel?"

The rasp of his name echoed for a beat. "What ... why are you helping me?" I was genuinely confused, trying to catch my brain up on what was going on.

He shrugged. "Lexen is my best friend. He's been with me

through more shit than I could even explain. I will always have his back. Family first, you know."

My throat went all funny as I tried to ask my next question. "Is Lexen ... all the Darkens, are they okay?"

Daniel nodded, which sent shots of relief through me. "They're fine, searching for you. Lexen..." I was desperate for him to finish that sentence, but he cut himself off, handing me a clear pouch that looked to contain water.

"It's legreto," he told me, the word rolling off his tongue. "It will help restore your energy, speed up the healing."

I eyed him closely, lifting the spout to my lips and tipping it back. I had no choice except to trust him. On my own I was dead. And right now I needed to rehydrate more than anything.

"I cleaned and stitched your wounds," he continued. "I can't do much more to help you because using my powers will alert Laous. Overlords are connected, and for now we're staying off the grid. Off the network."

As more of the cool liquid slid down my throat, I sighed. It was sweeter than water, almost like it had been flavored with fruit. Before I knew it, I had emptied his pouch.

"Crap, sorry," I said, holding it out to him. "I didn't realize I was drinking so much."

Daniel just waved me away, those rich cinnamon eyes flashing as he watched me. "That was all for you. I'm well aware of Laous' penchant to starve and dehydrate his prisoners. Makes them more pliable."

"How are you related to Laous?" I asked, unable to see one thing about that crazy asshole in Daniel.

Daniel's face took on a dark expression, giving him what I had dubbed "the Lexen look." "He is my uncle. He killed my father and took the overlord major position, even though it should have rightfully gone to me. Laous' marks were not inborn, they were placed there through a marking ceremony. This can happen if there are no naturally-born overlords, but since I was alive, it should never have gone down like that."

That urge to hug him came over me again. He was a plethora of contradictions, clearly a bad boy on the outside, but his eyes ... shit, they spoke to me on a level of pain that I'd rarely seen in another.

Sensing both of us needed some relief from the unexpectedly heavy topic we'd found ourselves in, I changed the subject. "I really appreciate the rescue—"

"Not rescued yet," he interrupted. "I only got you out of Shaken Ridge. There's still five more justices, and the next is my least favorite. Flames of Ether."

I nodded, swallowing hard. The land of fire – no doubt that explained why it was so hot. We were close.

"I need to get out of here and make sure my guardians are okay, because Laous will think I escaped. And he will punish them." There was no way for me to know if they'd received any help from the Darkens yet, so my worry was very real.

"He's going to suspect his man did something with you, so we have some time while he deals with him."

A slight relief, but still not much. "When did you know I was here?" I asked.

"As soon as you were taken ... Lexen lost his mind. While his family tried to calm him down and use diplomatic channels to find you, I came straight here. If there is something underhanded going on, Laous is usually involved."

Wishing death on someone was not a common thing for me, but the Imperial overlord was the exception. He was pure insanity. He needed to die.

"Lexen never brought a female to any of our meetings before," Daniel said; immediately I was paying attention. Of course I was; it was information about Lexen. "You were different. We all saw it, and I won't let my friend lose someone important to him."

I sucked in a hard breath, those words having a strong and dramatic effect on my body, on my heart. "I miss him." The very soft words escaped before I could stop them.

Daniel stared at me, probably unsure how to reply to that. I shook my head, trying to knock some sense into myself, but all that happened was a fierce headache slapped me with a wave of pain.

Even though I tried not to cringe, I still crumpled forward, hand pressed to forehead. "You need to rest," Daniel said.

I shook my head, more gingerly this time. "No, I can't rest until I'm out of here. We should go."

It was his turn to shake his head now. "I'm waiting on a package, so best make yourself comfortable."

His tone brooked no argument, so I sank to the ground, sprawling out, head cradled on my right bicep. "I'm just going to rest for a minute," I murmured to the now silent Daelighter. "Wake me as soon as you're ready to go."

I held his gaze until he inclined his head, and then I closed my eyes, seeking respite from the head pain. Exhaustion pulled me under almost immediately. It was a relief to escape reality for a short time.

Sometime later, low rumbles of conversation broke through my unconscious state. As I struggled back to the land of awake, the words became clearer.

"You got here much quicker than I expected." Daniel sounded surprised, but also kind of relieved.

"I was already in House of Imperial," came the short reply. That voice, the smooth husky accented voice, was enough to set my heart rate off.

There was a brief pause, before Daniel groaned. "Fuck ... Lex, what did you do?"

"Laous forfeited his life the moment he touched her. If my father hadn't stopped me, your overlord would already be dead. The council will deal with him, and then when they're finished ...

I will find him. Prepare yourself, you're about to get a promotion."

I'd never really feared Lexen, even in those first days of being a hostage, but his voice brimming with so much fury sent tendrils of adrenalin through my body. My instincts were telling me that he'd never hurt me though, and I wasn't just saying that because it was pretty clear I was half in love with him. I had no delusions he cared about me in the same way, but he always protected me.

I would stake my life on that.

Gentle hands brushed across my cheeks and I pressed into his touch. As my eyelashes fluttered open, the hard, dark lines of his face came into full view. His eyes were on fire, white flaming lights filling the dark depths.

"Hey," I said, my voice raspy.

Lexen's hand briefly clenched on my cheek, before he gentled it again.

"Hey," he started, before a rumble of anger shook his body. And the walls around us. It was already hot where we were, but Lexen was emitting even more heat. It was like he was a volcano about to erupt.

"I'm okay," I tried to reassure him, but he seemed beyond words again.

Then he kissed me.

As his lips crashed into mine with more force than I expected, but also far less than I needed, everything stilled. The pain in my body fell away. The worries churning in my mind disappeared. My body burned as hot as Lexen's as I pushed up into his hold.

He lifted me so I was straddled across his lap, our mouths clashing together, tongues sliding across each other, hands touching wherever they could reach. I was completely mindless; there had never been a kiss like this in my life before.

It was the kiss to end all kisses.

A throat cleared in an amused sort of sound and a sliver of clarity returned to me. And apparently to Lexen, because his hands gentled, as did our mouths. He pressed his lips to mine once more, slowly pulling away.

Sweet alien world. Did that just happen? Did Lexen Darken just kiss me like his life depended on it?

"I'm so damn sorry I left you alone," he murmured as we both stared, breathing a little deeper than was usual. "I left you and those bastards stole you right out from under me."

I lifted my arm, wanting to touch his face, but pain shot through my shoulder. Ouch ... wrong arm.

Lexen's head snapped to the side as he zeroed in on my white bandage. "What happened?" The question was asked slowly, deliberately, and for a second a shadow slithered across his face, like a specter of something more than the Daelighter he was.

"One of Laous' men threw her off the incubation level," Daniel said with bite in his tone. "She's lucky she landed in the trees. Had she hit the ground at that speed, the land would have crushed her."

Lexen didn't turn to his friend, lifting his gaze to meet my eyes again. "What else did Laous do to you? I need you to tell me everything."

Nobody would disobey Lexen when he spoke like that ... he was scary. Wasting no time, stumbling once or twice, I told them both what had happened from the moment I woke in the egg cage, leaving nothing out. "And he has ... or had a Draygo," I finished. "That's how he found out everything about the treaty. He used the power of the four houses by sending you all to Astoria. To find my family." As I finished, a stony sort of silence filling the cave, Lexen finally looked away from me, turning to Daniel.

"Like I said before, prepare to be overlord," he bit out. "Laous is a dead man."

Daniel swore a few times, rubbing a hand over his face in a tired manner. "A Draygo? I knew that my father had a draygone friend who visited. Maybe that was why Laous killed him. To get access to the Draygo..."

"He needs to be stopped," Lexen bit out. "And the council has to be informed of this new information."

He stood without dropping me on my head. I'd never had a guy carry me like that before, with such ease, as if he'd forgotten he even held me in his arms. I liked it more than I expected. The independent woman part of me rebelled, but another primal part liked the way he wrapped me up tightly, holding every part of me together, sharing his strength and comfort with me.

Still, now was not the time for me to be carried. I wanted to stand on my own two feet. So I struggled to be let down, and he immediately set me down, keeping me close to his side.

"We need to move fast." Daniel was serious as he glanced between us. "Laous is going to come for her, and he has way too much control over the justices. We can't beat him here, in his territory."

"Has anyone ever made it through the full six levels to reach the seventh?" I asked.

Daniel and Lexen both shook their heads.

Great. I should have guessed that. "So how are we going to get through it, then?" I asked, trying not to sound as pissed off and worried as I felt.

Lexen and Daniel exchanged a grin. The pair of them way too cocky and gorgeous for any girl to keep her sanity. "We're over-lord minors," Lexen told me. "We have one or two tricks up our sleeves. We can't hook to the network, but our individual strengths should be enough to get us out of here."

Daniel started to move, walking to the rounded stone doorway of this cave. There was another stone tunnel behind it, and at the end of that everything looked red. As we got closer, the heat increased to the point where I started to feel faint.

"Explain to me properly about this network you all use?" I asked, looking for information and a distraction.

"The network is an energy grid which spans across Over-world, connecting everything," Lexen said. "It runs just below our land, and flows between the magical elements. In Darken it's the stone of our mountains. Imperials have the Cascading Justices. Royale have a current through their legreto, their water. Leights are the forests, all of them connected, all of them alive."

"It's mostly where we get our energy and powers from," Daniel added. "Overlords have extra ties with the network. Ties we are born with. Especially within our own section."

"So Laous is pretty powerful right now?" I mused, realizing that the danger was far from over.

Daniel nodded. "Yes, he is. In normal circumstances I could call for a clear path to the exit from this place, but to do so now would alert Laous' warriors..."

I sucked in some hot air, trying to calm myself. Lexen or Daniel getting hurt was too awful to think about.

Further conversation was cut off as we stepped out of the cave for the first time. We stood on the edge of Shaken Ridge, in a section that almost seemed like an in-between place, where the ground didn't try and throw us around, but we weren't on the fire step yet either. Below us was a world of red. Heat smashed against me hard enough that I took a step back. This was impossible. There was no way for us to get through without burning to death. There didn't look to be a single path, just an ocean of lava and spouting fire holes.

"There are two paths through this land," Daniel said, reading my mind. Or the disbelief that was no doubt on my face.

"One requires a level of athletic ability which might be difficult for you," Lexen added, sending a smirk in my direction.

I flipped him off. "You saw me in one gym class." Which was exactly the same as every other gym class I'd ever been to, but I could totally pretend I had some sort of athletic skills hidden away.

"So what's the other path?" I looked between both of them, hoping it wouldn't involve climbing.

Lexen took a few steps back, lifting his arms in the air and dropping his head forward. I stumbled toward him, worried about what was happening, but before I got more than a step, Daniel grasped my biceps, holding me back. A rumble had both of our heads shooting up. Lexen was staring at me, his eyes a pure shining white. All of the black was gone. What looked like white electricity was streaming across his body, but I couldn't tear my gaze away from his eyes long enough to see what was happening.

"I'm going to let you go," Daniel said slowly. "Lexen's having some problems sharing. But you have to promise you won't go to him. He could hurt you if you get too close."

"I promise," I choked out.

Daniel released me, placing both of his hands in the air. He seemed to be silently communicating with Lexen. I was missing a lot of the finer details because I couldn't seem to focus on anything but the Daelighter standing before me covered in white light.

An icy blast hit me, stinging my hot skin. Wings burst from Lexen's back, huge and black, spanning out ten feet on either side. His skin took on a scaly texture as his body grew bigger, until he was almost twice his normal size. The white bolts of power that still ran across him slowly died off as he changed.

I swallowed hard, pressing my hand to my chest as I stared. "I'm starting to understand what he meant when he said he took on attributes of his dragon," I spluttered.

Daniel snorted, crossing his arms over his chest. "This is the power of the Draygo people. There are not many of them left, and Lexen is the only one to be born an overlord. Which makes him extra powerful. He does this hybrid shift using Qenita's energy, which means he is undetectable through the network. A power unlike any other."

Shut. The. Hell. Up! Seriously. I just kissed a freaking dragon-man.

"Will he be able to fly us the entire way down?" My question was far tamer than my thoughts.

Daniel shook his head. "No. Technically, we should be dead to even exist here. The Cascading Justices drain the living, even Imperials. It's why we mostly remain on the incubation level, where the network is the strongest and feeds our energy."

This was all too technical for me, especially when trying to wrap my mind around being dead. "Lexen will be able to skip at least two of the levels," Daniel added. "I can get us through the rest."

I nodded, sucking in a few much-needed breaths. Lexen tilted his head, his movements less human-like than ever before. The last of the light across his body faded; only those flames in his eyes remained. As he stepped closer to me, I was surprised by the fact that I had no urge to run. It was just a twelve foot man, parts of his skin covered in white and black scales, with huge wings towering above us ... no worries.

I examined his face, the same stunning and masculine features, a sheen of scales running down his cheeks and across his forehead. He still felt like Lexen to me ... an amazing, beefed up, dragon version. I mean, who didn't think dragons were cool? When he reached us, he swept me up into his arms, chest rumbling loudly as I sank against him.

Daniel was silently waiting, watching closely. I could tell part of him didn't trust dragon-Lexen as much as he did normal-Lexen. I wondered why I didn't have that same reservation. Maybe I was naturally stupid.

After a few moments I was adjusted to one side so Daniel could step in and grip onto the other, free side. Then, without any warning, Lexen's wings burst out to their full lengths and we were flying.

18

I'd thought flying on the magic carpet was scary, but it was nothing compared to the sensation of soaring like this. Lexen's powerful wings lifted us high and out over the flames below. I tried my best not to look down, because if I started to panic I would wiggle and he'd probably drop me.

I must have said something out loud about being dropped because Lexen let out a rumbly chuckle. "Trust me, little human. I'm not going to drop you."

His voice was at least ten octaves deeper than usual, a hybrid of man and beast, just like his body. "When are you going to quit with the 'little human' stuff?" I said, needing to find a distraction from the possibility of falling into flaming lava.

There was silence, just the whoosh of wings and the roaring of flames below. "It doesn't mean what it used to," Lexen finally said. He left it at that, and I found I was satisfied with his answer.

I'd sort of known that already; his voice used to snarl over the word "human," but now it was gentle. It had gone from an insult to a nickname.

"You two should stop fighting the inevitable," Daniel said. I twisted my head, my heart aching as I stared into his tortured eyes. How could there be so much emotion in a pair of eyes? Seriously.

"What's the inevitable?" I asked, voice barely audible above the crackling noise of fire and lava around us.

His lips twisted into a grin and I realized there was a deep dimple carved into his cheeks. Je-sus ... Lexen had hot friends.

"Emma doesn't understand our world," Lexen interrupted Daniel. "She doesn't understand what this sort of relationship would cost her. I ... won't do that to her, no matter what my draygone soul wants."

A growl ripped from his throat then and I was startled enough that I jolted. "Can you maybe not speak in code any longer?" Annoying Daelighters. "Tell me exactly what you mean for once."

His growls halted in an instant, and I almost died of shock when he answered me straight up: "Draygones have one mate – choosing someone who calls to their souls. It's an eternal bond. As a Draygo, I have a draygone soul within me. It is what makes me different from other Daelighters."

"Your dragon has chosen me?" I choked out, tears already springing to my eyes. I swallowed a few times, willing away the damp pressure. I'd always felt a link between us, so this explained a lot.

"Fuck," Daniel cursed. "She's going to cry, Lex. You know I don't deal well with crying females."

I snort-laughed. "I promise not to dry my eyes on you, Daniel."

He still wore a slightly panicked look, very at odds with his overtly masculine badass façade.

"Why did that upset you?" Even with his dragon voice there was a layer of concern tingeing Lexen's words.

I had to clear my throat a few times. "I felt a connection to you from the first moment I saw you. Before that, actually. Your house would always draw my eye and curiosity. Like that time you slowed your car next to me and cracked the window. There was this draw to go closer." Fear had made me run, but part of me wanted to open that car door and see who was inside.

Lexen nodded, clearly remembering what I was talking about.

"Then when you kidnapped me and were such a bastard," I continued, "it was easy to hide those feelings ... focusing instead on my animosity and annoyance. Only the more I got to know you..."

"The stronger it got," he finished for me.

"Yeah, pretty much."

I was about to ask him what he had meant about his world and dragging me into it, when I noticed that we were now past the land of flames, moving across an entirely new landscape.

"Gauntlet of *Malinta* ... monsters," Daniel said, following my line of sight. "Be grateful that Lexen will have the strength to bypass it also."

Grateful didn't even begin to cover it. It was a land of swirling sand. Which doesn't sound that terrible until you take into account that every time one of those huge mounds of orangey sand shifted in the breeze, claws would emerge. There were thousands of monsters pushing their way in and around the sand, fighting each other, ripping wisps of what I assumed were souls to shreds. Creatures I had no names for, creatures that would probably haunt me. The screams were very loud now that we were flying above it, and I had to tear my eyes away because I was starting to feel nauseous.

"Focus on me, Emma," Daniel said when I looked down again. "You can't help them. That's the first thing to learn about the justices. It's every Daelighter for themselves."

"How can you stand living near this place?" I murmured, my jaw clenching hard as I fought to stop the tears. Seeing those souls beg ... cry ... scream ... it was too much for me to handle.

Daniel's features were hard, his eyes flat. "Like Lexen, I have no choice. Born to the Imperials. Royal blood and all. I will fulfill my destiny to curate and punish the dead."

Which was clearly the last thing he wanted to do, judging by that tone.

"Are there any Daelighters who go straight to the land of redemption at the bottom?"

Daniel shrugged. "Imperial is the underworld for all of Over-world, all of the different lands and sectors. Some of them are brutal. Some are gentle. But very few beings make it straight to freedom. Most land in the bottom three platforms, though."

"We're also very long lived," Lexen reminded me. "Daelighters don't die from natural causes. Our lands and the network keep us young and strong, so we have generally lived a long life by the time we end up in House of Imperial."

That long life was still a concept I wasn't quite able to wrap my head around. No doubt it was one of those things preventing Lexen and me from having a chance together. Seemed pretty unfair that fate wanted to throw us together – his soul choosing mine as the one and only – and then I was going to die in sixty years. I mean, I'd take those sixty years, but I wasn't sure Lexen would want the same thing.

Shit, why was I even thinking about this? I was only seventeen years...

"What date is it?"

If anyone was surprised by my random question, no one showed it. "We have a different calendar to you," Lexen replied. "But I keep track of both. It's September 16th."

My birthday was yesterday.

I had turned eighteen and didn't even know, probably because I'd been stuck in an egg prison at the time. I'd turned eighteen without friends or family, without a single happy birthday or gift. Without my parents.

Lexen's hand pressed into my spine and he couldn't move it without dropping me, but somehow he managed to shift his thumb slightly. Letting me know he was there. "Breathe, Emma. Just breathe. I got you."

The rumble of those low words in my ear jolted me from the soul-crushing sadness tearing through me, tearing me down. A hand brushed my cheek and I whipped my head up and locked eyes with Daniel. We stared for an infinite amount of time, a sense of understanding between us. We both lived with a pain inside that was threatening to destroy us.

"Don't let the demons win," Daniel said, his tone solemn. "Keep fighting them, badass."

I actually laughed, shaking my head. I wasn't much of a fighter. It fell a little too close to exercise for my liking. Maybe I could read the demons to death. That was more my speed.

Lexen dropped a little lower as we passed the gauntlet of monsters. I tilted my head back so I could see his face better. My position was awkward, but I saw enough to know he was fatiguing.

"How much longer do you have?" Daniel asked, his gaze lowering to the land below us.

"I'm going to make it another two," Lexen bit out.

He was going to kill himself trying to save us, that was for sure. "Don't push yourself, just go as far as you can," I said. A thought hit me then. "Would it have been easier just to fly back up the top justice level?"

"There is no going back up to the top," Daniel told me. "This land works very hard to keep you in the justices. It only lets you move in one direction."

Great, we'd stumbled into the Overworld version of Ikea. We were screwed; we were never getting out of here.

"It'd be good if you can make it past the Maze," Daniel said to Lexen. "It's filled with tricks and riddles to solve. If you don't use your wits, you could be trapped there forever. We'll get through no trouble, but it will take some time. Time we don't really have."

We were above that land now. I blinked as I watched it below, trying to wrap my mind around the sheer size of it. From our angle, it was sort of easy to make out a path through the massive green hedges, but if we'd been on the ground, and had to navigate through the miles and miles of twists and turns, it would be next to impossible.

Lexen dropped a little lower again. We were only about twenty feet up from the top of the maze now.

"Go left!" I shouted down at a figure standing near a crossroads.

Daniel covered my mouth. "No helping, remember," he warned me again.

I shook my head, dislodging him. "You're not the boss of me. I'll help if I want to help."

Annnd I was back to belligerent teenager. Being told what to do was a huge pet hate of mine. Lexen laughed and Daniel wisely said nothing more. We dropped a little more, and I thought that Lexen's wing flaps were slowing. Lifting my hand, I pressed it to his chest. I wished I could send some of my energy into him, my clumsy, unathletic energy.

On second thought, that might be more of a hindrance.

His thumb caressed my spine again, and I swear I felt it all the way to the tips of my fingers. My hand was tingling where it remained pressed against him. I was wondering if our energies were clashing together somehow, because it felt like heat shifted between us, when Daniel cleared his throat. "Legreto level," he said.

Legreto level...

We had left the maze and were now over a platform of water. Sunlight brushed across me. For the first time it was warm, almost like I was outside. Pure magic, because there was still only darkness above. The Land of Legreto was stunning. I'd never seen clearer water, aquamarine in color as it thrashed around its level. There were pockets of land scattered along the body of water, land which disappeared at each rise and fall of the tide. It looked like you'd have to have perfect timing to be able to cross, jumping from one to another. I could see a plethora of creatures swimming in the depths of the water. Some looked huge and were shaped like sharks, so I was guessing it wasn't ideal to be caught in the waters.

We were going to find out, because Lexen was dropping rapidly now.

When we were about six feet above the water line, Daniel pointed toward a reasonably large domed section of land. "Put us down there, Lex. I see a clear run through."

"I ... can ... make it." The labored words were calling him out on his lie. But I knew he was going to give it a shot. He was practically gliding by this point.

I patted his chest, drawing his attention. "Just land. You still need enough energy to make it past the obstacles of the next level, and if I'm deducing anything from Daniel, it's that your energy is not going to come back. The justices will keep draining you."

I thought he was going to argue, but he tilted us just enough to glide the rest of the way down and land on the island Daniel had pointed out. His feet hit the ground, followed by his knees as he collapsed forward, flinging us free. I braced myself with my arms, stopping my face from smashing into the rocky ground.

Daniel was up and on his feet in a heartbeat, using his superior height to check out where we had to go next. Ignoring him, I took two steps back to Lexen, who was still on his knees. In his dragon form we were almost eye to eye. Actually he was still taller. I placed both hands on his cheeks, not liking the ragged way his chest heaved up and down.

"Are you okay?" I asked.

He gave me one of those rare smiles with all of his teeth, the one where it felt like I'd been punched in the chest. "Going to protect me, badass?"

I snorted. "You two – and Jero – need to work on your nick-name skills. You all suck."

His eyes shuttered for a moment as he sucked in a deep breath, then with a rush of light and energy he pulled the dragon form back into himself. Scales disappeared as he shrank to his normal giant size. The wings were the last to vanish, disappearing into his back somehow.

"I can conserve more energy like this," he explained as he got to his feet, with less grace than normal but still more than me.

"We need to move," Daniel interrupted.

Before I could say a word, he had turned and snatched me up into his arms. I opened my mouth to protest just as he leapt from the island, landing us in a small patch of water. It was only ankle deep when he landed, but by the time Lexen joined us, it was already to their knees.

I tried to ignore the weird creatures swimming close by, some with long lacy-looking tendrils. "I can take her," Lexen grumbled, staring his friend down.

"You can barely walk," Daniel shot back. "Accept my help for once. I'm not going to hit on your girl."

His girl. I stupidly enjoyed the sound of that, and Lexen didn't deny it. In fact it sounded like he mumbled "Better not" under his breath. Which made that enjoyment even greater.

Daniel leapt again, stumbling but managing not to drop me when we reached the next section. "You don't have to carry me," I protested, embarrassed to be such a burden. "No one has to carry me."

Daniel just laughed. "Lexen told me about gym class, as did some of my other House of Imperial classmates. This is safer."

Before I could inform him that all of the gossiping Daelighters could kiss my ass, a dark shadow splashed out of the water to our right, and in a move which should have been impossible, Daniel bent backward in some sort of *Matrix* shit and a huge blue thing sailed right past. I caught a glimpse of a million razor-sharp teeth, pointed nose, and huge bulbous eyes, before it splashed into the water again.

"Hang on," Daniel told me, turning to Lexen. "We're going to make three jumps in a row. That should get us out of here. You ready?"

"I'll still have more than enough energy to kick your ass when we get there, Dan. Don't forget that," Lexen shot back.

Daniel grinned, jumped and landed with ease. His feet were on the ground for a split-second and then he was jumping again. Each leap was minimum six feet long. There was no way in any world I could have made them on my own. When we reached the edge of the water, Daniel took a flying leap that sent us right over that step and down into the land below – the next level of the justices. I had an immediate flashback to my long fall into trees from the incubation level; screams ripped from my throat before I could stop them. My eyes were squeezed shut tightly because I really didn't want to see my death coming at me.

Daniel landed with a soft thud, jostling me only the smallest amount, before he set me down on shaky legs. Blinking a few times, I waited for my heart rate to settle. Lexen was mid-jump down the hundred-yard drop. He also landed gently, barely even making a thud. What in all that is holy? Both of the boys had landed like it was a three foot drop.

I narrowed my eyes, looking between the two of them. "So ... on Earth I'm athletically challenged. Here I'm what, the equiva-lent of a rock?"

Lexen just shook his head at me. "You're doing pretty good for a rock. And don't forget, a rock is the power which keeps both of our worlds functioning."

I grinned. That was a nice way to look at it. I could really get used to non-asshole Lexen.

Focusing my attention out into this last level of the Cascading Justices, I let out a long, exaggerated breath. "I could *really* use some good news. What is this level?"

Turning back, I caught Daniel and Lexen's grimaces.

"Well," the Darken Daelighter said. "This is the level of desires."

"What the hell does that mean?"

How could a land of desires be something hard or dangerous? Their expressions indicated they thought this was worse than the previous six lands.

"I see that look on your face," Daniel started, "and I promise you're wrong. This land will give you a ghost of everything you crave in life, the deepest hopes you hold in your heart. You will waste away chasing after something, only to find that it is not real, that you've been pouring your hopes and dreams, your literal soul into a façade."

Lexen let out a ragged huff. "I think we should rest for a little while. We're in the section between again and I can feel an ease on my energy. I need all the strength I can to resist ... especially with—" He cut himself off, but with the way he was staring at me, there was no doubt in my mind what he'd been about to say.

I looked again, across what looked like a beautiful snow-filled field. "What's with the snow?" I asked, wondering if that had something to do with desires. I had personally always found snow to be magical, but I knew for a fact not everyone felt that way.

"We don't see the same thing as you," Daniel told me. "This land shifts to each individual fantasy. The basic layout is the same, but I'm not a fan of snow, so I don't see that."

He didn't say what his land was, and no doubt it was quite a personal thing to ask that, so I didn't.

"I see snow," Lexen said, drawing my full attention. "Winter is my favorite season. I have fire and ice in my veins, but like Qenita, ice is where my heart lies."

Obsidian eyes flashed with white light. I could barely stop myself from touching him. The draw was getting stronger, especially since we had both acknowledged our feelings. Since we had kissed.

"I'll keep watch if you two want to rest," Daniel said, interrupting my fiery thoughts. "I'm the least battered and bruised."

I'd gotten quite good at ignoring the low aching throb in my injured shoulder. But as soon as Daniel mentioned it, the pain seemed to surge out with force. Together with my many other scrapes and my overwhelming hunger ... I was not feeling my best.

"A rest would be good," I murmured.

Daniel nodded. "I can give you an hour, no more. The council might have detained Laous, but he will figure out a way to come after us. We do not want to be in the justices when that happens."

Hell no we didn't.

Lexen held out a hand to me and I found myself smiling as I fitted my palm to his, our fingers interlacing. "Come on, badass little human. Let's get some sleep."

Fatigue was very faintly visible across his face. You'd have to be looking close to notice it, but it was there. I was going to make sure he definitely got some rest. He led me to the wall of the step, dropping to the ground and fitting his spine against it, pulling me down so I was lying in front of him. I could feel the heat of his body all the way down my back. I wasn't sure what to do, having never—

"Stop thinking so hard," he interrupted, murmuring into my ear. "I won't sleep unless I know you're safe. The only way for me to know that is if you're in my arms."

Everything in my body went boneless; I sank against him, letting my head fall to his bicep. It was a little too muscled to be comfortable, but it was definitely a step or two up from the ground. Daniel settled in a little away from us, perched on a flat rock, looking relaxed but somehow still alert.

I was so tired, but my mind just wouldn't shut down enough for me to sleep. All these new emotions, the strength of my feelings, the new experiences ... it was a lot. I was processing as fast as I could, but there was only so much "new" I could handle.

Lexen's hand, resting near my hip, started to move slowly. At first the gentle caresses sent fire through my body, but when he didn't touch anywhere other than that one spot, and the movements gentled, I found a haze washing over me.

My eyelids fluttered a few times, my breathing evening out, easing into something slow and rhythmic, and then I was fast asleep.

19

Not a single dream disturbed me. I don't think I moved a muscle until gentle nudges had me rising from unconsciousness with no concept of where I was. Or what had happened. It wasn't until I opened my eyes to see a darkly tanned arm that I remembered Lexen. More accurately, me sleeping on Lexen.

He shifted behind me and I rolled over so I could see him. He was wide awake, not an ounce of drowsiness in his gaze.

"Hey," I squeaked out, clearing my throat. "I hope I didn't kill your arm."

He wore a knowing look, like this half-smirk, half-smolder thing that he did so well. It was sexy as hell, especially teamed with the tousled dark hair. "Takes a lot more than a human to kill my arm."

I smacked his chest, instantly regretting that decision. Ouch. "You know what I mean. It must be dead from me lying on it." I let out a huff. "Last time I try and be nice to you."

He laughed, tightening both arms around me and rolling onto his back. I had no choice but to go with him, sprawling out across his chest. "I think I'm addicted to you," he murmured, our mouths brushing together. His expression sobered then as our gazes remained locked. "I'm starting to understand why Daniel wants to shirk his responsibilities. I've always accepted mine as part of my duty, even if I didn't particularly like the restrictions they placed on me. But now I'm wondering if the sacrifice is just too great."

"You've always accepted being overlord? Never fought against it?" I wanted to know the real Lexen, the foundation that built him.

He nodded, slowly, like he wasn't sure he was being completely truthful. "I've been groomed since birth, and I was ... fine with that. I like to be in control. I like to protect my people. I'm very good at doing both of those things. I'm the ideal candidate for overlord."

"But..." I started ... because I sensed a *but* there.

"But there were moments I contemplated jumping on Qenita and taking off. Soaring through the sky, traveling to other worlds." He paused, eyes focusing past me, before they came back to my face. "Until you, though, I've never had a good reason to truly question my duty."

I bit my lip, trying to stem the waterworks. I'd probably cried more in the last eight months than I had the previous eighteen years, so now I tried not to just sob for no reason. But Lexen was talking the duty in his life making no room for us. And that cut me deep.

"What would happen if ... you and I ... were together...?" I broke off.

He used his free hand to brush some of my disheveled hair back. "I have no idea. No human has ever bonded to a Daelighter. Especially not an overlord."

Rigid rules bothered me. I often disregarded them. But it wasn't my place to suggest that we ignore the very important traditions of his world. I also wasn't sure what bonding exactly entailed. I would like to start with dating, move on to bonded after that. If we didn't kill each other in the meantime.

The hand that had moved my hair settled against my face, cupping it. "You're worth fighting for, Em. I'm going to figure this out. There has to be a way."

My eyes filled and flowed over as I lost my battle with the tears. I couldn't stop from pressing my lips to his, just for a brief second so I could breathe him in. I pulled back as fast, giving him a watery smile. "This isn't just because we're in the level of desire, right?"

Lexen laughed again. There was a relaxed nature to him that I had never seen before. "No, this is all real."

He lifted his body up into a sitting position, bringing me with him, and stood. I was set on my feet, his huge body crowding round me for a beat, before he moved a little away.

"Where did Daniel go?" I asked, staring at the empty rock.

I'd forgotten about him. Since waking, Lexen had been the only thing on my mind.

"He's just gone to check if a certain path is there for us to use," Lexen said, his gaze scanning above my head.

Daniel appeared in that same moment, like we had summoned him. He waved us over, and as soon as we joined him he took a sharp right through two trees, leading us out into a wide, open field of snow. Well, snow for me anyway.

"Focus ahead," Daniel said, his voice even more rumbly than usual. Probably because of how rigid his jaw was. "Nothing you see is real. Don't let it sway you. We just need to cross this field and then we will be able to step into redemption. From there, I can get you back topside."

Bouncing on my toes a little – I was filled with nerves and I had to pee – I set my sight on what looked like the end of this platform. I could do this. I could ignore everything I saw, no matter what it was.

Feeling eyes on me, I lifted my head to find Lexen staring at me. "You ready, Em?"

Dammit, I was starting to like the sound of *Em* from him. The accent. The fact he wasn't sneering and calling me human. I was a goner.

"I'm so ready." I bounced again. "Ready as anybody here. I was born ready. Running is my thing."

So many lies.

I was trying to convince myself as well, so hopefully the pep talk worked. Lexen and Daniel just shook their heads at me. "Try not to fall over, badass," Daniel finally said.

I very maturely stuck my tongue out at him, receiving a glimpse of dimple in return. With a wink, he faced out across the snowy plain again. I saw him taking a few grounding breaths, before he nodded his head. "Let's do this," he growled.

Then we were running.

Now, under normal circumstances I have the grace of a hippo on land, all wobbling and roaring, jaw flapping in the breeze. Add in some snow to that mix and I turned from hippo to fish – flopping around, gasping for breath, dying second by second.

And I was wearing a dress.

We were all going to die.

Sure enough, I almost went down in the first five steps. Somehow Lexen snaked a hand around my waist, catching me with speed and grace. Athletic bastard. He didn't stop moving, flying along behind Daniel, who was pumping his arms rapidly, head firmly facing forward.

My feet weren't really on the ground now, so I kind of just skimmed my feet along as Lexen ran. At what looked like the halfway point, I started to feel hopeful. We were close. We were going to make it. I hadn't seen anything that would hold me up at all.

Daniel let out a roar then. "Leave me alone!" he shouted,

starting to slow. As we drew even, his eyes were squeezed tightly closed and he swung out blindly.

"What's happening," I asked Lexen.

There was no answer, so I tore my gaze from Daniel and looked up at the Darken. Those fires were back in his eyes; he watched his friend closely. "Will you be okay, for a second?"

Lexen's soft question jolted me, but I nodded rapidly. "Yes, I'll just stand right here."

He focused on me. "Don't move from this spot. Daniel ... he needs a little help right now. But ... don't move, okay? Can you do as you're told for once?"

I huffed, crossing my arms, rubbing them to create some warmth. It wasn't cold here, despite the snow, but a chill still ran along my body. "Just go," I finally snapped. Bossy dude thinks he just has to give me an order and I'll obey. I had been more than happy to stay in this spot, but the moment he ordered me to, well ... I immediately wanted to move.

"Stubborn little human," Lexen said with a grin, before turning away and slowly approaching Daniel. I narrowed my eyes on him, trying to drill a hole through those broad shoulders. Why did I not have the ability to shoot lasers from my eyes? Why?

That would be such a useful skill.

White drifted past my eyes, and I was startled to realize it had started to snow. Within seconds the snow was thick, blizzard-like, even though no breeze disturbed me. I lost sight of the boys, and despite Lexen telling – *ordering* – me not to move, I took a few steps closer to where I'd seen them last.

"Lex?" I called out, blinking rapidly to see clearer.

No reply. Well, not at first, but then I heard a faint whisper. I walked closer again, sure that I should basically be running into them now. Only they were gone. "Lexen!" I called louder.

The reply came from the last voice I'd ever expected to hear again.

"M&M ... baby ... it's Dad."

I ground to a halt, examining the man standing across from me. Chris Walters looked exactly like he had the last time I saw him: tall, strong, dark inky-black hair that was just starting to get a few grays at the temples; eyes two shades lighter than my cobalt, with one or two laugh lines around them.

"Dad?" He was the only one to call me M&M, my favorite candy and a play on my name. Apparently, when I was two, I snuck into his office and stole a bag and managed to eat a bunch before my parents found me. I'd always had a sweet tooth.

"I've been waiting for you to get here. We have so much to tell you." He took another step closer, the white snow swirling between us, but somehow not blocking my line of sight to him at all.

Hot tears were sliding down my cheeks, silently falling. "You're dead, Dad. You and Mom ... there was a fire."

He held out his hand. On his face was that kind smile he pulled out when I was worried about something. The sort of smile that happened in the eyes as well as the lips. "I'm so sorry we left you. If there had been any choice, we would have chosen differently."

My tears were falling so fast and furiously now that I was starting to choke on them, unable to breathe. "*This is not real, this is not real,*" I started to chant to myself, but I couldn't turn away. I just stood there, breathing in the sight of someone I loved more than life. Someone I had been missing with every part of my body and soul for months.

"Do you want to see your mom?" he asked me. "I can take you to her. We've made our home here in the afterworld. You can stay with us..."

Yes! I screamed loudly in my head. *Yes, God, please. I want them back.*

My feet were moving, stepping toward him, closer and closer. Snow mingling with tears was a weird sensation. Especially without the cold that would normally chill the water on my face. My dad waved me on, a brilliant smile lighting up his face.

"Just a few more steps, sweetheart."

I hesitated, something bothering me. "What's wrong?" Dad asked.

"I ... don't know. Just ... where did you say Mom was?"

She was always with Dad. They were nauseatingly in love, one of those couples where you had to leave the room when they were in it together. Especially when you were their kid. It was gross, for sure, but it also made me believe strongly in love. In finding the one.

They had been each others' ones. So why was Dad standing here alone?

"Where ... is Mom?" I repeated slowly.

That benign smile slowly faded away; his eyes took on a slanted groove of disapproval. I gasped as light swirled across his skin, and then the rich caramel skin tone, dark hair, and blue eyes faded away too. Standing there now was Laous, dressed head to toe in black. "Almost had you," he said jovially. "The land of desires is a difficult one for Daelighters to resist, and impossible for humans. Apparently since you are something between the two, you can fight the pull of desire."

I turned tail and ran as fast as I could in the opposite direction. "Lexen! Daniel!" I screamed.

For a brief moment I'd forgotten about them. Seeing my dad again ... it was a torture I would wish on no one. It had been amazing and absolutely devastating. My heart was crushing in my chest as I tried to run and breathe through all the snot and tears I had going on. The branch piercing my shoulder felt like a pinprick of pain compared to the sledgehammer to the chest I just got.

"Help," I cried out, coughing as my tears overwhelmed me. In the same moment I tripped, plunging forward to the hard ground. White might have coated the surface, but it was not soft like fresh snow. Kind of felt like I'd just face-planted onto an asphalt road, and I didn't even care.

Rough hands flipped me onto my back and I stared up into a face so dark with anger that it almost wasn't recognizable as Laous.

"Tell me what I need to know!" he screamed in my face. "Tell me where the key is or I will kill your family, your friends – every single person you have ever cared about in your life."

I felt a sharp pain in the back of my neck, but there was no time to worry about what it was. Laous wasn't kidding, that much was clear, but it was impossible to reveal something I didn't know. "You have the wrong person," I snarled at him. "I don't have any idea what the key is."

I was starting to get the feeling that my blood was never able to lead him to the key. It sounded like he needed me to give it to him all along. Otherwise why would he waste so much time trying to get me to tell him?

Laous let out a roar, and then in a flash slammed his fist down close to the side of my face. I flinched at the thud.

Tilting my head back, I gritted my teeth. "Maybe you shouldn't have killed the only people who would have been able to help you."

"You know, grubber. There is no way you don't know, and you have pushed my patience too far."

He might not have been able to kill me because he needed this information I apparently possessed, but that didn't mean he couldn't hurt me. His arm drew back again, his other hand wrapping around my throat. He hit me and agony exploded behind my cheek. My face went numb on that side immediately. He drew back and hit me again, same cheek, same blinding pain.

I tasted blood in my mouth as he swung for a third strike. Before it could land, something crashed into the side of him, sending him flying across the white land. I wriggled to the side, trying to put some distance between me and Laous.

Huge black wings caught my attention and I let out a low cry. Lexen. He was okay, and he had somehow found me. Daniel appeared at my side. "Emma, fuck, I am so sorry. My brother ... died in the cascades ... this is my fault."

I tried to answer him, but it was difficult to make my jaw work. So I simply shook my head multiple times. *Not your fault*, I told him with my eyes. This was all on Laous, that ... fucker.

Daniel fitted both of his hands under my arms, lifting me to my feet. The moment I was standing, blood rushed to my pounding head; everything went dark around the edges and I swayed on my feet.

"Rough day?" Daniel tried to joke, whilst carrying me in the opposite direction of where Lexen and Laous were now trading blows. The Darken overlord was much larger than the Imperial, his blows seeming to inflict a crap-ton of damage whenever he landed one. But Lexen was also very drained of energy, so I had no idea how long he could keep this up.

"No," I garbled out. "Stay ... Lex."

Daniel ignored me, picking me up and dragging me further away. I started to fight him, before nausea had me gagging and almost vomiting right down his shirt. Which would have served him right.

No matter how hard I fought, Daniel didn't move an inch. "Lexen is going to be fine," he said through gritted teeth. "He could destroy Laous with his eyes closed, two hands tied behind his back, and one foot removed. Lexen could take out all four overlords and not even break a sweat. He's the only one the four houses fear. He's the draygone lord."

"I d-d-don't ... care."

Goddammit, this was not the time for my face to be beaten in and swelling rapidly. I really needed my words right now. The ground started to shake as Daniel moved me further away. We were almost to the edge of the field. I could only just make out

Lexen in the distance. All of a sudden we stopped. Daniel let out a low curse.

"He wouldn't," I heard him say, disbelief in his voice. "Laous has lost his goddamn mind."

I had no idea what he was talking about, until I noticed that the white snow was changing again, this time to a black substance. Some landed on my arm, leaving behind an ashy smudge.

"What's he doing?" I asked, panic allowing me to fight through the pain and speak semi-clearly.

"He's going to purge the justices," Daniel bit out. "Which means every being on it will be wiped out. Like a fresh start ... a reset, if you will."

"We have to help Lexen," I yelled, flinching at the sharp stabbing in my face.

Daniel shook his head. "The reset is an ultimate power. Overlord power. There is nothing I can do to stop it. We would not make it to Lexen in time."

"What happens to all the beings in the purge?"

"They are reborn, back to the incubation level. They will have no memories of their previous life."

I knew my eyes were so wide that my eyeballs could have fallen right out with no resistance. "We can't leave!" I screamed at him.

"I'm sorry, badass. Lexen would want me to get you out. We're close enough to make it."

"Daniel, I will never forgive you. We cannot leave Lexen!" I tried, pleading, with just a hint of bite. "I mean, are you even sure? Why would Laous reset himself?"

He lifted me with ease and sprinted. The ash was falling faster, swirling around us, and just like the snowy blizzard from before, almost all visibility was cut off. "Overlord majors are never reset," Daniel shouted.

I screamed and kicked out, flailing my arms at the same time.

I refused to do this. Laous would not reset me if he needed whatever information he thought I held. Which meant he knew Daniel was close enough to get me to safety.

This was all about Lexen, about taking him out of the equation. Daniel moved so fast my head was literally smacking into his shoulder as he ran. The darkness increased until it was all I could see. Then we were flying. I'd done this enough times recently to know that Daniel had just jumped off the edge of the last justice. We were heading toward redemption, and I was wishing with all of my heart that I could somehow go back the way I'd just come.

Our landing was soft, barely a jolt compared to the way he'd been smacking me around when he ran. I'd had my eyes closed for the drop, but opened them as soon as we hit the ground. The falling ash was gone; now it was all bright lights, warmth, fields of green, oceans in the distance, stunning little homes nestled in the hills.

"Redemption is pretty," I said flatly.

Daniel took an extra look around, coming back to me. "Yes, if you make it this far, you will have peace."

I felt like I was a thousand years old. I had been through a lot, too much, and I wasn't sure I was going to survive losing Lexen too. Peace was not possible for me, not even if I lived here forever.

Daniel tilted his head back, staring up the edge toward the level of desires. For a second, hope sprang to life within me. I thought he was waiting for Lexen, but then there was an explosion. Dark ash burst across the sky in a puff of black, before it dissipated out into nothing.

"No!" I cried, hoarse and desperate. I grabbed Daniel's shirt, digging my fingers into his skin as I pulled him toward me. "Lexen will be okay, right?"

There was no answer. I appreciated that he wasn't going to lie to me, but as that sliver of hope disappeared I died a little more inside. Drawing on everything I had learned in the last eight months, I tucked the agony deep inside, pushing it down so far down I could no longer feel anything at all.

"So, what do we do now?" I sounded detached, which was exactly how I felt.

Daniel was watching me closely, those sad eyes dissecting me. I didn't care. He could stare all he wanted; there was nothing more for him to see. I had been a mess for eight months, a mess who had started to see the light at the end of the tunnel of darkness. Only to now be right back to that same dark place.

"I'll get us out of here. Stay close." Daniel was as emotionless as me, and through my own desensitized brain I realized that he had just lost one of his best friends. Daniel might have had fewer people in the world than me to care about, and he'd just lost one of them.

A part of my heart thawed just enough so I could step forward and wrap my arms around him, taking both of us by surprise if his tense body was any indication. "I'm so goddamn sorry," I whispered, choking up on the last word.

He remained tense, and I was just about to pull away, because awkward, when his arms came around me and he returned the hug with force. I was level with his chest, and I could hear the rapid race of his heart as he clutched me closer. His body shuddered a few times, as if he was fighting against the emotions consuming him.

Consuming us both. Overwhelming grief.

"Five minutes. I've been gone for five minutes and you're already moving in on my girl."

It took longer than it should for the voice I was hearing to register. Daniel and I pulled apart and a hoarse cry left me. Lexen was shirtless, his upper body looking like it was carved by the gods themselves, all rippling muscles and bronze skin. His wings were out, curving down around him.

"Lexen..." The disbelief in my voice was strong. I wasn't sure if this world was creating him, or if he was really standing before me.

"How?" Daniel asked, taking a step toward his friend. "How the fuck are you alive?"

Lexen shrugged, his face turning haunted for a second, before wiping clean. "Apparently dragon lords cannot be reset. The moment Laous realized that, he took off, and I came after you two." His wings and scales faded away in a brief lightshow, then he was back to regular Lexen. Minus a shirt still.

I ran for him as fast as my clumsy legs would carry me. I wasn't even that close when I leapt at him, but luckily he had all the skills I lacked, stepping forward and scooping me up, pressing me close to his chest.

"I thought you were dead," I sobbed, smacking him on the chest. "I thought you had left me ... alone."

He dropped his forehead down on mine. "I thought I was dead too. Your face was the last thing I saw. The Draygo in me has decided. I can't let you go. It might be selfish as hell, but if you want to give this a shot with me, I will do everything in my power to make sure that you and I have our chance."

I kissed him, cutting off whatever he had been about to say next. The pain from my bruises hurt for a beat, but the moment he took control, the moment his tongue stroked mine, mouth moving over my lips with a skill and precision that had my body turning to jelly, I forgot all about my injuries. His hands cupped under my butt as he hauled me further up his body, my legs wrapping around his waist as I pressed into him.

Lexen captured the moan that escaped from me with his mouth. The kiss was just getting to the point where I felt like I was about to self-combust when he pulled back. I huffed, breathing embarrassingly deep, meeting his star-lit eyes. "Reall-lyyy glad you didn't die."

Lexen dropped his head back slightly, laughter bursting from him. "Me too, little human. Me too."

Daniel's drawl distracted us. "Why is it that I always feel envious and slightly awkward when I'm around you two?"

Lexen set me on my feet, tucking me in close to his side, before holding out his other arm to Daniel. The pair did some sort of fist bump, half-hug bro thing.

"Thanks for getting her to safety," Lexen said, turning serious.

"Thanks for not dying. That would have sucked."

Daniel was the overlord of understatement too, apparently.

Happiness lifted me up. I had to press a hand to my chest because it felt like my heart might actually beat right out of it. As I rubbed the heel of my hand across my sternum, I paused at the lack of bump there. Not the normal chest bumps, my boobs were still very much in their normal position, but there was something missing.

My necklace.

I rubbed the back of my neck and felt the sting. I must have lost it on the desire level, when Laous attacked me.

Lexen noticed my expression. "What?" he asked, his voice rumbling out as he stepped in front of me, surveying our surroundings.

I wrapped my hand around his left wrist. "It's nothing. I just noticed that I lost my necklace." The last thing I had from my parents.

Lexen brushed back my hair, sliding his thumb across my cheek. "We'll find it. Once this reset is cleared, I'm going to figure out a way to search the justices. It is somewhere, Em."

I smiled at him. "It's okay. Apparently I'm dating a guy who can get his hands on a ton of starslight stone."

Lexen's eyes darkened, which meant they were pitch black in that moment. "I've got mountains of it. I can literally shower you with starslight stone. It's just ... none of it will be from your mom, and I know how much that one piece meant to you."

It had meant a lot to me, but I would always have my memories of my parents. I would always have them in my heart. Losing the necklace wouldn't take that away from me.

"I saw my dad in the desire level," I told Lexen, my voice cracking. "Walking away from him was the hardest thing I've ever done. But ... I knew it wasn't real. Laous didn't understand how I could resist, but I think it was because there is a bond already between us, Lex. You, me, and your draygone soul. The bond gave me the clarity I needed."

I was hauled up and into his arms in a flash, his lips pressing delicious kisses along my jaw and to my lips. "What do humans call it?" he murmured, as he continued to torture me with kisses. "Ride or die? You're my ride or die, Emma Walters."

Finally his lips found mine and I went completely mindless, lost in the sensations of kissing this guy.

Eventually Daniel called out to us. "Come on, you two. Enough with that ... we need to hitch a ride on the next transporter out of here."

I let out a breathy sigh as I collapsed against Lexen's chest. "Not sure I can walk. Might need a moment."

He laughed, hooking an arm around my waist and half carrying me to where Daniel stood, bemused expression on his face.

Despite the beauty of the redemption world, none of us looked back. There was nothing for me here, no reason to want to stay. I was ready to move forward, with Lexen, with the rest of my life.

And I was ready for some answers.

20

A multitude of faces stared back at me. The council seemed to be stuck between explaining what had happened and trying to dissect me with their eyes. At least a healer had somewhat dealt with my face and wounds, so now I was no longer in pain while I waited for them to get to the point.

"Get to the damn point!" Lexen snarled, reading my mind. His hands clenched on the table as he glared at each of them.

As soon as we had taken the secret transporter out of the level of redemption, Lexen had summoned the council. We were in House of Darken, in a room with a table large enough to hold everyone, which included Lexen's parents, Star, Marsil, and Jero, all of whom had greeted me with hugs and shouts. They'd truly been worried about me, and their delight at seeing I was back safely – Lexen too – was enough to mend a few of the broken pieces of my soul.

A female council member stood. Like almost every other Daelighter on the council, she looked to be in her early thirties. She had straight dark hair and large reddish-brown eyes.

"Laous has disappeared, and based on your testimony of his recent actions, he will never rule House of Imperial again. Daniel will be stepping in as overlord for the interim, until he can be initiated into the position."

Her speech was interrupted by Roland. "If Laous is going after the second secret keeper, how are we going to figure out where he is to stop him?"

Another council member, a blond male who was probably from Royale, let out a breathy sigh. "It appears that Laous has been planning this for a long time. We really should have seen it sooner, but he was always very uninterested in the treaty whenever we discussed it. He never showed any sign of wanting to destroy it."

"He needed a key," Lexen informed them. "He was trying to get Emma to tell him where it was."

The councilman's eyes shifted to me then. "Did you divulge the location to him?"

I shook my head. "I have no idea where the key is. My parents never told me."

"Did they ever give you something of value? Something from this world perhaps?" another woman on the council asked, pushing back her long ringlets of ashy blond hair.

I stilled. "Like ... a piece of starslight stone?" *Holy shit I was slow.* Was my stone the key? I'd been so focused on a literal key, something metal and long which could open a lock, that I forgot about the stone I wore. I'd never even considered the possibility, but it made sense.

"I had a necklace ... that possibly had a piece of starslight stone on it," I said slowly. "It disappeared in the justices. I'm not sure exactly when, but it could have been when I was fighting with Laous."

The blond man let out a huff. "So now he will be heading for the next secret keeper, the one born in House of Imperial."

Well, shit. "We need to find them first!" I demanded, on my feet as my chair screeched across the floor.

"We're working on it," the council informed us. "It is

extremely difficult to find these humans without the piece of stone you had. That stone was a sliver from the original piece gifted in the treaty."

Saywhatnow? I'd been wearing something that important for years and had no idea. My parents really should have told me, but knowing them as well as I did, they no doubt wanted to protect me for as long as they could.

"What will the necklace do? How is it a key?" I asked.

A small woman with silver hair stepped forward. She had been hovering at the back of the council group, not sitting. The moment she pushed to the front, all conversation died and everyone turned to her. She was definitely someone important.

Her silver hair threw me off at first, but her face was unlined, her eyes almost as dark as Lexen's.

"Did you bleed on the stone, at all?"

Her question took me completely by surprise, and I was a little slow to reply. "Uh, yeah, I probably did." I touched my now healed shoulder. "I got stabbed by a tree. I had blood all over me."

The woman gave a single nod. "That sliver of stone is the key to finding the original stone. It can be used as a scrying tool, when activated with the right blood. Your blood on it will lead to the second secret keeper, the Imperial born human. Then it needs to be dipped in the blood of the second secret keeper to track the third, and so on."

That was why Laous reset the justices. He wasn't trying to make sure any of us got to safety. He had found my necklace and knew he had what he needed. So he'd tried to kill us all.

"What is our next step?" Marsil asked. As he stood tall, decked out in all black, with shit-kicker boots on and a heavy expression, he totally looked like a warrior.

"With Emma's permission, we'd like to take a little of her blood and see if we can track the second secret keeper ourselves." She looked directly at me, and I nodded without hesitation. I would do anything to make sure Laous didn't get his hands on him or her.

She continued: "While we do that, everyone else will return to their normal lives. The treaty is not under any direct threat."

Ambra stood. Her graceful form seemed frailer than the last time I'd seen her. "Will the overlord families return to Astoria? To Starslight Prep?"

Everyone on the council nodded this time. "Oh yes, they must finish their school year," the silver-haired woman answered. "Laous might have initiated it for the wrong reasons, but the human government is loving this sign of 'trust.' It's important to keep up appearances, especially now."

School, right, totally forgot we still had that thing going on. Ambra joined her sons in looking unhappy, all except Lexen, who was watching me with an amused expression.

The entire council stood. Each lowered their head into a half bow toward Roland and Ambra.

"We will be in touch when we have any information," silver-haired lady told the Darkens. She then turned to me. "Do you mind?" she asked, holding her hand out. Rising to my feet, I took a step toward her, and she reached out and placed her hand in the crook of my elbow.

A brief prickling sensation followed, and when she pulled back there was a thin trace of red following her fingertips. "That should be enough. Thank you," she said, lowering her head slightly to me. *Much easier than a blood test, that was for sure.*

She faced Lexen. "I'm really glad you and your draygone mate are okay."

Dead silence filled the room. I wiggled a little on the spot, immediately uncomfortable.

Lexen was the only one to still look relaxed. In fact the asshole laughed, like she'd just amused him immensely. My mouth dropped open as he crossed to her and wrapped his arms around her shoulder, dwarfing the tiny female. "Colita, I never could keep anything from you."

My stunned face must have tipped him off to my astonishment, because he released Colita and stepped over to me. "She's my *drenita,* or as humans would call it, godmother. She's also a powerful seer, able to scry visions of the future in the sacred legreto."

"The same sacred waters I was born in?" I asked, my eyes flicking between him and Colita.

She nodded. "The very same. And you'll be happy to know, that having been born in those sacred waters, you – and the other three secret keepers – have the longevity of life that is part of all Daelighters. Even though you are almost completely human, in your blood runs some of our energy."

Jero laughed. "Are you telling me that pretty girl here is hooked into the network? That's fuc ... damn awesome."

Roland, who seemed to find Jero amusing – had to be the only one who did – let out a chuckle. "We can show her how to plug in – one day, when she isn't due back at school."

That sounded like a good idea. I was full up on new experiences at the moment.

"Wait," I called, halting the council just as they were leaving. "If secret keepers live forever, what happened to the ones before us?" I knew that all four had to be born in the same year, so I assumed the other three with me were all around my age. But the treaty had been active for over a hundred years.

Colita answered: "There was only one set of four before you. One of the men was hit by a car and killed. Luckily his wife was pregnant at the time. His daughter became one of the secret keepers in your four."

"So if one dies, you have to replace the entire four?" I wondered out loud.

Her smile was kind. "Yes, because the bond is broken."

They left then before I could think up any more questions. I had probably learned enough that day to keep my mind busy for a lifetime anyway. As soon as the door closed, Star burst up from her chair and threw her arms around me again.

"I can't believe you were in the land of Imperial. You were in the justices. You could have been reset!"

She'd been saying this over and over since we all got back, her arms strangling me like she was worried that if she let me go I would disappear. The only time she had stopped was when the council arrived.

Untangling her arms, I sucked in some deep breaths. "I'm fine," I reassured her again. "Lexen and Daniel were with me almost the entire time."

I turned my attention to the overlord major. "Are the Finnegans still okay?"

"Yes," Roland answered immediately. "As soon as they got word to me, I stationed guards on them. They're keeping Daelight Crescent locked down. The Finnegans have been informed that you are safe. They can't wait for you to return home to them."

I swallowed the rough lump in my throat. Ace had really come through for my family. Apparently he had been in on the big secret. All of the security was. And he had a means to get a message to Overworld.

"Will I be able to return to Overworld?" I asked, needing to know while also dreading the answer.

Lexen let out a rumbling growl that sounded very animalistic. Some of his dragon soul was making an appearance. "You're one of the few humans who will always be able to wander between the worlds. Once you learn the network, you can use the transporters just as we do."

He tore his gaze from mine to meet each of his family's. "Colita was correct, my draygone soul has chosen Emma. We're going to take it slow, but if I have anything to do with it, my little human is going to be around a lot."

The guy had smooth moves, that was for sure. I couldn't

disagree, because in my heart there was nothing I wanted more than to stay here in Darken. In this house filled with a family I adored. With the man I more than adored. It was bittersweet, learning the truth of my parents' deaths, and my true purpose as a secret keeper. But there was also some hope. Hope that I might eventually find happiness and a home again.

Roland and Ambra both walked over to stand before me and Lexen and I waited to hear their response. How would they feel about a human and their future overlord together? I knew from Lexen it had never happened before...

Ambra's hug took me completely by surprise as she squeezed me so tightly all the air exited my lungs in one big oomph. "Welcome to the family," she cried. "I couldn't have chosen someone better for Lexen. You have a strong heart and soul. You're a survivor."

Do. Not. Cry. Do not cry!

"We're going to be sisters!" Star squealed.

I snorted, swallowing down my emotions. "Hold up, let's not get ahead of ourselves here. I only just turned eighteen."

I was so tuned into Lexen that I noticed immediately when he stilled. "We missed your birthday?" he asked me.

I smiled, shaking my head at him. "Not a big deal, seriously. It's just another day."

"We don't celebrate birthdays here," Jero said. "But we know they *are* a big deal on Earth. We've seen all the squealing teens when they turn the big one-eight. You should have told us."

I shrugged, aware that Lexen still looked upset. "I didn't even know. It was only when Lexen told me the date in the justices that I realized my birthday was yesterday."

"You spent your birthday being held captive? Hurt?" Lexen was pissed, and before I could answer he swept me up in his arms and was marching out the door.

Laughter sounded behind us, Jero calling out a few suggestive things, which no doubt had my face turning an interesting shade of pink.

"Put me down!" I struggled against him, wanting to walk.

Lexen ignored me, his march losing no speed even as I struggled. "My draygone soul does not like that we missed a special day for you, Em, so please let me make this up to you."

His voice was gruff, but not quite as rumbly as before. Conceding defeat, I relaxed back into his arms. "Fine, but I am warning you, if you continue to use your strength to push me around, I'm going to fight back. And I fight dirty."

The hard rigidness to his jaw relaxed a little. "Is that right? Well, rest assured, I will never use my strength to do anything other than protect you. Your body. Your heart. Your soul."

As lines went, that one was pretty freaking stellar. My friends back home would have said it was cheesy, but I never understood why someone expressing a strong level of caring for someone was deemed corny. I found it sweet.

"I'm not sure I understand this dragon thing," I said quietly. "But I'm really glad your soul found a mate in mine."

He growled, pulling me closer and burying his head into the space between my head and neck. As he pressed his lips to my bare skin, I tried not to breathe embarrassingly loud.

"I'm a mess," I whispered, biting my lip to stop from saying anything else.

Lexen lifted his head, his lips tilted enticingly in a half-smile. "You're about as far from a mess as is possible. Even if you were, where we are going it won't matter.

Okay, then. I was two parts relieved and one part seriously disappointed when Lexen finally set me on my feet. A girl could get used to being carried, but mostly this girl liked to stand on her own two feet. Let's say ninety percent of the time.

I expected to be led to the basement with the transporter, so I was astonished when we ended up in Lexen's room. He opened the glass doors. Qenita's giant white head popped in almost immediately and I managed not to scream or pee myself.

"Do you trust me?" Lexen asked, holding his hand out for me. I didn't even hesitate. "With my life."

He helped me up onto the back of the massive dragon, her hard, cold scales scraping across my bare skin. The dress was pretty much done, and I was really looking forward to getting out of it.

Lexen settled in behind me, his warmth chasing away the chill of Qenita's hide. I was extra grateful for his support when Qenita's huge wings started flapping on either side of us, and then far more gracefully than I had expected, we were up and soaring across the sky.

Nerves had me tense at first, but her gliding was so smooth that I soon settled back against Lexen. He wrapped his arms around me and I could have died right then a happy human.

Qenita rose higher and higher, flying in a zigzag pattern through the underground. The heat and brightness increased as we got closer to the dragon fire that filled the top of the cavern. I was just about to ask if Lexen was taking me to a fiery death when Qenita veered off to the left, toward a huge opening in the side of the mountain, five times the size of the one we'd used in the lower sections to enter.

Like her own special dragon entrance.

Once we were out in the open, soaring in the cloudless sky, I lifted myself up so I could see absolutely everything. "It's so beautiful," I said with a sigh. "Mountains and snow and the brisk air. I've always loved this. I literally begged my parents every year to take me to Big Bear during the winter."

I twisted so I could see him. "If this was where I was born, why do you think we lived so far from the mountains?"

"Probably because they were trying to stay hidden. Be in the last place that would be expected."

Made sense, like someone from Royale hiding in the desert.

The less water, the less obvious their location. Or was it more obvious ... because somehow Laous had still found us. The council had said he used the energy of the four overlord minors, as I'd suspected. Still, it kind of felt like he would have needed more than that. Did someone betray the secret keepers? Tell Laous where to start looking?

Qenita banked to the right, distracting me from those heavy thoughts. I let out a low gasp as she glided down toward a range of mountains, three or four all closely linked. Unlike a lot of the ranges here, these had flat tops. I leaned over to see the sparkling aquamarine-filled craters atop them.

"These are not the sacred springs," Lexen started to explain. "It's forbidden to use them recreationally, but this is a sister spring to them, fed from the same underground reserve. Blessed by the dragons."

As Qenita came to land, I pretty much sprang off her, and would have fallen flat on my face if she didn't catch me with her wing. Damn my lack of athleticism.

"I'm so sorry," I said, rubbing my hand across the rigid spines which lined those majestic wings.

She blew a ring of cold into my chest and I knew it was all good.

Lexen joined me, far more gracefully, and we crossed to the first of the pools. Steam rose up across the lot of them, the twinkling water even more enticing from close range. "Can we just jump right in?" I asked, already preparing myself for Lexen to see my body. Weirdly enough, I wasn't that worried about it. He'd seen me in various states of undress anyway, and I had underwear on.

"Yep, jump in, the pools all feed into each other, so you can explore as far as you want."

Amazing. The water literally ran for miles ... on top of a mountain. Each pool broke into sections through natural rock formations, and there were even a few waterfalls in the distance. I didn't wait a moment longer, stripping off the rag that used to be a designer gown.

"This legrato has healing properties," Lexen said, his eyes filled with fire as he watched me. "It will help with the last of your injuries."

I still had the bandage on my shoulder. There'd been no time to remove it, so I lifted my arm and tried to reach the end of the white gauze. But, of course, Daniel was an overachiever in bandaging, and it was too tight for me to budge.

"Let me help you." Lexen appeared at my side, shirtless now, wearing a pair of shorts that fitted his body far too well. I was probably going to touch him because I couldn't help myself.

His hands were gentle as he worked the end free, fingers brushing against bare skin as he unwrapped it over and over. He then dropped down lower and removed the bandages still on my legs. One at a time. Torturously teasing me as he dragged his finger across my body.

"There you go." His voice sounded a little rougher than usual, his eyes telling me that he was definitely feeling the burn between us.

Neither of us moved as steam rose up around our half-naked bodies. "You're going to have to stop looking at me like that, little human," Lexen growled. "I only have so much restraint, and ... we're taking it slow."

As much as I wanted to disagree with him, I also knew there was no need to rush our relationship. Apparently we had forever to figure it out. Sucking in a shaky breath, I turned around and jumped straight into the warm pool. I went under completely; it was deeper than I expected. The sensation of the water caressing my skin, cleaning away the remnants of the battle I'd been through, felt like the second best thing to happen today.

The first was the kiss, of course.

Lexen joined me, and together we rose to the surface, kicking our legs to stay afloat in the hot springs. Swimming over to the edge, there were seats that seemed to be naturally formed in the rocks. Lexen and I both settled back into them. I let my legs float up in front of me, moving them slowly through the water. I waited for the cuts and grazes that littered my body to sting, but instead they felt soothed, especially the one on my shoulder.

"How often do you come up here?" I asked, turning my head so I could see what Qenita was up to.

She was not where we left her. It wasn't until a cascade of water washed over me that I realized she was bathing in the next pool over, one large enough to fit her giant form. I chuckled as she played in the water, acting very puppy-like.

"Before my time on Earth, Qenita and I would come here at least once a month," Lexen answered me. "One of the benefits of being dragon lord."

The urge to press myself into all of his smooth chest muscles just got too much, and as I scooted closer he draped an arm around me. "Leaving Qenita was one of the reasons you hated going to Earth, wasn't it?" My quiet question fell on his chest, my face pressed against it as it rose and fell gently.

"Yes, it's painful for us to be apart for extended periods of time. Plus, I missed her."

Such a simple answer, but the emotions behind those words were not. It had been more than a little difficult for him. I sat straighter, wanting to meet his eyes. "I'm sure you can petition the council to remain behind. As long as most of the overlord minors are there, no one would know, right?"

Lexen's lips hit mine, taking me completely by surprise. I recovered in a heartbeat, straddling him in a single movement. The going slow thing died almost instantly as the fire between us exploded. Hands were everywhere as Lexen's tongue caressed mine and I lost all sense of reality.

The scrape of skin, the taste of him on my lips, the rumble of his chest under my hands. Lexen was beyond hot, everything about him physical perfection, but it was so much more than that which had my attraction levels soaring into the sky. His loyalty. Heart. Caring nature.

It was too much. But I definitely would not complain.

When it was breathe or pass out, I wrenched my mouth from his. Our bodies remained locked together, all of his hardness pressed against my softness.

"That was certainly a nice response to my suggestion of staying here on Overworld."

He grinned, cupping my face with both hands. I loved how much he touched me; it was like he couldn't help himself. And I was a sucker for all of it.

"While I would love to stay with Qenita," he told me, "there's no way you're going back to Astoria without me. I have no idea what Laous is up to. I have no idea what the future holds for the treaty, but the one thing I know for certain is that I can't be away from you."

I groaned. "Tell me again why we're taking it slow." I rocked into him, because my body ached. He did things to me that I didn't even know were things. And I was not exactly innocent. Well, I had thought I wasn't innocent, but I was starting to see my lame introduction to sex was nothing compared to what Lexen would bring to my world.

And I wanted to experience it all with him.

"We have all the time in the world, *melerde*."

The unfamiliar word, in his sexy-ass accent, was enough to have my pulse racing. Except it wasn't completely unfamiliar. I was pretty sure I'd heard it before, but I couldn't remember.

"What does that mean?" I asked.

He pressed another kiss to my lips, his hands falling from my face to wrap across my back, pulling me even more firmly into him. "My love," he replied, between the touches of our lips.

I jerked back from him, sucking in a shot of air through my nose. "You love me?"

Way to go, Emma ... so smooth.

Laughter burst from Lexen. "Despite the fact that you look horrified right now, I'm confident enough to confirm your suspicions. I do, in fact, love you. Everything about you. You've constantly surprised me, from the first moment you broke the rules and followed us on Daelight Crescent."

I managed to smooth my expression, sucking in another fortifying breath. "You're wrong, Lexen Darken. There's nothing horrifying about what you just said. More like overwhelming, unbelievable, absolutely amazing." I breathed deeply again, finding the next words easy to say: "And while I'm not exactly an expert on love, I'm almost certain I've loved you since you kidnapped me."

"I felt it from that first moment, too," he said, his eyes holding me with their intensity. "I'm sorry about the kidnapping. I just needed you to be safe, and I used whatever excuse I could to make that happen."

"Are you still worried about me being in your world?"

He brushed a hand across my cheek, caressing it gently. "I still worry that you're going to get hurt from being in my world, but it's clear that you were always meant to be here. I won't fight fate. I will take my gifts."

I smirked. "So I'm a gift now?"

He flipped me over, so now he was the one pressing into me. Smooth rock lined my spine, and I held my breath, waiting for him to make his move.

"Always tempting me," he murmured, running his hands up and down my legs.

Holy shit.

21

ONE MONTH LATER

*T*he bell rang and I hauled my books up, almost smacking myself in the face. I was so ready to get out of my last class.

"What's the rush, sprout?"

I glared at Jero, shaking my head. "Sprout? Really? I think you've officially run out of nicknames."

He waited for me to finish stacking my textbooks. He, of course, had no books to retrieve. The Daelighters were still rocking their bookless genius status. Meanwhile, I was studying my ass off because I had missed so much school and I was not keen on falling behind. No way was I repeating my senior year.

Thank God for Lexen and his superior intellect. I didn't even care anymore that he was smarter and more athletic than me, because I reaped the benefits of those skills secondhand.

Jero took the heavy pile of books from me, slinging an arm across my shoulders and pulling me into him. Despite the fact that all of the Darkens were quite handsy with me, and had been for the past month at school, multiple gasps and hooded looks still shot in our direction.

"Girlfriend! The gossips love you," Ben trilled as he walked by us.

I just shook my head at him, glad that I'd managed to explain away my absence to Ben and Cara. Both of them accepted a lame story about an impromptu road trip which ended up with me in hospital. I had the scars to prove it, so they'd fawned over me, and I'd been grateful for their friendship.

Ben waved, heading toward the drama room. It was coming into the winter season of plays, which was apparently a big deal. Or so he liked to remind us. I knew Ben hid his pain in school activities. He was still having a lot of trouble at home, but he seemed to be able to handle it. Mostly.

I wanted to smack his parents in the mouth, but Lexen had me on a strict no smacking ban. Apparently I needed to stay out of trouble.

"Are you excited about tonight?" Jero asked, a shit-eating grin stretching his mouth.

Trying my best not to blush, I shrugged. "You know, we're just watching a movie and having dinner..."

Despite the fact Lexen and I had never been closer, we'd hardly had any alone time since returning from Overworld. Sara and Michael suddenly developed some very real rules, and I was to return home at exactly 5 P.M daily. Since I'd almost lost them, and they in turn thought for days I was dead, I had been indulging their overprotectiveness. We were bonding over the new knowledge of the supernatural we all possessed.

Michael and Sara might have always known there was an "alien" species on Earth, but they never expected it to be what it was. Me and my family's ties to it, more than anything, astonished them.

Jero interrupted my thoughts with a laugh. "Lexen has the entire house to himself while the rest of us return to Overworld ... and you're just going to watch a movie?"

I shrugged his arm off me, narrowing my eyes on him. "I'm not discussing my sex life with you." Or lack thereof. A fact that would hopefully be rectified tonight.

Jero hooted with laughter. "Lexen is going to have his hands full with you." He waggled his eyebrows. "Literally."

I was just about to break my smacking rule when tall, dark, and deadly entered the hall we were in. I took off as fast as my lazy legs could go. Lexen caught me with ease, lifting me up so that our mouths could meet.

"You know, you're barely even puffing," he said when we pulled apart.

I snort-laughed. "Yes, because an evil sadist has been making me go jogging with him."

Setting me on my feet, he brushed some of my wavy hair back. "You've been three times, and I had to promise you ice cream before you'd even get dressed."

I folded my arms over my chest, tilting my head to the side as I gave a rueful shrug. "It's never going to be my thing. You should just give up, accept that I have strengths in other areas."

"Yeah, she did knit you that wicked scarf," Jero added as he caught up to us.

I wanted to glare at the sarcastic asshole, but he kind of had a point. I was so distracted when I tried to knit around Lexen that I kept missing stitches and loops. My last creation was both holey and lopsided.

But he'd worn it. Inside, at least.

"Jero..." Lexen warned his brother. Apparently he didn't have a smacking rule, so Jero heeded that warning and held both hands up in surrender, veering to the right, heading toward the moving sidewalk that would take him to the parking lot.

"Have fun tonight, kids," he called as he jumped on. "Don't do anything I wouldn't."

And I was blushing again.

Lexen took pity on me, not calling attention to my pink cheeks. He just held his hand out and I placed mine in it, our fingers linking together.

"Jero stole my books," I murmured, trying desperately not to think about the fact that Lexen and I would have the entire night together. Our first true alone time in a month.

"He'll leave them at home. You always do your homework there anyway," Lexen reminded me. "Have the Finnegans left yet?" he asked after another moment of silence.

I nodded, pulling out my brand new cell phone. Being a member of House of Darken came with some additional perks – on top of Lexen's abs. And no one took no for an answer. Pushy aliens. "Yep, Sara just texted me and said that they were halfway to California."

They'd won a weekend away, skillfully set up by the Darkens. They hadn't wanted to leave me, but I told them I would be perfectly safe with Lexen, and since they loved him to death they eventually agreed it was time for them to loosen the strings. Sara even set me up on birth control, because they were too young to be grandparents to a little *humalien* baby.

Michael's word, of course.

Birth control was not something I wanted to discuss with my guardians, but at least it meant they were accepting that Lexen was part of my life – for the long haul.

"Come on, little human. Let's get out of here."

We walked hand in hand to the car. Lexen opened the door to his low-slung sports car and I slid inside. We roared out of the parking lot. Daelighters loved to drive fast, and I was slowly acquiring a taste for it. The gates were open to our street when we arrived, no delay for us to enter, and then it was on to Lexen's mansion. I eyed my shoebox house on the other side of the street, not at all sad that I wouldn't be sleeping on that rock-like mattress tonight.

While we were waiting for the gate to open, Lexen met my gaze. "Everything okay? You're quiet."

As my smile grew, I arched an eyebrow in his direction. "Are you saying I talk a lot?"

"Yes," came his reply without hesitation. "You talk constantly. And I love it. I never thought I could handle the need humans have to chat constantly, but now, when you're quiet, I miss your voice."

I laughed derisively. "There's still an asshole hidden under your sweet side, I see."

He didn't deny it as we traveled down the long driveway. It was kind of nice that he never lied to me or tried to hide who he was. The truth was, Lexen could be cold and lethal, like he was when I first stumbled into his world, but he also cared more deeply than anyone I'd ever met. His heart was huge, and the fact that even a small part of it loved me ... that was more than I ever thought I would have.

As soon as Lexen pulled into their underground garage, he was at my side in an instant. My door was open and I was hauled up into his arms before I could blink. "It's okay if I carry you this once, right?" he said as he hurried inside. "Your human legs are just way too slow, and I want every second we have to be alone."

Yeah, I was definitely not going to complain. As soon as we were inside the stunning ground level, ocean crashing in the distance outside the window, Lexen crossed into the white kitchen. He sat me down on the island bench, stepping between my legs. I wrapped my arms around his neck, and then we both took a moment to enjoy the closeness.

"What do you want to do first?" he asked me, leaning in close, his lips skimming across my throat. "Movie? Food?"

Instead of answering, I let out a breathy sigh, digging my fingers into his shirt and pulling him closer. He had ditched the coat and was wearing the school-issued button-down shirt open at the collar, untucked, sexy and disheveled.

"I ... I want..." I sucked in another breath, trying to string a sentence together. His lips were on my neck now and I was self combusting. "Room," I finally got out. "Take me ... to ... your room."

Lexen pulled back, fire in his eyes. "Are you sure? There is no rush, *melerde*. We have an eternity together."

An actual growl ripped from my throat, and the heat Lexen naturally exuded flared to life, sending hot trickles along my skin. He didn't move though; he was waiting for me to say the words. "I'm sure, Lex." I placed my hand on his chest, right above his heart. "I choose you, us, this ... always."

Lexen's hands went under me as he hauled me up and into his body. My legs wrapped around his waist and our mouths found each other again as he blindly strode away, heading in the direction of the stairs. He stumbled once, but quickly gained his footing, despite the fact that we couldn't seem to separate ourselves. Not even for a second.

In his room, the extra soft bed cushioned me as Lexen dropped me down onto it. He crawled over the top of me and I drank in the sight of him. I must have ripped a few of the buttons of his shirt – totally didn't remember doing that – because I was catching delicious glimpses of bronze skin and muscles.

Working my bottom lip between my teeth, I decided I might as well finish the job. Dropping on my back, I gripped his shirt on either side and yanked hard.

Nothing happened.

"Stupid buttons," I groaned.

Lexen laughed, lowering his body down, pressing me into the bed. "Maybe you should leave the buttons to me."

Somehow he managed to remove my shirt and his own before I could even blink again. His eyes skimmed down the top half of my body, clad only in a plain black bra now. He pressed his lips to the swell of my breast and I moaned, threading my fingers through his hair, running my fingertips across the etchings in the side of his hair.

Lexen moved lower, paying close attention to every part of my bare skin, kissing and licking. My body was moving against him, an unraveling feeling inside taking over. "Lex," I gasped, pulling him back up so I could taste him, feel his lips.

The rest of our clothing disappeared in the same magical way as the shirts, and for a moment I was shy, because I was not often naked around smoking-hot dudes. At the same time, it was Lexen, and I trusted him more than any other.

I lost all sense of time after that. It was just taste and touch, skin brushing across skin, spiraling sensations that took me to places I had never been before. Our bodies moved together, so in sync, almost as if we'd been designed to love each other exactly like this. The bond which had already been forming between our souls solidified. The love in my heart swelled.

As I arched off the bed, everything inside of me came apart. "I love you, Lex," I breathed, unable to stop the words from escaping.

He captured my mouth, along with my heart and soul. "Love you, always."

I shattered then, light exploding behind my eyes. Lexen followed me over the edge soon after.

A million years later, or maybe only a few minutes, my breathing started to slow down as I curled myself closer to Lexen. He shifted to remove the condom, which I was thankful he'd remembered. I might be on birth control, but doubling up never hurt anyone.

He wrapped me up in his arms, pulling me as close as he could. "You okay?" he said, his hands running up and down my arms. I was so relaxed I almost closed my eyes.

"Better than okay," I murmured into his chest.

He chuckled, chest rumbling under my head. "Come on, baby girl ... a quick shower before you fall asleep."

The next thing I registered was warm water hitting me from multiple directions. Lexen, towering over me as he always did, adjusted the showerheads so the spray was softer, washing down over us.

"Thank you," I said, tilting my head back so I could see him, almost groaning at the sight of the water slicing across him, sending his hair up in spiky tendrils, those long dark eyelashes framing obsidian eyes.

"For what?" he asked me.

I grinned and winked. "Mostly for kidnapping me."

His laughter joined mine. "Now that I've got you, I'm never letting you go."

"Goddamn Stockholm syndrome," I moaned. Because I did not want him to let me go, not now, not ever.

The shower turned out to be one of the best of my life, although I did get dirty a few times before I got clean again. When my skin was nice and wrinkly, we dragged ourselves out. Lexen threw me one of his shirts to wear, along with a pair of boxers. I followed him downstairs again and we dumped some pre-prepared meals into the oven.

"Want to pick out a movie while we wait for the food?" he asked me.

I nodded, jumping down off the barstool, and followed him down the hall to a huge cinema room. There were a dozen chairs, a massive screen, and an entire library catalogue of movies. I flicked through them, jokingly suggesting a few romances, before finally settling on something with action and drama. Lexen didn't seem to care. I didn't really either, because the reality was I prob-ably wouldn't see half the movie.

"Did Jero, Marsil, and Star head home just to give us some privacy?" I asked as I settled myself into a lounger. My body ached a little as I sat, but I kind of enjoyed knowing that love was the reason. It made the pain feel a little different somehow.

Lexen joined me. "No, Father has some update for us, but he

said it wasn't so urgent that they couldn't tell me when they returned." The Daelighters had recently been trying to pass all pertinent information in person. They might be tracking Laous through the network, but he could do the same with them.

So far there had been no peep about Laous and what he was up to on Earth. Word from the council indicated that the second secret keeper family was still secret, for now. But they had requested more of my blood to try something new. My necklace would lead him to the second. We all knew it was only a matter of time. From there he would find them one by one, then the treaty would be void.

Our talk turned to things far less serious after that, and when our food was finished we curled up together and watched the movie. Despite the fast-paced storyline and heavy action, I couldn't keep my eyes open.

Lexen's phone went off, startling me awake. He swiped the screen, read the message quickly, and then stood, pulling me with him.

"What's up?" I asked, yawning, my mouth stretching wide open in what was no doubt a hugely attractive expression.

He pulled me out of the cinema room, toward the front door of his house. "Daniel, Xander, and Chase are here. They have some news."

I glanced down at my clothes, thankful that Lexen's shirt fell almost to my knees, covering me pretty well. As he pulled the front door open, three Daelighters filed in, filling the wide, open space and making it seem smaller.

I'd seen all of them at school over the past month, but since they never advertised this friendship between them, we'd done no more than exchange some nods and smiles. It was nice to have them here in a more relaxed environment. Lexen led everyone to his main living area, settling into a double couch, pulling me down with him. I covered a yawn with my hand, trying to wake myself up.

Pretty sure I was in a sex coma, if that was even possible. Duh, it was Lexen Darken – of course it was possible.

As soon as everyone was seated, Lexen leaned forward. "What have you learned?"

Daniel mimicked his pose, his hands clasped in front of him. "I've just been updated from the council. They have figured out a rough location of the second secret keeper. They want one of us to head there and pick her up before Laous figures it out."

I swallowed hard, trying to work down the lump in my throat.

"She's in New Orleans," he said.

I was on my feet in a flash; the sense of kinship I felt for this person was second to none. They were just like me. Human, born on Overworld. And they were in danger – their family was in danger. We had to help them.

All eyes turned to me. "We have to get to NOLA now, before he finds her."

Daniel also stood. "Since the second was born in House of Imperial, this is my responsibility. I'm going to head down there tonight. I have some friends in the area, allies if you will, and I think that one of us going has a better chance of staying under the radar."

No one argued with him, but I thought it was a terrible idea. These four shouldn't split up. An idiot could tell that they were stronger together, as a team.

Daniel must have noticed my agitation. "I promise to call as soon as I find them. I won't try and take Laous on alone."

Knowing there was no real choice, I nodded.

"Are you heading out right now?" Lexen asked, all of us moving toward the door.

Daniel nodded. "Yes, I'm going to have to fly out. A transporter is too easily traceable."

"The council is holding off on sending anyone," Chase added, his braids twinkling in the lights above. "But we don't have long.

They're dying to take Laous out before humans even know there is a problem."

"I'll take care of it," Daniel added. Then he surprised me with a quick hug before he left. "Glad to see you looking healthy and whole, badass."

I shrugged. "What can I say, life with Lexen suits me."

He appraised me for an extended moment, then nodded. "So it does."

Once he and the others were gone, I leaned heavily against the closed door. Lexen interrupted me before I could make a suggestion: "I think we should pick this up in the morning." I had been about to propose some research time. Somehow he always knew.

"Bed sounds pretty good, actually."

I conceded defeat for now, secure in the knowledge that Daniel was on his way to New Orleans and that he would keep us updated. Once we were in the room, I barely managed to crawl my way across the bed before collapsing face-down on it. Lexen pulled the covers over us both.

"I need to brush my teeth," I mumbled.

There was a rustling and then Lexen was back with a new toothbrush still in the package, toothpaste, and a glass of water. "That's very thoughtful," I said, smiling around the brush.

I made quick work brushing and rinsing my mouth out, finally surrendering to the super soft bed. My eyes were closed by the time Lexen rejoined me, once again pulling the covers over us, spooning his body behind me.

"I'm not going another month without you in my arms, in my bed," he said into my hair. "My draygone was impossible to control. I almost climbed through your window."

"When?" I asked, twisting around so I could see him. Only the faintest light shone through his nearby window, but it was enough to make out his features.

"Every night."

Wrapping my arms around him, I let myself relax against him, and as he captured my lips in the most gentle of kisses, I decided that Lexen was right. As usual.

No more time apart. We were a team. We would figure out whatever battle was coming for us and we would not be defeated, because we would fight together. Always.

HOUSE OF IMPERIAL - SECRET KEEPERS #2

RELEASE JUNE 30TH 2018

hapter One

WWW.AMAZON.COM/HOUSE-IMPERIAL-SECRET-KEEPERS-BOOK-EBOOK/DP/B07D1YQLPL/

THE FRENCH QUARTER was a place I wanted to tell my children about – not that kids or family were an actual possibility in my life – but this city ... it was a world worthy to be passed on, to be spoken about in stories and song. There was something special here. I had felt it the first moment we arrived.

As I strolled along the colorful street that led into Jackson Square, I wondered what my life would have been like if I'd been born here. I mean, not right here on this somewhat grimy pavement, but in New Orleans. Maybe I would be reading tarot cards like the woman on my right, set up at her small white table, long dark curls spilling out from under the jeweled headpiece adorning her forehead, purple nails flashing as she placed cards down for an eager tourist.

Or maybe I'd paint. That always looked like a fun way to tell a story. Street artists were everywhere, expressing their creativity in a way that I couldn't imagine doing. I'd never held a paintbrush, not even as a child. Circumstances from before my birth dictated that my life would never be my own.

Something I'd grown numb to over the years.

As if to prove me wrong, a haunting saxophone tune started up from a jazz musician leaning close to the wall of a café; the low reverberations hit me deep in my soul, in the place that had been cold and dormant for a long time. I basked in that feeling for a moment, closing my eyes and letting the music take me away.

I probably looked like a crazy person, standing in the middle of the Quarter, face lifted to the sky, shoulder-length ash-blond hair sticking out in a million directions. Okay, so it was NOLA, I no doubt fit in perfectly, but for someone who had always tried to blend, being in public like this was making me uneasy. It was just that for the first time in a long time I felt alive. I wasn't sure if letting myself feel things was a good idea, but I couldn't seem to stay away. I kept coming back here, to experience this world filled with life and vibrancy, watching the tourists as they took their spooky tours and filled their bags with fancy masks, religious trinkets, and hot sauce. I envied their laughter, and ability to afford copious amounts of beignets. Those puffy balls of magic were everything. I'd had one my first day and since then I must have thought about their deliciousness at least seven times a week. I was addicted ... and totally okay with it.

Mostly, I envied them their happy moments and families. That existence was not for me, but at least by being here I got to experience a small sliver of *that* life. Glancing at my watch, I stifled my groan: 3:50 P.M. I'd already been gone for two hours, wandering the streets.

It was Wednesday. I was supposed to be at the farmers market on Peters Street. My mom allowed me to make this once-a-week trip from our tiny condo in the Marginy to gather some groceries. I'd be punished for taking my time today. We had strict rules in my family – my mom and me – and one of the most important was that I never put us at risk of exposure. We were to always stick to the shadows and live like ghosts.

Most days I felt about as substantial as a ghost, so she had achieved one of her goals.

With reluctance, I turned away from the square and started my trek back toward the market area. It was only a few blocks, but in this million-percent humidity it would feel longer. Heat didn't usually bother me, but I hadn't quite understood the true scope of "sweating like a pig" until we moved here.

As I walked, I let my eyes roam across the streets, waiting for the next new and crazy sight. One literally never knew what was going to happen here. We'd only lived in New Orleans for a few months. To the locals I'd always be a tourist, but I was okay with that. I would take that title in exchange for getting to experience this world. I was fascinated with it all. This city was hard to truly describe, a place like no other, and considering I'd moved two to three times a year since I was born, that was really saying something. Its French influences, not only in architecture but food and culture ... I loved them all.

I'd started hoping each night, before I went to sleep, that nothing would spook my mom into running again. We should still have at least another two months here, if she kept to her normal timeline.

I was not giving up one second of NOLA – not without a fight.

Far too quickly I arrived at the market, hurrying about to finish my shopping before it closed. The walk back to our condo would take forty minutes, but I'd brought some bags with cold packs for anything that could spoil in this hot weather. As I left the market, a group of kids pushed past me. They'd probably just finished school for the day, coming straight here with their parents.

I'd been homeschooled. Sort of. I wasn't sure there was an actual name for what my mom did, which was teach me the basics, lecture me incessantly about the dangers in our lives, and fill my young mind with the sort of scary stories that not even adults should hear. I was probably one of the few kids who had wished to go to school, instead of being stuck inside a small house ninety percent of my life.

My mom literally never left our home; never worked. She told me that neither of us could leave a paper trail, which included social security numbers and tax declarations. We lived off a large settlement payout from my father's death. He was killed when my mom was pregnant with me. It had been a big deal, something to do with a workplace accident. Whatever the cause, I lost a parent, one who might have actually loved me, and in exchange, we got enough money to live like nomads.

The money was almost gone now. Eighteen years of being on the run was pretty expensive, even if we did live in rundown, no-names-asked rentals.

"Callie!"

The shout had me spinning on the spot, heavy bags swinging against my legs. There were only two people in this town who knew my name. One was my mom, the other was a pain in my butt.

Turning away again, I yelled over my shoulder. "Not in the mood, Michaels. I have to get home."

Jason Michaels was a persistent bastard, I'd give him that, but even after he'd challenged me and I'd kicked his ass in the gym, he still hadn't given up. What his endgame was, I had no idea. He never asked me out, or even implied that he wanted to go on a date. He just ... asked too many questions and was always around. If my mom got any hint of his consistent presence in my life, my one other piece of freedom would be yanked away from me.

Along with New Orleans.

I was not letting this tenacious bastard take this place from me.

"Are you training this afternoon?" he asked, falling into step beside me.

"No," I replied shortly.

He just laughed. "You always say no, and yet you're always there."

Spinning on my heels, I swung back in his direction, startling him enough that he blinked wide eyes at me. Michaels was a good-looking guy, tall, broad shouldered, bleach-blond tousled hair, the same as I'd seen from surfers when we lived in California – but in manners and speech, he was all Southern.

"What exactly do I need to do to make you go away?"

He just shrugged, flashing me that slow smile. "You like me, I know it." He turned to walk away, calling over his shoulder. "See you this afternoon, *cher.*"

I glared at his retreating back, before shaking my head and hurrying along again. After powerwalking for a block, I turned back once to make sure Michaels wasn't following me. Leading him home would be the best way to kick Mom into flight mode. The street was empty of all tall blonds, so I felt safe in continuing – navigating the path to get me home quickest, while also being somewhat safe. We didn't live in the best neighborhood, but during daylight hours, I hadn't had too many issues. So far.

When I finally reached the stairs to the condo, I paused and took a deep breath. I had to prepare myself. My mom was about to lose her shit at me. Some days I was just tired of this life, of my existence.

You're eighteen now...

The stupid voice in my head had been reminding me of this for the last few months. My birthday had been in June, not that anyone remembered or mentioned it. But I knew, because it marked the moment I no longer had to follow my mom around. I could leave, get a job – paper trail be damned – rent my own shitty apartment and live an actual, normal life. But the same part of me that continued to hold people at a distance, the part that believed her stories, wouldn't let me make the final break.

With one more deep breath for courage, I started up the two flights, mentally bracing for the fight which was to come. As I put my key in the lock, the door pushed inwards, which didn't surprise me. Mom was no doubt waiting right on the other side for me. But as the empty living area and kitchenette came into view, I ground to a halt.

What in the...?

Stepping forward again, my senses were firing as I catalogued everything, searching for something out of place to explain what was going on. I left the bags of food near the front door, wanting both hands free. I wished my hair wasn't hanging loose; I didn't like to fight with it in my face. I had at least just cut it back to my shoulders, so it shouldn't be too much of a problem. As if to prove me wrong, strands of ashy blond fell in front of my face; a flick of my head put them back into place. The ceiling was low in here, and since I was five foot eleven, I ducked under the arched accents in the hallway. The last thing I needed was to smash my head and alert whomever was inside that I was here.

My Converse were quiet as I crossed the threadbare carpet heading toward the first small bedroom, just off the hall. The bedrooms were across from each other, the bathroom at the back. That was all there was to this place. Nowhere really to hide.

It was deathly quiet, a bad omen, because my mom played Mozart and Bach constantly. She said it helped ease the turmoil of worry that plagued her mind. I wasn't sure how I felt about classical music – I was starting to think I was a jazz girl at heart – but I sure as hell missed it now.

Because something was wrong.

Using my foot, I nudged my door open to reveal the twin bed, white dresser, open closet – or locker as they called it here – with my few clothes spilling out onto the floor, but nothing amiss. Ducking my head inside, I looked around to double-check, but as far as I could tell, the room was empty.

I sucked in some fortifying air and crossed the hall to my mom's room. In normal circumstances, I would never enter her domain. She was fiercely private, totally crazy, and prone to smacking me with wooden spoons. But this was no normal day. Her door was firmly shut. I twisted the handle, wincing at the tell-tale creak of the lever lifting. Stepping back, I swung the door wide open and waited a second for something to jump out at me. When nothing did, I peeked around the edge.

Her bed was twice the size of mine, neatly made with a faded green duvet. Her closet was closed, not a single item out of place, not even a shirt on the floor. I let my eyes run over everything, even dropping down to glance under the bed.

What was happening? Where was she?

Just as I was straightening, a creak from the living area sent a shot of adrenalin through me. I froze and unfroze almost in the same instant, crossing back to the door. I took two deep breaths, ducking my head out to look along the hall.

Holy fuck...

A man filled the doorway to the condo. I mean *filled* to the point where there was no space around him and he had to almost bend himself in half to fit inside. I was tall, but he had to be at least six inches taller than me. Our eyes locked across the room. Since my first step into the condo, everything had felt like it was going in fast forward. But right then, I couldn't move.

He stepped inside, untangling himself from the doorframe, only to find that the ceiling in the rest of the place wasn't much higher. With a scowl, his body hunched forward and he took another step toward me.

"You need to come with me. You're in danger."

His accented demand was low and husky. For an instant I craved to hear some sort of music or song from him, because he had a voice like an instrument, deep and rich, vibrating right through my body.

"Did you hear me?" The snap of his question knocked me out of my stupor and, managing this time to ignore the way his voice made me feel, I sent a scowl right back at him.

He took another step toward me and I straightened, shifting into a fighter stance. "Who the hell are you? Where is my mom?"

Those intense eyes remained on my face. I couldn't even tell what color they were; the lighting was shit in here, but they looked dark and ... somehow also light at the same time. I wasn't sure I'd ever seen a man like him before. He looked to be a few years older than me. A shaved head. A crap-ton of ink – from what I could see. Very well-toned biceps and chest muscles. This dude was ripped, and yet, despite his bulk and height, he moved smoothly, which was the most worrying thing so far. Every now and then, there'd be a fighter like him in the gym. They were lethal: strong, athletic, able to kick ass without breaking a sweat.

I needed to get out of here.

We were only a few feet apart now and I remained outwardly calm, hoping to distract him enough that he would be unprepared for my sudden breakaway. "Where is my mom?" I repeated, mostly to keep him talking. I did not expect an honest answer. He clearly hadn't been in the apartment when I first entered – no way could I miss him – but he might have already taken my mom and was back now for me.

"I have no idea. I got here just after you did."

My stomach clenched at that voice again. On top of that he had the sort of raw masculine beauty that I generally thought existed only in Hollywood. Why was it always the physically-perfect men who were deranged psychopaths?

"You need to leave. Now!" I was slowly edging to the right, aiming for a clear path to the door. "Or I'm going to call the police."

I would never call them, of course. We didn't trust police.

They were corrupt, blah, blah, blah. Even when my mom wasn't here, her voice was still in my head.

Tall, dark, and deadly paused, tilting his head to the side. "You're caught up in a world you have no idea of. The police can't help you, Human. I'm your only hope. Right now, I don't have time to enlighten you, so you're just going to have to trust me."

Panic like nothing I'd ever felt before hit me, so hard that my knees went weak and I almost dropped to the ground.

A world I have no idea about...

Oh, he was wrong. So very wrong. I reacted then without another thought.

Dive-rolling forward, I popped up right before him. As I rose, I slammed my fist into his groin and he let out an angry rumble. I continued rising, smashing my fist into his gut with a power hit, and then finally into the side of his head. I was fast; it was my greatest asset, and I knew exactly what angle to use and how hard to hit for maximum impact.

He let out a low groan, dropping to his knees, eyes wide as he cupped himself, blinking at me. The shock on his face was almost laughable; he had definitely not seen that coming.

Never underestimate a woman. You'll end up on your knees holding your balls.

His eyes, only inches from mine now, locked on to my face and it felt like I'd been the one punched. They were even more beautiful than he was, and that was saying something. The color was an unusual light brown, cinnamon dusted with gold. These gilded circles cut through the deep amber color. They were also framed by ridiculously dark and thick lashes.

Focus, Callie...

I called on my years of training – this was what Mom had been preparing me for. The only reason she allowed me to fight and train was because one day I would have to deal with this other world. One day the Daelighters would come for me.

Looked like today was that day.

ACKNOWLEDGMENTS

Thank you to my amazing readers. Five years strong; I almost can't believe that this is my life. It's truly a dream job. I am so grateful for you all.

Thanks to my release team. You all rock!! The support means the world to me, and without your enthusiasm for my books, I would not have half the motivation to get them out fast. Hugs.

Thanks to my Nerd Herd. You guys are so much fun! I love reading the posts, I love all the book recommendations, I flat out love the lot of you. Don't change.

Huge, extra special thanks to my PA extraordinaire, Heather. Girl, I could not do everything I do without you. Peanut butter to my jelly. Or as I like to say, Timtams to my milk.

As always, thank you to my family for putting up with having an author in their lives. We're not alway the easiest to live with, I may be slightly high strung at times (prove it, I dare you), but there is nothing in the world I adore more than you all. Love you, always.

Thanks to L.C Hibbett, you make this world a little less serious. And a lot more sarcastic. #irishtwin. Thanks also to Everyly Frost, Kelly St Clare, Amber Lynn Natusch, Heather Renee, Teresa, and Mary for beta reading this series. You all rock!

Lastly thanks to Leia Stone for being the best bestfriend a person could have, for offering advice on all 45367 versions of the blurb, and for actually reading this book even though it was over 100k words. I heart you.

ABOUT THE AUTHOR

Jaymin Eve is the USA Today Bestselling author of 25+ YA and NA fantasy/romance novels. She lives in Australia with her husband, two beautiful daughters, and a couple of crazy pets. Since 2013 she has sold over a million ebooks, and has no plans to stop writing anytime in the next 30-50 years.

facebook.com/JayminEve.Author

twitter.com/jaymineve1

instagram.com/jaymineve

ALSO BY JAYMIN EVE

Secret Keepers Series

Book One: House of Darken

Book Two: House of Imperial (1st July 2018)

Book Three: House of Leights (1st August 2018)

Book Four: House of Royale (1st September 2018)

Curse of the Gods Series (Reverse Harem Fantasy)

Book One: Trickery

Book Two: Persuasion

Book Three: Seduction

Book Four: Strength (2018)

NYC Mecca Series (Complete - UF series)

Book One: Queen Heir

Book Two: Queen Alpha

Book Three: Queen Fae

Book Four: Queen Mecca

A Walker Saga (Complete - YA Fantasy)

Book One: First World

Book Two: Spurn

Book Three: Crais

Book Four: Regali

Book Five: Nephilius

Book Six: Dronish

Book Seven: Earth

Supernatural Prison Trilogy (Complete - UF series)

Book One: Dragon Marked

Book Two: Dragon Mystics

Book Three: Dragon Mated

Supernatural Prison Stories

Broken Compass

Magical Compass

Louis (2018)

Hive Trilogy (Complete UF/PNR series)

Book One: Ash

Book Two: Anarchy

Book Three: Annihilate

Sinclair Stories (Standalone Contemporary Romance)

Songbird

CPSIA information can be obtained
at www.ICGtesting.com
Printed in the USA
BVHW031811171021
619163BV00013B/173